ALSO BY TOVA MIRVIS

The Ladies Auxiliary

THE OUTSIDE WORLD

THE
OUTSIDE WORLD

Tova Mirvis

To Lisa,
Best Wishes.

Alfred A. Knopf

NEW YORK   2004

THIS IS A BORZOI BOOK
PUBLISHED BY ALFRED A. KNOPF

Library of Congress Cataloging-in-Publication Data
Mirvis, Tova.
The outside world / by Tova Mirvis.—1st ed.
p.   cm.
ISBN 1-4000-4161-9
1. Jewish families—Fiction.   2. Brooklyn (New York, N.Y.)—Fiction.
3. Conflict of generations—Fiction.   4. Orthodox Judaism—Fiction.
5. Parent and child—Fiction.   6. New Jersey—Fiction.   I. Title.

PS3563.I7217O95 2004
813'.54—dc22   2003058923

Manufactured in the United States of America
First Edition

For Allan

THE OUTSIDE WORLD

— ONE —

T ZIPPY GOLDMAN was a good girl. Yet she lay awake and wished she could run across the living room, fling open all the windows and all the doors, and scream. Tzippy is crazy, the neighbors would say, unfit for our sons, our nephews. But no, Tzippy would reply, not crazy, not unfit. Just sad. And maybe a little angry.

To scream would be like battling the laws of nature. Still, she let herself imagine it, now that it was late at night and she was alone. Her parents were at the Rosenbaum wedding in Monsey, and the house that normally teemed with her four singing sisters was temporarily still. There were reasons for Tzippy's urge to howl. It was because of an unjust world, an unfair God. It was because bad things happened to good people, because fortune and luck were doled out in unequal portions. It was because Tzippy Goldman was twenty-two and still not married.

She and her mother had spent years planning imaginary weddings, deciding on color schemes before she was old enough to find a groom. Her mother used to tuck her into bed and, with her finger, draw flowers and rings and wedding cakes on her back. They discussed chiffon and organza, compared silk shantung and satin. They selected Venetian-lace wedding dresses, rhinestone tiaras, and veils with cascading tulle. When they finished planning the wedding, they moved on to the marriage house, the dream space Tzippy and her husband would one day occupy. In the marriage house, everything was new. Everything was white and clean and fresh. There were new sheets and white lace tablecloths. In the marriage house, there was never anything to worry about. The dishes never needed to be washed, the beds never needed to be made. The phone didn't ring, the doorbell didn't buzz. The dinner table was set for two, and there were long evenings with nothing to do but be together.

This dream was supposed to be waiting for her. Both Tzippy and her mother had always assumed that she would finish high school, get set up on shidduch dates, meet the right boy, get engaged, and have a beautiful wedding with lots of white lace and pareve vanilla cream frosting. She was born for this. It was possible to imagine that somewhere, in an alternate world, Tzippy had a home set up, children born, and dinner long prepared. But, in this world, it hadn't happened as she had expected, and she had passed four years waiting and worrying.

There were so many ways to be set up: my rabbi knows your rabbi; my mother knows your mother; my neighbor, your neighbor. Tzippy had been set up by teachers and friends, and by her mother, who was omnipotent and omniscient. Setting up an eighteen-year-old was a hobby for people. Finding a husband for a twenty-two-year-old was a national emergency. Well-meaning neighbors called constantly with suggestions. Tzippy's name was in the file box of every professional matchmaker in Brooklyn. Her virtues had been sung to every neighbor, every neighbor's cousin, everyone who had a son, nephew, or acquaintance of marriageable age. Before a first date could take place, so many questions had to be asked. Is Tzippy thin? Is she pretty? Is the family rich? Will they support a husband while he learns? Is there a history of divorce or mental illness? Are there any distinguished rabbis in the family? Do they own a television set?

Once the right answers were given, the match was made and the boy was allowed to call for a date. Tzippy wore the right clothes, said the right things, and nodded at the right times. She tried to convince herself that she should want to marry one of these boys. But she felt nothing for the strangers who sat across from her. She had always imagined that she would feel a rush of passion, of excitement, a rush at least of something. She had always hoped that her heart would pound and she would know when she found him. But the only thing she ever knew was that she wanted to go home. She felt as if she had been on the same date a hundred times before. She could close her eyes and a different boy would be sitting across from her.

Sometimes the boy wanted to go out with her again. Sometimes she convinced herself to go out with him. Sometimes the ones she wanted to go out with weren't the same ones who wanted to go out with her. Even if they were both interested, it never lasted more than a few dates. No matter what the reason, the explanation was always the same: "It's not shayach." This could mean that there was no chemistry. It could mean that the family wasn't prominent enough. Perhaps the boy was hoping for a more religious girl, a prettier girl, a fancier girl. Perhaps the girl was hoping for a boy not quite so short. She wanted someone more outgoing, someone more serious, less serious, a boy who would learn in yeshiva full-time, a boy who wore a black hat only on Shabbos and would every once in a while see a movie. That it worked for anyone seemed to defy the laws of nature that God, in His infinite wisdom, had set down.

Yet her former high school classmates seemed to have no trouble defying nature. One by one, another engagement was announced, a party held, a ring flashed. Tzippy bore it with great dignity, smiling tightly when her friends recalled that at their high school graduation they had bet that Tzippy would be first. And though she had modestly protested—no, not me, surely Rochel Leah or Sara Bracha first—she had assumed that their predictions spoke the truth. But four years had passed since she possessed that certainty. And tonight she stayed home while her mother danced at the wedding of a nineteen-year-old girl who got engaged to the first boy she ever went out with.

Tzippy had things that were supposed to keep her occupied until she got married. She took an early childhood education class at Brooklyn College. She worked as an aide in a nursery school. She helped her mother with her four sisters: Zahava, who was fifteen; Malky, who was eleven; Dena, who was seven; and Dassi, who was five. But Tzippy worried that her real life would never begin. She would live eternally with her parents, while her married friends moved into new apartments. They would sleep next to their husbands, while she became the pity of the neighborhood. Girls three years younger than she would get married, then girls five years younger. With their hats and their homes, they would become women, while she remained a girl.

"Don't be negative, Tzippy," her mother always told her. "You need to have faith. If you think it's never going to happen, maybe it won't.

"You need to smile. No one wants to marry a lemon," her mother reminded her.

Outwardly, Tzippy acquiesced to her mother's suggestions and tried not to lose hope. She knew that it was bad to be angry, bad to want more than had been allotted to her. She reminded herself that she was supposed to look at her situation and understand why God wanted it this way. Her mother said that her prolonged single state should be an atonement for anything she had ever done wrong. Every unmarried girl in Brooklyn felt the pressure, but for Tzippy it bore down with such weight that it was hard to breathe. To protect herself, Tzippy screamed silent rebuttals in her head: Why do I need to smile, Mom, if it's in the hands of God? If you like him so much, why don't you go out with him? Maybe I'll never get married. Maybe I'll become the world's first Jewish nun.

Hiding inside these silent retorts was a voice that was willful and disagreeable. Tzippy knew that this voice was probably her yetzer harah, her evil inclination, which she was supposed to ignore. But it liked to suggest that maybe she would never get married. It also liked to challenge her. What if she yelled at her mother in public? What if she refused to help out with her sisters? What if she insisted on getting her own apartment far away from Brooklyn? The presence of this voice scared Tzippy. She worried that she might open her mouth and this voice would emerge. Even if she managed to keep it quiet, people might be able to sense its presence inside her. Just by looking at her, they would know that she felt things she wasn't supposed to feel. The only way to make it go away was to get engaged. Her friends who had been delivered safely into marriage surely didn't hear such voices. But left on her own, the voice could take over. After a date hadn't worked out or another one of her friends had gotten engaged, it tempted her to test God. If You don't find me a husband, I will eat this cookie without making a blessing, Tzippy had once warned Him. When the phone didn't ring, a matchmaker on the other end, she had taken a bite and waited for God to strike her down.

It hadn't ended there. Once, when Tzippy had an afternoon to herself, she went to Lord & Taylor and wandered through the section of evening gowns. Long and satin, with beads and no sleeves, sheer, short, slinky, spaghetti-strapped and sequined, they lured Tzippy. Praying that no one would notice, she snuck a strapless black gown into a dressing room. In front of the mirror, she first saw only the absence of the required sleeves and high neck; she couldn't get over so much naked skin. But as she kept staring, she soon saw not what the dress was missing, but what she had. Tzippy was slight, barely five two. Her brown hair was thick and straight and long. She wore long jean skirts by day, flowered pajamas by night. But in this dress, she looked like a grown woman. She was surprised at the body she saw—as if the thin ballerina arms, the small waist and hips, weren't her own. Under her uniform of long skirts and long sleeves, they were hidden not just from others, but from herself as well. She loved what she saw. She would leave the dress here as long as she could bring home this image of herself.

This voice, these feelings, made it hard to fall asleep. Ever since Tzippy quietly turned twenty-two, the pressure had mounted exponentially. On this night, she wasn't the only one who couldn't sleep. Dassi, her youngest sister, woke up, besieged with bad dreams of monsters and dogs. Eyes half-closed, she appeared in Tzippy's doorway.

"Can I come in your bed?" she asked.

"Of course," said Tzippy, and took Dassi in her arms.

Tzippy's room was tiny, really a small box, but Tzippy was the oldest, so she had it to herself. There were no posters of rock bands, no soap opera stars. Instead, there was a picture of Jerusalem's Old City on the wall, a collection of china dolls on top of her bookcase. A fading border of ballerinas danced high on the wall. The bedspread was pink. The walls were a matching shade. There were two kinds of bedrooms Tzippy would occupy: the one of her childhood and the one of her marriage. Since one was supposed to follow closely upon the other, neither Tzippy nor her mother had seen the point of redecorating.

Dassi could make herself comfortable anywhere. She knew how to find the soft spots and burrow in. As Dassi went back to sleep, Tzippy smoothed her hair and whispered that everything was okay. Dassi had one arm draped across Tzippy's stomach, and Tzippy risked waking her by running her fingers across her baby-like cheeks. Her previous urge to scream was no match for the soft, steady breathing of her sister. As Dassi turned in her sleep, Tzippy melted back into the gentle, helpful, and kind girl that everyone knew.

But Tzippy still couldn't sleep. She tried to calm her anger by thinking about the date she had tomorrow night with Yosef Schachter, whom her mother was so excited about. She told herself that it was wrong to assume that this boy would talk about himself the whole night, forget her name, and then tell the matchmaker how off the mark it was. Maybe her mother was right. Maybe Yosef Schachter was The One. Tzippy had been taught that God was busy day and night pairing everyone up. She believed in the God of Abraham who introduced him to Sarah, the God of Isaac who matched him with Rebecca, the God of Jacob who gave him both Rachel and Leah. Tzippy wanted to believe that she would soon be the bride who floated down the aisle, her face shadowed with tulle. She wanted to close her eyes and be led to the future that awaited her.

No matter how many weddings she attended, Shayna Goldman never got tired of them. She was in love with weddings. When she heard of an engagement, she waited for the cream-colored calligraphed envelope to drop through the mail slot. The wait made her giddy with expectation. The Rosenbaum wedding had played coy with her. She tried to stave off a sinking feeling of disappointment as her friends received their invitations. She kept up a brave face, afraid to let her friends see her worry. When her invitation finally arrived, she felt more relief than pleasure. Being invited was like a soothing voice that said you are doing everything right. She immediately returned the RSVP card and posted the invitation on the refrigerator.

At the wedding, lattice-cut vegetables and platters of fruit were displayed on draped tables. Chefs carved paper-thin slices of scarlet beef. They dished Chinese vegetables onto white cocktail plates. Flanked by two great-grandmothers, four grandmothers, and two mothers, the bride entered the hall like a queen arriving for her coronation. Sisters in lavender satin posed behind the bride's white wicker throne. Shayna stared at them, at the flowers, and at the food. She didn't need to eat a thing and she would still come away full. She stayed until the end. When she finally pulled herself away, she wrapped five pieces of cake in a napkin and tucked them into her purse for her daughters.

Once Shayna got home and took off her makeup and dress, the wedding seemed like a dream. The house was too quiet, too lonely. Her husband, Herschel, hadn't come home with her. When the wedding ended, he had bounded over to her and said he was going to work. At eleven o'clock, he was just getting started. Shayna tried to sleep, but every time she closed her eyes she imagined the music from the ten-piece Neshama band. A wedding danced in her head, keeping her awake.

Though the house was dark, she knew she wasn't the only one still awake. When she came in, she had heard Tzippy rustling in her room. Tzippy had pretended not to be bothered by the fact that they were going to yet another wedding. She pretended not to notice that she was rapidly becoming the last in her class to get engaged. But Shayna saw beyond the calm Tzippy projected. Shayna knew she wasn't the only one in this house who was worried.

Shayna got out of bed and stuck her head into Tzippy's room. "I thought maybe you wanted some company," she said.

"How was the wedding?" Tzippy asked.

"It was nice. The usual," she said, and for Tzippy's sake swallowed any descriptions of dresses, flowers, and desserts. "Has Dassi been in here a long time?"

"She came in an hour ago. She says she's afraid of her room. I don't know what we're going to do with her."

Dassi opened her eyes. "Did you bring me a treat?" she asked when she saw her mother.

"I did," Shayna said. "I'll give it to you in the morning. A piece of cake for each of you."

"Tell me a story," Dassi said.

Shayna sat on the bed. "Once upon a time," she began, as she did whenever one of her daughters had trouble falling asleep, "there was a beautiful young princess named—"

"Tzippy," Dassi said.

"Yes," Shayna continued, "only when she turned eighteen, everyone started calling her by her full name, Tziporah. And this Princess Tziporah was a good girl who helped her mother and took care of her sisters. She was gentle and sweet, and she happened to be looking for a husband."

"Like our Tzippy," said Dassi.

"Yes, like our Tzippy. And also like our Tzippy, this princess was lucky to have a helpful and knowledgeable mother who summoned the available boys from all the finest yeshivas in the land. They came before her father, the king, and each one made a case for why he should marry the princess. The first boy said that he had a bank account filled with money to buy beautiful jewels for the princess. The second boy said he had no money, but he knew the whole Torah by heart. The third boy said he had no money and didn't know a lot, but he had a heart of gold filled with love for Tziporah."

Usually Dassi chose which of the boys would marry the princess and Shayna would finish the story, always ending with the princess's life-long happiness, her beautiful home full of grateful and well-mannered children. Shayna and Tzippy looked down at Dassi and waited for her to make her selection. But she was fast asleep.

"I can move her back to her bed," Shayna whispered.

"You'll wake her," Tzippy said. "It's fine. She can sleep here."

"Are you sure? I don't want you to be uncomfortable."

"I said it's fine," Tzippy snapped.

Shayna looked at her in surprise. She couldn't understand the anger that periodically erupted from her sweet, agreeable daughter. Not knowing what else to do, Shayna put up her hands in surrender and stood up to leave.

"Don't leave me in suspense. Which one does she marry?" Tzippy asked.

Shayna sat back down on the edge of Tzippy's bed. "You tell me."

"What if she sees something missing from each one and decides to marry none of them?"

"Come on, Tzippy," Shayna protested. "And anyway, I didn't finish. I was just getting to the fourth boy, who has all these qualities and more."

"Really," Tzippy said.

"Yes, and it just so happens that he's from Boro Park, and he learns half the day and works in computers the other half, and his name is Yosef Schachter."

Tzippy turned to face the wall.

"I'm telling you, I have a good feeling about him," Shayna said. "I really think he might be The One."

"So tell me really," Tzippy said. "How was the wedding?"

"You're sure you want to hear?"

"Ma, it's fine. Tell me."

"They had the most gorgeous flowers I've ever seen," Shayna said, and told her about the elaborate centerpieces and the bridesmaids in lavender and the tiny pearls sewn to the bride's veil. She told her whom among the five hundred guests she had known—who had said hello to her, who had not. She counted how many hot-food stations the smorgasbord had and described for Tzippy each of the multi-layer cakes at the Viennese dessert table. "Maybe if you get married in the summer, we could do everything in lavender and—"

"Stop," Tzippy said.

"You said you wanted to hear about it."

"I wanted to hear about Leah Rosenbaum's wedding, not about mine."

"I'm just trying to help," Shayna said.

"I'm sorry," Tzippy said when she saw the wounded look on her mother's face. "I didn't mean it. And you're right. Doing everything in lavender is a great idea."

Shayna kissed her daughter good night and stood up to leave. "You're a good girl, Tzippy," she said. "It will happen for you too. I know it will."

When Tzippy finally fell asleep, she dreamed not of angry girls who wanted to scream in public and kill their mothers in private, but of a princess who was good and kind, and who married all the yeshiva boys at once. They bought a beautiful home in Boro Park, and had many children and lived happily ever after.

Though he wasn't expected until seven that evening, thoughts of Yosef Schachter filled the next day. "What do you think he looks like?" the sisters wondered. "Where do you think he'll take you?" Shayna asked. "Yosef Schachter, Yosef Schachter," Dena and Dassi chanted. "You're such a Yosef Schmuchter," Zahava teased. "I'm going to Yosef Schmachter you if you don't watch out," Malky warned.

They were downstairs in the living room. It had been recently redecorated, as rooms were in every house in the neighborhood when one of the children reached marriageable age. Once Tzippy had graduated from high school, the imperfections in the decor leapt out at Shayna. She saw worn edges of fabric, scratches in the wood, ragged patches of carpeting. The house, too small for the seven of them, was a two-family attached. The beige carpeting upstairs had yellowed and the paint was cracked around the doorframes. Shayna had become convinced that these flaws stood between Tzippy and a husband. They would prevent her from being set up with the best young men. The only thing to do was fix what she could, hide what she couldn't. Now the living-room furniture was dark wood antique. The couches were formal, their beige fabric covered in plastic to protect against sticky hands. Shayna's desires had been transformed into wallpaper, her dreams embodied in patterns of brocade.

The living room was also the only room with air-conditioning. It was hot in Brooklyn during the summer, and anyone who could went away to bungalow colonies in the Catskills and Vacation Village, where the children played, the mothers shopped, and the fathers drove up before Shabbos. The Goldmans didn't go away. Instead, Malky, Dena, and Dassi went to day camp in the local Beis Yaakov high school, a city camp, where instead of swimming and archery, they did arts and crafts and took field trips to the pizza store. Zahava was a counselor there and complained bitterly about what hard work it was. If she had her way, she would lie on the couch while her sisters tended to her needs.

When the girls got home from camp, there were still five more hours until Tzippy's date with Yosef Schachter. They didn't know what to do with themselves. The only television in the house was stashed in Shayna's room, and they weren't allowed to watch it. They weren't even supposed to know it was there, its presence an unacceptable connection to the outside world. It had long ago been smuggled into the house in an air-conditioner box to hide it from the neighbors, all of whom had done the same thing. Instead, the girls played with their Barbies—only Barbie had been renamed Frayda Baila, while Ken was called Avraham Dovid. The two dolls snuck forbidden glances in shul and went out on shidduch dates. If only there were a pink plastic Barbie Hotel Lobby instead of a Malibu Pool Party. If instead of the pink Barbie sports car, there were a father's Lincoln Town Car for Barbie to go out in. They dressed their dolls in outfits that were sometimes modest, sometimes revealing. Sometimes Frayda Baila made Shabbos dinner for Avraham Dovid. Other times she took off her clothes and lay down on top of him.

"What are you doing?" Tzippy called to them.

"Nothing," they said, and Frayda Baila was quickly pulled off Avraham Dovid and everyone's outfits were put back on.

Shayna hummed with activity. She had woken up at six to begin cooking the Shabbos meals for her family and eleven guests. She had challah dough rising, which she would braid later that night. She had gotten the younger girls ready as if they were on an assembly line. She brushed hair, made breakfast, packed lunches. When they were finally out of the house, she davened, cleaned, and did the shopping. Then she came home and baked three cakes, one for Shabbos, one for a friend whose daughter had gotten engaged, one for a neighbor whose mother had died. Now, with the date approaching, her hopes for Tzippy filled her with extra energy. She organized closets and polished silver. She climbed a stepladder to dust the crystal chandelier.

"Do you really think he cares about the chandelier?" Tzippy asked.

Shayna had never seen Yosef Schachter's house, but she was sure that it was perpetually clean. The chandeliers never grew dusty. The couches had no plastic slipcovers. If they got stained, the Schachters would simply buy new ones. But for Shayna nothing came so easily. Keeping up with the house was a daily battle she waged. And marrying off her daughter was becoming, if not a war, at least a military operation.

The date with Yosef Schachter had been arranged through an elaborate circuitry, transmitted by connections once, twice, thrice removed. Shayna had always looked longingly at the Schachter family. Reuben Schachter was executive director of the Orthodox Coalition's kosher division. Shoshana Schachter had perfect clothes and perfect children. Her manners were as unflappable as her appearance. If Shayna couldn't actually be Shoshana Schachter, then she would settle for a closer connection to her. When Tzippy had started dating, Shayna thought constantly of Yosef Schachter. His name popped into her mind every time Tzippy came home from an unsuccessful date. And then, with absolutely no nudging on her part, her friends began suggesting the match. "What a coincidence," she had said, beaming. "Someone else was just talking about him for my Tzippy." Shayna used this as proof that God was alive and well and living in her world. His hand was there for those who knew how to see it.

But she didn't have to rely solely on God. Yosef Schachter was universally acknowledged to be a great guy. The crown jewel of Brooklyn, Shayna insisted. In addition to his impeccable family, Yosef learned half a day and worked the other half. A learner and an earner, Shayna trilled when she elicited this bit of information. Every time she called her friend, who called his aunt, who called his mother, she was told that Yosef had just started dating someone. Three weeks later, she would call back and find out that he had broken up with that girl but was now dating someone else. It took patience and persistence, but finally Shayna activated her network at the exact moment when he was between girls.

"Mom, stop it," Tzippy said. "It's making me nervous just watching you clean."

"So don't watch."

"I promise you, he's not going to look in our closets."

"Closets, closets," the girls chanted. "Yosef Schachter, Yosef Schmachter."

"Maybe some people don't have to worry about the closets. But I'm not going to give anyone a reason to say something against me," Shayna said as she left the room.

"But what if I don't want to go out with him?" Tzippy asked.

In the kitchen, Shayna had begun to scrub the refrigerator. "We're not going to talk about that," she sang out.

Shayna was not going to talk about the refrigerator, which remained old no matter how hard she scrubbed. She was not going to think about the decorating magazines that made her wish for a fairy godmother who could wave her wand and bring forth stainless-steel appliances. She was not going to talk about the fact that she was the only one of her friends who didn't have stainless steel. The more she cleaned, the easier it became not to think. She stared at the sponge and focused on creating a spotless surface of white.

Shayna didn't understand what had gotten into her daughter. Apparently Tzippy would have to learn the hard way that it *did* matter. In this neighborhood, it wasn't only God who saw everything. The neighborhood had eyes, always open, always watching. This made her careful. Shayna Goldman had once been Susan Cantor. She had grown up in Rochester, far from the Orthodox hub in which she now lived. Her parents were Holocaust survivors who had become nonobservant. Her father had died when she was young, and her mother was often too sick or too sad to get out of bed. Looking for something she couldn't name, she once went to an Orthodox shul on a Saturday morning. It was a small congregation of older people, and they were thrilled to see a young face. After services, they gathered around her and treated her like a long-lost granddaughter.

She went back every week. She ate lunch at the rabbi's house and learned about keeping Shabbos and kosher. She was amazed at each new ritual. There was a blessing to say when she finished going to the bathroom. New dishes needed to be dunked in the ritual bath before she could use them. She peered into the Orthodox world as if it were a doll's house, furnished and decorated with no detail overlooked. When Shayna began thinking about college, the rabbi's wife sat her down and told her about Stern College in New York City. It was an Orthodox school, where the girls took both secular and religious classes. Shayna had been amazed that such a place could exist, and she understood that there she could start over and make herself anew.

Of her daughters, only Tzippy knew that Shayna hadn't grown up Orthodox. Shayna had gotten pregnant with Tzippy right away, but then years had gone by without her getting pregnant again. She believed that everything, including this undesired spacing of her girls, happened for a reason. God may have resided in the heavens, but He worked in this world. Everything that happened—war and car accidents, upset stomachs and sales on groceries—was the will of God. He caused her to forget her keys. He caused her to trip. He caused her stockings to run. In this world, where a new baby every year or two was the norm, she had considered her trouble getting pregnant a punishment for her irreligious past, a public demonstration that she wasn't who she appeared to be.

But Shayna was desperate for one of the large, bustling families that she saw all around her, and she was willing to fight for it in the only way she could: with the words of her prayers. Shayna had learned how to pray. For her, God wasn't a remote concept, a distant being. She prayed as if He were a close friend. Holding nothing back, she shut out the world and poured out her worries and wishes. She was sure He was up there, listening and weighing her requests. If she only prayed with more feeling, with greater concentration, she could assuage Him. After years of prayers, every day, with lips moving, body swaying in hope and sorrow, it had worked. He was convinced.

The girls had come every few years. Just when Shayna started to feel the earlier dread that she would have no more children, she was pregnant again. By the time the younger girls were old enough to understand, there was no need to tell them that she hadn't grown up religious. Her mother had died soon after she got married. There were no relatives who drove to their house on Shabbos, no non-kosher kitchens to visit where she had to bring her own food and serve her girls off paper plates. With nothing to give her away, Shayna hoped to seal herself off from her past, so that no one would know.

She had all but succeeded. Shayna dressed like the other women in the neighborhood, in long skirts and long sleeves, her hair always covered with a hat or a wig. She had acquired a slight Brooklyn accent, and she sprinkled her sentences with bits of Hebrew and Yiddish. Her house could be mistaken for any other Orthodox home on the block. The bookshelves were lined with Hebrew books. Polished menorahs were displayed in the breakfront next to silver kiddush cups and spice boxes shaped like windmills, chariots, and castles with flags atop. She knew the ins and outs of this community. If someone needed silver candlesticks, she could rattle off the three best places to buy them. She knew who could make a hat to match a dress, who could build custom bookshelves large enough to fit the oversized volumes of the Talmud.

But no matter how hard she tried, Shayna still felt new to this world. She had been Orthodox for more than twenty-five years, and she worried that she might make a mistake. She might heat food improperly on Shabbos. She might not understand a Hebrew phrase that everyone else did. Then her neighbors would see through her, to her past. They would strip off her hat, her long skirt, and her stockings, and expose her as an impostor. They could burrow down to the bottom, innermost layer, where they would find the teenage girl who was all alone and knew nothing.

Now her past made her even more nervous. Finding a husband for Tzippy was the truest test of whether she really belonged. When it came to dating, the watchful eyes became more attentive. Having a mother who hadn't grown up Orthodox would make it harder for her daughters to find husbands. Blights far less serious than this were uncovered through a spy system that operated in the aisles of Kosher-Mart. So if others stopped eating at a certain restaurant no longer considered kosher enough, then Shayna would too. If others used only white tablecloths for Shabbos, she would too. If she had to inflate their wealth and let it be known that Herschel was willing and able to support a son-in-law while he learned in yeshiva, so be it. There were rumors of eighteen-year-old girls going on Valium when it was time to start dating, but that was how it was, and she wasn't going to be the one to challenge or question and let her daughters suffer because of it.

Finally, it was time for Tzippy to get dressed. She had spent the day wishing that seven o'clock would never come. Zahava was painting her nails red, even though her mother had forbidden her to leave the house with that color on. Dena, Malky, and Dassi had put aside their dolls and were playing wedding. Malky had a white lace tablecloth on her head, folded over so the wine stains weren't visible. Dena and Dassi were being forced to take turns playing the groom.

"You stand here," Malky instructed Dena. "And you stand here," she said to Dassi. "Now both of you sing, and I'm going to walk down the aisle."

She walked across Tzippy's room, hands clasping an imaginary bouquet. She stopped to give further instructions. "Sing louder. And you"—she pulled Dassi over to her—"need to hold my train."

"My turn to be the bride," Dena and Dassi cried.

"Not yet," Malky said. "We still have to play marriage."

The bride disappeared into her parents' bedroom. She came out wearing one of Shayna's hats and a pillow stuffed into her shirt to make a pregnant stomach. "Now I'm going to tell you what I'm making for dinner. And you have to listen and then tell me what you're making."

Dena smashed into Malky and yanked the hat off her head. Dassi grabbed the pillow from her stomach and hit her with it. They bumped against Tzippy, who was brushing her hair in front of the mirror.

"Girls," Tzippy said, "I'm going to be late if you keep distracting me."

"You look pretty," Malky said.

"Do you love him?" Dassi asked.

"If I were him, I would definitely marry you," Dena said.

Tzippy put down her brush and wished she could stay home with her sisters. She wished she were still their age, when veils were made of tablecloths and bride-and-groom was a game to play when she got bored. She grabbed Dassi and Dena in a hug, opening her arms to reach for Malky, who had tied the lace tablecloth into a cape around her neck and was pretending to fly, like Superbride, around the room.

The doorbell rang and four pairs of eyes peeked out from behind the door. The sisters had witnessed all the boys who came and went. They kept track of their favorites and made bets as to whether there would be a second date. They cried when Tzippy came home and pronounced a boy hopelessly unsuited for her. They cried even more when a boy reported to the matchmaker that he wasn't interested in Tzippy. They often wished they could come along on the dates. They imagined riding in the front seat of the car and being proposed to themselves. Sometimes they hoped their mother would succeed in giving Tzippy away, so there would be a wedding and they could get new dresses with lots of lace. Other times they wanted to grab on to Tzippy and keep her home forever.

"Tzippy, dear," Shayna called upstairs. She smiled at Yosef Schachter and invited him to sit down. She put out a plate of cookies and gave him a glass of orange juice.

"My husband will be so sorry he missed you," she said.

Malky, Dena, and Dassi were usually sent to bed as soon as the doorbell rang. But their father hadn't yet come home and his absence made Shayna so nervous that she forgot to chase them from the room. In exchange for this unexpected reprieve, they decided not to mention that just ten minutes ago their mother was leaving urgent messages for their father, reminding him about the date. Zahava went upstairs, uninterested in Tzippy's latest set-up. But the other sisters made themselves comfortable on the couch next to Yosef Schachter and took a closer look.

The girls knew that when it came to dating, first impressions were often faulty. They knew that you could get a reputation for being too picky. They knew that by the tenth date you were expected to know, if not one way, then the other. They knew that the boy was judged on the basis of which yeshiva he learned in and who his family was. They knew that a girl needed to be thin if she wanted to find a husband. They also knew that she was allowed to gain all the weight she wanted once she was married. They knew that their mother had once said, under her breath, that she would die if Tzippy was the last from her class to get married. They knew that she had made a flurry of phone calls to bring Yosef Schachter to their house.

And here he was. Dassi giggled and Dena elbowed her in the stomach. Yosef smiled at them and asked what grade they were in. He remembered their names after being told only once. When he handed each of them a cookie, their decision was made. He was the one for Tzippy.

"Tzippy, dear," Shayna called again.

Tzippy came downstairs, blushing. Her mother and sisters were huddled around her date, and she wished the evening were already over. Yosef Schachter waved good-bye to them, and Shayna felt the urge, which she restrained, to whisper in his ear, *Tzippy is a good girl.* As if she knew what her mother was thinking, Tzippy hurried out with the boy, looking as though she were being led to the gallows rather than to the lobby of the Brooklyn Marriott Hotel.

On this, her forty-second date, Tzippy dropped a lemon wedge into her Diet Coke and felt as if she were drowning. A hotel lobby was the standard first date, because the boy wasn't expected to buy dinner before he knew if the relationship had potential. They sat at a small cocktail table, one couple amidst many others, and didn't say a word. All her life, Tzippy had been taught not to talk to boys, not to look at them, not to think about them. So sitting across from one, what was she supposed to say?

Tzippy stared over his shoulder at the other dates. She could tell who was on a first date, who was on a second. She envied the old-timers who had made it to a third. She hated the girls who talked and laughed, and made it look so easy to sit across the table from a stranger you might end up marrying. It never happened that way for her. She had been on dates where the boys didn't stop talking. *Shut up,* she had imagined screaming. *Don't open your mouth one more time.* She had been on dates where the boy followed, word for word, the conversation topics suggested in the religious dating guides. She had been called Rivky instead of Tzippy. Even so, when she rehashed to her mother every horrible detail, it was never a question of whether she had liked the boy, only of whether he had liked her.

She asked her friends how they felt when they were on dates. Was she the only one who felt suspended above the moment? Was she the only one who wanted to flee? In contrast, her friends compared who went to fancier places on their dates. They talked of boys who were greeted by name at the lounges they frequented, boys who flew in from out of town and had dates booked at two-hour intervals. They compared their favorite marriage proposals. There were stories of scavenger hunts, the final clue leading to an engagement ring. Proposals were advertised on scoreboards, slipped into fortune cookies, broadcast on the news ticker in Times Square. They all knew the story of Esther Tuckman's faked kidnapping. The unsuspecting bride-to-be was taken hostage and was terrified, until her captor removed his mask and held out a small velvet box. "But when you're on a date, do you ever think about doing something crazy?" Tzippy asked her friends. The conversations stopped. "What," they asked, "like saying you'd rather go to a different restaurant?"

It used to sound easy. How hard could it be to determine basic compatibility? On their dates, they were allowed to laugh and have a good time. But the main objective was to discover if there was potential for marriage. Do you want to live in New York or in Israel? they asked. Would you allow a television in your home? Do you go to the movies? The yeses would be tabulated against the nos and a decision would be made as to whether the person sitting across the table was The One.

The rabbis assured them that their way of getting married was so much better than in the outside world. There, people gave advice about which college to go to; these days, even about which nursery school to choose. People had financial advisors and personal trainers. No one would dream of buying a new couch, God forbid, without calling a decorator. But when it came to marriage—the most important decision of all—you were supposed to rely solely on your own feelings. To prove their point, the rabbis pointed to the national divorce rate. See, they said, even living with someone first wasn't a guarantee. The religious girls and boys were supposed to trust their parents. They knew that real happiness was based on shared values, not on fleeting feelings of love and attraction. Their parents had been set up. So had their grandparents and great-grandparents. Love came later, a byproduct of companionship, family, and hard work.

"Israel," Yosef Schachter was saying. "I spent three years in yeshiva there and I loved it."

This statement brought her back. Tzippy had never been to Israel. Many of her classmates—those who weren't on the brink of engagement—went to seminary in Israel the year after high school. Tzippy had wanted to go. She loved the idea of going away for a whole year. "You're not going to leave me," her mother had responded when Tzippy had broached the idea. "What would I do without you?" Shayna asked. "The girls will barely know you if you're gone for a whole year." Hearing these words, Tzippy squelched her desire to go.

"What did you like about it?" Tzippy asked.

Yosef Schachter grew flustered. "Not just the learning. Not that I don't like my yeshiva here. Not that I don't like being close to my family." He used a flurry of double negatives, protesting against anything that might later be used against him. He spoke haltingly, as if what he had to say was too personal for a date. "But the yeshiva was in the middle of nowhere, and sometimes, when no one was looking, I went outside and ran as fast as I could, just for fun. I kept running until I was so out of breath I thought I might collapse. But by then I was so far away and it was so quiet, and I felt like I could be myself."

"Is that allowed?" she asked bitterly, throwing everything he had heard about sweet Tzippy Goldman out the window.

He laughed nervously. "I don't know," he replied.

Tzippy laughed too, and for the first time all night, they looked each other in the eye and smiled. She stopped thinking of him as Yosef Schachter and surprised herself by thinking of him simply as Yosef. He was actually a nice guy. He wasn't showing off; he wasn't making her feel as though she were at a job interview. If she were not so worn down by what her mother wanted for her, she might have been interested in going out with him again. But for the past few months, she had heard of nothing but Yosef Schachter. She had become tired of him even before she had met him. With each new piece of information from her mother, Tzippy felt as if there would be no choice. By virtue of her mother's love for him, they would end up married with a house full of kids even before they finished their first conversation.

Faced with the intensity of her mother's desires, Tzippy wasn't sure what she wanted for herself. But whatever it was, she was going to find it on her own. Tiny flitting pieces of Tzippy emerged and refused to behave. She envisioned standing up and joining hands with the other girls here on dates. At first they would cluck in surprise at her breach of dating etiquette. Then they would see the wild look on her face and start to feel it too. Something would break loose inside, and they too would need to cast off where they were, who they were. The soft background music would become louder, and Tzippy would dance the girls around the room, through the closely spaced tables and on top of the bar. From underneath their skirts, long graceful legs would come kicking out. Then she would kiss Yosef Schachter on the lips. All the girls would smack their dates on the lips and flounce from the room. Then Tzippy would go home to her room and close the door. When her mother and her friends gathered outside and demanded that she explain herself, the one window in the room would open and she would jump out. She would become a bird and fly away.

Indulging in dreams that were big and white and made of satin, Shayna heard keys in the front lock and rushed to the door, assuming it was Tzippy, maybe Tzippy aglow with a good date. But instead, three hours late and with no apology, it was Herschel. He walked in the door, trying to restrain his excitement. Herschel was all jingle and clink. He had a cell phone clipped to one pocket of his pants, a beeper to the other. A key ring was attached to his belt loop. On it dangled keys to the house and the car, keys to buildings he no longer worked in, houses he no longer lived in, cars he no longer owned. He carried stray keys he found around the house, duplicate keys to keys that opened nothing.

"This is the one," he exclaimed. "All these years, I've been saying it's only a matter of time. And now, here it is—"

"You were supposed to be home hours ago," Shayna interrupted.

When Herschel looked at her blankly, she reminded him, "Tzippy is out with Yosef Schachter." He looked as if this were the first time he had heard the name. "Yosef Schachter? The boy I've been talking about all week? The boy who I really think might be The One?"

Shayna sat on the couch, and Herschel joined her. "Shayna, listen to me. That's all I'm asking. Then you'll understand why I'm so excited."

In front of her friends, Shayna plastered a smile on her face and said that her husband was in the kosher food business. This was the best way to explain his enterprising ideas. But she wished that he worked somewhere more prominent. If he had to be in the food business, at least he could work in the Orthodox Coalition's kosher division with Reuben Schachter. This job, these connections, would secure their place in the community. Instead, Herschel had inherited a small catering business from his father. He changed the name from Kosher

Kitchen to Kosher Ventures and was always trying to expand it, always about to discover the next big thing. But some small problem always postponed his dreams. At the last minute, a contract didn't go through. There were unexpected health department regulations about shipping pizza worldwide. Freeze-drying wasn't as simple as he had imagined. But this never stopped him. By the time one idea failed, he had already moved on to the next one. Herschel lived in a string of continuous futures. He only saw what would be, what could be.

"Frozen hydroponic vegetables," Herschel announced. "Marketed to the kosher consumer."

He was standing again, and Shayna leaned back into the couch and looked up at him. Herschel had dark hair and a short, neatly groomed beard. His white shirt was perfectly pressed. Though he was shorter than she had wanted her husband to be, from this vantage point, he still loomed above her. He held up a business plan for starting a new line of frozen vegetables. He had two partners, three potential investors, and a signed endorsement from a rabbi.

"It's a niche market. Think about it. You could buy raw broccoli and spend hours looking for bugs. Or you could buy ours. One hundred percent bug-free. Guaranteed."

Worrying about bugs in vegetables was the latest stringency in their community. Certain vegetables, once presumed kosher, were no longer considered so. In the florets of broccoli, in the leaves of spinach, cabbage, and lettuce, tiny bugs lurked. These bugs weren't only undesirable; they were also non-kosher. Happy to have a new stringency in order to prove their devotion, people no longer ate these vegetables, unless they were guaranteed bug-free. Or they soaked and checked them. They held spinach to the light and laid cabbage leaves on paper towels to examine. They installed fluorescent light tables in their renovated kitchens.

"Shayna, think about it. You have five kids. How many pounds of frozen vegetables do you go through every month?"

She didn't say anything.

"Come on. Take a guess. How many do you think?"

"I don't know, Herschel. Just tell me."

"For argument's sake, let's say twenty-five pounds a month. And how many Orthodox Jews do you think there are in the tri-state area alone?" He didn't wait for an answer. "Believe it or not, there's a frozen food company out there looking for a buyer. So do the math. If we appealed to the kosher consumer, we'd triple the business they're doing now."

He saw the idea as if it had already come to fruition. The final product was stacked in the freezer section, baked into casseroles and kugels. But Shayna first saw the problems. Herschel constantly traveled to meet potential investors, while she stayed home and worried about money that was promised but never came. She thought about what everyone else had and about her five daughters who needed the same. Worried that he would embarrass her, she was often ready to hold her hands up and declare that she had had enough.

But Herschel could always sense this moment coming. And that was when he came home, cardboard boxes in hand, and announced that it was pizza night. He rifled through his pockets and pulled out presents for each of the girls. He kissed Shayna and handed her a velvet box. The piece of jewelry inside was just the thing she had seen on someone else and been wishing for. Then he plied her with assurances, and she listened. One part of her tried to say no, while every other part softened. She always joined him in his dreams, which were large enough for two.

"If my idea works, we're going to make a fortune. We're going to be famous."

He told her that the girls would have whatever they wanted. While they were still young, he would shower them with toys, dresses, and dolls. When they got older, the phone would ring off the hook with people wanting to set their sons up with his daughters. Shayna could remodel the kitchen and next year remodel it again if she wanted. She could live in a continuous state of redoing. He would be asked to serve on the board of every Jewish institution in Brooklyn. His picture would be in *The Jewish Press*. When someone mentioned Herschel Goldman, everyone would know who he was. His name alone would unlock doors.

"Maybe," Shayna said.

"It's more than maybe. You can see it, Shayna. You believe it too."

"But if it doesn't work, promise me that will be it. You'll do something else. You'll get a real job."

He hugged her and she couldn't breathe. "Believe me," he said, "it's not going to come to that."

Keys turned in the lock a second time. The door was opened and slammed shut.

"So what did you think?" Shayna called.

"You've got to hear this, Tzippy," Herschel called. "You're going to love it."

Tzippy walked into the living room, her cheeks blazing. "I want to go to Israel for the year," she announced.

Shayna stared at her. She had sent Tzippy on a date and, instead of returning with a romantic glow, she had brought home more of her inexplicable anger. Her daughter was becoming someone she didn't recognize. It was getting late for Tzippy. Didn't she know that at this stage in the game there was only one thing to want?

"Frozen hydroponic vegetables," Herschel announced.

"Yosef Schachter," Shayna wailed.

"What about him?" Tzippy demanded.

"Didn't you have a good time? He seemed so nice. I really thought maybe . . ."

"No," Tzippy said, and swept her arms out to either side of her. "Not him. Not any of them."

Herschel didn't register what Tzippy had said, except to think that whatever she wanted, she could have. Soon they would all have whatever they wanted. Shayna felt the dream once again slipping away. It never happened as she wanted it to, and she wondered if it ever would. But if her daughter was going to act this way, at least it would happen far from the watching eyes. Shayna hid her disappointment by formulating the explanation she would offer. "She's a serious girl. She was supposed to teach nursery school this year, but she decided she wanted to go to seminary in Israel instead," she would say to her friends when they asked about Tzippy. "She's barely twenty-two. We still have some time." And in the small part of Tzippy that was allowed to entertain thoughts that were not nice, not sweet, not appropriate, all she thought about was escape.

— TWO —

Two dish racks had appeared overnight, and they sat in Naomi Miller's kitchen sink as if they had always been there. This wasn't the only unusual occurrence in the house. On Monday, the mezuzahs disappeared from the doorposts and were brought to the rabbi to be checked for any smudged or missing letters that would render them non-kosher. A day later, having apparently been declared kosher, they were put back up. On Wednesday, large plastic cups intended for morning ritual washing appeared in each of the bathrooms. And now, Thursday, it was dish racks. It was as if a team of religious elves had been let loose in the neighborhood. Instead of green hats and turned-up shoes, these elves wore black hats and white beards and scurried from house to house, waving wands and leaving kosher in their wake. But Naomi knew who was behind these transformations. It wasn't her daughter, Ilana, or her husband, Joel. It was her son, Bryan, who had just returned home from his second year of yeshiva in Israel, filled with religious fervor and a love for the letter of the law.

He had gone to Israel between high school and college, as all his friends had done. This was the path Joel and Naomi had laid out for their kids, this line of moderation, this Modern Orthodoxy. They believed in being part of the modern world. They believed in the integration of religious and secular. They sent their kids to Jewish day schools that doubled as feeders for the Ivy League. In coed classes, in jeans and sneakers, they studied English and math half the day, Jewish law and Bible the other half. They kept Shabbos and kosher and played on basketball teams wearing blue and white uniforms with matching yarmulkes. And before they ventured out of this world where everything was consistent, or at least consistently inconsistent, they spent a year in Israel.

Before he left for yeshiva, Bryan had worried whether he would have enough time to play basketball. But after a few months, having undergone some transformation his parents couldn't understand, he worried that he didn't have enough time to learn Talmud. He begged for a second year, and Naomi and Joel had reluctantly agreed, in accordance with their principle that kids need room to grow and explore. And in accordance with their principle that two years in yeshiva was more than enough, they made him promise that after his second year in Israel, he would attend Columbia University as planned.

But, instead, he came home and informed them that he no longer wanted to be called Bryan. He wanted to use his Hebrew name, Baruch, which they had given him in memory of Joel's grandfather. But they had never intended it for use in the outside world. Because Baruch carried with it the dreaded *ch*, the modern-day shibboleth. As in Chana and Chaviva and Yechiel. Chaim, Nechama, Zacharyah, and Achiezer. Not a *Ch* as in Charlie, not a *Sh* as in Shirley, but a guttural sound that came from the back of those throats that had been trained to utter it from birth.

They thought his fervor was the result of his age, the kind of certitude only a nineteen-year-old could muster. They had seen their friends' children pass through this stage of fervent religiosity. They had heard stories about children who came home from Israel and carted off all the dishes in the house to be dunked in the local mikvah. If they could, these children would kidnap their parents and dunk them too. They rattled off every commandment their parents overlooked, eager to let them know why they and all their friends were hypocrites. And these were the more pliant children. Others refused to set foot back on American soil. The only way they would leave Israel was kicking and screaming.

Roots to grow and wings to soar, Naomi had written on birthday and graduation cards. Until Bryan had taken this far too seriously and searched for roots that went deeper than Laurelwood, New Jersey, where they lived. Their son wanted to pass through Ellis Island in reverse, to find a Poland, a Lithuania, a Galicia, he was sure still existed somewhere. And when he found where these roots led, he had taken the wings they had given him and flown right off the deep end. But still, they didn't expect their son to permanently join the growing ranks of the nouveau yeshiva-ish. They reassured themselves that all it would take was a few weeks back in America for Bryan to even out. Bryan had been home for five days now, and in the hope that he would soon return to a more comfortable middle ground, they were tiptoeing around him and waiting.

Baruch was in his bedroom, wrapped in the black leather straps of his tefillin ("And it shall be as a sign to you on your hand and a memorial between your eyes"—Exodus 13:9). Jet lag and laziness had conspired against him, and he had slept late, through minyan at shul, which he was commanded by God to attend ("He should not separate himself from the congregation when they pray"—Shulchan Aruch 90). Before he left yeshiva, his rabbi had warned him against being lulled into the complacency of his parents' so-called Modern Orthodox world ("You shall not walk in the ways of the other nations"—Leviticus 18:4). Five days in America and this was what had happened.

He was trying to make up for his failure with an extra measure of concentration. He burrowed into the prayers he recited every morning. The familiarity soothed his guilt. No matter where he was or how he felt, he uttered these words. Now, at home, they reminded him who he had become. Between the words of the prayers—until it became a prayer in itself—he told himself that he had changed, he had changed for good. Before Israel, he had raced through the davening. He had never felt as though he were standing before God. In yeshiva, when he davened, he saw arms wrapped in tefillin, bodies cloaked in the black-and-white stripes of the tallis. He saw lips moving and bodies swaying, and he felt the presence of God. After davening, Baruch had sat in the beis midrash, the yeshiva's book-lined study hall, and learned Talmud. He ate lunch, then learned more. At night, he returned to the beis midrash to review the pages that had been covered during the day ("And you shall be occupied with it day and night"—Joshua 1:8). He had studied Talmud before, in high school for the fifty-minute period between algebra and American history. But when he spent the whole day immersed in Talmud, he saw the shadow of God peeking out from behind the words.

If two men find an object, the Talmud read, they should split it. But what is meant by "find"? What is meant by "object"? He who sees it first or he who holds it first? What about a case in which each man claims it is his? What about a contradictory text, a standing principle? A proof text was brought from here, an opposing opinion from there. The folio pages of the Talmud became Baruch's world. The tiny black letters became small square huts with triangular roofs. They lined up and became rows of houses, stacked themselves and became modern skyscrapers. They changed shape again and became open doors and tunnels, pathways, caves, and alleyways leading deeper into this world. Behind every door, he found another door. Behind every answer, another question.

But at home, this world, which had existed so fully in yeshiva, threatened to collapse. The stereo in his sister Ilana's room was blasting the same rock music he had once loved, and he suspected an act of deliberate provocation. Since he had come home, Ilana had sent probing glances his way, but she had said little to him. She took the changes he had made as a personal affront and looked at him as if he had morphed into some creature she didn't recognize. He didn't want this distance. Before he had come home, he had hoped that she would follow in his footsteps, the two of them allied against their parents. He had imagined that they would work together against the laxity that ruled the house, just as they had once teamed up to combat their mother's one-hour-of-television-a-night rule. Always able to find the loophole in their mother's plans, Ilana and Baruch had rolled their eyes and chosen different one-hour shows to watch. "If I happen to be in the room while she's watching her hour, that's not my fault," he had argued. "And vice versa," she had added on cue. Remembering this, he wished he could take off his tefillin and go into Ilana's room. He wished he could laugh and joke with her as he had once done.

Baruch pushed away this desire, and reminded himself that it wasn't possible to change and still fit back into this family. God worked in strange and wondrous ways, and here He was using the music of the Top 40 to test his resoluteness—just as He had tested Avraham on Mount Moriah, Moshe in the desert. The only way to pass this test was to seek refuge in his prayers. Baruch put his siddur in front of his face. He swayed with more fervor and tried to summon his belief that when he prayed, he stood before God, Master of the Universe Himself.

When none of this helped—the bass of Ilana's music imbedded too deeply under his skin, mingled with his prayers—he looked heaven-ward. Perhaps God would see his desire to daven and deliver him from this house of sin. In the meantime, he would have to say something to Ilana. But he was no longer the kind of person who would barge into her room and tell her to shut off her goddamn music. He was a Ben Torah, and he would have to act in a way befitting such a person. He wasn't supposed to interrupt his prayers. But there were exceptions to this prohibition: if one had to use the bathroom, if there was a noise that made it impossible to concentrate, if Roman soldiers appeared suddenly in the shul.

He knocked lightly on her door, then loudly. Finally he gave up and opened the door.

"Ilana, I'm trying to daven, and I'd appreciate it if you would lower the music," he said.

He restrained himself from adding that he wished she understood who he was now. He also wished that they could somehow remain close. But shackled by the new awkwardness in their relationship, none of this could be said. All of it became one more heartfelt, if futile, prayer.

During the first week of summer vacation, in the thirteenth year of her life, Ilana was lying on her bed, talking on the phone.

"Come in," she said, and hung up the phone.

Ilana took her brother's presence in her room as a hopeful sign that he was finally back. Five days before, he had come home from Israel a different person. Her parents had clearly noticed, but they were try-ing to pretend that everything was fine. Her mother kept making unprompted declarations that it was so nice to have everyone together again. Her father watched TV and tried to block out everything going on around him. Ilana knew, though, that nothing was fine. She and Bryan had once been close, but since he had come home, she had barely spoken to him. She had tried, but even when she did say some-thing, it was met by silence or disinterest or worse.

In the doorway, he shuffled from one foot to the other and looked away. He braced his arm against the doorframe, as if he dared not enter. His serious, self-righteous expression made her feel as if she shouldn't be lying down. She had the urge to tuck away anything that might be incriminating.

But there was nothing she could do about her room. Once-worn clothes were draped over her desk chair. Dirty clothes were inside out on the floor, in the vicinity of the hamper her mother had placed there as a suggestion. A tangle of shoes filled the remaining floor space. The mess in her room was well past the stage where she could be told to clean it up. It had taken on the dimension of a family project, something for which several days would need to be allocated. In her defense, she claimed her room was a vehicle for creative expression. "I know you think it's random," she liked to say, "but a lot of thought goes into it." She smiled and coaxed from her parents their agreement that they wouldn't interfere with her personal sanctuary.

"The music," he said. "Would you turn it down?"

"Okay, Bryan," she said and lowered the volume, hoping this gesture would ease the tension brewing between them.

"I've asked you to please call me Baruch now," he said.

She leaned back into her pillow, surprised. No matter what she did, it was wrong. She was starting to see that nothing would satisfy him. She gave an exaggerated sigh and rolled her eyes.

"That might be what you're making us call you, but technically your name is still Bryan. You can ask us to call you by a different name and we can agree if we want to, but you can't say we have an obligation to listen to you."

"If I want to use my Hebrew name, why would you object to that?"

"I'm just saying that for some of us, it's still a free country and you can't force us to do anything we don't want to do."

"No, I can't force you. But I am *asking* you, as your older brother, to respect my wishes and call me Baruch. And I'm also trying to daven. And that's why I'm *asking* you to lower the music."

Ilana didn't say anything, and she hoped he would leave before her tough exterior gave way and revealed her bafflement. She didn't understand why she was caught in this blast of disapproval. She was a good girl. She listened to her parents. She got good grades. She davened when she remembered to. She went to shul on Shabbos. She wore shorts and watched TV and didn't see what there was to be so conflicted about.

It brought back the hurt feelings she had been nursing since his return. At the airport, she had shouted his name and thrown her arms around him. He didn't stop her, but his shoulders tensed and his body drew back as he perfunctorily returned the hug. She was so happy to see him that she hadn't worried about it. Later that evening, she sat on the floor of his room and watched him unpack. Still so excited to have him home, she moved to hug him again. This time he didn't just tense; he disentangled himself.

"Ilana," he had said. "It says in the Shulchan Aruch that after the age of bar mitzvah, a brother isn't allowed to hug his sister."

Still in hugging range, she stared at him.

"What are you talking about?" she asked.

"It's assur," he said. Forbidden.

"No, it's not," she argued.

"Yes. It is."

"That's crazy."

"It's not saying that there would be anything going on. Just that it's improper."

It was all so impersonal: a theoretical brother, a theoretical sister, a theoretical hug. She stepped back and held up her hands in surrender. "Fine. No problem," she had said, and wondered if the rabbis would object to her smacking her brother. In their estimation, was that sort of contact inappropriate as well? But inside her anger, she also felt ashamed, as if these rabbis and her brother were accusing her of an incestuous rabbinic sluttiness.

But that was five days ago, when she still had been naive enough to think that having her brother home meant having him back. She wasn't going to listen to this new Baruch boy who had returned in her brother's body. She scowled at him, and as he left her room, she hurled after him as if it were a curse word: "Bryan."

Opening his bedroom door, Baruch sang aloud: "Shema Yisroel, Adonai Elohaynu, Adonai echad."

Hear O Israel, the Lord is our God, the Lord is One. These words ought to be able to hold out against "I want to kiss you, I want to love you, please let me touch you." He imagined his words like soldiers armed only with their piety, going off to fight the corrupt words of whatever teenage pop star his sister was listening to.

"Mee cha-mocha ba'elim Adonai, mee cha-mocha nedar ba'kodesh," he sang. *Who is like You, God, in Your glory and majesty, in Your manifestations of holiness, in Your goodness and Your truth.*

She opened her door too: "I want to rock all night, come on baby, dance with me."

When it was time to recite the silent Shemoneh Esray prayer, he could think of no rabbinic source that allowed him to say it out loud, even to combat the evils of rock music. He let her music play, while he stood, feet together, lips moving, and blessed the God of Abraham, Isaac, and Jacob. When he finished, he resumed his battle cry.

"Ashrei yoshvei vaytecha." *Happy is he who sits in God's House.*

"Aleinu leshabe'ach la'adon hakol." *It is incumbent upon us to praise the Master of all.*

His first year in Israel, Baruch had tried not to be one of those boys so influenced by the rabbis that they gave up everything. In yeshiva, he spent the first six months trying to escape Rabbi Rothstein's inquisitive eye. But he also wasn't one of the boys who snuck off to the beach in Netanya or hung out at the Underground Bar. He went to shiur most of the time and spent his evenings on Ben Yehudah Street. Then he grew bored with going out, and there was nothing to do but learn. He immersed himself in the Talmud. When Rabbi Rothstein delivered shiur, Baruch saw that he wasn't simply lecturing, presenting, explicating. He was living the words. In his eyes, he saw truth reflected back at him. It was the same look emanating from the eyes of the Torah greats whose pictures adorned the walls of the yeshiva. In their browns, their blues, their hazel greens, they seemed to reflect the light of heaven.

Once Baruch saw this, it was like trying to walk against the wind. He realized that it was all true: It was true that God existed; it was true that He had given the Torah on Mount Sinai; it was therefore true that Baruch was required to follow its every commandment. Faced with such certain, blinding truth, how could he turn away?

Rabbi Rothstein said that the Torah covered every second of life. He said that adherence to God's law paved the way to happiness and truth. He also warned the boys against the dangers of the outside world. It didn't matter that you could find bits of goodness here and there. Rabbi

Rothstein preferred a clean cut, an unambiguous separation. It wasn't only their generation that had to deal with this problem. The great rabbis had had to wrestle with influence from the Philistines, the Greeks, the Romans. But Rabbi Rothstein made sure to emphasize that the question was particularly pressing these days: The filth had risen to unprecedented levels. And with everyone claiming, in the name of tolerance and acceptance, that there was nothing wrong with these influences, it was even more important to be vigilant. "You don't want your mind to be so open that your brain falls out," he told the boys.

After a few months, Baruch agreed with Rabbi Rothstein when he said that the Modern Orthodox had simply come up with a rationalization for their lack of faith, a way to feel better about being seduced by the charms of the outside world. "Face it," Baruch had said to his friends who were struggling with the same questions. "What our parents do isn't really right." His parents were minimally, nominally Orthodox. They went to shul. They kept kosher. But they didn't, he was sure, see the law of God as binding. They practiced a watered-down version of the truth. They did what was convenient or palatable, and ignored what wasn't. Picking and choosing, this was their true religion. In this family, where anything could presumably be discussed, all he wanted to ask his parents was if in their hearts, with all their souls, with all their might, they believed.

Because Baruch believed. He had peeled back his outer layers of doubt and cynicism, ego and desire. Underneath, he found a hard luminescent core of faith. He knew that if confronted, his parents would extol the virtues of moderation and secular education. They would talk about integrating and assimilating the best of both worlds. They would claim that math and science, art and literature, also came from God. His mother would talk about faith, struggle, and doubt. She would say that we can each hold mutually exclusive beliefs and all be right. His father would roll his eyes and attribute Baruch's belief to youthful extremism. If pressed, he would extol the benefits of living in two worlds. His parents wouldn't understand that Baruch wanted one world, authentic and whole.

There was something else his parents didn't know and wouldn't understand. Baruch had agreed that in two months he would be starting his first year at Columbia, his father's alma mater. His parents, he was sure, imagined him wearing the blue-and-white Columbia sweatshirt they had bought for him when he went for his interview. They imagined their son living in a coed dorm, enrolled in classes in literature, science, and philosophy. But as soon as Baruch worked up the courage, he would tell them. He wasn't going to college, not this year, not next year, not ever. Instead, he was going back to yeshiva.

With this announcement, Baruch would traverse the outermost limits of his parents' tolerance. For them, a son choosing yeshiva over college was an embarrassment. They worshipped the Ivy League. He had been raised to think that only Harvard, Penn, and Columbia were good enough. Law school, medical school, and business school were his parents' most heartfelt dreams. He had once accepted this as the word of truth. He had worked hard to get into Columbia. He had wanted to be a corporate lawyer like his father. Now he saw that his parents worshipped the false idols of achievement and success. Learning for the sake of learning, because it was the will of God, was of no value to them.

He had friends who submitted to the will of their parents and considered themselves passive resisters as they attended their first-year orientations. At the Ivy League school of their parents' choice, they read the books on the syllabi, but didn't allow them to penetrate their minds. He had a friend at Yale who returned from Israel and refused to live in the dorms. He organized his classes around minyan and shiur. Another friend attended Penn under protest and claimed that he was majoring in "honoring my mother and father." And by the end of their sophomore year, after incremental steps toward the middle ground, both of them were going to parties and studying comparative religion.

Baruch wasn't going to be one of those boys. He was going to immerse himself in the study of Torah day and night. Eventually he would become a rabbi, the one occupation his parents had never encouraged. And he wasn't interested in becoming a Modern Orthodox rabbi with a Ph.D. in Bible, at a shul where his congregants did one thing in front of him and another thing behind his back. He wasn't going to officiate at weddings where the mixed dancing started as soon as the table of rabbis cleared out. He wanted the real thing, the unadulterated God.

Rabbi Rothstein said that change starts at home, so Baruch took a look around his room. On the surface, it looked innocuous. He had always been neat. He was the only member of this family who made his bed every day. But this outer neatness hid the inner contradictions.

A Yankees pennant hung on the wall. His bookshelves were lined with spy novels. His bulletin board was covered with old sports schedules and pictures from camp with his arms around various girls. From his desk, he pulled out a stack of *Playbill*s from shows he had seen. He made a pile in the middle of his room, and he added to this his high school yearbook, his guide to the SATs, his copies of *Sports Illustrated* (regular and swimsuit). He tossed in the knit yarmulkes he had once worn. They were a Modern Orthodox mating ritual, crocheted by girls as flirtatious gestures and inscribed in contrasting colors. "To Bryan, Luv Hadassah," one cooed. "Friends 4-ever," another promised. The knit yarmulkes came in hot pink and hunter green, trimmed according to the fashion of the day, argyle and PacMan giving way to Bart Simpson and Nike swooshes. They were the religious equivalent of a sports car, and Baruch had traded his in for a somber four-door: the black velvet yarmulke.

He paused only when he came to his Yankees cap, which hung on the inside of his closet door. The white lettering on it was now faded and frayed. The inside rim was sweat-stained. And it was the sole item he couldn't bear to give away. He had once loved baseball above all else. He had once believed with perfect faith that the Holy One, Blessed Be He, guided the outcome of the World Series. One year, when the Yankees played in game seven of the World Series on Shabbos, he convinced Ilana to accidentally bump against the television and turn it on. In high school, he rarely left the house without his Yankees cap covering his yarmulke. He would never wear it now, but he wanted to keep it as a souvenir. He tossed it to the back of his closet. One day he would take it out and marvel at who he had once been.

Having allowed himself this one weakness, Baruch worked more fervently through the rest of the closet. Toward the front were the new clothes he had bought in Israel: identical black dress pants next to identical white long-sleeved shirts. Pushed to the back were Tommy Hilfiger shirts and Gap blue jeans, Nike sneakers and cable-knit sweaters. Rabbi Rothstein had made it clear that such clothes were a way of imitating the non-Jews, a modern-day idolatry. Baruch piled them up, filling bags, until all he had left in his closet was empty hangers and the starkness of black and white. The clothes would go into his mother's give-away pile, but if it weren't illegal in Laurelwood, he would have made a bonfire and set them aflame. Instead of a ram and two he-goats, this would be his karban olah, his burnt offering. In the time of the Holy Temple, one who wanted to repent was required to bring two sacrifices. So he added to the top of the pile a karban chatat, his most heartfelt sin offering: the blue sweatshirt with the white letters proclaiming COLUMBIA.

Dish racks in hand, Naomi listened to Baruch and Ilana fighting. She was used to knowing what to do with her kids. She had read all the right books, switching from Dr. Spock to Penelope Leach and back to Dr. Spock. She had studied the entire Adele Faber canon, and committed to memory *Siblings Without Rivalry* and *How to Talk So Kids Will Listen, and Listen So Kids Will Talk.* She believed in Harriet Lerner and *The Dance of Anger, The Dance of Intimacy, The Dance of Motherhood.* She subscribed to late toilet training, emerging literacy, and anger management. She didn't yell, didn't—God forbid—hit. Instead, she had said, "No, Bryan, little sisters are not for biting. Dustpans are not for eating." "I know you want a chocolate-chip cookie, Ilana," she had learned to say. "Wouldn't it be great if the whole world were one giant cookie and we could take a bite whenever we wanted?"

"Don't Adele Faber me," Ilana had once responded. At age ten, she had taken *How to Talk So Kids Will Listen* from Naomi's nightstand and read it too.

Even with this setback, these books, with their opposing opinions and contradictory experts, had coalesced into something of a philosophy. Naomi wasn't going to force her kids to do anything. She might suggest, encourage, recommend, persuade, but she never resorted to a stuffing-food-into-their-mouths, throwing-them-into-the-swimming-pool sort of parenting style. And, as a result, they were good kids. They had nice friends, they played on sports teams, they got good grades. Naomi tried to be accepting of whatever ideas and friends they brought home. She and her husband were considered relatively cool by her kids' friends, who felt comfortable in their house, where the only rule was that no one should do anything too crazy. This openness, she believed, was the way to turn out good kids: Give them space and let them grow.

She would wait it out. She would be here when Baruch wanted to talk, sit back and stay calm when he didn't. Meanwhile, she would try to enjoy her summer. Naomi didn't work, at least not officially. But she was at the center of a hundred projects and organizations. Unable to say no to anyone, she flitted from project to project, from one organization to another. She did fund-raising for the United Jewish Appeal. She made papier-mâché centerpieces and delivered fruit baskets for the Hebrew Academy PTA. In the summer, the projects and requests slowed down, and she wanted to make good use of this rare extra time. At the shul, she was taking a weekly class, Women of the Bible, and she took out the page of photocopied commentaries she was supposed to read in preparation.

This week, they were studying Rebecca. Naomi fumbled her way through the fantastical midrash, the terse Rashi commentary, the cryptic passages of Talmud. She was proud of herself for taking the class. She wanted to wrestle with ancient words, ask questions, and come up with her own answers. But she had trouble keeping track of which rabbi said what about which matriarch. It was hard to care about the minute details the rabbis exhumed. Every time she looked at the black letters on the page, her mind wandered back to her life, to her family.

Finally she gave up. This week she could answer the questions on her own. With the battle upstairs raging, she understood the biblical Rebecca, who, according to the midrash, carried the warring Esau and Jacob in her womb. When she passed a house of prayer, she felt a kick from one side of her belly. When she passed a house of sin, she felt a kick from the other side. What a schizophrenic baby, Rebecca must have thought. He doesn't know who he is or what he wants. Then she realized that she carried not one baby, but two. And not only two babies, but two ideologies, two nations.

But this was her family. These were her children. Rebecca must have loved both sons equally. The text may not have been explicit, but Naomi saw past the actual words. She filled in the white spaces with her own commentary. After a few more moments of listening, she heard the noises from upstairs begin to blend. Soon, it sounded as if Baruch were setting the morning prayers to a rock beat, as if Ilana's music were incorporating a cantorial undertone. With some deep breathing and a sense of humor, maybe the summer wouldn't be so difficult after all. She put the dish racks in the cabinet under the sink, and as she left the kitchen, the music created, at least to Naomi's ears, a cacophony that was pleasurable, a harmonious blending of worlds.

An hour later, Naomi went back into the kitchen and the dish racks were in the sink again. She narrowed her eyes at them, and once again, she put them away. But she wasn't going to give up so easily. She wasn't going to be put off by Baruch's righteousness, which so easily veered into self-righteousness. Since he had come home, they had been peering at him from a distance, trying to locate any remnant of their funny, easygoing son inside the vestments of a different world. She had tried to broach the subject. "It's hard to come home. Anyone would have culture shock after being away for two years." But Baruch didn't accept these invitations to talk. He was polite and respectful as he shrugged her off and sought refuge behind the closed door of his bedroom. But now she had him cornered. If he, for a reason she didn't yet understand, wanted dish racks, he was going to have to talk to her about it first. Positive attitude in hand, she sat at the kitchen table, drank her coffee, and waited.

Two cups later, Baruch emerged from his room. It was ninety degrees outside, and he was wearing black wool pants, a dark blazer, and a white dress shirt. On his head, his black velvet yarmulke proclaimed that there was a God above. He headed straight for the sink. He pulled out the dish racks and was about to return them to their new locale.

"Is there a reason you've taken an interest in dish racks?" Naomi asked.

Baruch startled and feigned innocence, or at least incomprehension.

"The dish racks?" she asked, reminding herself to keep her voice friendly, her face relaxed.

"Oh," he said. "Right. Maybe you didn't know, but with porcelain sinks, you're supposed to use dish racks."

This already was a kosher kitchen, but it could always be more kosher. The rules were details upon details, and they could always be applied more strictly. Keeping kosher originated with the biblical prohibition against eating certain animals, against cooking a kid in its mother's milk. But most of the details of keeping kosher weren't in the Five Books of Moses. They were detailed in the oral law, compiled in the Mishna and interpreted in the Talmud. They were expanded in the vast rabbinic commentaries that spanned the generations. In these texts, the rabbis outlawed the mixing of all foods meat and milk. They extrapolated from not eating them together to not cooking them together, to not using the same pots or dishes for one and the other. They debated what to do if mistakes were made. What if a piece of meat falls into a vat of milk? What if a non-kosher knife cuts a tomato? What if it cuts an onion? Is the tomato still kosher? Is the onion?

And so, Baruch explained to Naomi in the singsong tune of the Talmud, it would have been one thing if their kitchen sinks were metal, which was non-porous. Even if they had been used previously for non-kosher, pouring boiling water over them would make them kosher again. But porcelain was porous, so the non-kosher had become, so to speak, part of the actual sink. Which meant that the sinks couldn't be made kosher. Which also meant that her otherwise kosher dishes couldn't touch the porcelain without themselves becoming non-kosher.

"Okay," Naomi said, though he had lost her somewhere along the way. "That's fine. But I'd like you to show me where it says that."

"Trust me. Rabbi Rothstein says that—"

She shook her head. "If you want dish racks, you're going to have to show me."

"I'm not making this up," he said. "Do you think I'm pulling this out of thin air?"

"Come on, Baruch. Humor me."

He went to his room and scanned his books, most of which he had just finished unpacking. Baruch found the book of rabbinic responsa he needed, thanks to Rabbi Rothstein, who had emphasized this law for the boys, knowing that in the land of the Modern Orthodox this detail was often overlooked or deliberately ignored.

Baruch brought it to his mother. "It's right here."

Naomi looked. At least according to this book, this rabbi, Baruch was right: Porcelain sinks without dish racks weren't allowed. In this text, the rabbi applied ancient principles to modern times. He quoted the early-twentieth-century Mishna Brurah, which expanded on the sixteenth-century Shulchan Aruch, which referenced Maimonides' twelfth-century codification of Jewish law. At the dawn of the twenty-first century, she and her son were fighting about dish racks, and he could pull a book from his shelf and trace their argument back to rabbinic conversations from centuries before, stretching all the way back, she imagined, to Sinai. Because he could point out this passage to her, she too felt connected. She relaxed at this feeling of inclusion. Her son was inviting her to step into the pages of his texts, and she was eager to follow.

"The alternative would be for me not to eat in your house," he said.

The pleasurable feeling that she was bound up in rabbinic tradition dissipated, as did her ability to remain calm no matter what he said.

"Are you crazy?" she asked. "This is a kosher kitchen. Remember? What if we didn't keep kosher at all? What would you do then?"

"At least it would be clear," he said.

He looked away from her, down into his book, and she regretted what she had said. She had seen, a second too late, the hopefulness in his eyes as he thought he had found an ally. She had also seen, for that moment, her son. It didn't matter what he wore or what he said his name was.

Pick your battles: This was the advice her friends had offered. In hushed phone conversations this past week, they had compared whose children had returned from Israel the greater strangers. Everyone was afflicted with this new malady, this fierce, fervent virus. And they, the parents, couldn't figure out how to treat it. In Laurelwood, they thought they had successfully combined tradition with modernity. They lived their lives on the seam of this compromise. Like Orthodox Jews anywhere in the world, they spent Saturday at shul, praying to God. Like suburbanites in any other neighborhood in New Jersey, they woke up on Sunday and loaded their kids into minivans. They went to Little League games and stopped for pizza on the way home. Here, they didn't have to choose. They belonged to state-of-the-art health clubs. They ate kosher sushi. They had no problem with interdenominational dialogue or R-rated movies. They didn't feel the need for the added strictures of separate seating at weddings. They believed it was necessary and valuable to be involved in the secular world. They managed to find space for the modern, and possibly problematic, concepts of pluralism and multiplicity of interpretation.

Now this middle ground was shrinking. Maybe in fifty years, it would be gone altogether. In this community, they debated the alternatives. If they kept the kids home from the customary post–high school year in Israel, they would go straight to college and leave Orthodoxy behind. If they let them go to Israel, they would come back too religious and not go to college at all. Naomi knew of people who made their kids sign contracts that they would come home after one year and attend the Ivy League colleges where they had been accepted. Some parents visited Israel every six weeks to monitor and mitigate any changes. Naomi had never considered these measures. You have to trust your kids, she had always said. Let them become the people they are going to be.

Now it was her turn to put the advice she had dispensed into practice. She didn't really mind if Baruch chose something different for himself. But she did mind if he wouldn't eat in her house, if her grandchildren would one day look upon her as non-religious, if her whole family wouldn't sit together at the same table.

"If it means that much to you," she said, "the dish racks can stay."

The dish racks had been on the table, awaiting her verdict. With their fate decided, Baruch returned them to the sink. As he was about to walk off, Naomi called him back.

"You could have asked me. You didn't have to sneak them in," she said.

"I didn't sneak them," he said.

"But you put them there without asking. You just did it by yourself. That's what makes me angry. You could have talked to us about it. We would have listened."

"You would have listened?" he challenged.

"We would have. You know that, Baruch. We don't want you hiding out in your room like we're the enemy."

"So let's talk about it," he said. "Because as long as we're on the subject of the kitchen, there are a few other things that you're also doing wrong."

He told her that it wasn't okay to leave the oven on during Shabbos and to warm up food during the day. When making tea on Shabbos, she shouldn't pour the boiling water directly over the tea bag and possibly cook the tea leaves, breaking the prohibition against cooking on Shabbos. He said that she should be more careful about keeping her meat and dairy Tupperwares separate; he had found leftover chicken in one meant for dairy. Her every action, inaction, or misaction apparently had been remembered and recorded. She wasn't sure she believed in God's omniscience watching and weighing her every move. But who needed God when her son was doing that on his own?

It was a different world. Twenty years ago, no one checked inside anyone's pots or measured the length of anyone's skirts. She used to consider herself Orthodox in an all-purpose kind of way. Growing up, she hadn't worried whether she was of the modern, serious, strict, open, centrist, or liberal variety. There had been no need for this epidemic of adjectives. Now they meant everything. They divided the community into smaller and smaller camps. In Laurelwood, Naomi was firmly in the modern camp. Right-wing Orthodoxy had strongholds in Monsey, Lakewood, and Brooklyn. But apparently they were closer than she had realized. Even though she hadn't changed, she was suddenly less religious than she used to be. It was as if God had laid down a newly revised and expanded set of commandments.

Naomi felt simultaneous urges to shake her son and hug him. "I thought maybe we could all do something together today," she said instead.

"Thanks, Ima," he said, using the Hebrew word for mother, "but I can't. I have some things I need to do in Brooklyn." As if to make up for this, for all of this, he kissed her on the cheek, one thing which—according to Baruch, his rabbi, and their laws—was apparently still permissible.

In bed next to Joel that night, Naomi asked, "Do you think Bryan is right about us?"

"Are you serious?" Joel responded. "Don't tell me you're going to listen to his rabbi."

"It's just that I wonder where this is all coming from. Maybe there's something we should have done differently," Naomi said.

"It's coming from being twenty years old and thinking that you know everything. It's coming from spending two years in yeshiva, where you're taught to obey whatever your rabbis say. And what the rabbis say is that the outside world is bad, that your parents are bad, that college is bad and working is bad, that everything except sitting and learning all day is bad."

This was the most Naomi had heard from him these past five days. Since Baruch came home, Joel had given monosyllabic responses to any attempt at conversation. Even when he was home, he sat in the living room and kept to himself. He could go into hiding while remaining in plain sight. For Joel, one-word answers and shrugs of the shoulders sufficed. But Naomi wanted spools of dialogue, long extended conversations where she could unravel her swirling thoughts.

"Have you told him how you feel?" she asked.

"I'm sure he's more than aware."

"Today he told me that we need to put dish racks in the sink. Because there's no way to kasher porcelain."

"I hope you told him that when he has a kitchen of his own, he's welcome to use all the dish racks he wants."

"I told him we'd use the dish racks. He said he wouldn't eat in our house otherwise."

Joel groaned. "And what about his next request? Are you going to start covering your hair when he tells you that he's embarrassed to be seen with you?"

"Of course not," she said. "But he showed me where it says that you need to use dish racks."

"Look, Naomi. For every rabbi who says one thing, I can find you two who say the opposite."

"What do you want me to tell him? We want you to be religious, just not this religious, to take it as seriously as we do, but no more, thank you?"

"That might work," Joel said. "Maybe in the morning, you could sit him down and say that."

"You're kidding."

"I'm not."

"How could I say that? It goes against everything we've always taught them, about being independent thinkers, about forging their own paths." Naomi looked at him again. Though he was staring at her deadpan, she saw at the corners of his mouth the start of a smile. "You *are* kidding."

He didn't answer, but she wondered if, in the scheme of things, they were getting off easy. While some of the kids in their community were becoming more religious, others were leaving it behind altogether. They cloaked inside their school-sanctioned outfits the thrusts of rebellion. The boys wore ever-shrinking yarmulkes on top of gelled, angry hair. The girls had on skirts so tight that it was a wonder they could walk. She wondered what lay behind their cool impassive faces. Through their guises of nonchalance, an anger burned.

"You know what? I think it's going to be okay," Naomi said. "He just needs some time. It's hard to come home. He's having culture shock."

"*He's* having culture shock?" Joel said.

"I mean it," she said. "By the end of the summer, he'll be back to himself, and we'll look back at this and laugh."

They differed on how to deal with their newly pious, perhaps fanatical son. Lay down the law, Joel said. With a gentle hand and patient heart, Naomi believed. But despite this disagreement, they were more or less on the same side. They laughed and curled toward each other. This newfound crack in the family didn't separate them into opposing camps.

With Shabbos starting in an hour, there wasn't time to think about the dish racks or ideological divides of the previous day. Shabbos started eighteen minutes before sundown, and Naomi couldn't be late. Though some rules could be bent, when it came to Shabbos, there was no room for negotiation. Once it was Shabbos, the house would be calm. The food would be ready, the table would be set, and the candles would burn. But until that moment, Naomi was in her pre-Shabbos whirl, doing three things at once, playing the weekly game of beat-the-clock.

Naomi had friends who knocked themselves out cooking for Shabbos. By the time their guests showed up for Friday-night dinner, they were ready to crawl into bed. They were up on each new kosher cookbook that came out. The latest trend was to disguise traditional foods in the ingredients of the gourmet. They made gefilte fish from salmon and served it with lemon dill sauce instead of horseradish. Instead of bean and barley cholent, they made lamb and rice stew. But Naomi didn't do fancy, she didn't do organized. She had learned to live with a clutter of books in the den, with newspapers on the kitchen table, with Ilana's clothes on the floor in her room, seeping out into the upstairs hallway and beyond. Naomi flew through the house in a whirlwind as company was walking up the driveway. She ignored the new and always improving appliances that filled her kitchen. Joel loved gadgets: He had bought a bread maker, a cappuccino maker, and an indoor grill. Learning to use them would take her more time than they would save, so they sat unused. She cooked her own way, without a recipe in sight, everything done from memory and estimation. She added dashes of this to pinches of that. She stirred in more noodles, added extra sauce, and came up with something new. When she ran out of one ingredient, she substituted another.

Now, three pots of water boiled in front of Naomi. She tried to remember which pot needed rice, which colander of noodles needed egg and oil, which mixing bowl needed a final dash of seasoning. It was a perfectly run system tottering at the edge of chaos. But as long as no one interrupted her, she could finish on time and pass through into the quiet space Shabbos would create.

Naomi had high hopes for Shabbos. It was the one time she knew everyone would be home. Joel was a corporate lawyer in Manhattan, and he worked long, grueling hours. The family had grown accustomed to his absence. She had spent most of their married life trying to coax him home earlier. She reminded him that the work would still be there the next day. She wanted to know why he couldn't say he was tired, say it was dinner time, say he had a family waiting for him. He always laughed at how little she knew of the corporate world. But like it or not, Shabbos was the one time he had to leave work behind. For the twenty-five hours of Shabbos, he couldn't answer the phone, check his e-mail, or listen to his voice mail. None of them would watch television, use the computer, or drive the car. Without these distractions to hide behind, it would be easier to connect. Naomi wanted everyone to sit at the Shabbos table and talk. In their clamorous, disharmonious, sometimes tone-deaf voices, she wanted to sing the traditional Shabbos songs together.

Out of the oven came two roast chickens, the vegetables, and the kugels. Naomi lined them up on her countertops and checked her watch: one hour to go. This week, she wanted to bring Shabbos in calmly. She wanted to have everything done ahead of time, so she could sit back before lighting candles and reflect on the week that had passed, the week that was coming.

"You should go to shul with Bryan tonight," Naomi had urged Joel that morning, though he didn't usually go on Friday nights.

After a lot of coaxing, Joel had eventually agreed. She called him twice at work to remind him, and her nudging paid off. He walked in just as she was taking the last kugel out of the oven: thirty minutes to go. She kissed him, and he went upstairs to get ready. Now, with twenty minutes until Shabbos, all she needed was for the cake to finish baking and everyone to get along.

———

In his room, Baruch was ironing his white Shabbos shirt, distinguished from his white everyday shirt by a variation in the white-on-white pattern and by the fineness of the stitching ("For the honor of Shabbos, one's weekday clothing should not be like his Shabbos clothing"—Maimonides Hilchos Shabbos 30:3). He had on the *Miami Boys Choir Shabbos in Jerusalem* CD. With their high-pitched, prepubescent voices, these boys were the Orthodox equivalent of the rock stars Ilana worshipped. But whereas her music roused thoughts that Baruch was doing his utmost to avoid, his music made him think about God. Fresh from his pre-Shabbos shower, he had to force himself not to dance.

Or to dance with proper thoughts in mind. Dance because of the joy of the approaching Shabbos. Dance because these twenty-five hours were a chance to cloak himself in holiness, no matter where he was. Shabbos was supposed to offer a taste of the world to come. In yeshiva, they had savored it, in the sweetness of the prayers, in the radiance on their rabbis' faces. Even the mediocre yeshiva food had a succulence that was otherworldly. At home, Baruch would have to create this feeling for himself.

He had to admit, the smell of Shabbos did fill the house. His mother's food beckoned to him. She was trying to root him out of his room with roast chicken and potato kugel. But it wouldn't work. In their discussion about the dish racks, he had seen that she was only pretending to be accepting. In yeshiva, Rabbi Rothstein had emphasized the importance of outreach. He was supposed to set an example, to spread the word of God. But his family had no desire to listen. His mother allowed the dish racks to remain not because she was interested in learning and growing, but because of her belief that people can be different and still coexist. She tolerated him because she thought that everyone was entitled to a point of view. But she didn't see the value of adhering to every detail. With his insistence on dish racks, she thought he was being too literal, a slave to minutiae. She wondered whether he hadn't lost sight of the big picture. But his parents didn't understand that the world wasn't created with broad strokes alone. He was intent on seeing the big picture; only his version was like a pointillist painting, made of thousands of tiny dots.

Baruch started to get dressed. He opened his closet to get his suit—and there, to his surprise, was his Yankees cap. It had somehow worked its way to the front of the closet and become one more temptation, one more test from God. This time, he succumbed. He picked it up and put it on his head.

"Hey," he said to the mirror, "what's up?"

In this mirror, he had once practiced looking cool. He had flexed his muscles, he had fussed over his outfits, he had gelled his hair. Now, as he looked in the mirror, his recently acquired humility left him and his body changed. Baruch could see it; the mirror was sensitive enough to pick up every drop of evil inclination that lay dormant within him. He stood differently: shoulders tall, hips jutting out, muscles flexed. He saw a proud boy who worshipped at the temple of music, sports, and girls. He had spent the last two years rooting this boy out. He went after him with words of prayer. He tried fasting, he tried not talking. He traveled to Safed, city of mystics, and immersed himself in the ancient mikvah, whose freezing waters were said to bestow complete and ever-present concentration on God. He studied Talmud day and night. After a day, a year, a life of study, he was supposed to emerge whole and pure. He woke up every morning with this wish on his tongue. He wrapped his tefillin around his arm, binding this hope to his body. But it didn't matter. The old Bryan was still peeking out. He could feel him in there, like a second soul.

Baruch ripped the baseball cap off his head and buried it in a pile at the back of his closet. He readjusted his yarmulke to a prominent position on the crown of his head. In this world, but not of this world, he repeated to himself, his mantra of late.

"Shalom aleichem," he greeted himself, and the humble stance he had picked up in yeshiva returned. His shoulders rolled slightly forward and he bowed his head in submission to God, who was always above.

The only thing he needed to complete the look was his black hat. He placed a Borsalino fedora on his head, and instantly he felt better. The hat made him feel more religious. It wasn't just an item of clothing but a term of identity; not a description of what he was wearing but of who he was. To outsiders, it made a statement about where he belonged. But, more important, it reminded him as well. In their matching garb, the yeshiva boys were never alone. They always knew who they were. The ultra-Orthodox men whom he admired wore the long coats and black hats of an earlier century. They rejected modernity and proved that it was possible to live in a world apart. Why, they seemed to ask, do we have to live in the year in which we happened to be born? Who is to say that time travel is impossible?

As he and his friends made pilgrimages to buy their hats, they felt the weight of this past. They put their hats on, and they were no longer nineteen-year-old boys from America. They slipped out of who they had once been and became part of another world. But he knew his parents wouldn't see this. They would decry it as an example of being overly focused on the externals. So he had bought a sturdy hatbox and packed the hat into his suitcase, so he wouldn't have to explain its presence to his parents until he was ready.

It was nearly Shabbos. Baruch switched off the music and took a final look in the mirror. He was ready. This was who he was now.

Baruch went downstairs, walking carefully, self-consciously, as if he were balancing a melon on his head.

"Good Shabbos," he said to his parents.

They were standing by the front door, conferring in urgent, hushed tones. They looked at him. No, they stared at him. His father's gaze didn't leave the hat. His mother glanced at it quickly, then looked everywhere but at his head. Baruch searched for something to say, not knowing whether to make it better or worse. He could emulate Aaron the high priest, who pursued peace at all costs. Or he could be like Pinchas the Zealot, who raised his sword and saw no shades of gray.

"Are you planning to wear that when you're at Columbia?" Joel finally asked.

"I'm not going to Columbia," Baruch said.

"What do you mean?" Naomi asked. "Of course you are."

"No," Baruch said. "I'm going back to yeshiva."

This wasn't how he had planned to tell them. He hadn't planned how he would do it, but he was relieved that it was out. Now there was no turning back. His parents exchanged glances, a quick plotting of how to handle this new issue. We could ignore him. We could yell at him. We could humor him. We could punish him. We could reason with him. We could bribe him. A silent, coded negotiation passed before his eyes.

"Remember, honey," Naomi said, "we had an agreement. You were going to go back to yeshiva for one more year and then—"

"I know," he said. "But I've changed my mind. This is what I'm doing."

"No, you're not," Joel said. "A deal's a deal."

"I need to stay in yeshiva. That's what matters to me now," Baruch said.

"You need to go to college. Everyone does," Naomi said.

"Rabbi Rothstein says that—"

"This isn't up to Rabbi Rothstein," Joel said.

"Why don't we talk about this later," Naomi said. "It's almost Shabbos." She checked her watch. It was time to light candles, and she called upstairs to Ilana. Naomi wanted her daughter next to her as she lit the candles.

They were in the final minutes before Shabbos began, the eighteen minutes of leeway intended for emergencies but used widely as a buffer zone. All over Laurelwood, preparations for Shabbos were coming to a hurried end. Squares of toilet paper were being ripped, refrigerator lightbulbs unscrewed, bedroom lights turned off, bathroom lights left on. Automatic timers were set, ovens switched off, and Crock-Pots turned to low.

"You two need to get going if you're going to make it to shul on time," Naomi said, and called Ilana once more. "It's already ten past."

Joel and Baruch still weren't moving. They didn't want to walk the five blocks to shul and either have to continue this conversation or come up with another one in order to avoid it. They looked at each other and, in a brief, unintentional meeting of minds, they wondered: This is my father? This is my son?

With one minute to go until Shabbos, Ilana came downstairs. "What took you so long? Do you realize that Shabbos is starting right now?" Naomi asked.

"I made it, though, didn't I?" Ilana said and looked at her watch.

Ilana kissed her mother, then her father, on the cheek. She flashed her most innocent smile. She didn't know why they were standing there, not moving or speaking to each other. Clearly something had happened. Or was about to. But whatever it was, she wasn't going to be dragged into it. She walked past them. On her way into the living room, she turned back.

"Oh, and by the way, Bryan," she called, "nice hat."

— THREE —

ALL THE GIRLS wore skirts—long ones that billowed parachute-like into full circles, straight ones that passed the knee and kept going until the ankle. Skirts that were pleated and plaid. Skirts that had floral prints and required slips underneath to compensate for the sheerness of the fabric. Skirts that were denim, faded light blue or black. Skirts whose slits had been sewn shut. Skirts that hid figures, skirts that inadvertently accentuated the roundness of hips. Skirts that had so much extra material that if the need arose, they could divide themselves into two.

The girls who wore these skirts were studying at B'nos Sarah, a seminary in Jerusalem for American girls. Jerusalem was filled with these schools. They offered the girls a chance to immerse themselves in religious studies before marriage or college, whichever came first. At B'nos Sarah, the girls studied Bible and Prophets and Jewish law. According to the brochure, the school stood for the qualities of perfection and refinement of the whole girl, for growth in areas as varied as the love of God and the fear of God. "We are committed to turning out young women who will create meaningfully observant Jewish homes," it read. "Our students embody the values of Jewish womanhood as put forth by Sarah, Rivka, Rochel, and Leah. We value such ideals as modesty and humility. We instill a love of prayer, a capacity for continual growth." The sweatshirts the girls were given as welcoming gifts were emblazoned with B'NOS SARAH: MOVING IN THE RIGHT DIRECTION.

All summer, Shayna had waited for Tzippy to change her mind about going to Israel. She still tried to set her up on dates, hoping that the right boy would distract her. But Tzippy refused to be set up, and Shayna had given in. While her mother started to think about whom she could date in Israel, Tzippy waited for the summer to end so she could finally leave home.

Now, at the beginning of the school year, Tzippy sat in class and wrote down everything the rabbis said. One day she was glad she had come. The next day she put her head on her desk and wondered why she was here. In class, the girls learned that they must pray even if they weren't in the mood; if they waited to be in the mood, they would never pray. They learned that the Torah was to be interpreted literally. Any seeming contradictions in the text could be explained. They learned that no matter what modern science said, the world was not millions of years old, but a youthful 5,760. They learned about the perfection of the patriarchs and matriarchs. They learned that God created man and woman, but they weren't the same. It was only modern foolishness that insisted otherwise.

After class, the girls went through their closets, rooting out any immodest clothing.

"I can't believe I ever wore this," Devorah said, pulling from her closet a denim skirt that covered the knee when standing but not when sitting.

"That's not so bad," Esther Leah said. "Look at what I used to wear." She held up a blouse that in a certain light was nearly sheer, and whose sleeves in any light ended above the elbow.

"But look at the slit," Devorah said.

The short skirt and sheer blouse were thrown into the growing pile of clothes, all of which would be donated to the less fortunate, and presumably less modest. As they stuffed the discarded items into bags, the girls progressed to other areas: whether it was wrong to see movies, to read secular books, to go about without stockings. Tzippy had no clothing to get rid of. The only immodesty she needed to root out was in her mind, and she wished it were as easy to throw angry, hungry thoughts into a pile. Being in Israel was supposed to quiet the unrest that buzzed inside her. But as she sat with the other girls and their recharged fervor, the voice inside her was still there, growing steadfastly.

———

Tzippy woke from a dream that she was at home with her sisters and they were bored. There's nothing to do, they complained. Nothing to do, they said, pulling at her. She set them up at the kitchen table and handed out sheets of white paper that she ordered them to fold. Then she cut out paper dolls. Her sisters unfolded the paper, opening a chain of identical figures joined at the hands and feet. They scribbled faces and hair, then ran off, leaving Tzippy with strings of half-finished dolls. She heard the snipping of scissors. Blades opened and shut like long, bare legs. The dolls had her features, colored in with crayon. They were wearing the immodest skirts and shirts her friends had discarded, and in these clothes, the different Tzippys came to life and danced. Sometimes it was a slow, deliberate ballet. Other times the dance sped up, and one of the Tzippys pulled the other Tzippys and they made a wild, looping circle.

Tzippy had been to the ballet once, when she was twelve. After worrying whether it was appropriate, her mother had taken her to Lincoln Center in Manhattan for a performance of *Coppélia*. Tzippy watched the happy beginning of Franz and Swanilda in love. Then Franz mistook the doll Coppélia as real and fell in love with her. The doll came to life—Swanilda in disguise—and shook off the constraints of her wooden body. Her hands began to move, her legs to plié. She slipped the bonds of her maker and danced freely.

When Tzippy was fully awake, she remembered this ballet. Her blankets were tangled around her, and she felt hot. During the day, she knew who she was supposed to be. The girls bustled from one class to another, where they carefully recorded the truth in their notebooks. The dorm was in an apartment building, and through the thin walls they heard the hum of babies crying, children laughing, and mothers scolding. The girls were close with these neighboring families. They baby-sat for them, ate Shabbos meals with them, and imagined the families and homes awaiting them in the future.

But in the dark, this certainty didn't exist. In the privacy of her room, under her covers, Tzippy let herself imagine that none of this might be waiting for her. She might never get married. She might never have children. If that happened, she couldn't imagine who she would be.

Tzippy heard her roommate breathe and realized that she was also awake.

"Esther Leah," she asked, "are you okay?"

"I'm fine. What about you?"

"I don't know," Tzippy admitted.

Esther Leah, formerly Ellen Louise, had become Orthodox two years before. At Hebrew University for her junior year abroad, she went to the Western Wall one Friday night and was asked by a friendly rabbi if she had a place to go for Shabbos dinner. She said no and was taken to a family, who opened their house to guests from all over. Two weeks later, she enrolled at B'nos Sarah. Esther Leah didn't talk about her family, but dropped hints about hard circumstances. The other girls viewed Esther Leah with awe. They watched what they said around her, mindful of her refusal to gossip. They joined her for hours of singing around the Shabbos table. She was always the last to finish davening, and it made the other girls daven more slowly, with greater concentration. Tzippy shared the admiration, but she also wondered why Esther Leah had become Orthodox. Wanting to know what made her appear so certain, she waited for Esther Leah's holy demeanor to slip so she could see what lay beneath it.

"Esther Leah," she asked, "do you ever doubt?"

"Doubt what?"

"I don't know. Anything? Everything?"

"Everything? No. Well, I wouldn't call it doubt exactly. It's like Hashem is right there on my shoulder, like He's a bird and He's whispering into my ear all day. But sometimes I'm not sure what He's saying," Esther Leah explained. "Why, do you doubt?"

"No, it's just that sometimes I wonder what would happen if it didn't work out like it's supposed to. What if I decided to try something else?" Tzippy asked. "Of course I would come back to this. But just to see."

"How can you say such a thing?" Esther Leah said. She sat up in bed and switched on the light. This was the first time Tzippy had seen Esther Leah angry. "You should take it back. Right now," she insisted.

"I'm sorry. I didn't mean it." Tzippy put her hand to her mouth as if she could still catch her words.

"Believe me, Tzippy. I've tried other things and it's not worth it. You have everything you need right here. Do you know what made me become religious?" Esther Leah asked. "It was the families. They have so many kids and on Shabbos they gather around the table and everyone listens to the father make kiddush and they all just look so happy." Esther Leah turned the light off. She lay back down and smoothed her blankets around her. "It's going to work out. You'll see. In a few years, we'll both be married and have lots of kids and you'll look back and laugh at how silly you were to worry."

The next morning, Tzippy brushed away what had bothered her at night, chalking it up to strange dreams and evil inclinations. To doubt that everything would work out, that this was what she wanted? Someone could just as oddly have asked her whether she believed in the existence of her parents, whether there was such a thing as night and day, grass and trees. Even the Tzippy who wanted to scream didn't think of traveling that far. The earth was indeed flat, and it ended with a sharply drawn line at the edge of Brooklyn, with those who kept Shabbos and kosher and believed in the Torah. Those who dared to sail beyond that horizon would fall off the end of the world.

The girls cooked pots of spaghetti with tomato sauce and cheese. They baked brownies for dessert, breaking the diets they had vowed to begin. They were always starting strict regimes of cabbage and ten-calorie soup for dinner. Then, when they passed Angel's Bakery, they bought whole challahs fresh from the oven, smeared them with chocolate spread, and ripped them apart with their bare hands.

The kitchen where they sat had a graying stone floor. The small freezer needed to be defrosted with hairdryers every month. The porcelain sink was cracked and stained. The chipped plates, thin tin pots, and plastic colanders melted on one side were passed from one generation of B'nos Sarah girls to the next, all of whom were waiting for the day they would have wedding registries to get their good stuff. The girls ate and retold the story of Raizy Geller, who last year went on a third date and came home engaged. Once you were sure, she told her astonished and envious roommates, there was no reason to wait.

The older girls who were a few years out of high school had begun to date, and they filled the younger girls in on what they had learned. They had made lists of what they wanted in a husband, and they compared notes. Some of them kept notebooks where they wrote profiles of the different boys they had been out with. Each boy had his own page.

His name was written at the top, his statistics below: who set them up, where they went on the first date, what they talked about, what she wore, how many times they went out, and who ended the relationship and why.

They veered off toward the philosophical and debated the necessary properties of bashert. They knew that they were all looking for their destined match. But were they required to believe that there was only one person out there for each of them? The romantic and the fervent among them insisted that they were. God matched boys to girls before they were born. The more practical girls challenged this notion. What about people who died before they got married? Did that mean they never had a bashert, because of course God knew that they would die young? Or did it mean that somewhere out there, the second half of this couple was hopelessly searching for a bashert who was dead? And what about divorce? Was it possible to get married and discover that your spouse wasn't actually your bashert? If so, did this mean that your true bashert was still out there? Or could it be that God had gotten it wrong?

They grew hungrier. They stirred second pots of spaghetti, baked more trays of brownies, and enumerated the reasons to jump in. If you waited to start dating, the best guys would be gone. And there was the risk of waiting too long; no one wanted to remain unmarried past the age of twenty-two. They couldn't imagine life without husbands and children. They saw no point in dating for months, no reason for long engagements when a wedding could be planned in a matter of weeks.

"Take it from me," said Devorah, who had a serious boyfriend of five weeks. "It's hard. Especially for the guys. Shmuel would never talk about it, but it's driving him crazy. I can tell by the way he looks at me."

Esther Leah told stories from her college days, of coed dorms, coed suites, and coed bathrooms. Imagine, she said, the feet under the stall next to you might belong to a boy. The first time she had seen a size-eleven pair of Nikes next to her, she had assumed they belonged to a very large girl. Until the stall door opened, and this so-called girl had emerged, the boyfriend of her next-door neighbor.

"Really?" they asked. "How terrible." And then, "Tell us more."

But religious girls didn't think about such things. It was almost as if they didn't exist. Almost, almost, but hints were everywhere and nowhere: in the flush on a married girl's face after a Shabbos nap; in a young husband's unexplained absence at shul; in the shy look on a newly married classmate's face when she said that no, next Shabbos wasn't a good time to have guests. These thoughts were always on their minds and always put aside until the right time, the right place.

Tzippy waited for one of the rabbis at school to say that he had someone for her. These rabbis also taught in the boys' yeshivas, and they often paired their students up. She dressed up each day, hoping to catch their eyes. She imagined a pageant of boys twirling round. The judges would deliberate, their scores would be tallied, and one of them would be crowned her bashert.

But none of them ever said anything to her, and when Tzippy went back to her apartment, she had to hear who was expecting a phone call from a boy, who was getting dressed for a date. She feigned happiness when Rivkie Markowitz boasted that she had a list of guys waiting to go out with her. In her nightgown and unmade face, Tzippy sighed while Devorah waited for Shmuel to call, Chana waited for a Dovid, Esther Leah for a Yehudah Leib.

Soon Devorah was engaged. And so was Chana. When Tzippy came home one night a few weeks later, the girls were assembled for an engagement party for Esther Leah. For each engagement, the girls danced. The engaged girl stood inside a whirl of flying hair and swishing skirts, and she pulled in the other girls: Rivkie, Frumi, Bassi, Suri, Faigy.

When the bride-to-be had danced with everyone, the girls flurried. They wished one another "soon by you," while privately they prayed "soon by me." Circling the bride, hoping her good fortune would rub off on them, they wanted to hear how it had happened. They wanted to know how she knew and when she knew.

"It's bashert," Devorah shrugged, attributing the match to the hand of God.

"Suddenly, you just know," Chana said.

"You can't imagine anything else you'd want," Esther Leah explained.

While Devorah, Chana, and Esther Leah dreamed of weddings, Tzippy wandered the apartment. She called home and her mother asked, "Is there anyone?" She heard in her mother's voice how badly she wanted Tzippy to say yes, finally, there was someone. Her voice rose with hope, then sank as Tzippy said there wasn't. For the rest of the conversation, this disappointment lingered. Tzippy felt herself shrinking while her mother's hungering voice grew louder.

Tzippy tried to feel happy for her friends when they talked about how exciting it was to embark on their new lives, how beautiful to find the husband God intended, how thrilling to select china and sterling silverware. But she secretly hoped that one of them might break off her engagement. She consoled herself with the belief that those who struggled in the beginning were rewarded in the end. She took out a pen and paper and wrote in Hebrew, "Mitzvah gedolah liheeyot be'simcha tamid." It is a mitzvah to always be happy. But she had trusted God to work his wonders and find her a husband. She had reminded married friends and rabbis and nice old women in the grocery store that she was available. She had hinted and hoped. She had smiled and waited.

Under her bed, in a shoebox, Tzippy kept her list, which she had titled "In a Husband." In pristine handwriting, on heavy beige stationery, she had composed it when she turned eighteen. She was looking for a talmid chacham, a scholar who learned for the love of the word, whose tongue flew easily over the pages of the Talmud. He should be a baal chessed, a kind person who visited the sick, who remembered the suffering of others. But she also wanted someone with a sense of humor. In between all that learning and kindness, Tzippy wanted a husband who could make her laugh.

She crumpled up her list and threw it back into the shoebox. Inside, there were also letters from home and pictures of her family. She rifled through them. All the faces in the pictures were smiling. All the letters cheerfully assured her that God watches over and protects. Her mother's letters were filled with descriptions of boys with whom she could be set up once she came home. She tossed the letters back into the box and opened the chumash she kept by her bed.

Tzippy angrily turned the pages. She had been taught that there was no need to look beyond these words; they contained the whole world. Wanting to believe this, Tzippy scanned the pages until she came to the story of Sarah laughing at the news that she would bear a child in her old age. Tzippy imagined laughter that wasn't gentle and sweet. Instead it was angry and bitter and filled with disappointment. She read about Rebecca at the well and inserted into the text a coy smile and a bared ankle. She imagined desire pulsing underneath her modest act of offering to feed a stranger's camels. Rachel, who brought Jacob home to her father, was a woman who knew what she wanted. Even better, she knew how to make it happen. Then Tzippy turned the page and found Leah, who had to live with the fear that her pretty younger sister would get married before she did. She had endured the pitying looks and whispers. But then came her quiet, steely triumph. Leah remained silent under the veil. She may have burned with shame, but she still held on to her treacherous hope for a husband.

The matriarchs would have created a stir in Brooklyn. Cloaked in demure guises, they steadfastly pursued their husbands. Tzippy would follow after them. She had listened to the rabbis, who said that they should look for life lessons not in the silly advice columns of the modern world but in the Torah. She had waited for God; she had played by His rules. But no more. She was done with lists and done with waiting. This elusive husband—she was going to find him on her own.

At the beginning of November, it was hot in Jerusalem. Instead of cooling off, it grew hotter, a last late heat wave. Top buttons of shirts were left undone. Kerchiefs were pushed farther back on the head, away from sticky foreheads. And Tzippy, sweating the length of her long sleeves, was keeping her eyes open.

While her roommates left for class, she pretended to be sick. Then she quickly got dressed and ran down the stairs of her building. Tzippy checked out every yeshiva boy she passed. She watched them in the grocery stores and on the bus. There were boys with wisps of unfinished beards, boys with mischievous smiles, and boys who mumbled psalms as they walked. Sometimes she saw, hidden behind glasses, an especially piercing pair of eyes. She learned to appreciate a graceful back, a well-groomed beard. Pushing aside her modest instinct to look away and not cause the boys to have forbidden thoughts, she tried to catch their eye. Usually their hats were pulled so low over their faces that they didn't notice her. Or they blushed and looked away. But sometimes, they lifted their eyes and their gazes lingered and wondered.

When these looks made her stomach flutter, Tzippy understood a part of the world she was supposed to know nothing about. She and her unmarried friends feigned innocence. Their eyes protested too much that they didn't even think about such things. Boys were foreign creatures, observed through the slats of the mechitzah or across a school yard as the girls went in one door and the boys out another. They existed only in nighttime imaginings that weren't talked about the next day in school. Boys and girls were forbidden to touch until they were married. Even when they were dating, a hand wasn't allowed to stray across the interior of a taxi to find another hand. An accidental brushing of an arm couldn't turn into an intentional embrace. Boys and girls lived in separate physical worlds, and until marriage, there was no way to cross from one to the other. But then why did Tzippy feel as she did? Why could she imagine bodies, touches, she had never seen or felt?

There was one particular boy she saw every time she turned around. As he rushed past in the streets of Jerusalem, she caught glimpses of him from the side, from the back, from a distance. He was tall and had light brown hair peeking out from under his black hat. He wore the yeshiva uniform—the black pants, white shirt, black jacket—but he carried with him a maroon knapsack. Tzippy saw him in the grocery store and at the Western Wall, pressing his face into the crevices of the stone. She willed him to turn around and look at her. But he kept his gaze lowered, immune to her wishful stares.

One day, she saw him on the bus. She pushed through the crowd until she stood at arm's length from him. She still couldn't see his face, but she could have reached out to touch his back if she had dared. He got off the bus, and through the dusty window, she watched as he walked down the street, melted into the crowd, and disappeared. But at night he was there again. In her dreams, he turned around, smiled, and beckoned her to follow.

The heat wave hadn't broken, and Tzippy took off her stockings. She wiggled her toes, and the breeze worked its way through them and up her legs. She felt newly aware of the fabric of her skirt rustling against her thighs. She felt naked, as if she had left off something so vital as a shirt. The next time she saw him, she followed him from the Old City to Mea Shearim, one of Jerusalem's most religious neighborhoods. Here apartment buildings were crowded together. Lines of laundry hung window to window, clothes flapping like flags. Every time he stopped and looked around, she caught her breath. She thought about asking him if he needed help. But in this neighborhood, men and women didn't sit next to one another on buses. They looked away from one another as they passed. Girls with braids and long gray dresses moved in flocks. Boys traveled together, eyes averted, from yeshiva to home and back again. Signs plastered to the buildings warned against immodestly dressed women. Tzippy worried that the tznius police, the self-appointed enforcers of modesty, would see her bare legs. They would chase her down and banish her from the neighborhood.

But that didn't deter Tzippy. Her cheeks were flushed and her heart was pounding. Her hair had come unfastened from its barrette and fell into her face. Rivka had offered to feed the camels, though she must have been exhausted after a full day tending the sheep. Leah was willing to endure the shame of being the wrong bride. Suffering only from heat and exhaustion, Tzippy kept going. She ran after this boy, up the set of stairs that connected one street to another.

She took the stairs two at a time. She didn't watch where she was going, afraid that if she took her eyes off him, he would blend back into the mass of yeshiva boys. Her skirt caught under her and she tripped. She lost her balance inside the excess fabric, tipped forward, and let out a scream. Her skirt ballooned around her, and she was splayed, facedown, across the white stone steps.

The miracle she had been waiting for came to pass. The boy stopped walking and turned around. She was too embarrassed to look up. She wished she could pull her skirt over her head and hide.

"Are you okay?" he asked.

At the sound of his voice, Tzippy pulled herself up as gracefully as possible. For the first time, she looked at him face-to-face. In her mind, his hat flew off and was replaced with a small blue crocheted yarmulke with white lettering that read GO YANKEES. The black pants and white shirt were replaced by jeans and a sweatshirt. Gone too was his serious look, his averted eyes, and in their place was a teasing grin. This yeshiva boy became the fifteen-year-old who had played basketball in shorts and a tank top and made her blush.

"Bryan!" she cried out.

He was standing at the top of the steps, and he walked down to where she stood. She hadn't seen him in ages. Their mothers had been college roommates, and when they were younger, the two families had gotten together often. Over the years, they had done this less frequently until, at some point, they had stopped altogether.

"Hi," Tzippy said softly. She was still trying to catch her breath as he got over his surprise at seeing her and said hello.

"Are you here for the year?" he asked.

"I'm at B'nos Sarah. I've just been here for a few months," she said.

"It's my third year in yeshiva."

"Wow," she said. "I didn't know. I guess I haven't seen you in—"

"Years," he said.

She couldn't believe it was Bryan. She remembered the tingling feelings she once had in his presence. One time when her family was visiting, he was outside playing basketball with his friends even though it was Shabbos. She knew from her mother's conversations with Naomi that Bryan was a big shot on his school basketball team, though to her, the idea of a Jewish school with a basketball team was strange enough. She also knew that he was tall and cute and had a smile that was teasing and sweet at the same time. She had tried not to look at him as she walked by, taking her sisters for a walk. When he saw her, he stopped playing. He dribbled the ball and waved to her, calling "Hey, Tzip" as if they were friends. Then Bryan sang out, in front of all of his friends, "Tzippity doo dah, Tzippity day." "Very funny," she had said in a rush of embarrassment and excitement. She had tried to feign nonchalance in front of her sisters, but later, when she was alone, she had thought about the feeling he had stirred in her. She had held on to it and broken it into a hundred different parts.

Now, he smiled at her again, but then looked away as a group of Hasidim walked past, sent by a divine force to break up the moment.

"So maybe I'll see you," he said.

He waved to her and ran off, leaving her once again with a view of his back. Though he had looked away while they spoke, he had been glad to see her. She saw a flicker of interest in the way he stole glances at her. She would have jumped up and down, if only her ankle hadn't been sore, if only she had been the type to do this. But she saw in her head a miniature version of herself, in pink tutu and tights, leaping down the steps, pirouetting through the streets.

— FOUR —

A<small>T THE</small> J<small>ERUSALEM</small> P<small>LAZA</small> H<small>OTEL</small>, the revolving door went round continuously, bringing young men into the lobby. Their dates, whom they had never before met, were waiting in a row, and the boys didn't know how to tell them apart. They tried to match the voice with the face, the description with the girl. Which one descended from a long line of rabbis? Which came from a wealthy family? Who was Adina, who was Avigail? There was no time to waste with mistaken identities. Marriage and children waited in the wings. While the boys and girls sorted out who was meant for whom, the door went round again and Baruch came into the lobby, trying to remember how to talk to girls.

He had avoided going into town, avoided sitting next to girls on buses, avoided them wherever he could. Even so, images of them popped into his head uninvited. In the middle of learning, he saw shoulders and ankles and thighs, all the forbidden parts beckoning to him. Mea Shearim seemed like the safest place for someone trying to avoid these thoughts, so Baruch spent his free time there. He watched the Hasidim, wishing they would take him home and make him their own. He envied their wholeness, their history. He knew just a few words of Yiddish, the language that they spoke. His only exposure had been at shul in Laurelwood, when he sometimes joined the few older men, all Holocaust survivors, for a drink of slivovitz, a plum-flavored Hungarian schnapps. They forced on him a plate of herring, which he couldn't bring himself to eat, and spoke to him in a Yiddish he didn't understand. But the Hasidim spoke the Yiddish of their great-grandparents. Children jabbered it in the street. Baruch wanted to go back in time and rejoin his ancestors who had looked and lived like them. In his family, there was little connection to the past. But these devout Mea Shearim Jews seemed unaware that the cobblestone streets they trod weren't the same as those in their ancestors' villages and shtetls. The few hints of the twenty-first century—the bus stops, the advertisements on them, the phone booths that took telecards—stood out as anachronistic, not the people in their old-fashioned dress.

Baruch used to look at the Hasidim as an odd breed. Embarrassed by their hats and coats, he had wanted to make it known that he wasn't like them. He may have worn a small knit yarmulke on his head, but he hid his Orthodoxy whenever he could. Now, in the parade of bearded, black-hatted men, he saw the true bearers of the past. Epics were told in the shape and size of a hat, in the fabric of a coat, the length of one's pants. The men in fur-trimmed hats were the Belzers, whose rebbe had escaped the Nazis and come to Israel to rebuild. The ones with gold caftans belted over black pants were the Yerushalmis. They and their parents and grandparents had been born in Jerusalem and never left. The men in knickers and white kneesocks belonged to the Satmar. The men in suits offering passersby a chance to don tefillin were the Lubavitch, who hoped to usher in the messianic era any day now. The Breslover Hasidim left an empty seat in their shul for their rabbi, who had long since died. The Reb Arelach Hasidim spent their days in prayer, meditation, and song. The boys in yeshiva talked about the intensity of the Reb Arelach davening. The Hasidim sang and swayed until they seemed to take leave of the world around them.

Baruch walked through Mea Shearim, looking for this shul. There were no street signs, and everyone he asked for directions told him the same thing: "Yashar, yashar"—keep going, straight ahead. But each time he went straight, the road turned, and he was deeper into the neighborhood. The sun was setting over the buildings. The time for mincha would soon be over. Baruch hadn't missed saying the afternoon prayers in nearly three years, and sin chased at his heels. As he looked up and tried to decide which way to turn, a group of young boys clustered around him. They wore the same black pants and white shirts as their fathers. Their pale faces were swallowed under their ten-gallon hats. In his American-accented Hebrew, Baruch asked where the Reb Arelach shul was. They didn't understand him, and he tried again, in English. They giggled and whispered in Yiddish and answered him with one of the few English words they knew: "America, America."

When he didn't answer, they tried again. "New York? New York?"

Finally, one of the older boys stepped forward to help.

"Ani maveen," he said. I understand.

He pointed to a narrow set of steps sandwiched between two buildings. Baruch raced up the stairs. As he reached the top, he heard someone cry out. He turned around and there was a girl lying at his feet. All his efforts to avoid girls, and God placed one directly in his path. He recognized Tzippy right away, and any thought of shul and mincha suddenly dropped from his mind. He was too busy thinking about how pretty she had become. In high school, he and his friends had made fun of such modest dress. Full body armor, they had called it. They were too young to realize that covered was more alluring than uncovered.

The Reb Arelach Hasidim had finished davening and were streaming out of shul. As they went down the steps, they stared at Baruch and Tzippy. Their presence jolted Baruch and made him remember who he was. But before he ran off, he looked at her once more, wishing he could ask her if she wanted to get a cup of coffee with him. He wanted to talk to her without thinking that he was doing something wrong. He wanted to keep looking into her wide-open eyes.

Baruch hadn't thought he was ready to date. But in yeshiva, to be married at twenty-one wasn't an anomaly. Eighteen to the chuppah, the Talmud (Sanhedrin 42B) said. By that reckoning, he was already old.

Face-to-face once again, Baruch and Tzippy were formal with each other. They abided by every rule and custom. They didn't acknowledge that they had gone the back route of shidduch dating, first meeting on their own and then finding someone to set them up. Baruch had found someone who knew someone who knew Tzippy and asked to be set up with her. She had been busy with the same endeavor, trying to locate someone who knew him. When his intermediary called her, she feigned surprise at the suggestion, just as he did when hers called him.

Because Tzippy and Baruch had already met, they could skip the preliminary awkward moments of trying to find a way into a conversation. They didn't have to wonder why someone thought the two of them might want to meet and marry. They already liked each other. There was no wishing to flee, no surreptitious checking of watches. She didn't look around the room and wonder if she might be better suited for the guy at the next table. He wasn't thinking about the minutes ticking by, which could be better spent in front of his books. Instead, Baruch was noticing that Tzippy was unassuming, modest, and sweet. She noticed that he had adopted a Yiddish accent, as if he had grown up in Vilna or Volozhin instead of New Jersey. He watched her nod her head as he talked, and this made him smile. She noticed that he seemed more relaxed than the other boys she had gone out with.

Baruch told her about yeshiva and how much he loved to learn. After almost two and a half years, he couldn't imagine going home. She said that she too loved being in Israel. Baruch said that he wanted to continue learning. Tzippy said she was willing to support a husband while he learned. She wanted many children, many guests, a busy household, and a lot to do. When Baruch envisioned a home of his own, he imagined a Shabbos table spanning the length of the dining room. Everyone would remain around the table to sing and share words of Torah. They wouldn't wander off to sleep or read, as they did in his parents' house.

They finished their Cokes. This was usually the hard, horrible part of the date, when Tzippy couldn't think of anything to say. But she liked him. She could say what she wanted.

"So what happened to you?" she asked.

"What do you mean?"

"Come on, Bryan. I know you. You weren't always like this."

He flinched at her use of his English name, but he didn't correct her.

"I'll tell you," he said and swayed back and forth in his seat as if he were davening. "I grew up religious, right? Shabbos, kosher, the works. But we weren't really religious, not in a way that meant anything. You know what my family is like. We did what we did and that was it. Then I came to yeshiva, and for the first time in my life I saw what it really means to be religious. My rabbi wasn't just fitting Torah into his life. It *was* his life. I thought about my family, and I said to myself, I don't think they really believe. And then I had to ask myself the same question: Do I really believe?"

"So do you?" she asked.

"I think I surprised myself. Because the answer was yes."

"What do your parents think?" she asked.

He shook his head. "The way I see it," he said, quoting his rabbi, "each generation can get farther from Sinai and lose touch a little more. Or we can turn it around and regain that connection. We can build on the generation that preceded us."

"I guess that means they're upset about it," Tzippy said.

"You could say that," he said, and they laughed.

"So what about you?" he asked.

She shrugged. "I don't know. I'm still the same, I guess."

"It's funny. I feel like I know you and I don't know you. I remember some things, but it's hard to remember that that was you."

"I remember a lot," she said.

"So what did you think of me then?" he asked, afraid of her answer.

She took a deep breath. "I thought you were cute," she said, and they both blushed.

Now Baruch took a deep breath. "Do you want to walk?" he asked.

They left the hotel. The streets curved upward and the walls of the Old City became visible. Tzippy and Baruch wound through the cobblestoned streets to the Western Wall. Groups of men huddled to say the evening prayers. Across the mechitzah, women pressed their faces against the stone. Their mouths moved rapidly as they recited psalms from small, frayed prayer books. Tzippy and Baruch sat at the back of the plaza and watched the steady trickle of visitors, these modern pilgrims arriving by car and taxi, on foot and on the crowded number one bus.

The lateness of the hour made it easier for them to open up. They traded confessions. Tzippy said that her mother only wanted one thing for her. She had come to Israel to escape the pressure. She told him about her sisters and laughed when he couldn't keep them straight. She said that she loved them, but sometimes she felt like their mother and not their sister.

Baruch said that he and his sister no longer had anything in common. He knew that it was probably his fault. When he was home, he had been so intent on showing his family how he had changed that he had barely been able to talk to Ilana. Now it seemed impossible to believe, but before going home, he had entertained the fantasy that his family would be excited at how he had changed. He had thought that they might even want to change along with him. But they hadn't been interested. They recoiled at everything he said, or worse, they laughed.

"The truth is," Baruch confided, "my parents don't understand at all."

Baruch and Tzippy had progressed far enough that, for the second date, dinner was a sound investment. A second date meant that there was potential: finally, maybe, possibly, it was shayach. Sitting across from each other, they smiled. They smiled at whatever the other one said. When Tzippy went home, she was still smiling. She stayed up late, replaying everything Baruch had said. At night, in her dreams, he waved to her, and she followed him again through the winding streets. She fell and he turned, fell and turned, fell and turned. She cried out and he stopped, he looked, he smiled.

On their next date, Baruch and Tzippy went to the miniature golf course outside Jerusalem, where religious couples teed up on every green. They flocked here as an alternative to the hotel lobby, using the game as a way to loosen up and get to know each other. Baruch considered the course with a puzzled expression, as if he were deciphering a difficult passage of Talmud. Then he swung and the ball traveled down the green, through the red archways, past the fake flowers. The ball slowed as it neared the hole, curved along the edge, and fell in.

"You're good at this," Tzippy said.

He took a bow. "Well, you know, I've played professionally."

"Oh, have you?"

"Sure. On my yeshiva's golf team."

She laughed. "Maybe that's where I know you from. I've been playing for years."

"And what team are you on?"

"What, you don't think B'nos Sarah has a team? For your information, we're national champions."

To prove her point, Tzippy twirled around, golf club in hand. She hit the ball and it sailed over the wooden barrier. It bounced twice and landed, to the astonishment of the couple next to them, on top of the fake palm trees of the neighboring green.

At night, the girls huddled in Tzippy's room to hear about Baruch. They couldn't get over the fact that Tzippy had met him on her own.

"It's so modern," they exclaimed, first in disapproval and then in delight.

They bombarded her with questions and imagined how they might bring home boys of their own. They wanted to hear how she had picked him out from the throngs of yeshiva boys in Jerusalem. They loved that he was younger than she was; it made her escapade seem like more of a coup. Then they wanted to know what she liked about him. She answered that she could be herself around him. She said he was funny and sweet and cute. She liked that he was religious but also had a worldly streak.

But Tzippy was afraid to say more. If she spoke too soon, the future dangling before her might disappear. She didn't tell her friends that though she called him Baruch, she privately thought of him as Bryan. In high school, she and her friends had viewed their Modern Orthodox counterparts as living lives approximating those of the characters in the Sweet Valley High series she read in secret under her covers. They heard about the underground, unofficial proms, whose existence the Modern Orthodox rabbis condoned. In restaurants and at extended family occasions, they bumped into these boys and girls in their blue jeans and couldn't decide whether they still qualified as Orthodox. Once, her mother had gotten off the phone with Naomi and shaken her head in wonder. "Bryan is going to a sweet sixteen party, and apparently they have mixed dancing." Tzippy had tried to imagine it. But even in her imagination, a chaperoning hand had stepped in and sent the boys and girls back to their respective sides of the room.

Now she wanted to hear it. Baruch talked about high school and who he had been then. He spoke of his obsession with baseball, of the girls he had dated, the parties they had had. He always described them derisively, to show the shortcomings, the compromises. But Tzippy pressed him for details: She wanted to be able to imagine it exactly. What were the girls' names? What did they look like? What had he liked about them? Where were they now? She wanted to know if he had danced at these parties, if he had enjoyed himself, if he missed it now. Baruch was surprised and amused by how many questions she asked. "Why are you so interested?" he wanted to know. She quickly hid her wonder. "I'm just curious," she said.

She also didn't tell her friends that sometimes she and Baruch didn't say a word. They looked at each other and that was enough. She didn't say that she had worked up the courage to tell him how many guys she had been out with. "Forty-two," she said. He said he didn't believe her, and she grew quiet, assuming he was making fun of her. "No," he said. "What I mean is that I can't believe that forty-two guys let you get away." On one date, she presented him with her dating notebook as proof. He read aloud each name as if they were contestants on a game show. "Avraham Cohen, Yitzchak Kaplan, Yaakov Blumenthal, Yosef Schachter, come on down," he called out, and for the first time, she laughed out loud at her long, sad list.

On the phone, Tzippy didn't tell her mother about Baruch. If she were home, she would have spilled out the details as soon as her mother asked for them. But far away, Tzippy kept everything to herself. For once, it didn't matter what her mother thought. Tzippy didn't have to think about who his family was or what they had or how this match would reflect on her family. Sometimes an engagement seemed like it was for the sake of the community. They were paired girls to boys like princesses being married off to cement relations between foreign countries. The other boys she had gone out with seemed like nothing more than a series of qualities held up against the list of what she wanted in a husband. If it wasn't one of them, then it would be some other.

With Baruch, she didn't care about her list. Her feelings for him mattered more than what she officially wanted. She fantasized that her dates with Baruch didn't end with a good-bye at the downstairs door to her apartment building. Instead, she took his hand and led him upstairs. She wrapped her arms around him and lay her head against his chest. He ran his hands across her breasts. In her dream, she quivered without worrying that it was wrong.

She was emboldened by what she imagined. When they were together, her body took over. Her hands stopped listening to her. They found reasons to pass him things and accidentally linger a second too long. Her legs were also in on this rebellion. Sometimes they walked too close to him. Her mind tempted and teased her, posing questions and inventing scenarios. What if their arms brushed against each other? Would he move away first or would she? What if she took his hand and pretended it was the most normal thing in the world?

Tzippy and Baruch stayed out late into the night. For the sake of marriage, they broke curfews and missed classes. When they got home, they talked on the phone. No matter when they started talking, it was always three in the morning before they realized it.

"We should hang up," he said. "I have to be up at seven."

"I know," she agreed. "We really should."

Sometimes one of them fell asleep for a few minutes. Sometimes they were both asleep, cell phones pressed to ears. Then they woke up and began anew. In the middle of the night, it was easier for Tzippy to say whatever came to her mind. Any shyness or propriety was lost in the mix of late-night intimacy and sleep deprivation.

"I didn't just happen to be in Mea Shearim that day," she confessed. "I kept seeing you different places and I followed you."

He was surprised to hear it. "You did? For how long?"

"I don't know," she said, and hoped he wouldn't think badly of her. "Maybe a week or two?"

He thought it over. "I guess it was yad Hashem," he decided, the hand of God.

She smiled with relief. "I guess so."

They tiptoed close to the subject but never made it explicit. They began to include each other when talking about the future. Instead of saying "my home," Baruch had started to say "our home." He had taken to saying "we," where just two weeks before he had said "I."

Tzippy collected these slips of the tongue and made her own. "My roommates are so crazy," she said. "They say they're picking out china patterns for us."

"My friends are complaining that I'm distracted," Baruch said. "They keep teasing me that they've never seen me like this."

"What did you tell them?" she asked.

"I said that maybe I had spring fever."

"But it's only December."

"I know. That's why they didn't believe me. They thought maybe it was something else," Baruch said.

"And what did you say?" Tzippy asked.

"I told them that maybe they were right."

Tzippy and Baruch had been dating for ten weeks, long enough that the weather had turned from too hot to too cold. Three times a day they prayed for rain, and by late December, God had answered them with a steady drizzle. On the first day without rain, Tzippy and Baruch ventured outdoors. Bundled inside scarves and hats, they went to the Biblical Zoo. They tried to ignore the biting cold, but after a quick run past the deer, the gazelles, and the rams, they sought refuge inside the snake house.

"It's amazing," Baruch said. "God created so many different kinds of animals. I mean, why not just one snake, one lizard? Why all the different species?" This was a God, he concluded, who clearly liked variety.

Tzippy feigned interest, but was standing so close to him that their arms brushed against each other. Afraid to breathe, afraid to interrupt this accidental proximity, they stared into the cage.

"Have you told your parents about us?" she asked.

"No," he admitted.

"Me neither," she said.

"I mean, not yet," he corrected himself. "But I will. I was going to wait, until we talked, until we were sure."

"So are you sure?" she asked softly.

"Yes," he said, and stepped closer to her, until their jackets touched, layers of goose down and Polartec pressing gently into each other. They held up their hands as if to touch. They matched one gloved finger to another, letting the fabric touch and the skin imagine.

The rabbis were right. With a girl on his mind, Baruch couldn't pay attention to his learning. His mind battled his body. In the pages of his Talmud, he saw Tzippy's face. In the shiurim his rabbi delivered, he heard her voice. When he was supposed to be davening, he thought of how easily she blushed. The rabbis told them to evaluate a girl based on her modesty. They said to consider what kind of home she would create, what sort of mother she would be. Baruch had done that. He liked how religious Tzippy was. He liked that she was sweet and understanding. She filled all the criteria that he was looking for in a wife. But more than that, he just liked her.

"I think she's The One," Baruch whispered to Chaim, as they sat among the other boys studying late into the night.

He and Chaim had learned together for months but had talked about little but the pages in front of them. Even so, this was enough to connect them. The learning they had shared was as important as any personal information they might have exchanged.

At Baruch's announcement, Chaim jumped up from his seat. He never sat still when he learned. He paced, he gestured, he walked as he talked, his hands moving furiously in the air.

"The One," Chaim said, and his thumb dug into the air. "And what do chazal teach us about that?" He paused only to take a breath. "In Kiddushin, it says: 'If there is a question whether to study Torah or take a wife, a man should study Torah. But if the man cannot live without a wife, he should take a wife and then study Torah.'"

The boys were used to seeing Chaim in constant motion. In the beis midrash, they learned to block out whatever wasn't directly in front of their eyes. They studied in pairs and focused only on the voice of their partner amid the din. It wasn't unusual for boys to pace back and forth as they learned. Some boys cared so much about a line of text that they slammed their fists down on the table and yelled at one another in disagreement. But a discussion about marriage caught their attention and disrupted their learning.

In a singsong chant, Chaim continued. "Rav Yehudah said in the name of Shmuel: 'The ruling is, a man must first take a wife and then study Torah.'" Just when the boys began to look relieved, Chaim held one finger up in the air to warn them. "But Rav Yochanan retorted, 'With a millstone around his neck, is he expected to study Torah?'"

Before the boys began to date, they consulted with their rabbis as to whether they were ready. It wasn't a decision they took lightly. Once they were ready, their learning wouldn't be the same. The unmarried boys in the yeshiva lived in the dorm and were provided with three meals a day. They needed little besides their books. Once the boys were married, they were elevated to the kollel, a higher slot in the yeshiva hierarchy. But unwittingly, they had also taken their first steps toward leaving. Kollel boys stayed for as long as their fathers or fathers-in-law could support them. But the demands of the real world encroached. Their wives often worked two jobs, took care of many children, and the pressure was too much. They had to make a living. The smartest ones managed to get jobs teaching in the yeshiva. Some taught in high schools or elementary schools, and tried to have an impact on the communities where they lived. Others snuck college classes at night and eventually left yeshiva altogether. They worked in computers and struggled to make time to learn.

"But doesn't Rav Huna also say that 'he who is twenty and not married will spend his day in sinful thought'?" This came from Yaakov, who had just decided he was ready to date.

"Yes, but in Sotah it says that a man should first build a house, then plant a vineyard, and only then take a wife," Chaim said. He wasn't ready to look for a wife. There would be time for that later. He loved his books too much to divide his attention. He pored over them all day, took a cold shower at night, and by the next morning was back at his place in the beis midrash.

"But in Yebamot, Rav Tanhum says in the name of Rav Hanilai that 'when a man lives without a wife, he lives without joy, without blessing, without good,'" said Avrumy, who just two nights before had come back engaged.

They jousted texts back and forth. But what about other advice, they wondered. Where could they find examples of how the rabbis went from their all-male world and found what to talk about with the girls? Where did it say how to calm the nerves that beset some of them on dates? Which sage could they turn to for advice on how to decide if a girl's few irritating habits were enough of a reason to end it?

"How do you know when she's The One?" one of the single boys asked.

"If there's nothing you don't like about her," another boy suggested.

"If you don't feel after a few minutes like you're ready to go home."

"If you can imagine seeing her every day for the rest of your life."

"If you don't feel so nervous that you want to jump out of your skin."

"If you don't feel like she'll take away from your learning."

"If you want to be with her so much you can't learn at all."

"If your rabbi agrees she's The One."

"If your parents do."

"I think you just know," Baruch said.

Baruch called home once a week but didn't mention his impending engagement. With his father, he answered questions perfunctorily. His mother made it easy. She liked to talk. Were he to hand the phone to one of his friends, she wouldn't notice.

Before he had come back to Israel, he and his mother had tacitly agreed to disagree. She had brokered a tense peace between him and his father over his refusal to go to Columbia. In negotiations that went on behind the closed door of their bedroom, she had convinced Joel that they couldn't force him to go. What should we do, she asked, handcuff him to the lecture-hall chairs? Then, she had wanted something from Baruch in return. She cornered him the night before he left for Israel and extracted a promise that he would be tolerant and respectful. Separated not just by miles but by centuries, on planes of existence that never intersected, it was easy to go along with her solution.

Now, Baruch willed his news to come out, but it never did. He was sure that if he told them he was getting married, this tenuous peace would fracture. They would first be shocked, then furious. They would inundate him with questions. They would carry on that he had no way to support himself, let alone support a wife and family. Instead of listening to his answers, they would only notice how much he deviated from what they'd wanted for him.

But this was what he wanted. Getting married was his next step. His rabbi had met Tzippy and given his approval. Some of his friends in yeshiva were dating. They were starting to get engaged. In this world, getting engaged this young, this soon, was normal. He envied even more the boys born into the yeshiva world. When they got married at nineteen to girls who were eighteen, they didn't stand under the chuppah alone. They felt the force of an approval that was generations long.

One night, he and Tzippy were at a falafel stand in town. It was like a hundred others in the center of Jerusalem, with a once white speckled counter and a few maroon-topped stools. On the walls were faded posters of orange groves and tourists smiling from underneath bright blue kibbutz hats. Baruch added extra slices of fried eggplant to his already full pita, and he bit carefully to keep it from splitting open and spilling onto his lap. Tzippy was sitting on the stool next to him.

For the past two weeks, he had seen an expectant look pass across her face every time they went out. She was waiting and wondering when he was going to propose. She had been dressing up for each date, never sure which night was going to be *the* night. But tonight, she looked more relaxed. They had just met for a quick dinner, and she had on a jean skirt and a B'nos Sarah sweatshirt. It didn't enter the realm of possibility that they could get engaged here.

They ate their falafel and stole glances at each other. Tzippy wrapped a piece of hair around her finger and twirled it. When she glanced coyly at him, he stopped thinking about his parents and the fighting that would soon ensue.

"Tzippy," he said, and took a deep breath. "Will you marry me?"

Her whole life she had been imagining this moment. She and her friends had planned it out and dissected it and waited for it. They had thought about where it would take place, what he would say, what they would wear. But now that the moment was finally here, it didn't matter that she was wearing a jean skirt and that they were at a falafel stand with greasy counters and dirty floors and that her mother would be horrified if she knew that this was where Baruch had proposed. For the sake of those who cared, they would make up a better story later. For Tzippy, what mattered was Baruch and the love he was offering.

Tzippy said yes, and she felt herself changing. This was the moment Tzippy had imagined when people spoke of the world to come. She stood at the edge of this world and started to run. Suddenly there was nothing but blue sky all around her, and she sailed over the ocean that separated her former life from her current one. She reached that heavenly barrier, ready to cross over.

— FIVE —

WHENEVER BARUCH wanted both parents on the phone at the same time, Joel knew to expect trouble.

"Guess what?" Baruch said. "I'm engaged."

Joel's first thought was to remain calm. As far as he and Naomi were concerned, their son was still a child. As far as they knew, he didn't have a girlfriend. Last they heard, he didn't talk to girls. So all Joel had to do was wait for the haze to disperse, the explanation to emerge: I am engaged in finding myself, perhaps. Or, more likely: I am engaged in a mission to drive my parents crazy.

"Mazel tov, mazel tov," Baruch said. "I'm getting married."

"What!" Naomi said.

"To whom?" Joel asked with dread, not wanting to imagine what sort of wife Baruch would choose.

"Oh my God, when did this happen? How did this happen?" Naomi shouted.

Well, Joel thought, this is what it feels like to have a stroke. Or a heart attack. The room was spinning, and he was inside a loop of dizzying circles.

"What's going on?" Ilana asked, hearing the commotion.

"Get on the phone," Naomi said. "Your brother has some exciting news."

"What is it?" Ilana asked. "Just tell me."

Naomi made an exaggerated show of shrugging her shoulders and motioned for Ilana to pick up another phone.

Ilana went into the den for cordless phone number three and

brought it into the kitchen, where Joel and Naomi stood facing each other, eyebrows furrowed.

"That is so crazy," she said when Baruch repeated the news.

Naomi covered the mouthpiece with her hand. "Ilana, please!" Then she went back to the conversation. "Tell me more. How did you meet her? What's her name?"

"I'm engaged to Tzippy Goldman."

"You're not serious," Joel said.

At the same time, Naomi exclaimed, "Sweet Tzippy Goldman."

Joel's panic worsened. He hoped he had heard Baruch wrong. He hoped he might wake up and this would simply be a bad dream. But he wasn't waking up and Baruch wasn't saying that he was kidding. Joel pressed the phone against his ear. Tzippy Goldman was the daughter of two people he didn't like, whom he had always wanted less to do with, not more. He had thought he was free of them, and now he was about to become more involved with them than he had ever imagined.

He had married into the friendship. Naomi and Shayna had been close friends, and when he started dating Naomi, she talked about Shayna constantly. He imagined that whatever he and Naomi discussed was automatically reported to Shayna upon her return to the dorm. But it wasn't enough that the two women were such close friends. Shayna was dating Herschel, and Naomi was determined to double-date with them.

In the early years, Joel had made an effort. It hadn't occurred to him that he had a choice. But it grew harder. The more they were forced together, the more he withdrew. He was never one to talk a lot, but with them, he couldn't force himself to say enough to qualify as polite. He had no capacity for pretense. His voice took on a tight quality when talking to someone he didn't like.

He had nothing against Shayna. He found her mildly annoying, but that was typical of him. It was Herschel he couldn't stand. A sarcastic inner monologue ran through his head when he was in Herschel's presence. At that time, Joel was a hardworking young associate at his law firm and had so little free time. He hated to spend any of it with someone he found so distasteful. Slaving away at his job out of a sense of responsibility, he didn't have the patience to hear Herschel describe his grand plans for starting his own company, for making a million dollars without working a day. Herschel asked him why he didn't quit his job and start a firm of his own. He tried to convince Joel to invest some money in one of his ventures, to get in on the ground floor of a sure thing. Knowing that Herschel wanted something from him made Joel close up more. He listened to Herschel's plans and didn't believe a word.

After spending time with them, he and Naomi always fought. "Why couldn't you be friendly?" she asked. "Why do you always have to invite them?" he answered. He held his ground, and after nearly twenty years of fighting about it, Naomi had finally stopped making plans with them.

"It was a shidduch," Baruch was saying. "I met her by accident, but my rabbi knows her rabbi and they both thought it was a good idea. I wasn't planning on dating yet, but seeing her made me realize I was ready."

"Really," Naomi said casually, as if all they needed was a few more sentences from their son and they would know enough to feel calm and pleased.

"So we went out, and from the beginning we both knew there was something there. We understand each other and we have a lot to talk about and she's really great and she's what I'm looking for. So we're getting married."

Joel shook his head in disbelief, and Ilana returned a look of horror. Stunned, she waited for her parents to say something. But Joel had no idea what to say. At each point along the way, they had been willing to bend, from one year in Israel to two, to a third year, to no college at all. Just when they got used to one idea, Baruch surprised them with another. Any attempt Joel had made to put his foot down was held back by Naomi's insistence that it was a phase, their son merely taking the long road on his journey to find himself. For lack of a better option, Joel had chosen to believe her.

"Bryan, have you considered the fact that . . . ," he started to say.

There were a hundred ways to finish the sentence, but Naomi held up her hand to stop him.

"Baruch, we're not even sure what to say," she said. "This is such exciting news and you've caught us a little off guard. We need to catch our breath and digest this. But it's great. It's really great. And I'm sure you've given it a lot of thought and you know what a huge decision this is."

On three cordless phones, they stood there. Joel and Ilana were silent as Naomi tried to fill the void between them and Baruch. But there was nothing to say. Marriage ended their hopes that this was a phase. It locked these changes into place.

"What did you expect?" Naomi asked when they hung up. "That he was going to go to yeshiva for three years and then decide to go to college and date and go to parties and have a bunch of different girlfriends and then a few years later settle down? This is what they do, Joel. This is what it means to be part of that world."

"I'm sure he barely knows her. And they're both babies."

"I was twenty-two," Naomi said.

"That's irrelevant. It was a different world."

"It's just going to take some getting used to," Naomi said. "For all of us. Once we see him and Tzippy together, we'll feel better."

"And of all people," Joel said with renewed opposition. "He had to pick her."

"I've always liked Tzippy," said Naomi. "She's really very sweet. But I still can't believe it. Everything is connected. We think we lose touch with someone and then here they are again."

"I know," he grumbled. "That's exactly the problem."

"But we were such good friends. I can't believe it's been so long since we've seen them. I really wish we had stayed in better touch. I miss them."

"I don't," Joel said.

"I don't either," Ilana said.

"What do you have against them?" Naomi asked Joel. "They mean well. They're very nice. They've never done anything to you."

"Isn't it possible that I could just dislike them, for no reason at all?"

"You could have at least sounded happy for him," Naomi said.

"Are you crazy? 'Mom, Dad, I'm throwing my life away. Are you happy for me?'" Joel mimicked.

"Come on, it's not that bad."

"It is," he insisted. "If I didn't know better, I'd say you thought this was a great idea."

"Of course I'm concerned about it. I want to be sure he knows what he's getting into. But I also want to be supportive. He's telling us the biggest news of his life and to greet that with a barrage of critical comments isn't going to change his mind. It's just going to push him away. And he sounds so excited. I think he's really in love. Didn't you hear it in his voice?"

Joel hadn't heard anything except defiance. He was convinced that Baruch's newfound religiosity was the ultimate rebellion. Had Baruch come home with no yarmulke, he wouldn't have elicited this strong a reaction. But their son was too smart for that. He knew how to find their weakest spot and take aim.

"This is what he wants," Naomi said. "Not everyone has so much faith, but he does, and I think it's nice. Can't you concede that that's possible?"

This was their standard fight. They had been having versions of it since they were newly married. Naomi would say that Joel needed to be flexible, more understanding, more tolerant. Joel would say that she was unrealistic and impractical. She was living in her own world.

In subsequent phone conversations, Baruch gave them more details, none of which made Joel feel better. They were planning to get married as soon as possible. He would continue learning, in a yeshiva in New York for the next few years. She would teach nursery school to support them. "Spending the first years of marriage in yeshiva gives us a foundation for the rest of our lives," Baruch said, making Joel feel as if he were quoting sentences from a primer his rabbi had given him, *How to Become Religious and Alienate People.*

Until now, he and Naomi had had an unspoken agreement. The house and the children were her domain; earning a living was his. But now he couldn't retreat from what was going on. Naomi was too willing to accept whatever Baruch brought home. Joel preferred to argue every point. He was determined to find the holes in Baruch's reasoning. He knew they existed. Faith was always porous. Joel didn't believe his son when he offered up an airtight view of the world.

Joel presented his arguments to Baruch. "It's hard to really know someone after a few weeks, don't you think?" he said. "I know the important things," Baruch answered. Joel responded, "People grow and change over a lifetime. When you're twenty-one, it's hard to know who you are and how you want to end up." "So we'll grow together," Baruch answered.

Still not willing to give in, Joel tried the practical. "If you're really going to get married, how do you plan to support yourself? What if everyone learned full-time and no one had a job? It's not a self-sustaining system." He tried flattery. "You're so smart. You have so much going for you. Why not try college for a year?" He tried the theoretical. "I would hate for you to cut yourself off from other options that one day you might be interested in." In response to each of these, Baruch told him that the only thing worth doing was the study of Talmud. "Jobs," Baruch pronounced, "are at best a necessary evil."

"Right," Joel answered. "They're necessary. Otherwise, what do you plan to live on?"

Baruch answered that there were more important things to consider. They didn't want a lot. He was going to join the yeshiva's kollel for married students, and they would live on Tzippy's salary and the small stipend they paid.

"Do you have any idea how unrealistic that is? What if you have children? They're an expensive endeavor. Believe me."

"We'll do the best we can."

"But what does that mean? Translate it into a practical plan. Because if you think I'm going to pay for you to sit and learn, think again."

"You were planning to pay for Columbia. Why is this so different?"

"College at least prepares you for the real world. It gives you an education so you can become self-sufficient."

"You don't have to help us. Tzippy's parents will," Baruch said.

"Are you sure about that?" Joel asked. "I'd make sure Herschel is really going to do what he says before you count on him."

"He will, because *he* understands the value of learning."

At that point, Joel handed the phone to Naomi. He didn't want to hear about Herschel. He was still trying to formulate why supporting his son in college *was* different from supporting him in yeshiva. They had the money, so he could easily help them out if he wanted to. But he wasn't going to pay for something he so strongly disagreed with. There wasn't one single path he wanted Baruch to follow. He wasn't looking to replicate himself, nor hoping to vicariously fulfill any lost fantasy. He wasn't of the generation that insisted on their sons becoming doctors or lawyers. He would have been happy with his son the professor, his son the architect, his son the aspiring artist.

For his generation, it had been different. They had understood the need to sacrifice for later gains. They had expected to work hard and to support their families. Even if he had once wanted to do something else, he didn't feel he had a choice. Everything in their house was paid for on the back of his job. If day school cost $15,000 a year and camp was another $5,000, and shul membership was $3,000, then being a lawyer was what you did.

When the children were young, Joel had spent more hours at work than at home. The partners acted as if nothing existed beyond the walls of their office. Any family plan was made with the knowledge that it would be canceled if something came up. If the client wanted a revised draft of a document by the morning, Joel was obligated to give it to them. He often worked all night, keeping himself awake by pacing and eating chocolate bars from the snack machine.

But through the fog of unrelenting pressure, he had privately rebelled. He imagined that one day he would walk out of his office and never come back, leaving piles of paper on his desk and the red light of his voice mail flashing. He ascended the corporate ladder chronically exhausted. He missed weeknight dinners, Little League games, and school plays. Eventually he stopped minding. Now, as a partner, he had more control over his schedule. But hard work had become a habit. He had forgotten that it could be any other way.

But what was the point of all this hard work if his son had no interest in what he wanted to give him? Baruch wanted to throw everything away at the age of twenty-one, close off his options before he even had a chance to explore them. Joel had worked hard to give his kids whatever they wanted: music lessons and trips to the museum, tickets for plays and concerts. Their kids were supposed to be the generation that knew no limits. They could be anything they wanted: even vice president, Naomi liked to say. Presented with an abundance of choices, Baruch was selecting the most restrictive of possibilities.

"He's still our son," Naomi reminded Joel as he lay awake in bed the night before Baruch and Tzippy were to come home. "Try to look past the outer differences and see who he is on the inside."

Joel didn't answer. He had had enough of her optimistic advice. He had heard it before and it never seemed to work.

"It's going to be fine," she said. "Maybe this will even make it easier."

"Why would it make it easier?" he asked.

"I don't know. But who knows? I think it might."

There was no point in arguing. He couldn't tell what Naomi really believed. Sometimes she was just thinking out loud, her words a continuous stream of ideas, wishes, questions, possibilities. Now that Baruch was engaged, she had convinced him to come home. He could learn in a yeshiva in New York, she had told him, and he had finally agreed. Naomi had spent the day in eager anticipation of Baruch's homecoming. She had removed from his closet the overflow items from Ilana's room, stocked the house with his favorite foods, and returned the dish racks to the sinks from their sojourn in the utility closet. Now her eyes were closed. She rolled over, offering no other words of wisdom, and Joel went downstairs to pour himself a drink.

Now that Baruch was coming home, he would no longer be just a voice to fight with across the phone line. Joel surprised himself with his longing for his son, the old one. He paced the house and swirled the scotch around in its glass, wishing he could heed Naomi's words and see his son. But all he could see was Baruch's black hat. In his mind, it took different shapes. It flattened at the top, grew taller, and became a top hat. It curved out at the sides, sloped in at the middle, and became a cowboy hat. It grew larger until it swallowed him entirely.

He tried to push away the image of the hat and replace it with the familiar face underneath. But what *was* underneath? What lay inside? He wished he knew. His son justified his every action by claiming it was the word of God. Maybe it was, but Joel had trouble believing in the importance of each word, the law divvied up and parceled into the tiniest of applications. When he was growing up, people did what their parents did. They weren't looking to be more observant than their families. He could be an Orthodox Jew and be many other things at the same time. His religion didn't have to identify him, constrict him, define him. He wasn't like the young associates in his firm who wore their yarmulkes to work and organized kosher summer associate lunches. At formal dinners, they unwrapped plastic wrappers from kosher airplane meals and expected people to think it was normal. Joel wore his yarmulke when he left the house in the morning, through the commute into Manhattan. As he entered the revolving doors to his Midtown office, he palmed the yarmulke into his pocket. Mid-rotation, he tousled his hair to remove the circular indentation it left behind. By the time he came into the building, he looked like everyone else.

Now, at their shul in Laurelwood, the rabbis gave classes on the religious implications of using soap on Shabbos. They sermonized on the appropriate way to tie one's shoes. Every variation in observance was investigated and categorized. Joel witnessed the march of stringencies, a one-upmanship of who could be more religious. On Shabbos, he stood in shul and watched people daven and sway, only to hear that this one cheats on his taxes, this one cheats on his wife. He had seen hypocrisy masquerading as faith, and now he couldn't see beyond it. The more religious his son became, the more estranged he felt. He couldn't help but wonder where God was in what his son did and said. Was He under the hat? In between the plastic slats of the dish racks? Was His spirit sweeping through this house, a thrumming audible only to his son?

Joel stood in front of the living-room wall where Naomi had hung, from floor to ceiling, framed family photos. She had taken black-and-white photographs of the kids when they were younger, one of the many short-lived hobbies she had passed through. In archival frames with white matte borders, they hung close together, in no particular order. Ilana's and Bryan's baby pictures were next to Joel's and Naomi's baby pictures. Bryan in a basketball uniform was poised midair, a basketball caught in the moment of release. Three generations swam at the beach in Miami on summer vacations. Joel's grandmother, ninety years old, walked down the aisle at their wedding. Ilana, named after this grandmother, was dressed up in a long peach gown Naomi had once worn as a bridesmaid. Joel and Naomi's wedding photo was next to his parents' wedding photo. Next came Joel's formal bar mitzvah picture, a tallis draped over his shoulder, a white satin yarmulke on his head. Interspersed with these were older photos of great-great-grandparents that Naomi had dug up. She had interviewed older relatives and collected stories about the people in the photos. She hung old and new pictures together to show off the resemblances. Four generations of curly-haired women, the curl of an upper lip, the small foreheads and widow's peaks that showed up in every generation—the features the same, the contexts worlds apart.

There was one photo of Joel's pious Lithuanian great-grandparents. She was stern-faced and proud in a high lace collar fastened with a brooch, hair covered with a black kerchief. He wore a long black coat and had a somber face peeking out from behind a beard. Joel knew little more than their names and a few biographical details. He had never been one to listen to family stories, nor to keep in touch with cousins and remember who was who. All he knew was that they were the last European generation in his family. Their children, Joel's grandparents, had come to America before World War I. They had opened a grocery store in Baltimore, Maryland. Joel's father married a girl from Charleston, South Carolina, with a Southern accent. In just a few generations, his family had become American.

Joel had once thought of these photographed ancestors as the last of their kind, a remnant of a world that once existed. Now he wondered who would outlast whom. His family had come forward and now they were boomeranging backward. With Baruch somewhere over the Atlantic on his way home, Joel looked at this picture and didn't know if he was seeing the past or the future.

Joel and Naomi had been standing in the international arrivals terminal for an hour, wandering and waiting, when Herschel and Shayna rushed in, four daughters in tow.

"Well, here we are," Shayna said. "Finally."

"The bridge was backed up. It was the worst traffic I've ever seen. But, see, I told you, we have plenty of time," Herschel said.

"You look great," Naomi said, and she rushed over to kiss Shayna on the cheek.

"I have my girls to keep me young."

"They must be a handful."

Shayna didn't have to answer. The girls were already scattering in various directions, and she was constantly turning her head to keep an eye on them.

"Busy, busy, busy," Shayna said. "But they help me out. And, of course, Tzippy is the biggest help of all."

Naomi turned to Herschel. "And what about you? What are you up to these days? Last we heard, weren't you opening a pizza place?"

"No, no, no." Shayna dismissed this with a wave of her hand. "He hasn't done that for ages. He's with the Orthodox Coalition now, in their kashrus division. He's a vice president. He's been working with kosher food for years, on his own, and the Orthodox Coalition finally convinced him to come on board."

"That's exciting," Naomi said.

They looked at each other, Naomi at Shayna, Joel at Herschel. Each husband and wife eyed each other as well. Even in the crowded terminal, their silence felt conspicuous. The past pushed against them. They carried with them the shadow of their previous friendship.

After Naomi had gotten off the phone with Baruch, she had called Shayna. It had been a few years since they had spoken, and she was nervous as she waited for Shayna to answer. She had stopped calling Shayna, because she knew that at the end of every conversation there would be the inevitable moment when they were expected to make plans. Shayna was always inviting them for Shabbos or suggesting Sunday picnics. Naomi had come up with excuses until she ran out of them. She tried to cover for Joel's dislike because she felt bad about it, because it wasn't nice, because she didn't want to hurt anyone's feelings. But there was no wishing away the truth. Joel wasn't going to do things he didn't want to do. With this constant tension, it became easier to subsume her own wishes.

"Shayna," she had said, trying to fill in for the years of absence, "mazel tov. Can you believe it?"

"After all we went through, I can't believe it turned out to be someone we knew," Shayna had said. "Of course, Tzippy could have been married many times over by now. But what can you do? She's very choosy. She said she was waiting for the right one."

"We didn't even know Baruch was dating. We didn't know he was thinking about marriage."

"You didn't know he was being set up? I guess we weren't that surprised," Shayna said.

"Who would have thought, when we were in college, that our kids would get married," Naomi said.

"Who would have thought a lot of things," Shayna said.

"I'm sorry it's been so long," Naomi said. "Somehow, the time has just slipped away."

"Don't worry about it. That's exactly how it is for me too," Shayna said.

While Naomi had talked on the phone, Joel stood nearby, listening to her end of the conversation. Do you want to talk? she motioned with her eyes, her arms, her smile. Even though he was still recovering from the initial shock, she thought maybe he would. How hard could it be to say hello and sound, if not thrilled, at least not horrified. But Joel wouldn't budge. He shook his head and, when she persisted, he left the room.

Now, at the airport, Naomi wanted to step lightly on his foot, as if this might force polite conversation out of him. He likes to do his own thing; this was how she explained his reticence to herself and their friends. But in moments like these, she needed his help. She had imagined this would be a joyful reunion. It was true; the two families didn't have as much in common as they once did. But they had once been close. No matter how far they had drifted, the past surely had to count for something.

Shayna was trying to affect the same blasé stance Naomi had adopted— that these things happen, that friendships drift, that it's hard to stay in touch. Naomi wanted to pretend that in the crush of children, family, and home, their friendship had gotten lost, and neither of them remembered anymore how or why it had happened. But Shayna remembered. She remembered everything. Before they had finally drifted for good, she had always been the one to call. If she wanted to talk to Naomi, she had to pick up the phone. Whenever Shayna tried to make plans to get together, Naomi had an excuse. Shayna kept calling, leaving messages that went unreturned. With a sinking feeling, Shayna had finally given up. She tried to act as though it didn't matter, but that sinking feeling had created a small hole inside her where she always worried about what she had done wrong.

At Stern College, Shayna had been placed in Naomi's dorm room by chance. Shayna knew no one. Though Naomi had her own group of friends, she let Shayna attach herself to her. She brought her home for Shabbos, and Naomi's family became hers. Shayna listened to the stories Naomi told and the names she mentioned. When those same names came up again, she pretended she knew them. The stories became so real that she could have told them herself.

Newly religious, Shayna had watched the other girls carefully, as if Orthodoxy were a secret kingdom and she just needed to elicit the password in order to be admitted. She understood that if she wanted to be like everyone else, she needed to pay attention to what people did and said and wore. But she still made mistakes. She still hadn't rooted out the instinct to switch off the bathroom light on Shabbos. But in front of Naomi, she didn't have to pretend. "Don't worry," Naomi said, when Shayna stood in the dark bathroom and was so embarrassed that she considered turning the light back on. "That happens to me too. And I grew up religious. If anyone asks, we'll just say the lightbulb burned out." She had been so grateful to Naomi. She was the friend who knew her best. She had helped her become the person she wanted to be.

Now their children were going to be married. Waiting to see her engaged daughter, Shayna wasn't going to let anything pull her down. She wasn't going to think about having to smooth over a few details of the engagement for her friends—that it had happened at a falafel stand, that she hadn't been told ahead of time, that the parents hadn't talked before it was official. It was time to celebrate. The engagement was a battle won, a prayer answered, a breath released. A week before, Tzippy had called, sounding perfectly normal.

"What's new?" Tzippy had asked.

"Leah Klein had a baby boy, her second," Shayna reported about a girl only a year older than Tzippy. "The bris is Wednesday. Fifteen hours of labor, can you believe it? They thought it would be easy, because her last labor was only five hours. But apparently not. So how are you?"

"Fine. School's good. I'm learning a lot. Oh, and by the way, Bryan Miller and I are engaged."

At first Shayna thought Tzippy was joking and she started to laugh. Then she realized that Tzippy didn't joke like that, and she screamed so loudly that Herschel came running. The girls woke up and bounded downstairs in their nightgowns. Her hand shaking, Shayna held the phone in the air, as if they could see through to the engaged Tzippy on the other end.

"She's engaged!" she had screamed and burst into tears. She sobbed into the phone, while the girls jumped up and down in disbelief. Herschel grabbed the phone, while Shayna squeezed her eyes shut and pressed her fingers against them. But she couldn't stop crying. The tears drowned out everything she wanted to say. She had always imagined that she would feel nothing but joy when this moment arrived. Now that it was here, she felt weak from how badly she had wanted it. Her happiness was tinged with how hard it had been. She took the phone back from Herschel, but her voice still cracked and hiccupped when she tried to wish Tzippy mazel tov.

"Mom, it's good news," Tzippy had said.

"Believe me, I know," Shayna said, and pressed her fingers against her eyes to halt the flood.

"We're not going to be getting any sleep for the next few months. Planning a wedding is a big job," Shayna said now to Naomi.

"It's going to be fun, don't you think?" Naomi said.

"Of course. I didn't say it wouldn't be fun. Just a lot of work."

"Maybe we could do it together. We could divide up what needs to be done."

"Of course. But Tzippy's the boss here. Her whole life, she's been planning her wedding. I think she's had every detail down since she was five years old."

"What about you? Have you started thinking about it?" Naomi asked.

Shayna laughed. "Well, they've only been engaged for a few weeks. But of course we're starting to get the ball rolling. I've called around to a few halls and left a message with the band everyone uses. A lot depends on what's available in June."

"June? That's barely five months from now," Naomi said. "I thought maybe after the holidays, in October or November."

"It's going to be sooner than that. I wish it could be before Pesach, but the best halls are booked solid."

"But it's hard to pull it together so quickly," Naomi protested.

"It's plenty of time, believe me. Everyone does it like that."

Shayna felt newly confident as she spoke. She was finally getting what she wanted. Once, long ago, she had tried to remake herself in Naomi's image. She had looked at Naomi with such awe, marveling at how comfortable she was with herself. Maybe it was Naomi who had changed over the years. Or maybe it was she. Either way, they had switched places. Naomi now had a tentative quality in her voice; Shayna was the one who knew what to do. She belonged here. She knew all the rules.

Standing in line for customs, waiting to declare what they had returned home with, Tzippy and Baruch were as nervous as their parents.

"It's going to be fine," Baruch assured her.

"Of course it is," Tzippy said.

They looked at each other and giggled. It was not going to be fine. After getting engaged, they had waited a few hours before telling any-one. For that short time, the decision had belonged to them alone. The giddy freedom they had both felt began to subside as soon as they had called their parents. Shayna's desires bore down on Tzippy. The pres-sure was the same. Overnight, her mother had gone from worrying about dating to worrying about the wedding. She called every day, and as she carried on about dresses and caterers, dessert tables and fabric samples, Tzippy heard something ravenous in her voice.

Tzippy had secretly pored over the stash of *Bride's* magazines the girls kept in the dorm. Alone, she looked at the dresses and imagined herself in one. But as soon as her mother wanted to talk about the wed-ding, she clammed up. Holding back was the only way to protect her-self. If she opened her mouth, her happiness would escape. The diamond on her finger was reflected in her body, her love for Baruch a small hard circle in her chest. If she took it out and held it to the light to examine it, her mother would swallow it.

"Let's tell them we eloped," Tzippy suggested to Baruch.

One giggle led to another. They got a strange, hysterical pleasure from the knowledge that they had followed the rules, but not exactly. They had gotten engaged far from home with none of the requests for permission, none of the family summits. They hadn't even told their parents they were dating. They had done the equivalent of running off together.

Joel saw Baruch first, and instead of calling out his name and waving, he froze. He averted his eyes and waited until Shayna shrieked their names, until Naomi jumped up and down and waved her hands over her head. Then there was a great flurry of hugs and hellos. Shayna beamed at Baruch and hugged Tzippy tightly. The sisters hugged Tzippy, then hugged one another. They ran in circles hugging whoever would let them. Herschel put his arm around Baruch and welcomed him into their family. When Herschel finally moved aside, Joel shook his son's hand, but didn't meet his eye. He smiled at Tzippy, knowing not to touch her. But Naomi wasn't going to hold back. With her right arm, she pulled Tzippy to her and hugged. With her left arm, she pulled Baruch and hugged. Whether he liked it or not, she was going to hug her son.

— SIX —

WITH A SHORT ENGAGEMENT, there was no time to waste. Tzippy and Baruch had been home for two weeks, and every day was dedicated to crossing items off Shayna's list. Even the sisters were recruited in the effort. Shayna assigned them the job of flipping through issues of *Bride's* and turning down the corners of pages with flowers or dresses or china they liked. By the end of the week, every page had been turned down. Then they cut out pictures of wedding dresses and made paper dolls. They entered a contest to win an all-expenses-paid Bahamas honeymoon. They filled out questionnaires to determine what type of bride they were—old-fashioned or modern, practical or romantic. They ran around the house with lace tablecloths permanently pinned to their hair.

Shayna filled her days with preparations for the wedding. She was in a race against all other brides and their mothers. It was already February, and to get a date in early June, she had to wrest the best hall from another prospective bride. She ran from the caterer to the florist. The phone hadn't stopped ringing since Tzippy called with the news of her engagement. Shayna answered with a breathless hello and waited to be greeted with a mazel tov. It was a friend who never returned her calls, then a friend whose five daughters had each gotten married at the stroke of nineteen. Then it was the florist, the caterer, the dressmaker.

Shayna wasn't going to think about what the wedding would cost, not yet. She didn't have the money to pay for what she planned, but that didn't stop her. She consoled herself with the fact that they all stretched themselves thin to pull off these lavish weddings. Usually

Shayna bought everything on sale. She prided herself on her ability to pay less for their clothes, yet make it look as if they had the same as everyone else. But with a wedding, there were fewer ways to conserve. Everyone knew what it meant if you used one band and not another. Everyone knew who took second mortgages to pay for the most prestigious caterer. Everyone was so busy competing with everyone else that it was impossible to tell who was leading and who was following. There was talk of the rabbis imposing restrictions. They wanted to outlaw lavish centerpieces and open bars. They wanted to limit the numbers of guests invited. If this were to happen, her entire neighborhood would publicly complain but privately be relieved. But until then, Shayna had to do what everyone else did. She wasn't going to be first to cut back and let her daughter be the only one who had less. For years, people had pursed their lips and, half kidding, said, "Five girls! Have you thought about all the weddings you're going to have to make?" She had laughed along with them. Then it was still a distant dream. Now, at the dining-room table, Shayna made lists of what she had, what she needed. On the table were two years' worth of *Bride's* flagged with yellow Post-its. She had collected samples of paper, fonts, and fabric. She had saved invitations from every wedding to which she had ever been invited.

Shayna wanted this to be the standard by which all future weddings would be judged. She wanted to invite everyone she knew. She wanted everyone to wait with nervous anticipation for an invitation to arrive. She wanted her friends to gasp in awe as they entered the hall. Tzippy's dress had to be the most beautiful anyone had ever seen. Her own dress had to be the second most beautiful. The girls' dresses needed to match the hall. The tablecloths needed to match the carpeting. The chair covers needed to match the walls. She wanted Tzippy's bouquet of flowers to be so big that it would require two hands to hold it. The little girls would carry white wicker baskets filled with rose petals and wear wreaths in their hair. She wanted a smorgasbord of fresh vegetables cut and arranged to look like bouquets of flowers, bouquets of flowers arranged to look like platters of fruit, platters of fruit to look like small landscape scenes. She wanted a choice of beef, chicken, and salmon. She wanted a Viennese dessert table with cakes frosted to look like spring hats, cakes like treasure boxes, cakes like butterflies and castles, too beautiful to cut, too artful to eat.

———

"I'm ready," Tzippy announced as she came into the dining room.

In the two weeks since Tzippy had come home, the wedding had grown exponentially. Her wedding would soon take up the entire world. It would happen as Shayna wanted, whether Tzippy was there or not. She could be buried under yards of lace and tulle and no one would notice. Tzippy remembered the game of wedding planning that she and her mother had once played. Now it was coming to life, exactly as they had imagined.

But it was too late. Tzippy had had her fill of weddings. The wedding had become her mother's domain, and her only consolation was knowing that one day the wedding would be over and it would be possible to wake up and not hear about flower arrangements and table overlays. Until then, Tzippy preferred to think about the practical details of their lives. What came after the wedding, at least, still belonged to them. Baruch was going to learn in a Brooklyn yeshiva. They were going to live in an apartment near her parents' house. She was planning to work in a nursery school. She was making a list of the things they needed for their new home. She was trying to figure out how much money they needed.

It took her mother a few seconds to notice her. When Shayna finally looked up, she hummed "Od yeshama" at her, the wedding song that was the musical accompaniment to every hope she had for her daughter.

"Okay, okay," Tzippy said. "I'm going to be sick of that song before the wedding even starts."

"A bride never gets sick of 'Od yeshama,'" Shayna insisted.

Today's appointment was with the sheitel maker. More than the florist or the caterer, buying a wig meant that Tzippy was really getting married. Not even a wedding ring proclaimed the news as loudly. Shayna imagined the thrill of a married daughter sitting next to her in shul, her sheitel on her head like a crown of achievement. As each of her daughters got married and had children, Shayna would have a huge bustling family. In just one generation, she could create what she never had. Her grandchildren would grow up with a web of cousins. The sheer number of relatives would dispel any loneliness.

Shayna walked slowly down the street. They passed a Jewish bookstore, which stood next to a kosher pizza place, next to a kosher deli, next to a kosher bakery, next to another Jewish bookstore. This street was the capital of Jewish shopping. People came from all over to buy Jewish books and silver candlesticks, to pick out a tallis for a groom, a stack of hats for a bride. The music stores carried only Jewish music. There was Jewish classical, Jewish rock, Jewish folk. The clothing stores also catered to a religious clientele. The mannequins were buttoned up to their plastic necks. There was no need to stray from the confines of Orthodoxy. On this block, the whole world was made over in their image.

Shayna waved to everyone who looked familiar. She made Tzippy slow down and adjust to her promenading pace. These errands were the victory lap. For years, Shayna had held her tongue when her friends discussed plans for their daughters' weddings. She had endured endless questions about why Tzippy wasn't engaged.

"You remember my Tzippy," Shayna said now when they passed people she knew. "And I'm sure you've heard the news. She's engaged."

"I hope you realize how lucky we are to get this appointment," Shayna said to Tzippy. "Suri is usually booked three months in advance. But I begged her, so she squeezed us in."

When Shayna got married, she bought her wig alone. Her mother had laughed when Shayna told her she planned to cover her hair. If her daughter insisted on living in a world that no longer existed, she wasn't going to have any part of it. But Shayna had been eager to cover her hair. She didn't view this law with the same dread as some of her always-religious friends. She loved the idea that she would be marked as a married woman wherever she went. Shayna spent four hundred dollars, an amount that seemed like a fortune to her then, for the Classic, a honey-brown wig with bangs and shoulder-length hair that curled stiffly under. From a mile away, it was evident that it was a wig. But there had been so few choices then. Everyone had the Classic. From the back, it was hard to tell the women apart.

Now, she and her friends had their wigs styled in salons. They knew who had a Ralph, who had a Clairie, who could boast a Suri. They wore velvet bows and netting on their wool hats. In the summer, they bought straw hats with fruit baskets and botanical gardens on top. They wore brown velour snoods that gave the illusion of hair. When their husbands weren't around, her friends sometimes complained about covering their hair. Berets were itchy, hats were hot, wigs were expensive and needed upkeep. Their hair grew darker because it was always covered. Sometimes it grew thin or matted. Even with a natural-looking wig, they still longed for their own hair.

But Shayna never complained. She fastened her wig to her head with headbands, bobby pins, and combs, with the belief that doing so was the expression of God's will. A wig on her head was a foolproof way of belonging. The Modern Orthodox might overlook this law, but in her world everyone followed it. Covering one's hair had become the dividing line, the surest sign of where she stood. On subways, in department stores, and on the street, she wore her world on her head.

"About the flowers for the chuppah, tell me what you think because—" Shayna said.

"Whatever you want is fine with me," Tzippy said.

"I thought we could cover the chuppah with white roses and then line the aisle with matching flower archways that everyone could pass under."

"Why can't we do something simple?" Tzippy asked.

"Simple how?"

"I don't know. A few baskets of flowers? A regular aisle?"

"No," Shayna said. "We have to do more than that. I was at a wedding a few years ago where they transformed the entire hall into a garden. They had wrought-iron trellises for the chuppah and a gate that they looped flowers through. The lights were dimmed, and they hung lanterns and made the aisle look like a stone pathway."

"How do you plan to pay for something like that?"

"We'll find a way," Shayna said. "We've been waiting for this since you were born."

"It doesn't have to be one of those weddings that everyone talks about. I don't need that."

"But it's your wedding. Don't you want it to be a certain way?"

"I just want it to be a regular wedding."

Shayna stole glances at Tzippy. She had never seen her look so pretty. The only thing spoiling it was her reticence. At night, Shayna fell asleep to the sound of Tzippy whispering and giggling on the phone with Baruch. She tried to stay awake to hear her daughter's happiness. Around other people, Tzippy was happy to talk weddings. Shayna heard her on the phone with her friends, discussing flowers and dresses. She caught Tzippy fingering the swatches of organza and chiffon lined up on the dining-room table. Only with Shayna did she pretend not to care. The more Tzippy pulled away, the harder Shayna tried. To draw her out, she talked of a hundred tiny votive candles around the wedding cake. She described marzipan fruit glazed with sugar and wrapped in white netting for guests to take home. She suggested matchbooks decorated with a picture of Tzippy and Baruch, A PERFECT MATCH inscribed underneath.

Shayna tried to explain. "This is what everyone will remember. You'll be fifty years old, and people will see you and think about how skimpy the flowers were at your wedding."

"So let them think that. I told you, I don't care."

"What do you mean you don't care?"

"That I *don't* care."

"What kind of bride doesn't care?" Shayna asked.

Now it wasn't love but anger that blazed in Tzippy's eyes. "I guess this kind."

Shayna stopped walking. She had dreamed about this time since Tzippy was born. They had finally gotten what they wanted. All the years of disappointment could fade and become merely the buildup that dramatized the story of how Tzippy Goldman found her husband. But faced with her daughter's inexplicable anger, she missed the years when they sat on her bed and described imaginary weddings to each other.

Shayna looked around, making sure no one had overheard them. "Tzippy, do you have any idea how much work I'm putting into this?" she hissed out of one side of her mouth, while with the other she smiled.

"So don't do it," Tzippy said.

"Who else is going to do it?"

"But why does it matter so much?"

In front of Suri's Sheitels, Shayna forced a smile onto her face. If she wasn't careful, she would laugh with a long hysterical caw that would give way to tears. It did matter. She knew how much it did. Shayna squeezed her eyes shut and saw the wedding laid out in her mind. She clenched her fingers into fists with the force of her desire.

———

There were many sheitel stores in Brooklyn, one on every corner, but only one Suri. She was legendary for her ability to replicate a head of hair exactly. The girls nowadays wouldn't wear anything that screamed wig. They didn't want hair that was stiff and brittle. They wanted it soft and silky, to move when they did. The rabbis considered a married woman's hair to be the equivalent of nakedness, for her husband's eyes alone. When they first allowed women to cover their hair with wigs instead of kerchiefs, they hadn't foreseen the possibility of these natural wigs. But even so, the women were subordinating themselves to the will of God. The commandments weren't supposed to be unduly restrictive. So much was forbidden that they took delight in what was permitted.

Suri specialized in Orthodox women and cancer patients. She returned phone calls infrequently and professed to being nearly done with a wig she hadn't yet begun. Her inaccessibility only made her more popular. Brides happily paid the $3,000 she charged for a custom wig made with human hair. They set wedding dates based on Suri's estimate of how long it would take her to finish a wig.

The trick to making such a perfect wig wasn't in the actual hair but in the nylon net cap that lay underneath. Suri had come up with a way to make it look like a human scalp. The line where the wig attached to the head was in plain view and no one could see it. The old wigs had stood a quarter of an inch off the head and needed bangs to hide the unnatural seam. But Suri's wigs hugged the scalp. They replicated it exactly. She could part the hair in the middle or on the side. She could do ponytails. The flesh-colored cap peeking through the hair only made her creations look more realistic. Some wig makers specialized in curly, others in hard-to-match colors. Some could do cheap, some could do fast. But Suri turned out wigs that rendered themselves invisible.

Pale pink curtains covered the front windows of the store. On the windowsill, Styrofoam heads modeled Suri's most popular models. On the doors she hung posters of models in wigs. These models wore dramatic makeup and had provocative smiles. They seemed to be wearing their wigs to make a fashion statement, not a religious statement.

"Here she is," Shayna announced. "Here's the bride."

Tzippy and her mother weren't looking at each other, but Suri didn't care. She had seen it all. With the curtains drawn and their hair uncovered, the women who came here told Suri things about themselves they didn't reveal anywhere else. She knew who was happily married and who wasn't. She knew which brides stayed up nights worrying they were making a mistake.

Before she said hello, Suri took a lock of Tzippy's hair in her hand. "It's thick," she said, "and nice and straight. That's good. It makes it easier to duplicate."

She told Shayna and Tzippy about the bride who had fooled her fiancé and her father, neither of them believing it was a wig until she unhooked the clips and pulled it off at the dinner table. And about the bride who wore her custom wig to her sheva brachos, causing the guests to gape in disbelief that she wasn't covering her hair. She had customers who worked in law firms and investment banks. They wore wigs with their business suits, and no one ever knew.

"Once I had a girl walk in here with a head full of curls," Suri said. "I took one look at her and said there was no way I could replicate that. Either I could give her the curls but not the texture, or else the thickness but not so many curls. Unless you can find real curly hair to start with. Then it's a whole different ball game. But the girls with the naturally curly hair never want to sell."

"What did she decide?" Tzippy asked.

"Who, the girl with the curls? It turned out that she had always wanted straight hair. So everyone was happy." Suri clapped her hands together, ready to get down to business. "But enough about her. She has her sheitel, she's happily married, she looks beautiful. What are we going to do with you?"

Suri led Tzippy to a pink barber's chair, where Tzippy sat in front of a floor-to-ceiling mirror. On a tray in front of her, Suri assembled clips and brushes. Combs floated like seahorses in a jar of blue liquid. The store looked like a hair salon. The only difference was that here the hair wasn't attached to heads. It was dropped off to be styled and picked up when it was ready.

Suri pulled out small disembodied swatches of hair, each a different shade of brown. She held them up to Tzippy's hair, squinting to see if they matched. She selected several and explained that brown was never just brown. In Tzippy's seemingly ordinary hair, numerous shades were woven together. Then Suri pulled out a roll of what looked like Saran Wrap and molded it against Tzippy's head. Later she would use this as a model to make the cap.

"Now the fun part," Suri said. She kept a stash of ready-made wigs as samples, and she took them from their boxes. These wigs were inferior to what she would make, but the girls needed something to try on. Sometimes they bought one as a spare. All the wigs had names. The Tiffany wig had long curly hair. The Jacqueline sported a short, sleek cut with a spiky top. The Rochelle was a chin-length bob that fell over one eye. The Janice came in brown number 6, blond number 7, red number 9. It could be dyed any color in between. Straight wigs could be permed, curly ones blown straight. Suri picked out a long blond curly wig and shook it out. She pulled Tzippy's hair back into a tight ponytail and put the wig on her head. She straightened the wig and pinned it to her hair.

"See, you go like this, and then like this, and then you're all set," Suri said.

Suddenly Tzippy was a blond. Then she was a redhead, then a brunette again. She tried on wigs that were long, wigs that had bangs, wigs that were styled into braids and French twists. Some of the women used this as an opportunity to have the blond, stick-straight hair they had always wanted. At home, Shayna had five different wigs. She could go short or long, light or dark, to match every mood and outfit. Her wigs were lined up on her chest of drawers, each carefully pinned to a Styrofoam head. Often when Shayna left the house, the girls would sneak into her bedroom and try them on. They could choose which version of their mother they wanted to be.

But Tzippy said no to all of these wigs. She wanted to look like herself. So Suri pulled out the Clarice, a brown shoulder-length wig that was an approximation of Tzippy's hair, and fastened it to her head. This wig was good enough that those who didn't know would think it was real. But it was just stiff enough so that those in the know would understand that she was covering her hair. When Suri finished Tzippy's custom-made wig, everyone would have a hard time detecting its presence.

Tzippy had never doubted that she would cover her hair when she got married. She had loved to try on her mother's wigs and hats. But now that it was for real, it seemed so foreign, so strange to be wearing this on her head. She touched her hand to the wig, as if trying to ascertain that this was still her underneath it. In the wig, she seemed older. She also resembled her mother. Tzippy looked at herself and her mother's face stared back.

"What do you think?" Tzippy asked.

Shayna had been afraid to get too close, for fear the Tzippy before her would dissolve. But at Tzippy's invitation, she stepped forward and touched the wig.

"A married woman," Shayna said, and sighed.

Instead of looking directly at Tzippy, Shayna watched her reflection in the mirror. Tzippy did the same, and what they saw reflected back at them was a mother and daughter shopping for the wedding, smiling together. Neither of them could take their eyes off this image. In it, Shayna saw what she had always hoped for. She wanted her daughter to be at home in this world. When Tzippy walked with her friends, their long jean skirts flapping against their legs, Shayna often searched for a sign that she didn't belong. Could someone look at this group of girls and pick out which one had a mother who didn't grow up like everyone else? Now, with marriage looming, Shayna wanted her daughter to be like the women she envied, women who said the right thing and were perfectly dressed and served beautiful meals and always belonged. The wig on Tzippy's head made Shayna feel that it was possible.

— SEVEN —

O N THE PHONE with Shayna, Naomi listened to the continuous recitation of rules. From the way Shayna talked, these rules carried the weight of religious law, as if they too had been handed down at Sinai. These were the laws of FLOP: Flowers. Liquor. Orchestra. Pictures. The boy's family paid for these. The girl's family paid for everything else. These were the rules of engagement: An engagement was usually three months, but rarely more than five. Upon engagement, the bride's family bought the groom a gold watch and a complete set of the Talmud. The groom bought the engagement ring. His mother bought the bride a pair of silver candlesticks. Other presents were doled out over the course of the engagement. A piece of jewelry was given to the bride for every holiday that occurred during the engagement. A pearl necklace was given at the wedding, a gold necklace with a bezel-set diamond during the week of sheva brachos.

Today, the subject under discussion was whether to have separate seating for the men and the women during the wedding dinner. Baruch insisted that they needed to. This, he said, was how everyone did it. Joel said that forty years ago no one had even heard of separate seating. Then, even ultra-Orthodox men and women had mingled and thought nothing of it. But Shayna said she would rather die than have a wedding with mixed seating. She would be talked about for years to come. Naomi was trying to get them to compromise. She wanted three sections—one for men, one for women, one for both. But this would leave no one happy, including Naomi. She worried that one day they would have to further subdivide their wedding halls, a section for every belief and idea.

Shayna ignored their opposition. She had moved on to the type of mechitzah they should use to separate the men from the women. She was talking potted plants to keep the two apart. Dry ice to obscure the view with smoke. Fake palm trees. Ten-foot-high flowering plants.

"I don't know," Naomi said. "I thought we hadn't decided yet about the separate seating."

"But that's how it's done. It's what everyone does," Shayna insisted.

In the few weeks since the kids had been engaged, Shayna had made it clear: The wedding belonged to her. Except for paying their share, Naomi and Joel would be like guests who showed up when it began, went home when it ended. Naomi didn't want to carp or complain, but, despite her best intentions, the engagement had become a series of fights. The two families fought about when to have the wedding, how many guests to invite, how much to spend on flowers, whether the parents should carry candles down the aisle, whether Joel would agree to wear a black hat for the sake of the pictures. And for each of these battles, Naomi was stuck in the middle. To Joel, she defended Shayna's ideas, or she tried to fudge the details. If Shayna was talking about five hundred guests, Naomi reassured him that they were thinking about no more than four hundred.

"Could we have one day when we don't talk about the wedding?" he asked her.

"It's supposed to be fun," Naomi reminded him.

"It is?"

"Joel, of course it is."

But he greeted each piece of news with exasperation. Even before she mentioned a detail about the wedding, his patience was frayed and thin.

"We're having separate seating over my dead body," he pronounced.

"Is it really that big of a deal?" she asked.

"Yes. It is. And if I have to wear a black hat, I'm not going. You can tell Shayna I said that."

"I think it was only a suggestion. I'll ask Shayna about it," said Naomi.

"You'll *ask* her?" he said, shaking his head before turning back to his book.

If she mentioned any of Joel's reservations to Shayna, she found herself in the midst of a heated argument. Shayna had a reason for why they needed to spend more on the flowers, why a single videographer wouldn't be able to capture every important moment. Shayna had an endless capacity to focus on the details. Off the top of her head, she could offer extensive comparisons of the dessert selections offered by the top five kosher caterers in the tri-state area. Details like these didn't even pause in Naomi's head before flitting out. She didn't care how the flowers looked. She just wanted everyone to be happy.

Why can't we sit down and talk about it? Naomi wondered. Why couldn't she and Shayna pick up where they had left off? Why couldn't Ilana tell Baruch that she missed being close to him? Why couldn't Joel and Herschel lay their differences on the table and discuss them? Why do we need to? Joel would ask. Because we are going to be related, she wanted to answer. Because our children are going to be married. Because one day we will share grandchildren.

"So," Shayna said, calling her back to the discussion at hand, "what do you think?"

"I was thinking that maybe we could do something a little different. Maybe we could find a way to put our personal stamp on the wedding," Naomi said.

"I would call fifteen thousand dollars' worth of flowers enough of a personal stamp," Shayna said.

But Naomi didn't want a wedding that would be judged solely on its lavishness. Instead, she imagined what they might do to make it different. She wanted to write something, sew something, build something, dance something.

Ilana came downstairs and stood in the doorway. Naomi waved and mouthed that she would be off the phone in a minute. Ilana threw herself down at the kitchen table and waited. After two seconds, it was clear her mother was talking about the wedding. After five seconds, it was clear she was talking to Shayna.

The wedding had invaded their house. It was the only thing anyone talked about. Naomi spent her days in high-level negotiations with Shayna. Then, she and Joel talked about the latest plans over dinner.

They fought about it at night in their room. Before the engagement, they had talked about Baruch in urgent conversations that ceased the second Ilana appeared in the doorway. Even when he was away, he got most of their attention. Over the past year, these conversations had dwindled. There was nothing left to say, and they had made their peace or at least reached an interim agreement. Now, with the wedding, there were once again an endless number of things to fight about.

Ilana still couldn't believe her brother was getting married. She had thought he was distant before. Now he was gone altogether. The wedding would be their good-bye party to him. Except for the fact that she would have to attend, Ilana didn't want to have anything to do with it. She was tired of hearing about it, tired of the way it took center stage, tired of having to wait for her mother when she had promised they would do something special together. This was the first free Sunday they had been able to come up with since Baruch had returned home engaged six weeks before. Her mother extolled the value of quality time and individual attention, but these were just words she threw out. She hadn't yet noticed that there were things going on in Ilana's life too.

Until recently, Ilana had liked school. She had had the same two best friends since the second grade. Ilana, Rena, Michelle—their names were uttered in a single breath. She occupied a comfortable spot in the hierarchies of eighth-grade popularity. But apparently the rules had changed and no one had bothered to tell her. Her classmates had become different people. Seemingly overnight, they had begun to talk about music and movie stars and boys. They complained to one another that they were fat. They competed to bring the lowest-calorie lunch— small pop-top tuna cans and grapefruit—and last on it the whole day. They pored over fashion magazines and looked for ways to assimilate the latest styles into the Hebrew Academy dress code.

Rena and Michelle shook their heads in wonder and studied these changes as sociologists would, from a careful, disinterested distance. For the moment, they were content to remain on the outside and let the shuffling of the class happen as it would. They didn't take great interest in what they wore. They didn't call the boys on the phone. Instead, they went over to one another's houses and read. They swapped books when they finished. Around her two friends, Ilana acted as though she too didn't care. She tried to share in the solace they took in schoolwork, parental approval, and one another. But Ilana felt the pressure. She knew she either needed to change or be left behind.

Several times, her mother was on the verge of hanging up. Ilana's hopes rose, and then the conversation started anew.

"I thought we were going now," Ilana said, hoping it was loud enough for Shayna to hear.

"Hold on, Shayna," her mother said and put her hand over the receiver. "Give me one more minute, Ilana." Then she went back to her call and listened some more, nodding her head in apparent agreement.

"You're right," Naomi said. "The important thing is that they're happy. And it should be a beautiful wedding. If that's what we need to do, I'm sure it will be fine."

Giving up the hope that her mother would ever get off the phone, Ilana pulled from her knapsack a copy of *Seventeen* magazine that she had borrowed. This had recently become required reading for her classmates. A blond model or singer or actress whose name she was supposed to know smiled at her from the cover. THE SPRING FASHION BIBLE, it proclaimed in hot-pink letters. HOT NEW MAKEOVERS. SEVEN DAYS TO A BRAND-NEW YOU. If Ilana wanted to change, this was a good place to start.

Naomi hung up, and after a deep breath, she turned to Ilana.

"I'm all yours," she said.

"One minute," Ilana said, pretending to be immersed in an article.

"I didn't know you like *Seventeen*," Naomi said.

"Well, I do now."

"'Change your hairstyle, change your life,'" Naomi read over her shoulder. "It sounds like pretty heavy stuff."

Both annoyed and embarrassed, Ilana quickly closed the magazine. "What's wrong with that?" she asked.

"Nothing. I'm just surprised, that's all."

Her mother clearly didn't understand. She wore clothes that didn't make demands. She liked flower-print skirts that were loose and flow-ing, long beaded necklaces, dangly earrings, and bright Indian-print scarves. This afternoon, Naomi was wearing a cotton skirt that was missing one button and had bleach stains splattered on the back. Were Ilana to point it out, she would say that she hadn't noticed, and then, after a moment of wondering how that had happened, she wouldn't care.

"Let's not fight," Naomi said. "I want us to have a nice day together."

Ilana expected her to follow that up by saying that "we should use this as an opportunity to discuss our differences." She expected her mother to put on her sympathetic "I'm listening" face, where she leaned closer to Ilana and narrowed her eyes in concentration. To her surprise, her mother didn't say this or offer any of the similarly themed speeches Ilana had been raised on. She looked upset, and Ilana felt bad for starting up. Despite her protestations, she wanted this day with her mother. She wanted her all to herself.

In the car, she tried to find the part of her that, just an hour before, had wanted to tell her mother everything. Usually the car was Ilana's favorite place to talk. There was no phone to interrupt them, nothing to pull them away. But now Ilana felt herself close off. She rolled down the window and turned away.

"So," Naomi said, "what did you want to tell me?"

"Never mind," she said.

"Come on, Ilana. I want to hear what's going on."

"It's nothing," she said. "I just can't wait for school to be over."

"You have three more months. Isn't it a little early to be counting the days? And eighth grade is a real milestone. You don't want to wish this time away. You're on the verge, Ilana. It's very exciting."

"What's very exciting?"

"Growing up. Becoming a young woman."

Ilana snorted.

"Is something going on?" Naomi asked.

"Nothing's going on. It's just different around here these days," Ilana said.

"I know. It's a lot of changes at once."

"Everyone's changing," Ilana said.

Naomi looked away from the road, at her. When her mother looked at her like that, she sprouted a guilty conscience. But the only thing she was guilty of was wanting to be someone else. She wished she could open the pages of *Seventeen* and step inside.

Ilana and Naomi went for lunch in Laurelwood's main shopping area, which was lined with kosher stores. In this New Jersey town, every empty lot was an opportunity for a new kosher restaurant or a breakaway shul. On Friday afternoons, people bustled from the bakery to the butcher to the flower shop. They beeped at one another as they passed in their minivans, calling "Good Shabbos" out the window. A few hours later, those same streets were nearly deserted, because everyone was getting ready to serve Friday-night dinner. Or they were walking home from shul, three abreast, on streets they didn't expect to share with cars. They carried their keys and pushed strollers because of the eruv that encircled the town on telephone wires and utility poles, a symbolic enclosure delineating the boundaries of their neighborhood. At work and in the world, they had to explain who they were and what they did. They had to remind co-workers that they kept kosher. They had to fumble their way through explanations of why they couldn't make it to an event on a Friday night. They had to repeat that no, Chanukah wasn't exactly like Christmas. No, kosher didn't mean the food was blessed by a rabbi. But here, there was nothing to explain. In Laurelwood, the minority felt like a majority.

When Naomi and Joel moved to Laurelwood twenty-five years ago, the Orthodox community was fledgling. They came here because it was affordable. There was one Orthodox shul and that was enough. Now every house that was for sale went, in a bidding war, to a young Orthodox family with two kids and a third on the way. The community was filled to capacity. A NO VACANCY sign could have hung from the exit sign on the nearby highway. So they spread farther out, considering themselves pioneers as they started a string of satellite communities up and down the highway.

"So what's the latest wedding fight about?" Ilana asked over lunch.

"Oh, it was nothing," Naomi said.

"You don't have to tell me. I know anyway."

"What do you know?"

"I know that Shayna wants to have six hundred people, and Daddy thinks that it becomes a zoo when it's that big, and that the only reason people have such huge weddings is to show off. And you told him you'd say something about reining it in, because you also like the idea of something more intimate. But when you tried to say something, Bryan got mad at you and said that it wasn't up to you."

Naomi looked at her with a mixture of amusement and surprise. "What else do you know?"

"You think Shayna doesn't want you to be involved and so you feel left out. You thought it would be easier, but Daddy says of course it's not, because what did you expect—"

"Whoa," Naomi interrupted. "How did you pick all this up?"

"Oh, you know . . . ," Ilana said, and smiled in satisfaction. "Around."

"Some of it has been fun," Naomi said.

"But why do you always listen to Shayna?" Ilana asked. "You could tell her that it's not what you want. You could say that you're not going to go along with it, and if she doesn't like it, then that's too bad."

Naomi laughed. "It's not as simple as that, Ilana. Sometimes you have to give in on small things. You have to look at the big picture and decide what's important. And the details of the wedding aren't what matter. This is a happy occasion. That's what we should focus on. It's a very exciting time for all of us."

"Right," Ilana said.

"You could get involved in the wedding. You could spend time with Tzippy. You could reach out to her sisters and get to know them."

"What am I supposed to do, go sheitel shopping with Tzippy? Help her pick out her china?"

"Tzippy is really very sweet," Naomi said.

"That's not the point. The wedding has nothing to do with me. I'll go to it, but that's it."

"It sounds like you're angry," Naomi murmured.

"Really," Ilana said. "You think so?"

But her mother didn't hear sarcasm. It didn't register on whatever frequency she tuned to.

"Yes, really," Naomi said. "I know it must be hard, with everyone so wrapped up in the wedding. And Baruch is busy and starting a new life."

"I don't care about that anymore. Believe me, I've given up trying to be close with him. Tzippy can have him."

"Just because he's more religious doesn't mean he has stopped loving you."

"Bryan is acting like he's so religious, but I don't buy it. What about being nice to people? What about caring about how other people feel? What about respecting your parents? It's like he's decided that those don't matter just because he puts on a black hat and davens ten times a day."

"I don't think it's as simple as that, Ilana. And he still cares about you. I know he does. I'd hate to see you shut yourself off from him. It's only going to make you feel worse."

"That's just the way it is."

"But have you told him how you feel? Have you tried to talk to him?"

"Mom," Ilana said in disbelief.

She had done nothing but try. She had spent this past year while Baruch was away trying to get used to the idea of a very religious brother. She told herself that if she could get past who he appeared to be on the outside, she would be able to find what was still him on the inside. Since he had come home, she had tried to force this person out of hiding. She had stomped past his room trying to make him hear her. She had walked directly in front of him while he davened. She had planted herself on the stairs outside his room so he would have to walk past her. He could trip over her for all she cared—anything to make him notice. But he stepped over her and around her. Sometimes he actually stopped and said hi to her, and her hopes would rise that he might sit down to talk and they would have one quick moment like it used to be. But then he kept going, busy with Tzippy, the wedding, and his learning. She was back where she started, marveling at the stranger across the hall.

So in response to her mother, Ilana snorted again. She had told him how she felt in only about a hundred ways. The problem was that he had forgotten how to listen.

As they left the restaurant, Naomi stole glances at Ilana. She knew, of course, that they had been busy with the wedding, that the family had undergone changes, that Ilana missed her close relationship with Baruch. But still, she was surprised by Ilana's anger. Ilana had always had strong opinions and a strong will, but usually she and Naomi were on the same side. She had always been sure that she knew what her daughter was thinking. In the car, at the dinner table, when she tucked her into bed at night, Ilana had always opened up and poured out her day.

"You can go, Mom. You don't have to wait with me," Ilana said when they stopped in front of Judaica Express, where she had arranged to meet Rena and Michelle.

"I don't mind," Naomi said.

It felt good to be outside. Naomi turned her face toward the sun. Even though it was still cool, she felt the beginning of spring. She turned around and stared into the store window at a display of hand-made tambourines.

"I like that," she murmured. "They're so . . . ," she began, grasping for the right word.

Naomi felt a rush of desire to buy one. But it seemed silly. What would she do with it? she wondered. They were pretty, but it wasn't just that. She didn't want to look at it. She wanted to grab it and rattle it against her hip to shake out some greater feeling—as if this music could rouse her, her family, her friends, and their community.

The street was lined with kosher bakeries and hat shops, wine stores and bookstores, kosher butcher shops and pizza places. They had kosher submarine sandwiches and kosher cappuccino. Stores sold leather yarmulkes painted like basketballs and baseball sweat-shirts with YANKEES written in Hebrew. They had Hebrew computer software and Palm Pilots with the siddur downloaded onto them. On this block alone, there was everything one needed to be Orthodox— every gadget, every imaginable convenience, all supposedly in the service of God. But was this what it came down to? Naomi wondered. After so much fighting, she too felt an inner rumbling of dissatis-faction.

"I think I might get a tambourine," she said.

"Go for it, Mom," Ilana said, distracted by the arrival of Michelle and Rena. In the space of a few minutes, she had forgotten her anger. It was like a flash flood, quick and fierce, and then it was over. Naomi watched Ilana come to life in the presence of her friends. This is what it's like to have a teenager, Naomi reminded herself.

When Ilana disappeared into the giggling pack of girls, Naomi went into the bookstore and picked up the tambourine. Of all the characters they had studied in her Women of the Bible class, it was Miriam she had liked the most. Miriam picked up her tambourine and led the women dancing and singing after they crossed the Red Sea. She imag-ined that the women must have been reluctant. They probably hadn't realized they could get up and dance. But with the shaking of her tam-bourine, Miriam lured them closer and pulled them in. Naomi wished someone would pull her in. She wanted not so much the tambourine but what it would unlock. While she waited for her purchase to be rung up, she turned it over and examined it, as if it contained a hidden message.

"I want to make an engagement party," Naomi announced.

Dinner was over, and Baruch was in his room. Joel and Ilana were in the living room reading, buried so deeply in their books that Naomi felt she had to physically extricate them. She had to say it twice before they put down their books and looked at her.

She stood in front of them. "What do you think? It could be our way of giving a piece of ourselves to the celebration.

"We could do it here at home and keep it cozy and casual. We could do it sort of last minute, maybe in two weeks. It would be a chance for our friends to get to know Tzippy.

"We could blow up pictures of when they were kids, and, Ilana, maybe you could do a slide show about Baruch. You could invite your friends too. It's harder to do what we want with the wedding. But this could be our thing. We can do whatever we want."

Ilana and Joel had to restrain themselves from rolling their eyes. But it didn't matter, because Naomi realized how badly she wanted this party.

"We could make up a song. And we could tell everyone to come up with a poem about Baruch and Tzippy. It would be our chance to show them how excited we are."

Joel shrugged his agreement. "If you want to," he said and returned to his book.

Before Ilana went back to hers, she rolled her eyes and grinned at Naomi. "You're so cute, Mom," she said.

— EIGHT —

THIS TIME Naomi's desire coincided with the rules. There was supposed to be an engagement party. Shayna gave her stamp of
approval, and Naomi got to work. She invited all their friends. She went
through her photo albums and pulled out pictures of Baruch as a baby.
She asked Shayna to send her some photos of Tzippy, and she made col-
lages to hang around the house. She decided to keep the food and decorations simple. She wasn't going to fall into the fancier-than-thou mode,
where a bris was as elaborate as a bar mitzvah, a bar mitzvah was like a
wedding.

With a combination of bribery, force, and flattery, Naomi managed
to get both Baruch and Ilana to help her prepare. They were each busy,
or at least this was their excuse for what they didn't want to do. Baruch
was learning most of the day. He treated home as a hotel. In his mind,
he had already taken his leave. Ilana was busy with school and friends.
She spent hours on the phone, holed up in her room.

A few hours before the party, Naomi worried there wasn't enough
food. In a last-minute flurry, she tried to come up with another dish.
She took out two cans of cherry pie filling, lots of fresh fruit, three containers of Rich's Whip, and a carton of orange juice. She was still creating the recipe as she gave out instructions.

"Okay, Baruch, you open these cans. Ilana, you cut up the fruit."

"Don't worry, we won't tell anyone you helped cook," Ilana teased
Baruch. "Isn't it like a sin for a boy to help in the kitchen?"

Baruch gave an exaggerated sigh. "Maybe if you spent about five
minutes a day learning you would know the answer to that."

"No thanks," she replied.

As they bantered back and forth, Naomi was relieved. They were getting used to each other again. If nothing else, they acknowledged each other coming and going. Even if Ilana and Baruch didn't have long, involved conversations, even if Joel and Baruch never sat together in front of a Yankees game, they still lived under the same roof. They could veer off in different directions but find ways to come together. They were still a family.

"Do you really think anyone is going to eat this?" Ilana asked. She dipped the spoon into the bowl and the pink soupy mixture slid slowly down.

"It's going to be delicious," Naomi announced.

"What is it?" Baruch asked.

Naomi looked from them to the bowl. "It's like a fruit soup. It's called fruiterella," she decided.

"Served in all the finest restaurants," Ilana added.

Naomi glanced at it. "It just needs to be stirred a little more."

Ilana held out a spoonful to Baruch. "Taste it."

"No way," he said.

"Come on, Bryan, open up," she teased.

He reluctantly opened his mouth. "Delicious," he pronounced. "Now it's your turn to taste it, Ilana."

"Ilana, why don't you tell Baruch what you're doing these days," Naomi suggested.

"Sure, Mom," she said. "So do you want to hear about the soap operas I'm watching or the movies I've seen?"

"Both," Baruch said.

Ilana and Baruch laughed at Naomi's efforts to promote togetherness. They teased her, but they were having fun and so was she. She knew that they wanted to feel close again. They were taking hesitant steps toward each other and then away, not knowing how to reconnect. But here they were, together. Grab this moment and hold it tight, she thought.

"We're doing great," Naomi said. "After this, I'm nearly done. I just have to cut up the vegetables and work on my toast."

"Your toast?" Baruch asked.

Naomi had spoken at all the family occasions—at Baruch's bar mitzvah and Ilana's bat mitzvah, even at Baruch's bris eight days after giving birth. She had made up poems and put together slide shows.

"I wanted to say something about you and Tzippy," Naomi said and saw the nervous smile on his face. "Is that a problem?"

"No," he said, "not really."

"Why don't I believe you?" Naomi asked.

"It's fine. Give the toast."

"I will. But I just want to know why there would be an issue."

"Because," Baruch said, looking away, "it's not done."

"What's not done?"

"Women speaking in public."

"And why is that?" Naomi asked.

She tried to hide her hurt feelings behind a disengaged curiosity. But it didn't work. Baruch stiffened and looked like he was preparing to hold his ground. The relaxed look on Ilana's face also disappeared. She scowled at her brother and folded her arms across her chest.

"Do you really want to hear this?" he asked.

"We're listening," Ilana said.

"My rabbi said that it's inappropriate because 'Kol kavod bat melech penimah,' the glory of the king's daughter is inside. From this, we learn that women aren't supposed to be in the public eye. They have important roles to fill in the private sphere, and by speaking publicly, they blur these roles."

"But the rabbis were talking about a very different time period," Naomi said. "For them, that idea made sense. But the whole world has changed, and so maybe some of these things have changed as well."

"What's next?" Ilana asked. "Are you going to start making rules about how often we're allowed out of the house?"

Naomi turned to Ilana. "I don't think the rabbis mean inside, as in inside the house. I think they mean internal, that who you are inside yourself is what matters."

"Right," Ilana said.

"And even if it did mean that at one point, you can reinterpret it and make it meaningful for you," Naomi said.

"I'm sorry I said anything. I knew you wouldn't want to hear it," Baruch said when Ilana turned away and Naomi looked at him, annoyed. "Give the toast. It's fine."

His acquiescence didn't make Naomi feel better. It was fine with him only because he had given up any hope of fitting in with his family. He would let them do as they wanted, and he would go off somewhere else and do what he wanted. In the meantime, he was trying to slip out the kitchen door, just as Joel was coming in.

"Did you hear that, Dad?" Ilana asked. "Now we're not allowed to speak in public. What do you think? Is that going to become house rules around here?"

Eyebrows raised in disbelief, Joel stared at his son.

"What's the newest rule, Bryan?" Joel asked.

"I said to forget it," Baruch said.

"What do you think? If women speak in public, it will cause lewdness or something?" Ilana said.

"Ilana, that's enough," Naomi said.

"Whose side are you on?" Ilana muttered.

"We're a family," Naomi said. "We're all on the same side."

Ilana was staring at her brother, hurt and anger mingling on her face. Joel had looked annoyed even before he had heard what was going on. Baruch was facing off against both of them. And here she was, in her usual spot in the middle, wondering why these differences, minor compared to all the possibilities in the world, had to force them apart. A hundred guests were due to arrive in two hours, and instead of finishing her preparations, she was wishing plaintively, naively, maybe uselessly, that she could open her arms and force them all into a hug.

"Rough day?" Joel asked Naomi, when they were alone in the kitchen.

"No, it was good. I had them both in here, laughing, at least for a few minutes. Maybe I shouldn't expect it to last. And if they're going to disagree, that's okay too, because at least they're communicating. But I just wish it didn't have to always end up this way, with everyone so angry at one another."

Joel tried to decipher what Naomi was saying. When she was upset, it was like walking into the middle of a conversation.

"I want to give a toast," she explained. "But apparently it's 'not done.'"

"Surprise, surprise," he said.

"You knew?"

"A woman speaking in public? Scandalous."

"Seriously," she said.

"I am being serious. That's how they think about these things."

"I'm still giving it," she said. "He said he's not going to stop me."

"How generous," Joel said.

"Maybe it was a mistake to think the party could make a difference," Naomi said.

This would be the time to say "I told you so." Or to say that he wished she had thought about that before inviting a hundred people to their house. If she had caught him in a bad mood, he would have said all these things. He had been dreading the party. All afternoon, he had been hiding in the bedroom, trying to gear up for a house full of people. Naomi teasingly referred to him as a misanthrope. But that wasn't really the truth. He craved the rare quiet moments when he could think. Alone in his room, he felt the relief of not having to say a word.

Seeing her hopefulness, Joel softened. "It's going to be okay," he reassured her. "Look at it this way. If nothing else, it's a 'growth experience,'" he said, quoting one of her favorite phrases back at her.

She laughed. "Joel, are you happy for him?"

"I want to be, but I don't know if I am. I miss him. I miss who he used to be," he said.

Naomi opened her mouth, wanting to convince him that Baruch was still the same person he used to be. He had heard this speech, and every variation of it, too many times already. But instead she cut herself off before she began.

"I miss him too," she said.

She didn't tell Joel what he should be making himself feel. This time she wasn't talking about anger management, child management, or husband management. She reached for him, and he held her in his arms. They stood in the middle of the kitchen, next to the unwashed dishes and the trays partially laid out with pastries. It was messy and would stay that way for the remainder of the night, maybe for the next few days. But there was nothing to be done about that now. For the moment, Naomi had let go of all that she wished she believed in. She stood with Joel in his bafflement and dismay.

— NINE —

THEIR FRIENDS CAME—from Laurelwood and Woodmere, Great Neck, Riverdale, and New Rochelle. The lines of Jewish geography spanned the bridges and traversed the tunnels. There were rarely more than two degrees of separation. Naomi kissed her friends and enjoyed their mazel tovs. The crowd of people pushed away her bad feelings, and she was caught up in saying hello and making introductions.

"Don't tell me you did all this yourself," she heard from her friends, who crowded around her.

"June fourteenth," she answered when they asked about the wedding date.

"Yes, it is soon," she said, and made a face to show that the rush wasn't her idea.

Naomi hugged Shayna and kissed Tzippy on the cheek. Shayna air-kissed her in return. "Everything is beautiful," Shayna told Naomi and laughed. "It's very you."

It was, and Naomi wasn't going to let anyone spoil it. For this one night, she didn't have to think about the fights that had already taken place, the fights that would surely resume in the morning. Instead, she looked around her house, filled wall-to-wall with friends. A giant piece of butcher paper hung so guests could write notes to Tzippy and Baruch. Birds of paradise shot up from vases all over the house. The fruiterella filled a gleaming crystal bowl in the middle of a table decked with pastries.

"And look at all these beautiful girls," Naomi said of Shayna's daughters. Each of them in descending order was a reprint of Shayna. Feeling a sudden longing, Naomi reached out her hand.

"Come, let me introduce you," she said.

"My Tzippy is fabulous with the kids," Shayna said to Naomi's friends, who gathered around her. "Next year she'll be a head teacher. The kids love her. The other teachers say they've never seen anything like it.

"We were inseparable," Shayna said in response to the continuous barrage of questions. "At Stern College, we were like this," she said, and entwined two of her fingers. "Right from the start, we hit it off. We stayed in touch for ages. It's only these last few years that we weren't as good. But what can you do?" Shayna said, and forced a laugh.

As she spoke, Shayna stole glances at her daughters. Before ringing Naomi's doorbell, she had straightened their dresses one final time. Now she uttered a silent, fervent prayer that they stay perfect for ten more minutes, or at least until everyone in the room saw them. But it was too much to wish for. On her daughters, sashes she had fussed with for fifteen minutes came untied by themselves. Their hair unraveled from even the tightest braid.

Instead, she pinned her hopes on Tzippy, who stood by her side and smiled. Tzippy wore a lavender suit with pearl buttons. She had on matching pearl earrings. She was met and she was talked to. The scowl that had been laced through her smile was gone, almost letting Shayna think she had been imagining it. She wished she were. But a shadow of it lurked, as if waiting to get Shayna alone and lash out at her.

Now her one wish was that Tzippy's anger make no appearance. Interspersed between Shayna's every sentence was a silent plea to Tzippy: Please smile, please say the right thing. Please agree with me. Please don't embarrass me.

"My Tzippy always said that she believed in bashert. She always said she wasn't going to settle. She—"

"Was waiting for the right one," Tzippy said on cue.

Baruch wandered through the party, accepting the mazel tovs and smiles bestowed on him. His parents' friends who had known him his whole life were there, along with his friends from high school and his newer friends from yeshiva. They were reminders of the parts of his life that didn't match. Before he left yeshiva, one of the older boys gave him a piece of advice: Keep your mouth shut and then do what you want. Outwardly, he could go along with what his family wanted, while inwardly he would still believe it was wrong. As much as his parents claimed to have accepted him, they still expected him to find a middle ground. But he couldn't bend, because he wasn't talking about preferences or theories. When it came to God—His will, His rule, His law—there was no room for compromise.

Since he'd been home, he and his father had argued constantly. They jousted back and forth. It was like a game of chess being played out in the rooms of their house. If Baruch moved to a black square, Joel sought refuge on a white one. They moved sideways and across, over one, up two, waiting for a chance to challenge each other.

It hadn't always been this way. They used to have a quiet closeness. They had watched baseball together. They had gone to games on Sundays, when his father didn't have to work. The score, the stats, the standings, gave them something to talk about. Columbia had been the same. During his sophomore year of high school, he had announced that he wanted to go to Columbia, and Joel had taken it on as their special project. He put down whatever book he was reading to help his son with his essays. He turned off the television to conduct mock interviews. He took a day off work to show him around the campus. The day Baruch's acceptance letter arrived, he called his father first. He had come right home from work. He walked in the door and hugged him and whispered how proud he was.

Now it was hard to find things to talk about. Baruch wished they could go to shul together or learn together. Tradition was supposed to pass from father to son. But his father was skeptical by nature. When his father saw the world, it was fractured into a thousand parts that would never fit together. He hedged his bets, partly observing, partly doubting. Growing up, Baruch had wondered why Joel so often stayed home from shul. When Baruch was little, he had watched Joel put on tallis and tefillin in the morning. But instead of davening from a siddur, he wandered around the house or read the newspaper. No one had ever talked about this. Either they hadn't noticed or hadn't dared to ask.

Now Baruch wanted to ask his father if he had any idea what it was like to be sure you're right. Not to hedge, not to doubt, not to moderate, not to mollify. You dress differently, you talk differently, you eat differently, and though it's sometimes hard, it ultimately doesn't matter. Because the rest of the world is wrong: You alone hold the truth in your hands.

Tzippy waved to Baruch from across the room. She disentangled herself from her mother's grasp and went over to him. Seeing her, he felt better. With her, he could be serious and funny, religious and silly. He could be all parts of himself at once.

"Cake?" Baruch asked, and offered her a bite from the piece he was eating.

"No thanks," she said. "I think I've had enough cake to last me a lifetime."

"Do you want to go outside?" he asked.

They looked over their shoulders to see if anyone was watching. When the coast was clear, they slipped outside, where it was dark and quiet. Since they had been engaged, they barely had time to be together. They had decided they wanted to spend the rest of their lives together, and suddenly it was hard to find five minutes alone. But until someone came outside to steal one of them away, they were as alone as they had ever been. Tzippy sat down in the patio chair next to Baruch, ready to listen.

"It's hard to be home," he said.

"I know," she agreed.

"Last summer when I came home from Israel, I didn't really want to talk to my family. I couldn't stop thinking about how different I was from them. Now I want to talk to them, but it's too late. I feel lonely in my own home," he said.

"Come to my house. There's no way to feel lonely there. There's no space to even think about that."

"I'd rather be there than here," Baruch said.

"I like your parents," she said.

"I like yours."

They should switch, they decided. Or better yet, cast off both sets and start anew. They knew that engagement was a time to be endured. Underneath its seemingly sweet veneer, it was a tense time between families. Tzippy and Baruch were trying to stay out of the disputes. Baruch wasn't going to take his parents' side in the interminable wedding battles. For once, he didn't care about the details. Tzippy didn't listen when her mother complained that Naomi either didn't understand or didn't care that there was a way it was supposed to be done. Tzippy ignored her when she tried to pry information out of her: Do they talk about us? Do they like us? Do they like you? She didn't tell her that Baruch had admitted that his parents, especially his father, were upset about the wedding. Tzippy and Baruch hoped that once they were married, it wouldn't matter as much where they came from. The new family they created would be an antidote to every disappointment they had with their own.

"What about you?" he asked. "How are you doing?"

"I'm fine. See, I'm smiling," she said, and forced her lips into an exaggerated grin. "I think I'm supposed to smile all the time."

In the air, an inch from her face, he drew a looping smile with his fingers, and this made her smile for real.

"It's strange to see you at home," she said. "I don't know the Baruch who grew up here."

"You know what? I don't know him either," he said.

They sat next to each other, on chairs whose legs were touching. Tzippy's and Baruch's arms almost touched as well. She was scared of what she would feel and scared of how he would react, scared that he would pull away in horror and scared that he would not. But she couldn't stop herself. She leaned toward him and grazed his hand with two of her fingers. It was so light, so soft, that it could have been imagined or wished. She did it again, to be sure it had really happened. She ran her fingers across his hand, and her body tingled with the shock and pleasure of actually touching. Too thrilled and scared to move her hand, she waited to see what would happen next.

He held her hand. He gently stroked her fingers. He wanted to touch her face, which he had stared at these past few months. He wanted to kiss her mouth, which distracted him when he learned, when he davened, when he slept. He put his arms around her and she leaned in close, their bodies gently pressing against each other.

Just as his lips were about to find hers, a looming figure appeared in Baruch's head. It was the face of his rabbi, who whispered in his ear, "So you haven't changed after all." If he leaned any closer to Tzippy, these words would become true. One kiss and he would disappear. Guilt outpaced desire and he pulled away. He was surprised at her and surprised at himself. His married friends had warned him of the pitfalls of engagement. The knowledge of what you would one day be able to do threatened to overpower even the strongest self-control. It was dangerous to walk the edges. That was where people got lost. Baruch stood up and turned around. They both tried to pretend that it hadn't happened.

As they went inside, though, the initial touch replayed itself in their heads, mirrored back from every angle. A hundred hands reached for each other. A thousand fingers intertwined.

Joel moved from room to room, hiding behind bookshelves, joining in conversations he had no interest in, offering to help in the kitchen even though there was nothing that needed to be done—all this in a desperate attempt to avoid Herschel. He couldn't talk to him. How hard could it be? Naomi would chide him. Just be friendly. Be polite. But Joel couldn't do it. He had avoided talking to him on the phone. At the airport, there were enough people to hide behind. It had been bad enough when they were just supposed to be friends. But now they were expected to be family.

Herschel was standing near the buffet table and, feeling brave, Joel decided to pass within a few feet of him and grab some food. Joel's hunger was his downfall. As he grabbed one of the mini knishes that were rapidly disappearing, someone clapped him on the back.

"Joel, where have you been hiding?"

Herschel was popping knishes into his mouth and playing with a variety of corkscrews from Joel's collection of high-tech gadgets. One created a vacuum and lifted the cork right out. Another attached to either side and pulled. Joel enjoyed the innovation and the precision with which they each did their job.

"These are something else," Herschel said. "Who would have imagined so many ways to pop a cork?"

Joel grunted a response, a noise that was supposed to sound like an agreement without drawing him deeper into a conversation. Not that it would make a difference. He was going to be stuck here for a long time, maybe until the end of the party, maybe for the rest of his life. Herschel always acted as if they were good friends. He seemed to have no idea how much Joel disliked him. Or maybe he feigned ignorance simply to annoy him. This had always been infuriating to Joel. Herschel was impervious to his attempts to ignore him.

"With all these gadgets, it's the same. The idea is to think of something new before anyone else does. We're similar, you know, Joel. We both appreciate a good idea."

Joel could practically see the wheels spinning inside Herschel's head. He hadn't changed at all. He would talk and talk. And somewhere in the midst of all he had to say, he would come up with a business venture for the two of them. This was what he disliked most about Herschel, and it came up every time they saw each other. The more Joel thought he was going to be asked for something, the more he closed up. Joel hated the idea of getting something for nothing. He couldn't stand those who felt entitled, who let someone else foot the bill.

"There you are," Herschel said to Baruch, who was walking over to them. "We were wondering where you were."

Joel was relieved to see his son, hoping he would free him from being stuck with Herschel.

"Come, have something to eat," Herschel invited Baruch.

With the knishes now gone, Herschel moved on to the fruiterella. He spooned out some for himself, drinking it in one gulp. He held up the cup. "This is good. What is it?" He filled his cup again and offered some to Baruch.

"How about you?" Herschel asked, and held a cup out to Joel.

Joel put his hand up. "No thanks."

"Suit yourself," Herschel said, and downed that cup too.

"So, Baruch, what are you planning to do with yourself? You're not planning to stay in yeshiva your whole life, are you?" Herschel asked.

"At least for the next few years," Baruch said, not glancing in Joel's direction. Herschel either didn't notice the tension or didn't care.

"Yeshiva is nice when you're young. But how many years can you really do that?"

"I want to stay for as long as I can," Baruch said.

"Joel, I'll bet you're happy about that. Am I right?" Herschel asked and laughed. Joel grimaced and looked away.

"Not me," Herschel said. "I can't sit still like that. I need to be doing something. Do you want to know what I think? You need to take that learning and find a way to use it. If you just sit in yeshiva, what good does it do anyone? Let's say you had to think of something else. What would you do?"

"I don't know," Baruch said. "Maybe we would find a small Jewish community where we can make an impact."

Baruch told Herschel that some of the boys from his yeshiva joined out-of-town kollels, where they brought Torah to new communities. Baruch had learned about the value of outreach. With the rising rates of assimilation and intermarriage, the future of the Jewish people lay in a return to tradition. He would offer people their first taste of Torah. He would fill their Shabbos table with guests who had never before celebrated Shabbos.

"Why do you want to do that?" Herschel asked.

"Because I know what it's like to want something more meaningful," Baruch said. "So many people are looking for something. I think there's a hunger out there."

Joel tried to tune them out. He thought of his bedroom, where he could close the door and shut out the noise and the people he didn't like. But he knew it wouldn't bring him the relief he had imagined. He hated seeing his son talking to Herschel, and the betrayal he felt would follow him.

"You're right about that," Herschel said as Joel walked away. "There's a great hunger out there."

The crowd gathered around Naomi in the living room, as she nervously stood up and tried to remember why she had wanted to make a toast. Then she looked out across the crowd at her family and friends—the different strands of her life that had come together to celebrate—and she started to relax.

"To Baruch," she began, "and Tzippy. And all our family and friends."

All week, she had thought about what she would say. She wanted to talk about letting go and staying connected, about joining together and remaining individuals. But she had waited to write her speech, for fear it wouldn't come out as she had planned. She had hoped to have time that afternoon to put her thoughts on paper. In the rush of getting ready, the time had slipped away. Instead, she had scribbled down a few ideas and was going to trust that the moment would move her and the words would emerge.

She had decided to speak about the book of Ha'azeenu, which had been Baruch's bar mitzvah portion. "'An eagle stirs up her nest, hovers over her young. She spreads her wings and carries them,'" she read. "Just as Hashem carries us through the good and the bad, a parent also must do that. But there comes a time when the parent eagle stirs her young to leave the nest, to fly on their own wings."

She talked about the joy at seeing Baruch's independence and the bittersweet feeling of watching him set off on his own. She was brimming with emotion; she had so much she wanted to say. If only she had at her disposal the words to explain it all, to wrap motherhood and love, independence and connection, into sentences that would hold all that she felt. Soon, she was talking about birds and eggs, nests and trees, mixing together roots and wings. She had gone far afield from what she had intended and was trying to wind her way back. She looked at Baruch and Tzippy, who were flushed with the happiness that lay ahead. She choked up and rushed to finish.

"May you, Baruch and Tzippy, soar with the wings Hashem gave you, yet plant deep roots of connection to your family and your community."

When she was done, the guests sang "Simmen tov u'mazel tov." They looked at Tzippy and Baruch, and wished them "a good sign and great fortune, for us and the whole house of Israel."

When the party was over, Shayna and Naomi worked together in the kitchen to clean up. Baruch and Tzippy were outside, and Ilana had gone to her room. Herschel had cornered Joel in the living room, while the girls were asleep on various beds and couches. It was nice to work side by side. They stacked plates in the sink, and the wedding details felt far away.

"Do you remember?" Naomi asked.

"Remember what?" Shayna asked.

"Oh, I don't know. Everything."

Naomi felt silly; she felt young. She felt the rush of satisfaction that the party had turned out as she had hoped. She wanted to grab Shayna's hand and bring back the days when they were easy, close friends.

"Do you remember cooking broccoli in the bathtub?" Naomi asked.

"Do you remember lighting Chanukah candles together in the lobby?" Shayna asked.

They remembered Shabbos at college and the boys who were imported from Yeshiva University uptown to form a minyan. They all ate together in the dining room and then they danced around the tables and sang. They remembered discovering that the people in the buildings across the street from the dorm could see the girls changing when their shades were open. They remembered that there was never enough heat, and they used to put on their warmest pajamas, pile their blankets onto one bed, hide under them, and talk.

"Do you remember Herschel's Cadillac?" Shayna asked.

They reminisced about the Saturday night Herschel had pulled up in front of the dorm in a butter-yellow Cadillac. The car had belonged to his father, the one nice thing he had owned. Herschel had never been allowed to drive it. But when his father died three months before, the car had become his. Hershel was still in his year of mourning. He wasn't supposed to go to parties or hear live music. But after Shabbos at home alone with his mother, he had to get out. He took his father's car and drove. He ended up in Manhattan, at Stern College, where he posed in front of his car and pretended to be waiting for friends.

"Nice car," Naomi had said. She was the first to look away from their cluster of friends. The presence of a new boy made all of them look up. The Stern lobby and the sidewalk in front of it were meeting places for Orthodox young men and women. Then, before everyone started to become more religious and objected to this coed mixing, the rabbis approved of this mingling. A whole generation of Stern girls had met their husbands here.

Naomi and Shayna had walked over to Herschel and introduced themselves. They had both been curious about him. He looked older than the boys they hung around with. His white dress shirt was starched and pressed. A gold cuff link dotted each wrist.

"Are you at Yeshiva University?" Shayna asked.

"No, I'm learning at a yeshiva in Brooklyn. I was going to go to YU, but it didn't work out," he said. "My father just died."

"Poor Herschel," Naomi said.

"Want a ride?" he offered.

He had expected Naomi to get into the front seat. But Shayna had hopped in first. She confided to Herschel that her father had also died and that she had only recently become Orthodox. They discovered that they both had parents who were Holocaust survivors. Neither had extended families. He told her that he was going to take what his father had started and build something more. He had plans for the future. He wanted to open a kosher restaurant and a kosher grocery store. You have to be able to see it, he told her. You have to catch the trend before it starts to rise. Orthodoxy was experiencing a revival. Kosher was an idea waiting for its time. "You're part of it," he said. "Your becoming Orthodox is part of that trend."

The next night, he called Shayna, and they stayed on the phone for hours. She was happy to listen to him. She believed everything he said. A whirlwind of dating followed. That he lived in a cramped apartment in Brooklyn and not a sprawling house on Long Island, as he had originally told her, didn't bother her. That his father's business brought in a fraction of the amount he claimed didn't matter. For the next few years, she felt as if she were always riding beside Herschel in the Cadillac. Everything was breathtaking and fast, and she couldn't stop.

— TEN —

Sleep didn't interest Herschel. One of these days someone, maybe he, was going to invent a pill that rendered it unnecessary. Driving to his office at night, he cruised over the Brooklyn Bridge into Manhattan. The lights of Manhattan seemed like an endless streak of ideas, bulbs of inspiration overhead. He imagined that his father's soul twinkled behind one of these lights.

Today was twenty-five years since his father had died. His father was a survivor of the Russian labor camps, where he had worked in the kitchen. When he came to America after the war, he built a kosher catering business from nothing. He cooked and schlepped so Herschel wouldn't have to. He had wanted Herschel to stay in yeshiva. But the words of the Talmud swam in front of Herschel's eyes. He wasn't one for theories, for hypothetical situations. But Herschel knew intuitively the ins and outs of the yeshiva building. He knew what to do if the copy machine jammed. He had a key to the maintenance office and was in the good graces of the janitorial staff. He snuck the boys into the kitchen for late-night snacks. Soon Herschel was spending more time in the kitchen than in the beis midrash. He dropped out of yeshiva and joined his father's business. He took it over when his father died and tried to expand it. Now, with his father's soul hovering, Herschel wished he had more to show for himself. He had thought that by now he'd have a kosher empire so big that his father would see it from heaven.

From his collection of keys, Herschel took one and opened the office of the Orthodox Coalition. The OC, as it was called, did more than just give kosher certifications. It sponsored social services, youth groups, and rabbinic forums. But kosher supervision was its back-bone. Other organizations also gave kosher certifications. Many cities had their own rabbis and their own symbols: the OK, the Moon-K, the star K, K in a cowboy boot from Texas, K and the Seattle Space Needle, K in the state of Tennessee. But none had the universal recognition of the OC.

Herschel had succumbed to Shayna's desires and gotten this job. His official title was Vice President of Kosher Inspections for the Mid-west Region, but there were hundreds of vice presidents like him, each master over a tiny plot of land. He tracked the expansion of the kosher markets in his assigned region and oversaw certifications for newly kosher products. He traveled constantly, doing surprise kosher inspections at factories, restaurants, and bakeries. The biggest excitement was when a product bore an unauthorized OC and had to be recalled. But Herschel wasn't cut out for the drudgery of preparing reports, returning phone calls, and going to meetings. He liked to arrive when he was ready and leave when he felt like it. He wanted to get rid of the stacks of paper that sat on every surface in his office. If he had his way, he would open the window, turn on a fan, and let all the paperwork blow out across the city.

The only time he could stand to be there was at night, when the office teemed with silent ideas. The empty space became his imaginary command center. Kosher Ventures was miraculously transformed into a massive operation, bustling with employees, phones ringing off hooks, fax machines spewing paper. It had worldwide connections, a constellation of outposts, its finger on the pulse of the food industry, its products circumnavigating the globe.

Herschel had had so many ideas, all of which should have worked. The failure of the hydroponic vegetables still shocked him. Sometimes he woke up in the morning and had to remind himself that it hadn't happened. It was a fluke of bad luck that a company in Israel had beat him to it. Before the hydroponics, he had come up with the idea for the Travel-Kosher Suitcase. This insulated bag would fit into the overhead compartment of an airplane and be stocked with vacuum-packed food and a portable hot plate. It was designed for the kosher traveler who found himself in a city with no kosher food. Before that, he had hired a non-Jewish columnist to compare every kosher restaurant with its non-kosher counterparts. Herschel billed it as a chance to get a look from the other side. For six months, "The Food Goy" was the rage of the *Jewish Press* set. Herschel made plans to syndicate the column. He was going to be his agent, his producer. He was planning books and speaking tours, when it was discovered that the Food Goy wasn't a goy at all, but a rebellious former yeshiva boy who boldly ate treif and enjoyed the opportunity to stick it to his family and friends.

Herschel's ideas stretched back for miles, but he wasn't sure how to go forward. Now that he worked full-time, Kosher Ventures wasn't so much closed as on hiatus. He was out of money, out of investors. Even worse, he was out of ideas. They used to come to him in the shower, as he slept, in shul, and at home. Like nocturnal black bats whose eyes gleamed red, they circled until they found him. But ever since the hydroponics, he had had nothing except hope. He wanted to come up with an idea that would make him famous. He longed for money, but it was more than that. He wanted to make something, find something, build something.

He paced the halls, looking at the knickknacks on his co-workers' desks. He sharpened pencils in his secretary's electric sharpener. He helped himself to boxes of paper clips and fresh white notebooks. If he stayed here long enough, he would come up with a new idea. He studied the walls, with the history of kosher food mapped out in framed pictures and plaques. In the beginning, there was Crisco, an all-vegetable product, cheap and kosher, as its advertisements proclaimed in the Yiddish press. Underneath was a picture of a Jewish housewife using it to make strudel. A few years later, Maxwell House, Quaker Oats, and Post cereal became kosher and ran ads announcing this fact. In 1923, the OC, the first official national kosher certification, appeared on a can of Heinz vegetarian baked beans and a new world was born. In 1926, a dozen companies bore the OC imprint. By 1956, the OC was on a thousand products. Every historic highlight was hung on the wall: a picture of the first kosher cake mix, the first kosher bottle of Coca-Cola, the first kosher store-bought bread, the first kosher frozen pizza, the first kosher Budweiser.

All this history, and where was his place in it? Herschel wandered into the mailroom and found it. Stacked in boxes and waiting for the next day, he found a crate of Oreo cookies certified for the first time with an OC. Next to it was a box of newly printed magazines, the about-to-be-released issue of *Kosher Today.* On the cover, there was an Oreo cookie. KOSHER IS HOT, it proclaimed in a banner headline.

The Oreo was the final frontier. Its becoming kosher was a milestone no one would forget. It wouldn't get lost among kosher Entenmann's, kosher Pepperidge Farm, kosher Sara Lee. It was more earth-shattering than M&Ms and Snickers put together. Kosher keepers everywhere would remember where they were when they heard that Oreos had become kosher. In a few months, they would be in every kosher pantry, knapsack, and glove compartment. They would be stashed in bedrooms for midnight snacks.

An estimated ten million Americans bought kosher on a regular basis, Herschel read in the accompanying article. Eighty percent of these consumers weren't Jewish. After years of stagnant sales, kosher food was the fastest-growing sector of the food industry. Over ten thousand products now bore the OC imprint. There was kosher bubble gum and jellybeans and TV dinners, kosher "bacon" and kosher "shrimp." Requests for kosher certification were up twenty percent in the past year alone. Eighteen thousand grocery stores had some sort of kosher food aisle. Outside the New York area, kosher sales had nearly doubled. Over sixty percent of consumers associated kosher with words like "clean" and "healthy" and "quality." Perhaps it was because of the return to traditionalism sweeping the nation. Or perhaps it was the persistent yet useful misconception that kosher food was cleaner or unadulterated or blessed by a rabbi. The lactose intolerant bought. The Muslims bought. The Seventh-Day Adventists bought.

It was as if the hand of God had made its way through the steel girders of a Manhattan skyscraper, down the elevator shaft, through the hallway, into the office, and touched Herschel on the head. It was as if God were turning the pages of the magazine, telling Herschel that the time was right. At the bottom of a page, he saw a small ad: "Kosher restaurant wanted. Great opportunity. Investors available. Memphis, Tennessee." Until now, Herschel had concentrated his efforts on New York. But among the tall buildings and the crowds, there wasn't enough room for him. Herschel needed a place to stretch his wings, and now he had found it. It was time to take kosher to the far reaches of the country. Full of hope, Herschel went home, taking the case of first-edition kosher Oreos with him as his rightful prize.

———

"Close your eyes," Herschel said to Shayna when he returned that night.

Shayna lay in bed, surrounded by glossy eight-by-ten photos of cakes. They were shaped like butterflies, like lattice baskets, like spring hats. There were wheelbarrows holding marzipan vegetables, presents tied with bows, treasure chests filled with coins, all iced with pareve buttercream frosting. The bows on the hats creased like fabric. The butterfly wings were nearly iridescent.

"I'm not going to order them. I'm just looking, for fun," she said.

"Close your eyes," he said again.

Shayna closed her eyes and still saw the cakes. If she ordered them, they would be the last bite people tasted before they went home from the wedding. This would become the measuring stick against which future Viennese tables would be judged. Anyone who had them afterward would lay their tables with a lingering shadow of Tzippy's wedding.

"Good," he said. "Now open your mouth and make a mezonos."

She said the blessing, and he put something in her mouth. Hoping that he had read her mind and brought her one of these cakes, she chewed slowly. She was surprised at the crunch of something store-bought and the taste of ordinary chocolate. Then she recognized the taste. She had grown up eating Oreos, when they were made with lard.

The cookie wasn't that good, but he was so excited that she finished it. To Herschel, it didn't matter how it actually tasted. Its once forbidden status was the only ingredient that mattered. Over the years, Herschel had asked her to describe the non-kosher food she had once eaten. If he couldn't taste it, he wanted to hear what it was like. She pushed aside her memories of what it had been like to eat whatever, whenever, she wanted, and she told him that treif was nothing special; he wasn't missing much. She was unwilling to be his window onto the outside world. The last thing she needed was for it to be said in the streets of Brooklyn that Shayna Goldman has eaten treif.

"Kosher," Herschel said, and popped a cookie into his mouth. "At last. It's happening, just like I always said. And this is only the beginning."

He whispered his plan into her ear, and she listened. He had been distant since the demise of the hydroponics idea. He never lamented its loss, but he had seemed diminished because of it. Now, with a new idea looming, she saw a glimpse of the young man who had pulled up in front of the Stern College dorm. She almost expected that if she got out of bed and looked out the window, his Cadillac would be parked in their driveway, gleaming and new.

"About the cakes . . . ," she said.

"Order them," he said. "One of each." He put his arms around her. "I'm telling you, this time it's going to happen. I'm sure of it."

They fell asleep. Herschel dreamed of the house he would build once he had success firmly in his hands. He dreamed of cathedral ceilings, a grand staircase, and a high arched doorway through which all the important people would enter. He added more rooms until his house became a mansion. Next to him, Shayna was dreaming of yards of fabric and the dresses that could be made from it. She imagined spools of ribbon tying together sets of china and sterling silver. The furniture she selected filled the rooms he was building. The dresses she wanted filled the closets of his palace, which grew until it had taken over the whole neighborhood, until it became so grand that it was finally visible from heaven.

— ELEVEN —

Herschel was on the phone with three investors from Memphis. The only thing these men knew about the kosher restaurant business was that their community needed one. They and their families had lived in Memphis for five generations, and this detour into kosher was part business venture, part community service.

"Listen to me," Herschel said. "Not a restaurant, per se. A kosher department. With takeout. And fresh meat. And a few tables. In a grocery store."

"A grocery store," the investors drawled, worrying that they had made a mistake by agreeing to talk to this man who answered their advertisement brimming with ideas. But it wasn't easy to attract someone to Memphis. They had run this ad for weeks in succession, and he was the only one who had called.

"We were thinking of a steakhouse," one of them said.

"Or Chinese."

They wanted to go out to eat. Tired of eating plain lettuce at the nicest non-kosher restaurants in town, they wanted a place for a business lunch. They wanted a family-style restaurant, so their wives could have a night off. They also wanted a place that did takeout for Shabbos, pizza on Saturday nights, brunch on Sunday morning.

"No," Herschel told them. "That's not going to work for the same reason that none of the other kosher restaurants in Memphis have worked. Do you want to know the secret of staying in business in a community outside of New York? You have to attract the non-kosher customer as well. But what's going to draw people in? Why would a non-kosher customer seek out a kosher restaurant? It's more expensive. It's not open on Friday nights or Saturdays. It has no meat and milk together. So you know what you have to do? You have to put it right under their noses. Make it so convenient they can't help but go in. With the grocery store, they're already there."

These investors had hoped for so much more. They had gone out in search of a kosher restaurant. To return with less felt like an admission that their community wasn't as grand as they thought. But Herschel wasn't worried about their misgivings. The slightest hint of opposition made him more certain.

Herschel dreamed of seven lean cows and seven fat cows. The famine in Memphis was replaced by years of plenty. The members of the community bowed to him in gratitude. He woke from this dream at four in the morning, fully alert. There was no point trying to go back to sleep. Instead he went to his office.

Herschel researched the demographics of Memphis and compared them with other cities of the same size. He contacted suppliers and put together an estimate of start-up costs. He described for the investors the kosher departments he had seen in other cities. Dallas had a kosher bakery. In Atlanta, there was kosher Chinese takeout in the middle of Kroger. Toronto had something to behold: a grocery store the size of a city block lined with kosher counters. One counter was for raw meat, another for fish. There was a cheese counter, a prepared-foods counter, a bakery, and a grill. Herschel could spend his life there and never get hungry. He called all the grocery stores in Memphis to see who would rent him space. He faxed them the *Kosher Today* article and a proposal claiming that opening a kosher department would increase foot traffic by twenty-five percent.

A few weeks later, Kroger, the largest supermarket in Memphis, agreed to lease him the back portion of the store, which had been empty since the video rental had gone out of business. It was set off from the rest of the store and would allow them to operate independently. They could have their own kitchen, their own staff. There was room for several refrigerated-food servers, some shelves of kosher products, a few tables and chairs.

Herschel shifted the kosher certification requests to the back of the pile. Tacked up on his walls were charts and numbers about Memphis. He read restaurant-supply catalogues. He faxed sample menus and earnings projections to the investors. They called hourly with more questions.

"Ten years ago, I would have told you to serve Southern barbecue. I would have said go ethnic. But now we've come full circle. People want more than faux shrimp cocktail. They want the food to feel kosher as well," Herschel said.

"It's going to be part takeout, part café. We're going to have genuine Jewish food like your bubby made," Herschel told them. "Kasha varnishkes, potato knishes, matzo ball soup, kugel, homemade gefilte fish, chopped liver. I'm talking beyond bagels and pastrami. I want the real thing.

"As of last year, we're selling ten million pounds of herring and gefilte fish a year. Do you have any idea what that means? It means that herring can become as common as tuna. Gefilte fish can be the next sushi. You want to know why? Because people are hungry for something authentic. They remember when they used to eat it at their bubby and zaidy's house. They miss the past. Even if they never had it, they still miss it."

The investors were persuaded by his assurances that this was just a starting point. They were pleased to find a partner who understood as they did the community's capacity for growth. Their pockets ran deep, their dreams ran high. Soon they stopped talking in hypotheticals. They asked Herschel how much money he needed, when he wanted to open, who would run it day to day.

"If it were up to me, I'd move down there in a second and run the place myself. That's how sure I am it's going to work. But my wife won't hear of it. She would never leave New York. But trust me," Herschel said, knowing that this time they would, "I know just the person."

Herschel bought two tickets to a Yankees game, one for himself and one for Baruch.

"I don't know about you, but I needed to get away from all this wedding business," Herschel said to Baruch as they sat in the bleachers.

Herschel couldn't open the refrigerator without accidentally sampling the chicken Florentine that Shayna had brought home from the caterer for Tzippy to taste. He couldn't sit on his own couch without knocking over a thousand varieties of pearl beads.

"I used to go to the Brooklyn Dodgers. Now that was a team. My mother wrapped up Shabbos leftovers, and my father and I went to the game together, when he wasn't working," Herschel remembered.

"I used to be a Yankees fan," Baruch said. "But it started to seem so silly after my rebbe asked me what God thinks about grown men running around a field with no other purpose than to hit a ball. After that, I couldn't look at it in the same way."

Herschel shook his head. "Give up everything else, but not baseball. Baseball's like Torah. Look around," he said.

The stadium was dotted with men and boys wearing yarmulkes. Rooting for the Yankees was an acceptable foray into American culture even for those who usually shunned it. Herschel was wearing a Yankees cap over his black velvet yarmulke. He had no problem wearing it with the same black dress pants and white shirt that Baruch wore. He wasn't one to get caught up in the contradictions.

"Come with me, Baruch. I want to show you something," Herschel said between innings.

Herschel guided Baruch to the kosher hot dog stand located behind first base. It had the highest prices and the longest line. But the customers were willing to wait and pay. If they were hungry, this was their only option. The men were wearing black hats and Yankees batting-practice jerseys. The women wore long jean skirts and baseball caps over their snoods. There were also men in shorts, women in tank tops, men whose yarmulkes were hidden under Yankees caps, men who had come straight from the office and forgotten to put their yarmulkes back on. And kids in full Yankees uniforms with tzitzis hanging out, standing next to kids wearing baseball jerseys emblazoned YIDDLE LEAGUE. Mincha minyans formed to the right of the stand. They were like pickup games of basketball. As soon as there were ten, the prayers began.

Back in his seat, Herschel bit into a hot dog. It was the best one he had ever tasted. The extra flavor came from being able to buy it at the stadium like everyone else, and that was what he needed to bottle and market. The Yankees were now up by four. It had gotten dark, and Herschel looked out past the blinding brightness of the stadium to the dark city on all sides.

"Baruch, do you remember the discussion where the rabbis are talking about a new community and what to establish first? A new community springs up, and the leaders debate what should be established first—a cemetery, a school, or a mikvah? One rabbi says you have to create the cemetery, because you have to respect the dead. The second rabbi says the school, because without an education for the kids, the community has no future. And the third one says the mikvah, because without that, there won't be any children."

"According to the Rambam, that's only in a case where the community is—" Baruch said.

"Do you know what the answer would be today?" Herschel interrupted. "A kosher restaurant—that's what you should open first. Tell me if I'm wrong about you, Baruch. I think you're looking for something. You want to blaze your own path, but you're not sure how. I know you want to learn, but you also know you can't sit in yeshiva for the rest of your life. And I have the perfect solution. I want to open a kosher department in a grocery store, in Memphis, Tennessee. I have a space. I have the money. All I need is someone to manage it. The way I see it, this idea combines everything you want to do. You can bring kosher to a hungry community. You can have time to learn. And you can change people's lives. One day you can even teach classes there. It could become a center for Jewish learning. You said yourself that there's a hunger out there. Here's your chance to do something about it."

Herschel cracked peanuts and popped them into his mouth. He knew that Baruch probably looked down on having to work. Yeshiva boys like him treated the men their fathers' age as an unlearned mass. They imagined that if they went back a thousand years, they would find that the Torah was passed down only by those who sat all day in front of their books. The line of rich fathers-in-law must have stretched all the way back to Sinai. But Herschel knew the men of his own father's generation. They had worked their entire lives and still stood closer to God than these kids ever would.

Baruch turned his attention from the game and started to think about what Herschel was saying. Since he and Tzippy had gotten engaged, they had worried about where they would live, what they would do, how they would support themselves. He wasn't going to go to college. He wasn't sure he could stay in yeshiva. Their friends who stayed in yeshiva had parents who helped them out. Herschel had initially made it sound as though he would help. Once Tzippy pressed for details, he said he wasn't sure he could do it. Baruch had asked his parents for help, but his father refused. He railed against the impracticality of Baruch's desire to stay in yeshiva. He said that it was just a way to hide from the real world.

But now, in this idea of Memphis and grocery stores, Baruch saw a way to learn and make a living at the same time. Coming from Herschel, who saw the value in learning, such a compromise was easier to hear. Baruch liked Herschel. He too had learned in yeshiva and could quote from the Talmud. Baruch remembered Herschel from years before, but the main thing he knew about him was that his father didn't like him. He remembered Joel's snide comments about Herschel's ideas that never went anywhere. At the time, he had taken his father's judgment as the sole, irrefutable truth. He hadn't realized there was a different way to see the world.

— TWELVE —

IN BED, with the lights off, Tzippy whispered into the phone. It still felt shocking that a boy was allowed to call her. Even more astonishing was that she was allowed to talk to him. Though he was her fiancé, what thrilled her most was the idea of a boyfriend.

"How would you like to go far away?" Baruch asked.

"How far?"

"Very far."

"Even better. So tell me where you're taking me," she said.

"Memphis, Tennessee."

She laughed. "What are you talking about?"

"I'm talking about bringing people closer to God. About forging my own path. About starting something from scratch. "

"You sound like my father," Tzippy said.

"It's your father's idea. He wants to open a kosher department in a grocery store in Memphis, and he asked me if I want to run it. I'd oversee everything and do all the kosher supervision. And I'd have time to learn."

At first she thought he was joking. Even when they worried about how they would support themselves, the possibility of doing something other than yeshiva had never come up. This was the model for marriage she had been taught to believe in. It was reinforced in the marriage books she was reading, the sequels to the dating books she had once read. *Dear Bride, The Secret of Jewish Women, How to Build a Jewish Home, How to Be a Woman of Valor*—their covers were invariably pink and had fancy lettering with pictures of lace tablecloths and bouquets of roses. They advised the new bride to speak kindly and ask how her husband's day went. She should have makeup on when he came home and have dinner waiting. She was told not to complain, not to contradict, not to argue. These books expanded upon the blessings that would result when marriage was conducted according to the Torah. It was a recipe for happiness, and all the young brides needed to do was follow it exactly.

"What do you think?" Baruch asked.

"I don't know. I'm surprised."

"I know," he said. "But I can't stay in yeshiva forever. What else are we going to do? This at least seems like a good way to work and still have time to learn."

"I like the idea of going far away," Tzippy said.

"Me too," he said.

"But is this what you want to do?"

"Maybe. Will you at least think about it?" he asked.

She did, all night. She thought about her friends from high school who lived in nearby apartment buildings. Before she was engaged, she had visited them, and her envy was so strong that it was hard to sit in their living rooms. In their married apartments, their lives matched the fantasies they had sketched out for themselves when they were high school girls sitting on one another's beds. They looked like the same women they had once imitated in their endless games of dress-up. Only now they never had to take off their mothers' sheitels. They never had to go back to being girls who were waiting for their lives to begin.

Now Tzippy would finally have what they had. She knew exactly what her life would be like. She would live in this same neighborhood and see her mother every day. She would help out with her sisters until she had children of her own. Her friends would be the same girls she had grown up with. They would pass together from high school to marriage to motherhood. They would travel on a one-way road, each stop along the way decided in advance. Now is the time when everyone is getting married. Now is the time when everyone is having children. But one of the girls, Tzippy imagined, made a break for it. When no one was looking, she began to run and didn't look back.

Slowly, the idea that she and Baruch could go somewhere else began to take hold. Tzippy didn't want what everyone else had. She didn't want to be able to envision exactly how it would be. She wanted to live in a place beyond the boundaries of her imagination. She had never thought about Memphis or imagined Jews there. If she told her friends that they were thinking about Memphis, they would laugh and wonder what she could possibly do there. But Tzippy knew what she would do. Separated from her family by miles, she would be on her own.

— THIRTEEN —

FIVE DAUGHTERS and no sons. Wait until the girls get married, Shayna and Herschel had always been told. Then you'll have five sons. Now they had one. Baruch was always at their house, for dinner during the week and for Shabbos, sleeping at a neighbor's house to preserve propriety and hold temptation at bay. He spent more time at Tzippy's house than at his own. He was eager to entertain the girls, happy to talk to Shayna, willing to listen to Herschel. In the bustle of their house, he made a place for himself.

In the car on the way to dinner, Baruch was sandwiched between Dassi and Dena. In Brooklyn, where kosher restaurants were in abundance, they first had to choose whether they wanted meat or milk, McDovid's fast food or Jerusalem II pizza, Galilee Grill, Shalom Hunan, or Sushi Eden.

"I want pizza," Dena said.

"I want Chinese," Dassi said.

Shayna hushed them and they ignored her. Tzippy hushed them and they gave her dirty looks. Their enchantment with their sister the bride had faded. They had always wanted their sister to get engaged. But they hadn't realized that this would mean she would get all the attention and then go away and leave them. They had only imagined that there would be a wedding and a husband and lots of new clothes.

"Pizza."

"Chinese."

They argued until neither girl remembered which she wanted. If

Dena said Chinese, Dassi wanted pizza. If Dassi wanted Chinese, Dena wanted pizza.

"What if I want hamburgers?" Baruch asked.

They stopped arguing and broke into peals of laughter. Now they too wanted hamburgers, and they chanted this as loud as they could.

"Hamburgers it is," Herschel decided. "We're going to Lenny's."

Lenny's Barbecue claimed the world's first kosher buffalo wings, and for this feat alone, Herschel was willing to wait for a table. Everything at Lenny's was super-sized. The menu offered a choice of grand burgers or mega burgers. The fries came extra-long and extra-spicy. The wings came hot, super-hot, or super-super-hot. The ribs were so huge that when they were brought to the table even Herschel was silenced. He tied the complimentary bib around his neck. Rib in hand, Herschel held court.

"Girls, you probably think you could always get a kosher meal like this. You think hot dogs, wings, fries—what's the big deal? But trust me. It wasn't always like this."

He told them how, thirty years ago, Lenny's was a far-off dream. Now, of course, people complained anyway. More kosher restaurants per capita than anywhere in the world and still no one was happy. Why do they have to be so noisy? people asked. Why must they teem with children? Just because a restaurant is kosher, why must the service be slow? They asked the eternal, mystical, practically kabbalistic question: Why, why, why could you always tell it was a kosher restaurant?

But that was because people couldn't remember what it was like to have nothing. There used to be two places to eat out. If you wanted meat, you went to Lou G. Siegel's, a meat-and-potatoes place where Hungarian goulash and stuffed derma were always the specialties of the day. If you wanted dairy, you went to Ratners on the Lower East Side. They served pierogies and blintzes and the waiters scolded you if you didn't finish what was on your plate. When Shmulke Bernstein's opened and served kosher Chinese, people thought they had seen it all.

"But there's still farther to go," Herschel said. "This idea of mine is the next big thing."

"Can we come see it?" Dassi asked.

"What are you going to call it?" Dena asked.

"What about Malky's Place?" Malky said.

"No, Dassi's Place."

"No, Dena's."

Herschel waited for them to quiet down. "No," he said, "we'll call it The Kosher Connection. And of course you can come see it. You all can."

The sisters loved to hear him talk. Tzippy too had grown up believing everything he said. When Herschel described the restaurants he would open in every Jewish community in the country, they were sure every word would come true. Their last name would be as omnipresent as Manischewitz. Now their imaginations went with him to Memphis, where they saw their father presiding over a huge grocery store, his picture printed on the milk cartons, emblazoned on the shopping bags.

Herschel was persistent. He called Baruch every day with another reason why it was a good idea. He tried the practical, he tried the idealistic. Opening the kosher department, he said, was a marriage of the two.

Baruch wished he could ask his parents for advice, but instead he called Rabbi Rothstein. There were other rabbis in his yeshiva who had mastered more pages of the Talmud. They sat in their studies, lined floor to ceiling with books. If they needed to quote a passage, they always knew where the book was and what page it was on. The endless number of texts seemed to live, unfurled, behind their eyes. But Rabbi Rothstein could see into the boys' hearts, and he was the one to whom the boys turned for advice, on matters ranging from the mundane to the metaphysical.

Baruch told him about Herschel's offer, and Rabbi Rothstein listened. He had heard the same concerns from many of the boys who worried about going out into the world.

"How do they say it?" Rabbi Rothstein said finally. "You can't take it with you? Well, about Torah, they're wrong. You *can* take it with you."

When Baruch hung up the phone, he opened his Talmud and saw that this was true. Before, he had imagined that the rabbis never left the beis midrash. Now he saw that the rabbis he revered weren't just scholars. Underneath a brilliant legal opinion was a shoemaker. There, inside a logical proof, was a weaver. The great commentator Rashi was a vintner. Maimonides was a doctor. The author of the Shulchan Aruch sold fabric; the Chafetz Chaim owned a grocery store. Some may have worked out of necessity. Others did because they eschewed the idea of living off communal stipends. In either case, the great rabbis had been part of the outside world. In yeshiva, it had been easy to forget this. Even as the worries of everyday life hovered, they liked to pretend that they had slipped the bounds of the real world—as if they could live on words alone.

On Friday afternoon, Baruch sat with Tzippy as she finished preparing for Shabbos. Though his mother kept remarking, in a faux-casual voice, that they hardly saw him anymore, Baruch was spending Shabbos with Tzippy's family again.

Tzippy did two things at once. If she focused, she could do three. As she cooked, her sisters came in and out of the kitchen with what seemed like a revolving door of requests. Tzippy was hot from standing over the stove. Her hair kept falling into her eyes, and she twisted it and clipped it to the top of her head. She was wearing an old T-shirt that she liked to cook in. This was a Tzippy that Baruch hadn't been allowed to see when they were dating. Her mother would probably say that he still shouldn't see her in an imperfect state, for fear he would change his mind. But he loved seeing her this way. As she bustled, he saw a glimpse of how their lives would be. He imagined that the steady stream of high-pitched requests came not from her sisters but from their daughters.

"What?" Tzippy asked, feeling his eyes on her.

"Nothing. I just like watching you," Baruch said.

They hadn't touched each other since the engagement party, but having done so once made it harder not to do it again. Now, whenever they were together, the air felt ripe. They forced themselves to sit on opposite ends of the couch. They sat on their hands. When all else failed, they invited Tzippy's sisters to come join them in the living room.

Tzippy shook her finger knowingly at Baruch and handed him a spoon. "I guess I'd better put you to work."

"What are we making?"

"Noodle kugel."

"What should I do?"

"Don't tell me you don't know how to make a kugel," she said.

When he said no, she put her hands on her hips. "Well, you're about to learn."

She lined up the sugar and spices in front of him. In a matter of minutes, she had him mixing the noodles with the eggs and oil, while she checked the cakes that were baking. Meanwhile, she answered the phone and sent Zahava to the store for some missing ingredients.

"Your father should have asked *you* to run The Kosher Connection," Baruch said. "You could do it by yourself."

She laughed. "We could bring my sisters in as assistants. Just to really test my patience."

"I mean it," he said. "Maybe you could work with me. It could be both of ours."

She looked at him in surprise. "You sound like you're serious about Memphis."

"Maybe I am," he said.

"Maybe I am too," she said.

An hour before Shabbos, the sisters were dressed, the younger ones in matching navy dresses with white sashes. Comb marks were visible in their wet hair. The food was warming on the hot plate, chicken noodle soup in one pot, roasted chicken and kugels in pans. The white tablecloth was bleached and ironed. Seven white candles inside seven silver candlesticks were waiting to be lit. When the clock struck 7:14, Shayna was ready. She lit the candles and waved her hands three times in front of her face. As she covered her eyes and whispered blessings for each of her children, the men were leaving for shul.

Tzippy sat with her mother and sisters in the living room. Siddurs open on their laps, they took turns trying on Tzippy's diamond engagement ring. The ring was one and a half carats, circle cut, platinum setting. It was large and blinding for a young bride, but this was what everyone got. No one wanted a ring smaller than anyone else's. And they would grow into them. Twenty years from now, their rings would fit them perfectly.

Zahava grabbed the ring from Dassi. She put it on and held out her hand to admire it. "It's not bad," she said. "But emerald cut is so much better."

"Give it back," Tzippy said. "Now."

"Are you excited about the wedding?" Malky asked Tzippy.

"Of course I am," Tzippy said.

"It's not fair. I want to have a wedding too," Dena protested.

"Don't worry. Before you know it, it will be your turn," Shayna said.

"It's not the wedding that's important, silly. That part hardly matters," Tzippy said.

In response, Shayna hummed part of the davening out loud: "Lecha dodi likrat kallah, p'nei Shabbat nekabbalah." *Come my beloved to meet the bride, the Sabbath presence let us welcome.* These words confirmed that this bride was everywhere. She was in their house; she was in their prayers. She came decked in splendor, draped in satin. She filled the room with her presence, the house with her spirit.

At shul, the men sang the Lecha Dodi and swayed, black suits and hats in synchronous motion. Baruch sat next to Herschel. Almost his son-in-law, he was starting to feel like his son. Baruch felt part of this group of men. Most of them worked in business during the day. But they weren't like his father, whose job had become his world. They started their day in shul. They learned on the train going to the office. Instead of taking a lunch break, they stole away for an hour each afternoon to daven mincha and learn. They ended their day as they began it, back in shul.

When Herschel and Baruch came home, the family gathered around the table. Herschel began the Shalom Aleichem, welcoming the Sabbath angels into their home. They sang along with him. Little girl voices mixed with Shayna's and Tzippy's barely audible ones. Baruch and Herschel enunciated every word and swayed. Their eyes locked. Both of them saw angels and chariots. They heard the rustle of wings outside the window.

Herschel began the Aishet Chayil. *A woman of valor who can find. She is more precious than rubies. A husband places his trust in her and profits from that. She brings him good not harm all the days of her life.* He serenaded Shayna with these words of praise for the loyal wife. He pretended to hold a microphone and, with the finesse of a lounge singer, he gazed into her eyes. This week he got carried away. He drew his words out with a flourish that necessitated his kneeling before her on one knee. Shayna acted surprised and coquettishly held out her hand.

But Herschel wasn't the one singing with the fullest heart. The little girls giggled as Baruch sang to Tzippy. It was love across the Shabbos table. Tzippy blocked out the rest of her family and concentrated on Baruch's face. Since they had gotten engaged, they liked to tell each other stories about what their lives would be like when they were married. Now they thought about Memphis, where they would know no one. They would be on their own, away from their families. They let these fantasies carry them through the last waning weeks of engagement.

— FOURTEEN —

ILANA PRETENDED TO BE ASLEEP. It was Shabbos, and her mother was knocking on her door, telling her it was time for shul. Three weeks before the wedding, her mother had insisted that her family spend this Shabbos together. At the wedding, there would be a crush of extended family and out-of-town friends. But she wanted one last time as a foursome. She insisted that Baruch stay home instead of going to Tzippy's family. She told Joel and Ilana that she expected them to come to shul. Joel had listened to Naomi's request and belatedly joined Baruch, who had been at shul for an hour already. Ilana was still holding out. She listened as her mother got ready and called out one last hopeful good-bye.

Only when the house was finally empty did Ilana sit up in bed. She surprised herself with how much she didn't want to go to shul. She wasn't interested in this enforced family time. She had decided not to care. She no longer tried to bring Baruch out of his room. Engagement had permanently sealed him away.

At the engagement party, she had been bombarded with people telling her how excited she must be about her brother getting married. She nodded, then made a quick retreat. From across the room, she had watched Baruch and Tzippy. They made a show of not touching, always careful to maintain the required distance. But they got as close as they could. He leaned over to whisper something in her ear. She was always smiling up at him. Seeing him that way made Ilana feel shy. She could no longer try to rile him, tease him, provoke him.

She had eventually gone outside where she could hide. She walked through the backyard, and then she stopped and stood silently. Baruch and Tzippy were out there, and in the light of the porch, she saw them lean toward each other. They stayed, suspended in a near touch, for a moment as Ilana watched them. She wanted to pry them apart, then she wanted to push them together. She wanted them to see her. She imagined, with pleasure, their embarrassment. Her brother was so judgmental, but now she would leap out at him and yell "Gotcha!" She would unmask them. They who pretended to be so holy in public were just like everyone else in private. It confirmed what she had suspected: that it was all pretense. Everyone layered themselves in disguises and costumes, pretending to be something they weren't. Their whole world, she decided, was a masquerade ball.

It made her wonder about everyone she knew. What was underneath their guises of religiosity? Did they really feel it? Did they really believe? Her friends accepted it at face value. "But they're Orthodox," they would say when she wondered out loud. They didn't understand, as she did, how little that really meant. She wondered about those who stopped pretending. How did they do it? Did it happen overnight? Or did it happen so slowly that you could barely see the accumulation of a thousand moments of doubt? Ilana did what she was supposed to, but she wasn't sure she believed in it. In doling out portions of belief, maybe God gave hers to Baruch. She wondered whether being Orthodox was something she could easily shed. Alone now in the semi-dark, she wondered why, for example, she didn't flip on the lights. Did she truly believe that God cared one way or the other? Would a bolt of lightning strike her down? She had never paid much attention to the light switch before. Now it beckoned to her, like a dare.

Their shul in Laurelwood was the largest of five. In the past ten years, it had expanded twice. A capital campaign was under way to raise money for yet another expansion, though there was no space left on this lot for one more inch of building. They already stretched to the curb. The parking lot had long ago been turned into the youth wing.

The men came first, filling the main section of the shul. The women came later. When shul was more than half over, it became the mommy hour. Hoping to arrive at the end of services, they walked slowly, laden with double strollers. The walkway that led to the front door had been transformed into a parking lot of Peg Peregos.

In the sanctuary, children roamed the aisles, while the men and women whispered in their respective sections. They spent so much time at shul that they knew how to make themselves at home. The service was like a show they had seen before. They knew all the words. They knew exactly what would happen. Sometimes they paid attention. Other times the prayers became the background noise to their whispered conversations.

During the haftarah reading, some of the men left the sanctuary for the kiddush club. They gathered in the social hall, with plates of cookies borrowed from the kinder-congregation. They went from the words of the prophets to the sampling of single-malt scotches. In the social hall, a youth minyan screeched its way through the service. The teen minyan downstairs was next to the young couples' minyan, which had no upper age limit, so some couples never graduated to the main service upstairs. But even if they had wanted to, there wouldn't have been enough space. The congregation was bursting at the seams. All life-cycle events took place at once. In any given week, there was a bris and a bar mitzvah. A kiddush was sponsored in memory of one person's father, in honor of someone else's upcoming wedding. In three weeks, it would be the weekend of Baruch's wedding, and the shul would be filled with their guests. Baruch would be called up to the Torah, and after he recited the blessings, the congregation would shower him with candy. As the children scampered to collect it, everyone would sing, wishing him a sweet life, a happy marriage.

The Torahs were carried around the room as the congregation sang the Mizmor Le'dovid psalm. Naomi's mind had wandered, but this brought her attention back to the davening. No matter how many times they carried the Torahs around, Naomi always felt a renewed glimmer of pride. With their silver crowns on top, these parchment scrolls were vestiges of royalty. Only there weren't kings underneath these crowns but words.

As the Torah procession passed the women, a few of them sang out loud, but with the hope that no one would hear them. Most of them sang silently, lips moving but no sound emerging. Others whispered or looked off into the distance, watching the fashion parade of women coming in and going out. Were Naomi to really sing, her voice would soar above the rustles and whispers of the women's section. The words they were singing were so familiar that she rarely gave any thought to their meaning. This time though, she read from the English translation in her siddur: *The voice of God is upon the waters. The God of glory thunders. The voice of God breaks the cedars. The voice of God convulses the wilderness.* It came as a surprise that they sang this every week, so calmly, in such a matter-of-fact manner. Maybe the psalmist felt this power, but here, God's voice could barely shake them from their own thoughts. It couldn't break the somnolent feeling in the room. Naomi looked at the women around her. She had known many of them for years, through sisterhood luncheons and fund-raising projects. But now, as she looked at them, she longed to know what everyone was really thinking. She wondered what brought them back to shul each week, if they were really davening. She wanted to know what was inside them.

The procession of men and Torahs came to a stop in front of the open ark, and now they were singing Etz Chaim Hee. *It is a tree of life for those who grasp it. Its ways are pleasant and its paths are peaceful.* Trying to rouse herself, Naomi closed her eyes and imagined herself grasping onto this tree. She imagined herself embarking on a journey, following its pathways. When she opened her eyes again, the sunshine coming through the skylights was reflecting off the silver adornments of the Torah, sending rays of light into the women's section. They glinted off their jewelry and illuminated their faces. Naomi squinted, and in the brightness, the shul she stood in wasn't the same as it always was. The cantor's voice became ethereal. The whispering stopped. The children were still. The people she stood next to were transformed, and so was she. Suddenly, she could see inside them, to the quiet, hidden parts where they prayed. She could hear past the top layer of words being said, down to the silent, private wishes that were whispered or barely said at all. She heard the inner longings that accompanied the prescribed words. The air in the sanctuary was teeming with these wishes. The words had become real, and they were streaming out of their bodies.

Then Naomi blinked, the sun moved behind the clouds, and the light faded. It was shul like any other week. She looked around. Had anyone else felt what she had? Under the bedecked straw hats, was anyone else yearning? Everyone looked the same as they always did, and the feeling was passing. Trying to hold on to it, she sang louder and swayed. She realized that she wanted more from the laws she observed. She didn't want religion to be a garment she wore on the outside. She wanted the words of the prayers to be closely vested to her body, next to her skin.

Ilana came into the sanctuary and kissed her mother. She smiled at her mother's friends and opened her siddur to the right page. She was a master of quick switches. On the outside, she looked like she always did. On the inside, she thought about what she had imagined doing. The lights in the shul taunted her. She waited for them to single her out and expose her. She couldn't tell her mother what she was feeling. Her mother would stare at her in horror. Then she would call one of the family meetings with which she had been threatening them their whole lives. They had never actually had one, but she could just imagine how it would go. The conversation would begin with her mother saying, "We're not here to judge you, but we're worried about you." She'd probably have an appropriate book handy and give it to Ilana to read and discuss.

"I'm so glad you came," her mother murmured.

"It's not like I had a choice," Ilana said.

"I didn't force you to come," Naomi said.

"Yes, you did."

Naomi looked at her in surprise. "Why wouldn't you come?" she asked. "We go to shul every Shabbos."

"So? Just because we go every week isn't a good enough reason," Ilana said.

"Of course it is. It's Shabbos. It's what we do."

"That makes no sense," Ilana said, and was hushed by a woman behind her who, five minutes before, was talking nearly three decibels louder.

"What makes no sense?" Naomi asked.

"Forget it," Ilana said.

"Well, then I'm going to finish davening."

"Don't tell me you're getting religious on me too."

"I am religious," Naomi said.

"Mom," she protested. But hushed once again, she decided not to bother. She could fake it with the best of them. She would pretend to daven if it would make people happy: open her siddur, mumble, and bow. She watched her mother, who seemed unusually involved. Across the mechitzah, in the men's section, her brother was swaying with such fervor that she expected him to launch from his spot. It was lonely to be the only one not davening, and she took solace in watching her father, who was lost in his own thoughts. He stood merely in proximity to prayer. Ilana was the same. She could read the words, but they stayed rooted on the page. They didn't come to life for her; they didn't take flight.

Later that afternoon, Naomi, Joel, and Ilana sat together and read, all suffering from the same impatient Shabbos feeling. It was hard to heed God's word and rest. Thoughts of what they would do later that night, during the upcoming week, always encroached. As they checked their watches and calculated how many hours were left until Shabbos was over, Baruch came downstairs and stood awkwardly before them.

"Sit down," Naomi invited him, and moved over on the couch to make room. He sat next to her but still looked uncomfortable. Joel stopped reading long enough to say hello. Ilana didn't look up from her book.

Since lunch, Baruch had been in his room, taking a Shabbos nap. A few times, Naomi had thought about knocking on his door to see if he wanted to join them. Now she was happy that he had come down on his own. With her whole family together, Naomi wanted so much to talk. If only she found the right thing to say, the clamor of their disagreeing voices would subside and she would be able to hear their individual voices. Then those voices would come together and sing in unison. Naomi thought about telling them what she had felt in shul. She wondered if there was a way to explain what she had felt without having them think she was crazy. What would she say? I really felt something? I think I saw something, heard something? Skeptically, they would ask her what it was. And what would she answer—God? But maybe, she thought. Maybe it was.

"I have to be at shul soon," Baruch said. "I just came in to talk to you about something."

He folded his hands, then nervously unfolded them. He had waited to tell them for as long as he could. Now he had no choice. The wedding was a few weeks away. He and Tzippy were making plans to move to Memphis. But he didn't know how to begin. Even as he told himself he didn't care what his parents thought, he knew he still wanted their approval.

"Instead of going back to yeshiva, I'm planning to do something different," he said.

Joel sat up in surprise. A hopeful look passed across his face.

"Baruch, tell us," Naomi said. "What's going on?"

"Maybe I should have told you this before, but Herschel and I are planning to open a kosher food department in a grocery store in Memphis, Tennessee," Baruch said.

"Please tell me that you're joking," Joel said after Baruch gave them the details. He put his hands over his face, and shook his head.

"You're the one who says I need to support myself," Baruch said. "So you should be happy I'm not going back to yeshiva. I'm going into business."

"I am happy that you're not going back to yeshiva," Joel replied. "But don't kid yourself. You're not going into business. You're helping Herschel with a ridiculous idea."

"Why is it ridiculous? Herschel knows what he's doing. He's done this kind of thing before and he says that—"

"I'm not sure I'd listen to anything Herschel says," Joel said.

"Why? Just because you don't like him?" asked Baruch.

"Bryan, do you have any idea what the failure rate is for new restaurants?" Joel asked.

"What kind of restaurant is it going to be?" Naomi asked.

"Naomi, do *you* have any idea what the failure rate for new restaurants is?" Joel asked.

"The thing I give Herschel credit for is that he doesn't give up. He's always willing to try again," Naomi said.

"It's not even a restaurant," Ilana said. "Didn't you hear what he said? He's going to be working in a grocery store."

"What's wrong with working in a grocery store?" Baruch asked.

"Seventy percent of restaurants close in the first year alone," Joel said. "And that's for people who know what they're doing, professionals who have degrees in business and marketing, who've worked in restaurants and run them before."

"Anyway, it's not just about the food," Baruch said. "We're going to use it to bring people closer to Torah."

"I thought you were going to sell kosher meat," Naomi said.

"That's just our starting point. Eventually I'm going to give classes. We're going to teach people about keeping kosher, about being Jewish."

Joel laughed. "Let me understand this. You're going to sell someone a pound of chopped liver and the next thing you know, he's going to become religious?"

"What I'm doing is for the name of God," Baruch said.

"It's not for the name of God. It's for the name of Herschel," Joel said.

"It doesn't matter if you don't approve. I've already decided that this is what I'm doing," Baruch said. "Herschel found us an apartment in Memphis, and we're going to move down the week after the wedding."

"You've really lost it, haven't you?" Joel said. "You've really gone off the deep end this time."

"Why didn't you tell us sooner? Why didn't you discuss it with us?" Naomi asked.

Baruch stood up. "Why didn't I tell you? Why didn't I *discuss* it with you? Why do you think? Because every time I tell you what I want to do, every time I'm not exactly like you wish I was, you disapprove. You want me to be this person you have in your head. Well, it's not going to happen."

"I don't think that's true, Baruch," Naomi said. "But if you feel that way, then we need to talk about it."

"No, it is true, Naomi," Joel said. "I don't approve, and I'm not going to pretend I do. If you want to do something stupid, Bryan, go ahead. But don't expect me to cheer you on."

"Believe me, I don't. You'd only be happy for me if I wanted to be like you. What do you expect me to do? Work hard all day and not have time for anything besides a job I don't even care about?"

"Stop it," Naomi said. "Both of you, calm down."

"No, it's fine," Joel said to Naomi. "He's made it very obvious that he doesn't respect anyone who thinks differently than he does."

"What about you?" Baruch said. "You hate anyone who's more religious than you. You pretend it's about college and jobs and getting married too young. But the truth is, you hate seeing me believe in something so strongly, when you don't believe in anything."

His words hung between them. Naomi's first fleeting thought was to wonder if her son was right. And then, before she could consider the question, she was furious at Baruch for saying it. She was furious at him for all of this. Because how do you measure belief? Even if you could, who did he think he was? What gave him the right to judge?

"I'm going to mincha," Baruch said, and left the room. A few minutes later, Ilana did too. In the silence that followed their departures, Joel looked at Naomi.

"I hope you're happy," he said.

"Me?" she asked. "This isn't my fault."

"You're the one who said that he just needs time to find himself, that this was his 'journey' and we had to let him make it. Well, I guess this is where it ends. What did you think would happen if we never put our foot down? That he would come to his senses on his own? Well, apparently not," he said, and left the room as well.

Now she was furious at Joel too. The truce she had tried to hold in place had broken. With her family retreating to their own corners of the house, Naomi went into the backyard, filled with regret. No matter what she did to bring them together, her family insisted on pulling apart. She was glad she hadn't told them about her experience in shul. Even if she had found the words, they wouldn't have understood. They would have laughed and doubted and mocked it. And in the process, they would have ruined it for her. She would rather keep this feeling to herself, where at least it could remain intact. Naomi stayed outside, hoping for a recurrence of what she had felt before. It was a clear night, but instead of some uplifting sign from the universe, what she soon saw in the sky was three stars, the sign that Shabbos was over.

— FIFTEEN —

T HE WEDDING would never really happen. They would always be separated from it by increasingly smaller increments of weeks, days, and hours. They would live in a perpetual state of anticipation.

Until, to everyone's surprise, June 14 arrived. All the plans, once wishful dreams, had come into being and were now laid out on serving trays, draped across tables, entwined in the sisters' hair, carried in baskets and bouquets. Tzippy walked down the aisle slower than any bride in the history of the wedding hall. Shayna had made her promise to linger over each step. Tzippy practiced moving one foot forward, then slowly bringing the other foot to meet it. She was supposed to wait for a count of three before taking the next step. She was supposed to let it pass slowly, so that her whole life she could look back and savor every moment of this, her wedding.

With so much tulle, it was impossible to tell that Tzippy was moving her feet at all, just as it was impossible to tell that she had disobeyed her mother's most heartfelt pleas and, instead of white satin pumps, had worn white Keds sneakers tied with lace. Through the veil covering her face, Tzippy looked at the guests seated on either side of the aisle, at the flower-covered chuppah, at the photographer and videographers recording her every move. Everything was cast with an ethereal beauty. Her parents were on either side of her. Herschel smiled broadly and had to restrain his urge to wave. He felt like royalty; the guests were his subjects watching him pass by. Shayna had a smile on her face that wouldn't fade the entire evening. Until they had started down the aisle, she had been busy checking to make sure each detail was in place. She was giving last-minute instructions to the caterer and the photographer. But as soon as it was time to walk down the aisle, she stopped thinking about the details. She looped her arm through Tzippy's, and they set off.

Ilana had already hurried down the aisle, her face arranged into what she hoped would pass as a smile. The lavender bridesmaid dress was uncomfortable. It had long sleeves and lots of lace, and under the bright lights of the photographer, she felt way too hot. Zahava and Malky walked down the aisle together, using this as a chance to practice for their own weddings. Dena and Dassi were the flower girls, and so far, this was the greatest moment of their lives. With wreaths in their hair, sprinkling rose petals as they had practiced, they skipped down the aisle to the theme song from the Uncle Moishy Flying Kugel Eaters video.

Baruch had walked down the aisle accompanied by Naomi and Joel. Naomi wore a hat as a sign of respect, a small concession in exchange for family unity. Joel didn't wear a black hat, as a sign of defiance. He had decided that instead of arguing the point, he would simply do what he wanted. He was fairly certain that Shayna wouldn't chase him down the aisle, hat in hand. They left Baruch under the chuppah and moved to the side.

In his white kittel, Baruch swayed and recited tehillim. He tried to concentrate on God's presence, which rested under each wedding canopy. Decorated with flowers and greenery, the chuppah symbolized the house he and Tzippy would create. Like the tent of Abraham, it was open on all sides to allow guests to enter. But it was closed on top and had four pillars, to symbolize the permanence and ultimately the privacy of the home they would build.

The guests were reading this in the explanatory program that Naomi had insisted on. The guests from one side were trying to piece together the names and faces of the other side's wedding party. They were whispering about the dresses and admiring the flowers, whose budget greatly exceeded what had been agreed upon. The photographer was wishing they would hurry it up. The team of videographers had filmed thousands of weddings exactly like this one, and they felt as though they were watching reruns on television. Tzippy's married classmates were thanking God that it was finally her turn. The unmarried ones were reassuring themselves that Tzippy was already twenty-three. Even though she had married late, the end of the world hadn't yet come.

And Tzippy was still walking down the aisle. A bride had a direct line to God, and Tzippy had been told to pray for the sick and the unmarried, which she did. She had given her jewelry to the unmarried girls to hold for her, following the custom that all brides should be equal and unadorned. The single girls had begged to hold the pearl necklace and earrings, and most of all, the diamond ring. Like the bouquet thrown in another world, holding the jewelry was a sign that they would be next.

When Tzippy finally reached the chuppah, she circled Baruch seven times. With each revolution, she symbolically built the walls of their home and asserted the primacy of his role in her life now. With her seven circles, she also imitated God, who created the world in seven days. The rabbi then recited the first of the wedding blessings over a silver wine goblet filled with white wine. With these words, Tzippy was officially betrothed to Baruch. He took a sip of wine, and Tzippy's veil was lifted and she took a sip. Baruch and Tzippy swayed as if they were praying. They swayed and the rabbi swayed and soon their parents swayed too. The second set of blessings was recited, and they took another sip of wine. In Hebrew, Baruch said, "You are sanctified to me with this ring, according to the laws of Moses and Israel." He slid a gold ring onto Tzippy's finger, and they were married.

Seven other rabbis, chosen in an almost equal split between the two families, were called up to the chuppah to read, sing, chant, or mumble their appointed blessing. They blessed God who created the world and the human being. They praised Him for uniting man with woman, for creating happiness and joy, bride and groom, exultation, song, pleasure and delight. When they finished, Baruch stepped on the customary glass and broke it under his foot.

In the shattering of the glass, in the shouts of mazel tov and the keying up of the band, in the hugging and the wiping away of tears, the two families forgot about the fights and the anger. Joel didn't pay attention to the mysterious appearance of three extra members of the band. To his surprise, Naomi's assurance that it would be easier once Tzippy and Baruch were married held some truth. At least there was no more hope that they would change their minds. Naomi didn't try to run interference between Joel and Herschel. She was too busy trying to be in the moment. Shayna was too busy being congratulated on the beautiful wedding to notice that Dassi had walked down the aisle with a chocolate stain on her dress.

This was a wedding, and it was time to dance. After a few moments alone together, Tzippy and Baruch made their grand entrance into the banquet hall. To the sound of a deafening drum roll, with confetti and silly string flying in the air, underneath a row of crepe-covered arches and a barrage of outstretched arms, Tzippy was danced to her side of the room, Baruch to his.

On one side of the opaque curtain, decorated with potted plants, Joel danced with Baruch and hugged him. He found himself hand-in-hand with Baruch's rabbi. Herschel grabbed Joel in a hug, and Joel neither flinched nor pulled away. He was happier than he thought he would be, and drunk besides. The yeshiva boys knew when it was time to cut loose. They began with the yeshiva boy shuffle, and what they lacked in variety and footwork, they made up for in intensity. They had their arms around each other and stomped into the center. Soon these boys were kicking their legs and twirling, moving their hands through the air as if they were performing *Swan Lake*.

On the other side of the mechitzah, Tzippy stood in the center of the circle and pulled people in to dance. First she danced with Shayna, then with Naomi. She pulled her eager sisters and a reluctant Ilana into the center. Next she danced with Baruch's grandmother, his aunts, and his many cousins. She whirled around, still not believing she was the one in the middle. Soon, the order broke down, and Zahava danced with Naomi. Dena rode on Ilana's shoulders. Esther Leah clapped hands with Shayna, and they twirled and spun in front of Tzippy. Streamers waved, batons twirled. A maypole was brought out. Tzippy stood on a chair and held it while the girls danced the pastel ribbons around her. On the men's side, boys in clown costumes danced with rabbis. Yeshiva boys whizzed by on Rollerblades.

The dance floor was crowded, and the women accidentally spiked high heels into one another's feet. Circles formed and broke off and spawned new ones. Women in long sleeves and wigs who attended three weddings a week were dancing next to Joel's non-Jewish colleagues, who wore sleeveless cocktail dresses and had never before done a horah. They were holding hands with eleven-year-old cousins already dreaming of weddings. Concentric circles looped one way and then the other. They snaked in and out, some clockwise, some counterclockwise. From the sidelines, it looked like chaos. But from inside the circles, the intricate patterns they were dancing around the bride were evident. Inside the throng of people, Shayna found Tzippy and grabbed her hands. As they spun around, Tzippy dipped her head back, and a swirl of smiling faces, flowers, and tablecloths rushed by. She didn't want to stop. If she let go of her mother's hands, she wouldn't fall. She would keep spinning.

— SIXTEEN —

A THOUSAND MILES AWAY in Memphis, there was a hunger indeed. Month after month, it went unsated. The last kosher restaurant had closed two years before, and now, in this city sandwiched between Mississippi and Arkansas, there was nothing. One kosher establishment opened, then closed. Sometimes one opened and did well, so a second opened. And then they both closed. Until someone bravely ventured forth and opened another. And then it too closed.

The Jews of Memphis could tell their community's history through their restaurants. It began in the Pinch, the old Jewish neighborhood downtown. North Main Street was lined with dry-goods stores and pawnshops, and in the middle of them was Segal's Deli, the first kosher restaurant in the city. It eventually gave way to Rosen's Deli, then became Cooper's Deli, but they all served the same taste of the Old World.

The Jewish community grew and prospered. They left the Pinch and moved to bigger houses in Midtown. In the fifties, the city had had its heyday. For one consummate year, there was a kosher restaurant and four kosher butcher stores. In the seventies, they had The Fiddler on the Roof, which eventually gave way to The Posh Nosh, which gave way to a string of restaurants, none of which stayed open for more than a year. In the eighties, three pizza places opened and closed. The Jewish community was never big enough to sustain a kosher restaurant. But, still hoping, they tried Chinese food, then Middle Eastern food, then pizza once again.

And then there was nothing. They envied other cities where kosher

restaurants survived. They dreamed of New York as earlier generations did of Jerusalem. They made pilgrimages to the steakhouses, the
pizza places, the kosher Japanese and Thai restaurants. They read
restaurant reviews in *The Jewish Press* and planned vacations around
where they would eat. But this only temporarily sated their desire.
They knew that a community needed a restaurant if it was to be considered a viable place to live. In Memphis, they were proud. They had
built an elementary school, a fledgling high school. There were three
Orthodox shuls. Only a kosher restaurant eluded them.

The night before The Kosher Connection opened, Herschel couldn't
sleep. He and Shayna had been in Memphis all week, staying with
Tzippy and Baruch in their new apartment. Shayna was helping them
move in. Herschel was making last-minute preparations to get The
Kosher Connection up and running.

When it started to get light, Herschel quietly left the apartment. The
automatic doors to Kroger slid open, and from a long line of unused
grocery carts, he selected one. A grocery store was Herschel's idea of
heaven. It was open twenty-four hours, and in its cans and cartons, he
saw possibilities, packaged and ready to be opened. He dreamed of one
day when there would be no lines at the checkout, and everything would
be kosher. He'd walk up and down the aisles and never come to the end.

In Memphis, the grocery stores were huge. This one had a bank and
a florist. There were books and greeting cards. One day, maybe, it
would also carry clothing and electronics. There would be no need to
go anywhere else. In this city, there was more space than anyone knew
what to do with. There were wide streets and sidewalks, though no one
walked anywhere. The houses were big and inexpensive. In Brooklyn,
a small three-bedroom house. In Memphis, a mansion. In New York,
Herschel navigated his carts through crowded, narrow aisles. Here, he
spread out. He became as large as he felt.

He was getting close. He rounded the corner, past the bakery, past
the pharmacy and the dairy section. He had worked hard for this—so
many phone calls, so much finagling, so many promises—and now he
was almost there. He forced himself to slow down. Just before he
walked past the last freezer of vegetables, he abandoned his cart and
set forth unencumbered.

Herschel took one of his keys and raised the metal grating that sectioned off the back area. He flipped on the lights. A red neon sign overhead welcomed shoppers to The Kosher Connection. As the customers entered the space, they would pass from the world of Kroger to the world of kosher. Herschel had hung black-and-white photos of the Lower East Side to give the place an Old World feel. In honor of the grand opening, the walls were decorated with blue and white streamers. A banner loudly proclaimed: YES, WE ARE KOSHER! Signs advertised: DAILY SPECIALS. BUY ONE GET ONE FREE. ASK ME FOR A TASTE. An L-shaped, glass-fronted refrigerated-food case cut across the space. Inside, black ceramic dishes waited to be filled with whitefish salad, chopped liver, matzo balls, gefilte fish, and kugel. There were two white Formica tables and a few chairs. Along the walls were two shelves of hard-to-find kosher products specially imported from Brooklyn and Israel. In the back, the stockroom brimmed with cans of food. In the kitchen, pots large enough to bathe children hung overhead. Knives filled a butcher block. A Sub-Zero fridge was stocked and ready to go.

It was exactly as Herschel had seen in his dreams, and from here he could anticipate the future. The people would be drawn through the aisles of Kroger, to the back of the store. They would come, one by one, in groups of two or three, curiously, skeptically, in awe and in gratitude. Most of all, they would come hungry. An endless line of customers would stand in front of the counter. When one person was served, the line would remain just as long. Vats of chopped liver and trays of knishes would be dished out but never would be consumed. The walls would expand with every new person that entered. Herschel saw beyond these walls to Birmingham, Charleston, and Savannah, to a chain of Kosher Connections that would be fruitful and multiply and inhabit the earth.

— SEVENTEEN —

T HE CUSTOMERS CAME according to no logic Baruch could discern. There were either no customers or three at once, all of whom thought they were there first. Baruch tried to keep up. He waited on customers, supervised the chef, and made sure everything was one-hundred-percent kosher. He tried to scoop chopped liver with one hand while ringing up an order with the other.

"You're off to a good start," one of his customers said. "But do you know what you should serve? Pizza."

"Have you thought about adding a few green plants? You'd be amazed at how they'd brighten the place up," another customer said as she looked around.

Herschel had said that once things got under way, they would hire more counter help, maybe even an assistant manager under Baruch. He had assured Baruch that it would be easy. There would be long stretches with little to do. There would be plenty of time to learn. Baruch could eventually give Torah classes. He could offer a lunch-and-learn special. But on his first day without Herschel, Baruch realized that he had no idea what he was doing. He had never had a job before. His whole life had been school. He had graduated at the top of his high school class and gotten into Columbia. He had sat in front of the Talmud for five hours without losing his focus. But he couldn't work a cash register. He couldn't wait on customers without forgetting what they had ordered.

Nothing went smoothly. As Baruch struggled to fix one problem, another arose. The chef ran out of meat, and when Baruch called to check, the supplier claimed to have sent it two days before. The scale went haywire, and Baruch rang up a pound of chopped liver for five hundred dollars. He ran out of change. He dropped a matzo ball on the floor, and it rolled away to an inaccessible spot under the food server. Before turning to his next customer, he was thrown off by a phone ringing and a delivery arriving at the same time. It was Tzippy on the phone, and he assured her that he was fine. When he came back, a customer wanted to taste the chopped liver. She held up a sample to her nose and smelled it. She took a tiny bite and chewed slowly, not caring about the growing line behind her. All his customers were like that, oblivious to the fact that he had a hundred things to do. They asked him where he was from. They asked him for his life story. In Memphis, he was the only one in a hurry.

Baruch tried not to think beyond the immediate task in front of him. But voices of doubt assembled in his head. They said that it had been a mistake to come. He had given up college for yeshiva, and he had given up yeshiva for this. In yeshiva, he had tried to step past his physical needs. In yeshiva, the world of the spirit mattered above all else. In Kroger, he was at the epicenter of the physical world. The aisles were loaded with products people didn't really need. A hundred kinds of cookies, a thousand brands of cereal. It just tempted them into wanting more.

And it wasn't just any food; most of it was treif. The Kosher Connection was steps from the non-kosher meat counter. When Baruch walked in the front doors of Kroger each morning, a blinking neon sign advertising Boar's Head greeted him. The fish counter lay somewhere out there in the expanse of the store. There, lobsters swam lazily in a tank. Pink shrimp were laid out on ice, displayed like small jewels. When Baruch passed them on his way in each morning, he had to laugh. How the mighty had fallen. How far he was from who he had wanted to be.

"Can I taste the chopped liver?" his next customer asked.

"Can you make a hundred knishes for tomorrow?"

"What you should do," someone else said, "is have Chinese food."

"Kosher barbecue," his next customer proclaimed. "That's where it's at."

There wasn't a moment of rest. There were always three things he could be doing. And even if he did all those, he still wouldn't be able to keep up. In yeshiva, the boys lived with the fear of wasting time. They didn't play basketball; they didn't engage in idle conversation. They lived to the ticking of God's stopwatch and were loath to do anything but learn. But Baruch had no time to learn. There wasn't even time to think. He tried to review a page of Talmud in his mind while he worked. But every time he turned around, a customer approached and asked for chopped liver. Though they had begun the day with fifty pounds of it, they were almost out.

"Tomorrow," Baruch promised, and he sent them on their way, hoping that kugels and knishes would suffice.

And then, at last, there was a small moment of silence. There were no customers, no phone calls, no deliveries, not even the crackling voice of the store intercom. The grocery store had seemingly folded itself up and disappeared. His Talmud was stashed behind the counter, and Baruch pulled it out. He balanced the oversized volume on the scale, letting this replace the tabletop shtender he had used in the beis midrash. He scanned the words for where he had left off. At first he couldn't remember what was being discussed on the page, and he felt how long he had been away.

In yeshiva, he had begun his day by reviewing what he had learned the day before. His everyday thoughts had receded and the words on the page came to life. They expanded until there was no room in his head for anything else. Now he wanted to re-create this. He wanted to leave behind the clutter of mundane concerns. Previous generations had learned Torah no matter what was going on around them. They had shut out poverty and persecution. Surely he could close his eyes to the needs of his job. He stared into the page, and what soon became immediate were the words around him. *Rabban Gamliel said. Rabbeinu Tam disagreed.* A contradiction here. A proof text there. The words became so real he could almost hold them in his hand.

The service bell rang as if from another world. Baruch reluctantly closed his Talmud and went out front, expecting another customer, another demand.

"Surprise," Tzippy said.

She came in dripping with sweat. She had only walked from the parking lot, but this was Memphis in July. Every day they marveled at the heat. Whenever they walked outside, they were assaulted by it.

Tzippy reached for his hand, and instinctively Baruch pulled it away. She laughed, and so did he.

"I forgot," he confessed.

After being forbidden to touch for so long, it was hard to remember that now it was allowed. For Baruch, the world was divided into two categories, allowed and forbidden. With marriage, the two had changed places, but he hadn't yet become accustomed to it. He was so used to holding back his desire that he was shocked by every touch.

But God and the rabbis didn't deliver them freely into the land of the permitted. Their married lives were also divided into two: when they were allowed to touch, when they weren't. When Tzippy had her period, and for the week that followed, they weren't allowed to touch. Until she immersed herself in the mikvah, they were cast back into the land of the forbidden. The laws were even stricter than they had been before they were married. When they were forbidden to each other, they couldn't pass dishes between them. They couldn't sit on the same sofa cushion. They couldn't eat off the same plate. These laws were established by the rabbis, who understood something about the power of temptation.

The engaged boys prepared for the rules of marriage. They discussed menstrual blood and spotting on underwear. They referred to the female body, to her breasts, her thighs, to between her legs. But they used the Hebrew words, whose foreignness was enough to lessen their power. The words became disconnected from their meaning. Their class discussions proceeded as if they were talking about land to be surveyed, judgments to mete out, lost property to be returned. But now these theoretical scenarios had become actual touches, real-life quivers. The dry terms they had used in yeshiva had nothing to do with the soft skin of Tzippy's body. He wanted to touch her all the time. He marveled that he could. He also marveled that Tzippy felt the same way.

Now, he knew two Tzippys. There was the person who sat before him in her long skirt and buttoned-up shirt. Even in the sweltering Memphis heat, she wore these modest clothes. Now she also wore her wig, and even though it looked natural, he knew it was there. But there was also another Tzippy whom he was just getting to know. This one coyly suggested that it was time to turn in for the night. This one surprised him with black lace bras and tiny underwear. She told him that all the religious girls wore these. Boro Park was filled with underground lingerie shops, the chaste nightgowns up front, the racy lingerie hidden in boxes in the back. Underneath all those long skirts were string bikinis and see-through thongs. Inside every long-sleeved blouse was red or black or magenta lace.

Baruch took Tzippy's hand. My wife, he thought. He loved the way it sounded. When he looked at her, he could see his future. They would build a home together and fill it with children. Their lives would have purpose. He could finally relax. He didn't feel the need to defend who he had become. By marrying Tzippy, he had staked his claim. Marriage was the true coming-of-age in the community. It didn't matter that he was only twenty-one. Now, he was a married man.

He felt like a child only when he talked to his parents. He watched what he said, afraid that if he told them how hard the job was, they would say that they had been right. So he told them he loved Memphis. He loved the work. He had plenty of time to learn. To his surprise, they took what he said as a given. Since the wedding, there had been a quiet sort of acceptance. They no longer tried to change him. His mother carried on about what a good job he must be doing, how proud of himself he must feel. Then she tried to get Joel on the phone. More often than not, her attempts were unsuccessful. She came back to report that Joel was in the middle of something but sent his love.

When they did talk, each conversation between Baruch and Joel was a competition over who could say less. There were long silences and one-word answers, until one of them finally claimed to need to hang up. At the wedding, his father had been caught up in the moment. He had hugged him as they danced, and Baruch had thought that maybe they could once again be close. But the moment passed and left silence in its place. Their fights, however fraught, had kept them connected. Now there was nothing to talk about. Over the phone, there were so many ways to hide.

Baruch brought Tzippy a plate of food, and she perched on a stool behind the counter and talked to him as he worked. He speared bits of knish and meatballs with toothpicks and fed them to her.

"Why don't y'all have a taste?" he asked her in the Southern accent he was working to perfect.

"Why, thank you, honey, I think I will," she said in her own version.

Baruch circled his arms around Tzippy's waist. "Not bad," he said. "You sound just like them."

"Good. Because I love it here."

"Do you?" he asked.

"Except for the heat," she said, "I really do."

The farther they were from her family, the happier Tzippy seemed. He liked to see her this way. He didn't tell her that he had spent the day wishing they had never come to Memphis. He didn't want to dampen her enthusiasm. Instead, Baruch got back to work. It was almost time to close for the night. He put away the food and began to think about the next day. He had to make sure there was enough meat defrosted. He had to look over the supplies and fill out order forms.

"I'm sorry," he said after an hour. "It's taking longer than I thought."

"So I'll wait," she said.

An hour later, he was still working. "You should go home," he said to Tzippy.

"You can't leave it?"

"I wish. But it will only make tomorrow harder."

"It's going to be fine," she reassured him.

"Are you sure?"

"Of course I'm sure," she said. She kissed him good-bye, and as she walked away, he looked longingly after her. There again was that long pleated skirt that concealed so much.

When Baruch finally came home, Tzippy was lying in bed. "You know what I see when I close my eyes?" he asked, shaking his head as if this would rid it of its contents. "I see food."

"Come," she said. "Lie down."

Baruch lay next to her, and Tzippy pulled the blankets over their heads, making a tent.

"Hi," she whispered.

Their faces were so close that it was hard to see him. She still couldn't believe they were allowed to lie here together. They had been married for six weeks, and sometimes, when she first woke up, she forgot where she was. Then she remembered, and she felt the novelty of being married all over again.

When she closed her eyes, she could see the wedding. Despite all her protestations beforehand, she had loved being the bride. She had barely seen Baruch for most of the wedding. They were separated by the mechitzah that cut across the room. But after she danced with the women on their half of the hall, the men came over in a swarm. Tzippy sat on a chair and they lifted her high over their heads. A multitude of arms carried her to the other side. As she crossed over, the room was transformed from shiny, colorful satins, glittering necklaces, and clutch purses into a sea of black suits. Her dress was blindingly white against this backdrop. Baruch was lifted high on another chair. Some-one handed him a white dinner napkin, and he held one end of it toward her. She took hold of the other end of the napkin, and they were joined together, high over the heads of this crowd.

When the wedding ended, they had shyly put their arms around each other's waists. They said good-bye to their families and left the hall. They went to the Brooklyn Marriott Hotel and passed through the lobby where Tzippy had suffered one bad date after another. She remembered how she had felt then, her urge to run away. This time she wanted to be exactly where she was. She walked proudly past the few lucky dates that had lingered late, and she and her husband went upstairs.

Now they were allowed to go into a room together and close the door. They could stand as close to each other as they wanted. His face was close to hers, and she didn't have to pull away. He pressed his cheek against hers. She ran her hands across his face. He laced his hands through her hair. She lay her head against his chest. Each time they touched, they looked surprised. Even though they had waited for this, they had never really thought it would be allowed. Their lips met, lightly, quickly, sweetly. Then he really kissed her, and she gasped. All those months of waiting were released in that gasp. She became aware of all the parts of her body: her back, which arched and leaned toward him; the tips of her fingers and the soles of her feet, which tingled and burned. Her whole body was lit with small flashes of feeling.

This feeling, she realized, was the source of the mystified look that lay behind her newly married friends' eyes. They never said a word about it, but days after their weddings, they had always seemed so much older, separated from their unmarried friends by years. But she didn't want to think about them now, just as she didn't want to think about the wedding and all the guests. If she opened her mind and let them in, all five hundred guests might be assembled around their bed. She wanted to be right where she was. She wanted to allow this mystery to unfold.

The bodice of Tzippy's wedding dress was satin and fitted, and it came to a sharp V at the waist. The skirt had layers of tulle. Baruch fumbled with a lace-covered button, a hundred of which lined the back of her dress. "There's a zipper," she whispered in his ear. He found it hiding underneath the faux buttons and undid it, his hands trembling. Hers were too, but she wrapped them around him and steadied herself. He worked her shoulders out of the dress and then it slid off her. She stepped out of it, suddenly not shy or afraid. She stood before him, in her lacy wedding bra and underwear, the tulle of her dress in a shimmering white heap on the floor.

Shyly, slowly, with embarrassed laughter and fear, with awkward glances, they undressed each other and lay back on the bed, he on top of her. Scared and excited and wondering what it was they were supposed to do next, they kissed again. Their hands explored, making small forays into previously forbidden territory. Then they both opened their eyes and they were face-to-face. They stared into each other's eyes, which were now so close that they could barely see anything. Without clothes and the usual distance between them, he looked so different. Unable to believe that they were doing this, she didn't know who he was, or who she was underneath him. But then they started to laugh. He cupped his hands around her face and whispered her name. She whispered his name back at him, and with the glint in their eyes, in the bareness of their skin, they found each other.

Later, Tzippy fell asleep with the shock that it had happened at all. Gazing at her husband, she wondered if maybe they had dreamed it. Maybe they had just wished it. The wedding was followed by a week of sheva brachos. They shuttled back and forth between Brooklyn and New Jersey, each night a different dinner party, a different outfit. She wore her brand-new suits and her wig, as different sets of relatives and friends wished her mazel tov and kissed her on the cheek. And all the while, surrounded by so many people, she returned to the private moments between them. In her mind, she still lay in a tangle of sheets, under the crush of his body, in the circle of his arms around her.

When the week ended, they moved to Memphis. Herschel and Baruch spent all day at Kroger, and she and her mother bought furniture and set up the apartment. Using whatever energy she had left from planning the wedding, Shayna made sure that the marriage house was set up perfectly. She was still on a high, and she beamed at everything Baruch and Tzippy said. In this afterglow, it was hard for Tzippy to be angry with her mother. And it was only for a week. She had the rest of her life ahead of her. When her parents left, she closed the door behind them. She locked it just to be sure.

In Memphis, everything was new. This is the first time I am making dinner as a married woman, Tzippy thought. This is the first time I am doing the laundry, the first time I am buying groceries. Her whole life was a series of firsts. Their apartment was a small one-bedroom, but it was theirs. Tzippy unpacked, and each book she put on a shelf, each picture hung on a wall, cemented the fact that this was real. In case she forgot, proofs of the wedding pictures smiled back from every free surface in every room. The apartment glowed with their newlywed status. They hadn't finished unpacking and already the apartment was a wedding present showcase: eight silver kiddush cups, five challah boards, eleven challah covers, seventeen spice boxes. Boxes of bubble-wrapped china awaited her.

"I've never seen so many pounds of chopped liver. Imagine opening a refrigerator and there's nothing but vats of it," Baruch said now, in their bedroom.

Tzippy didn't want to hear about chopped liver, and she pulled the blankets more tightly over them.

"It's like everyone woke up today and decided they had to have chopped liver," he said. "One woman made me promise I'd put aside a few pounds of it just for her. And then, someone else called to place a special order for twenty-five pounds of it."

Tzippy let go of the blankets. "What is someone going to do with twenty-five pounds of chopped liver?"

"I have no idea. I didn't get a chance to ask. But I'm telling you, people are ordering it. Someone called from Hot Springs, Arkansas, to see if we could deliver it for a bar mitzvah." He closed his eyes again. "I'm afraid I'm going to dream about it."

Tzippy laughed.

"What's so funny?" Baruch asked.

"You," she said. "It's just funny to hear you talking about this."

She expected him to laugh too, but he couldn't. Alone with her, he couldn't hold back what he was feeling.

"I don't know what I'm doing," Baruch confessed. "I didn't want to say anything, but today was horrible. Every time I turned around, something else went wrong. And it's all I have time for. I've barely learned since we've been here."

She saw on his face not just exhaustion but fear. When Baruch first mentioned the idea of coming to Memphis, she hadn't thought it would really happen. When, to her surprise, it began to work out, she had been thrilled. She had only been able to survive the final few weeks in her parents' house by reminding herself of how far away she would soon be. Every time her mother wanted too much, every time her sisters screamed and danced circles around her, she imagined the calm, quiet place that awaited her.

Tzippy's mind worked quickly. She came up with the only solution she could think of.

"Call my father," she said. "If you ask him to come back down and help, he will."

Baruch looked relieved as soon as she suggested it. "Maybe he could come for one more week, until I feel more comfortable," he said. "I'm sure it will get better. It has to, I guess." He closed his eyes and rubbed his temples, starting to relax. "But this obsession with the chopped liver is something else. I'm telling you, I've never seen anything like it."

"Okay, enough with the chopped liver," Tzippy said. She put her finger to his lips and pulled him close.

— EIGHTEEN —

The WEDDING VIDEO, all seven hours of it, played in a continuous loop on the VCR, and Shayna couldn't pull herself away. The television had emerged from its hiding spot in the bedroom armoire and now occupied center stage in the living room. The first time Shayna watched the video, she had tried to take in the whole wedding at once. Then she watched it repeatedly, each time with a specific focus. She tried to gauge from Naomi's facial expressions what she thought of the flowers, the food, and the music. She caught the single frame when each of her daughters' hairdos had tumbled down from their elaborately twisted edifices. She knew when, exactly, chocolate sauce had spilled on each lavender dress. She looked to see which of her friends had danced the whole time. She wanted to see who ate what, who talked to whom, who left early. She wished the videographers had miked her guests so she could hear their every reaction.

Barely two months had passed since the night when her guests had worn beaded gowns and strolled through the tables of the smorgasbord. The women whose friendship she had always longed for carried rhinestone-crusted Judith Leiber bags and sampled the feast she had laid before them. At the reception that preceded the ceremony, they circled Tzippy on her white wicker throne and exclaimed how beautiful she was. When they leaned over to kiss her, they left the actual kiss floating in the air so as not to stain this vision before them. When it was time to begin the ceremony, the men danced to where Tzippy sat, and Baruch lowered the veil over Tzippy's face. A few tears had glistened down her daughter's cheeks, but Shayna kept her smile in place.

Her makeup was perfect, and she was not going to ruin it by crying. She stared at Tzippy in her gown, under the veil, and sucked in her breath. She would never again in her life see as beautiful a sight.

At the end of the evening, as the tables were undressed, the leftover food packed away, the orchestra disassembled, Shayna held her head back and cast her eyes upward at the mirrored ceiling, where the bouquets of long-stemmed white roses were reflected back at her. They hovered overhead, like flecks of white light. If they came loose, they would float down into her outstretched palms. She wanted to grab hold of them. She wanted to live inside this moment when she hadn't just belonged in this world; it had been hers.

"Did I tell you about the meat slicer I'm going to order?" Herschel asked Shayna as he walked into the living room.

"Not now. I'm trying to watch," she said.

He ignored her request for silence. "The thing to remember is that you can't fall behind on equipment if you're planning to grow."

She hushed him again.

Herschel glanced at the TV. "How many times can you watch this?" he asked.

He stood up and paced the living room, cutting in front of the television. Since they had come home from Memphis, he hadn't stopped talking about The Kosher Connection. He carried on about how much he had loved Memphis. If it were up to him, they would pack up and move there right now. For Shayna, there was only one piece of Memphis that mattered, and that was the marriage house, the apartment where her daughter lived.

Shayna had loved being there. She had helped Tzippy pick out the furniture. She had helped her go through all the wedding presents. With bated breath, she undid the wrapping paper, moved aside the white tissue paper, and pulled out a crystal vase, a bone-china place setting. She displayed them on the countertops. She lined up the silver in the new breakfront. With new flatware, new pots, new sheets, and new tablecloths, it really was possible to start life over again.

When Shayna was inside the apartment, it hadn't mattered where it was. But then she stepped outside and couldn't understand why her daughter was in Memphis. There was the heat, the small size of the

Jewish community. There were no familiar stores and, Herschel's plan notwithstanding, there was nowhere to eat out. What bothered her most, though, was that it was so far from Brooklyn. It was like living in exile. Tzippy didn't mind. She loved Memphis. She talked about how pretty it was, how much open space there was. But who needed that? What was the point of having eighteen china place settings and the right silver kiddush cups if no one was there to see them? Instead of open space, Shayna wanted a crowd of people who would peer into Tzippy's apartment and approve. She wished she could pick up the apartment and move it intact to her cramped backyard, where Tzippy could continue to live with Baruch. She could have her own life, but it could be in view of Shayna's back windows.

On the video, she watched as Tzippy and Baruch were, once again, married. As they were danced back down the aisle, Shayna caught the unmistakable signs of happiness on Tzippy's face. Seeing that now made Shayna want to talk to her. She wanted to ask if she remembered that exact moment.

Before Shayna could pick up the phone, it rang, and she knew it was Tzippy. She was connected to her daughter, no matter how far away she lived. She paused the video and went to answer it. But Herschel grabbed the phone before she could.

"Baruch, how's it going?" he asked.

She waited for him to hand her the phone. She imagined Tzippy standing next to Baruch, urging him to finish up so she could talk. But Herschel began to pace again, faster this time. He talked just as fast, his hands gesturing back and forth. After a few more minutes, he hung up and stood before her, ebullient.

"They need me down there," he announced.

Shayna looked away from Herschel, back to the television screen, where she and Tzippy were dancing together in the center of a circle of women. With the remote control, Shayna alternately pushed Pause and Play, letting this moment of the two of them last. Only this way could she have all she wanted of her daughter the bride.

— NINETEEN —

Herschel stood behind the counter, wearing a University of Memphis baseball cap and a white apron over his dress shirt and pants. He reveled in wearing plastic gloves meant for food service.

"You didn't think I'd abandon you, did you?" Herschel said. "Of course I was going to come back. I needed to do a factory inspection anyway, outside of St. Louis, so technically I was in the neighborhood."

It didn't matter what Herschel said or did. Baruch was just glad he was there. It hadn't gotten better. He still had more customers than he could handle. They all wanted to be served at once, and all thought they were in charge. After a few weeks, they expected him to know all their names and who they were related to. If he tried to hurry one of them up, they smiled with their mouths, but shot him reproachful looks with their eyes.

"First things first," Herschel said, and pulled from his bag a matching University of Memphis baseball cap. "You have to look the part."

Baruch put it on his head. "Very good," Herschel pronounced. "Next you have to smile. You'll see, Baruch. Once you get the hang of it, it's a piece of cake."

Baruch wanted to believe that. With Herschel there, it felt possible. He made it look easy. He always knew what to say. By the end of the week, he knew the names of anyone who had ever lived in Memphis. He was on a first-name basis with everyone who worked at Kroger. He wandered through the store striking up conversations. In the kitchen, he peeked inside bubbling pots. He dipped his finger into pans and licked them.

The customers sat at tables and asked Herschel how he had gotten into the business. He came out from behind the counter and told them about his father. He said that they were using his recipes from the old country, brought over in his memory and recorded the second he stepped off the boat. He asked them how their families had ended up in Memphis. He claimed that he had reason to believe that a distant cousin of his had once lived here too.

The investors and their wives came by, as they had every day. Baruch had grown flustered under their entitled, scrutinizing gazes. Herschel served them first, and gave them a discount and a double portion. He wiped off the table for them if they wanted to stay and eat their dinner. They, in turn, told him what to do. They offered decorating tips and menu suggestions. Herschel nodded at everything they said, and he promised to look into it, first thing in the morning. He gave them a tour of the kitchen. He showed them the top-of-the-line knives, the scratch-proof countertops, and the brand-new super-size refrigerator. He told them that they were doing well but were still coming up a little short. They conferred privately with one another and agreed to give him another round of money, because the food was good and the community was excited.

When Baruch waited on customers, he prayed they wouldn't order anything complicated. His goal was to make it through a transaction without making a mistake. Feeling Herschel watching him made him even more nervous. Baruch waited on a customer, and when all she wanted was some ground beef, he was relieved.

"One pound of ground beef? That's it?" Herschel asked.

"That was all she wanted."

"No, that's all she *thought* she wanted. Your job is to convince her she wants more. Watch me," Herschel said, and went out front.

Three customers were standing there, waiting for someone to help them.

"What can I do for you?" Herschel greeted the first customer. Before Baruch knew what had happened, Herschel was holding out a bit of chopped liver on the edge of a fork. "You've got to taste this," he said to the customers. "It's delicious."

Having convinced them, Herschel instructed Baruch to dish out two pounds of chopped liver for both of these lovely ladies and to throw in a few knishes on the house.

"Come on, Baruch," Herschel said when he came back into the kitchen. "You have to be able to see it. You have to believe. I know it's been a long day and you're tired. But trust me, Baruch, it's going to take off, and you're going to be part of it. In two weeks, you'll be a pro and you won't even remember that you felt this way. In another month, you'll be running this place during the day and teaching classes here at night. What do you think? You could line up the chairs over there, serve them supper, and teach Torah for dessert."

Baruch looked at Herschel skeptically. With all the hard work he had put in, he had forgotten about his idea of teaching. He no longer thought about elevating the physical to the level of the spiritual. He couldn't imagine preparing classes, let alone getting anyone to sit and listen to them. With so much to do in the here and now, who had time to think of anything beyond?

Behind the counter, Tzippy and Baruch stole moments together. In the storeroom and in the kitchen, they held hands and whispered. But with Herschel here, it was harder to find these moments. He always had something new to show them.

Before they moved to Memphis, Tzippy had insisted that The Kosher Connection would belong only to Baruch. But once they were there, she came by every day and helped out. There was a never-ending list of things to do. Most of it would never have occurred to Herschel or Baruch. She hung a giant chalkboard and wrote out the specials of the day. She bought tablecloths and organized the plastic silverware that cluttered the top of the counter. She added green plants and limited the number of salamis Herschel was allowed to hang overhead.

"Come on, lovebirds," Herschel called to them. "We've got work to do."

"What do you think this is going to be about?" Tzippy whispered and giggled.

"Shhh," Baruch said, but he laughed too.

Reluctantly, they pulled apart as Herschel came into the kitchen to find them.

"There you are," he said. "I have a great idea."

Herschel was thinking about the chopped liver. It was still their biggest seller, and he wanted to package it and ship it worldwide. He was considering dry ice and FedEx. He wanted to show Baruch the business proposal he had written. He wanted Tzippy to write up a brochure. He wondered if she could design the packaging.

"One thing at a time," Tzippy said, and showed him the menus she had redone.

"They're fantastic. You're a natural," Herschel said. "It's in your blood."

When Tzippy was little, she had sometimes woken up in the middle of the night and gone downstairs to find her father sitting alone at the dining-room table. He had a notepad in front of him and was staring intently just beyond where he was sitting. When she joined him—she in her nightgown, he still in his work clothes—he put his arm around her and told her that the ideas were out there. It was just a matter of knowing how to see them.

She had once wanted to work with him. She wanted to help him think of ideas and figure out how to bring them into being. Herschel had listened to her suggestions and nodded enthusiastically. He had bragged to his friends of the good head she had on her shoulders. But once she was old enough to start thinking about marriage, he had handed her over to her mother. Now, in Memphis, he showed her off to the customers who came by. He told them that he and Baruch were just following her orders. She was the one quietly running the place.

The women in the community gazed adoringly at Tzippy. They hoped that the presence of a new young couple would help revitalize the community. This was their constant goal, their eternal dream. They invited Tzippy and Baruch for Shabbos meals. They wanted Tzippy to join their committees, their various sisterhoods. Most of the women were her mother's age and looked at her as a daughter. The women who were closer to her age were busy with their children. They came to the counter, ordering food while rocking a baby. Sometimes, these women of Memphis seemed like they could inhabit the homes in her Brooklyn neighborhood. Some of them had the same skirts and the same wigs. They were the Memphis versions of her mother, of her friends from home. But they also came in greater varieties. Some of them wore shorts and tank tops and still ordered kosher meat.

Tzippy accepted their Shabbos invitations. She talked to the women when they came to shop. She was happy for their friendship and for making her and Baruch feel welcome. But she didn't want to become one of them. At home, she had always been surrounded by people. Her mother crowded guests around the Shabbos table, afraid to leave any space empty. She wanted to know who Tzippy was friends with. She was always counting them, keeping track. If on Shabbos afternoon Tzippy wanted to read alone in her room, her mother admonished her for her anti-social behavior and shooed her outside, to a friend's house. But now Tzippy was happy to be alone. To live in a new city, in her own apartment, with her husband—this was all she wanted.

Crates of cabbage and broccoli, leaves of spinach and lettuce, were stacked and waiting. In addition to managing the business, Baruch had to make sure everything was one-hundred-percent kosher. He had to rinse the vegetables and check for bugs. He soaked each leaf or floret and held it to the light.

Baruch stood over a tub of broccoli that presumably had been triple-washed and inspected. Some of it had already been cooked into kugels. But now, he saw something. He held it up to the light until he was sure. Crawling on a leaf was a tiny green bug. Herschel came in and stood next to him. Baruch didn't say anything. He just pointed.

"You know what to do," Herschel said, and put his arm around Baruch.

It was true. With a question about kosher, Baruch was in his element. It was the word of God, and it was at play in this kitchen. Baruch had pored over the texts that discussed every aspect of keeping kosher. He had spent months learning every variant opinion. He knew the majority views and the minority ones. In yeshiva, they had traced the evolution of every law and followed it to its practical application. They talked about fire-burning stoves and clay pots, vats of meat and drops of milk. They dissected the differences between glass and metal, hot and cold, and they did all this far away from an actual kitchen. The kitchen was no more real to them than the slaughterhouse, the planting fields, the bathhouse, the marketplace, the Holy Temple. But now, for Baruch, it had become real. One bug in the broccoli, and he had the chance to make a practical difference. He realized that he hadn't abandoned what he had learned. He was just looking from a different vantage point.

— TWENTY —

TZIPPY WOKE UP ALONE. She rolled over in bed, flung out her arms, and stretched. Now that her father was back in New York, the apartment felt bigger. The days felt wide open, the possibilities endless.

She was supposed to be figuring out what she wanted to do in Memphis. She was supposed to be looking for a job as a nursery school teacher. But she was enjoying her freedom too much. She couldn't remember a time when she wasn't doing two things at once. Her Saturday nights had been a string of steady baby-sitting jobs. She spent her summers as a counselor at a local day camp, pulling toddlers in and out of swim diapers all day. She had chased her sisters and fed and bathed them. She had learned not to want for herself, not to say no, not to be selfish.

But now she was allowed to slip out of this role. The rules had changed, the obligations lifted. Being married took up nowhere near as much energy as worrying that she would remain single forever. And that gave her rare extra time. She knew, though, that it wouldn't last. She would be called back to her regularly scheduled life soon enough. Pregnancy dangled like an ever-present possibility. The news from her married friends centered around who was having another baby. Adulthood came upon them so quickly, and there was no time to think about anything. Their lives were a cycle of pregnancies, births, and the fleeting time in between. For some of them, there was a wedding-night conception; for others, a few months' reprieve. When they were engaged, she and Baruch had imagined their house filled with children. She had assumed she would have kids right away. She wasn't yet pregnant, but it was too soon to be worried. She was having too much fun to be disappointed. For the time being, she didn't have to think about anyone but herself.

In Memphis, Tzippy loved to drive. In New York, she had been afraid. She had driven only in order to get her license and then never again. When she was a child, her recurring nightmare was that she was in the front seat of a car with her mom, her sisters loaded in the backseat. Then, with no warning, her mother disappeared from the driver's seat, and she would have to drive home to the sound of the girls' screaming. But here the traffic was usually light, and the other drivers were polite. You go, they motioned at four-way stop signs. No, you go, they waved to one another.

Tzippy turned on the radio and drove down Poplar Avenue, which took her from one end of the city to the other. The crowds and congestion of Brooklyn gave way to wide tree-lined streets, with sprawling houses. The lawns were green and lush. Sprinklers ticked circles of water all day. There was no hustle and bustle, no need to rush. There were never any people on the street. There were no children, no pedestrians. Only occasionally did she catch a glimpse of someone getting out of a car and disappearing behind the doors of one of the houses.

As she drove toward downtown, she passed strip malls and cathedral-size churches, one on every block. In Brooklyn, kosher stores and shuls were on every corner. Here, the white steeples that cut across the skyline made her feel even farther away. When she came to the Mississippi River and the M-shaped bridge that spanned it, she wanted to press the accelerator and fly across. It didn't matter that she would end up in Arkansas. That seemed as far away as another country, a different world.

Instead, she ended up at the library. On a day alone, in a city where she knew almost no one, when she had nowhere she needed to be, she walked in and shed the need to look over her shoulder. She felt the pleasure of no one watching her. Before she was old enough to worry about getting married, she had loved to read. The girls were allowed to read certain books, ones that had been carefully screened for anything objectionable or questionable. Because if they didn't read, they couldn't wonder. If they didn't see, they wouldn't know. Her mother had encouraged her to read the Orthodox equivalents of secular books, as many of her friends did. Instead of *Nancy Drew and the Haunted Lighthouse,* her friends read *Devorah Doresh and the Mystery of the Missing Tallis.* They read of the adventures of Beis Yaakov girls, who did good deeds and were always happy.

But Tzippy had hated these books. She didn't want to read about places she already knew. She read *Ann of Green Gables* and *Rebecca* and *Little House on the Prairie,* wanting to leave herself behind at the first page. But she had marveled at how much she had in common with them. In these girls who kept house, she found pieces of herself. When she finished with them, she moved on to *Sweet Valley High.* There, the world of boys and girls was so foreign she could have been reading about another species. She read these books secretly, under her covers. She hadn't envied the characters their proms or their football games. She hadn't wanted this life for herself. But she had wanted to know about it. She had imagined that the small window in her room would open and let her go visiting. She could travel in her nightgown, the edges of it trailing behind her as her books carried her farther from home.

Flush with the freedom that she could do whatever she wanted, Tzippy wandered the aisles of books. The library was huge, filled with cavernous spaces where she could wander. She wanted to read her way through the building. She wanted to consume everything in sight. She pulled a volume of fairy tales off the shelf and sat on the floor, her skirt folded over her legs. These were the stories her mother had once told her, changing the names of the characters to Jewish ones, reshaping and recasting the scenarios so they fit more smoothly into their world.

In Shayna's version, Cinderella hoped to marry the rabbi's son. It was a small leather prayer book she left behind. Wise, loving parents secluded young girls in towers for their own safety. They had kosher food delivered to them, and they were happy and content. The twelve dancing princesses who were locked in their room at night still awoke with their dancing shoes tattered and torn. But that was just a test of their father's faith in them. Usually they slept soundly. The only time they ever snuck out of their rooms was to visit the sick and to dance at the weddings of poor orphan girls. But now Tzippy saw that it wasn't as her mother had said at all. Her mother's protective veneer fell away, and the stories became so much more interesting. Tzippy understood now why the princesses' shoes were tattered each morning. She happily followed them out the secret passageway from their room, through a forest, to a palace where they danced with princes all night long.

Tzippy moved from fairy tales to novels. She went back to the library every day, and the world around her widened. She pored over travel books. In the huge reading room, silent except for the sound of pages turning, she saw the sculpted cathedrals of Tuscany, the canals of Venice, the châteaus of France. She took walking tours around Paris. She turned right at the Louvre and wished she could go inside and spend days there. She strolled through the Luxembourg Gardens. In coffee-table art books, she turned pages of water lilies and Degas dancers. She sucked in her breath at the beauty of light blue bows tied against feathery white ballet skirts.

Tzippy carried her books home with her. When Baruch came home at night, she was subsumed in them. She didn't look up as he closed the front door. He watched her and waited to see how long it would take her to realize he was there. After two pages, she finally looked up at him and blinked, letting their apartment slowly come back into focus.

"How long have you been standing there?" she asked.

"All day," he teased.

She put her book away and they sat down to dinner. She rarely cooked. Usually Baruch brought home the day's leftovers. She had always listened to her mother's friends trading ideas for supper. When Tzippy and her friends had imagined being married, they had thought that serving dinner would be one of the highlights of the day. They imagined the romance of placing gourmet meals before their husbands every night. But takeout was fine with Tzippy. It gave her more time.

She and Baruch sat across from each other. He told her the stories of the day, entertaining her with who said what, who did what, and how he handled it. He had finally gotten the hang of it. He said that he wasn't really the manager. His customers were the ones running the place, and once he accepted that, he was fine. He asked for their suggestions. He hung a request list where they could write down hard-to-find kosher products they wanted to have ordered from New York. He promised the mother of a certain three-year-old that he would find out if anyone, anywhere, made a kosher goldfish cracker.

"Sometimes I know what they're going to order before they open their mouths," Baruch said. "I could ring them up when I see them coming. But that's not how they do it here. They don't just come to shop. They come to talk. They want to tell me their life stories and only then will they tell me what they want to eat."

"So what do you do?" Tzippy asked.

Baruch laughed. "I listen. It's fun."

"What happened?" she asked. "It sounds like you're enjoying it."

"You know what? You're right. I am," he said.

If she were in Brooklyn, she would be expected to be concerned that he worked all day and had little time to learn. Her friends probably still sat around their kitchen tables and bragged about whose husband learned the most. She would have to sit quietly, hiding her shame that her husband barely put in an hour a day. But she had stopped calling her friends regularly. She blamed it on being busy, but the truth was, she didn't want to know what they thought. In Memphis, she could think whatever she wanted. The idea of a list of what she wanted in a husband—a learner always put first—was far away.

They ate and then they read. They faced each other on opposite ends of the couch. Tzippy sank back into her book. Baruch read *Restaurant Today*. The phone rang, but neither of them moved.

"Do you want to get it?" she asked.

"No. Do you?"

The answering machine came on, and Shayna's voice entered the living room.

"I knew it was her," Tzippy said. "I always know, just by the way it rings."

Her mother's words were muffled, but Tzippy could hear her willing them to admit they were home. Her family called daily, sometimes hourly. If it wasn't her mother, then it was one of her sisters.

"I have an idea," Tzippy said when it was quiet again. "We could open our own restaurant here. Just the two of us."

He laughed in surprise.

"Why not?" she asked. "We can do whatever we want."

"What about The Kosher Connection?" he asked.

"I don't mean right now. But maybe one day we could do something more with it. You know, like a sandwich place," Tzippy said. "Make your own sandwiches. On the menu, we'd list everything we had, and you could order any combination."

"Not me," Baruch said. "I'd go meat, all the way. I'd do hamburgers and hot dogs, ribs, steak, coleslaw, and corn on the cob."

They built a steakhouse and served perfect cuts of meat to adoring crowds. They closed it down and opened a dessert café. It became a bakery that made fresh bread and served sandwiches to go. Then it was an all-you-can-eat barbecue place. They stayed up late and whispered imaginary restaurants to each other. They fell asleep with these plans hovering between them.

The next day, Tzippy went back to the library, to the business section. She wanted to know how to translate her ideas into practical plans. Surrounded by more books than she could ever read, the voice that had once dogged her made its return. Before, this voice was held in check by another, louder one that worried and warned, "What if you never get married?" But now, with that fear allayed, the voice had grown bold. Free to say what it wanted, free to travel at will, it found its way down to Memphis, into the supposedly solid walls of marriage, where once again it began to speak to her.

— TWENTY-ONE —

In her room, getting dressed for the first day of ninth grade, Ilana rifled through her closet. Baggy T-shirts and long jean skirts were lined up like uniforms. A year before, she had liked them. Now they seemed as though they belonged to someone else.

For the past eight weeks she had been at camp. Away from home, Ilana didn't feel bound by anyone's expectations of her. She had shed her old friends the way she did her winter clothing. She and her new friends spent nights in their bunks doing one another's makeup. They dieted, they tanned. Ilana's curly hair had finally grown long, and she spent an hour each day with a hair dryer, blowing it straight. They borrowed one another's clothes, experimenting with all the different ways they could look. She wore tiny T-shirts with flimsy sheer skirts. She wore her shorts short, her shoes tall.

It was hard to come home. Ilana didn't want the summer to end. It had been a summer of changes. She was no longer the little sister who gazed adoringly at a brother who was leaving her behind. She was no longer the well-behaved girl whom her parents counted on even as they overlooked her. She was becoming herself.

Out of habit, and because she didn't think she had a choice, she put on one of her long jean skirts that skimmed the floor. So many of her friends would be wearing the identical skirt. To the delight of the yeshiva high school girls, these skirts had become fashionable. But that didn't matter to Ilana. She looked in the mirror and cringed. The skirt not only covered her body; it hid who she was. It was like putting on a costume, gearing up to play a role that wasn't her. When she was younger, she had loved to play dress-up. She had gone through her parents' closets and come to the dinner table in old bridesmaid dresses, topped with feathered hats. She had adopted accents and created characters who eventually became shadow members of the family. Now she was still playing this game.

Her mother had prepared a special first-day-of-school breakfast and was calling her to come eat. Ilana went downstairs and sat at the kitchen table, across from her mother's eager, expectant smile.

"You look nice," Naomi said.

"Thanks," Ilana mumbled.

She felt her mother wondering what to say. Since she had come home from camp, her mother had been waiting for her to open up. But Ilana didn't want to talk. In past years, she had written fifteen-page letters home. She had composed detailed accounts of exactly what they did and how she felt. She could document every moment of every summer with these letters, which her mother saved. This summer, she wrote short letters. It wasn't that she didn't have anything to say. She stayed up late writing in her journal. She wrote about the quiet thrill of looking up to see a boy staring at her legs. About pretending not to realize that her shirt dipped low when she bent over, pretending to be oblivious to the flash of her bra strap, the seemingly unintentional baring of a thigh.

But she couldn't talk about this with her mother. She shifted uncomfortably and pulled at her skirt. Suddenly, she couldn't stand it. Her legs felt too constricted. She felt like they might break into a rash from so much material. She longed for the exposed toes, bare legs, and naked arms of the summer.

"One minute," she said to her mother, and went back upstairs.

Ilana pulled off her clothes and left them in a pile at her feet. She rifled again through her closet and through the overflow piles on the floor. At the bottom of a heap, she uncovered a short jean skirt she had gotten in a trade with one of her bunkmates. At the beginning of camp, before she had lost weight, it had barely fit her. Now she wriggled into it. She liked the way she looked. The skirt was the right kind of tight. It was also a few inches above her knee and she tugged at it until it sat on her hips. When she stood up, it was within spitting distance of her knees.

Ilana went back downstairs, now running late. As she grabbed her knapsack, her mother looked her up and down.

"You changed," Naomi said.

Ilana bristled. Whether it was a mere statement of fact or a larger one of ideology, she couldn't tell. "What is that supposed to mean?" she asked.

"Nothing," Naomi said. "I was just saying that you changed what you were wearing."

Buried in her mother's words were layers of meaning, some intended, some not. Her mother was always trying to convey something without actually saying it. She was staring at Ilana in innocence, yet Ilana felt her judgment. Before Naomi said another word, Ilana gave her mother a smile to reassure her that everything was fine. Then she said good-bye and ran out the door.

Maybe it was just about clothes. The door slammed shut, and Naomi stared after Ilana, hoping this was true. She didn't mind if the skirt was a little short. In her day, they hadn't even known about these strictures of dress. As a teenager, she had worn sleeveless shirts and miniskirts and had thought nothing of it.

But still, Naomi was baffled. Ilana hadn't slowly grown into a teenager. In the few weeks she had been away, she had been swallowed into a black hole of clothes, makeup, and boys. Naomi tried to get used to the morning whirring of the hair dryer as Ilana stood in front of the mirror and pulled at her hair. She tried to get used to this Ilana, who looked like she had dieted, twisted, plucked, and shrunk every part of herself.

Naomi had never cared about clothes, hair, or makeup. She had never fussed over what Ilana wore. She laughed at women who pierced their babies' ears or tied pink bows into their two locks of hair. But she saw how much Ilana cared, and she tried to be encouraging. She had tried to tell Ilana in a hundred different ways that she looked nice. But whenever Naomi commented on anything, Ilana grew uncomfortable— as if her whole body were a pair of high-heeled shoes and she was just learning how to walk in them.

Naomi didn't want to make a big deal out of Ilana's behavior, when she was just happy to have her home. She had waited for her daughter all summer. Though Ilana had gone to camp every year since she was nine, this year Naomi had missed her so much more than usual. Without her around, the house was too quiet.

For a few weeks following the wedding, Naomi had basked in its afterglow. But that quickly faded, and she spent most of the summer on her own. Ilana had left for camp, anxious to get out of the house. Joel was working long hours. It reminded her of when he was a young associate. But he didn't seem to mind the hours now. He relished the opportunity to be away. Distancing had become his coping method of choice. Baruch, of course, had been away for a few years already. Memphis may have been a lot closer than Israel, but he felt farther away than ever. She talked to him regularly, but he filled their conversations with only the most superficial details of his life.

The clamor had indeed parted, as Naomi had hoped, but what it left behind was silence. She hadn't thought it possible that she would miss the fighting. But at least then they had been talking. The issues had been out in the open, and Naomi had thought that if they talked about them enough, they would eventually come to an understanding. But now she had none of this hope. The silence was too steady, too resolute.

It was Ilana's luck that, at school, this was the season of the crackdown. Each year, the girls had become more daring in their attempts to circumvent the rules. When a rabbi approached, they pulled their skirts down onto their hips to make them appear longer. They threw sweaters on over tiny, tight T-shirts. The rabbis bemoaned the return of the miniskirt. They decried the school's slide into the world of the Jewish prep school. They worried that their students were becoming no different from their non-religious counterparts.

On Ilana's first day of high school, the principal went into each classroom and laid out a new dress code. The girls couldn't wear platform shoes, skirts above the knee, sleeves above the elbow, shirts that were skimpy or exposed the collarbone. They couldn't wear skirts with slits that passed the knee or sweaters that could be deemed immodest or tight. The principal had come to them prepared. He had sources to back him up. He quoted the rabbis who declared what parts of them were off-limits. He cited the Talmud and the later commentaries to explain why their skirts needed to reach the knee, why their shoulders needed to be covered.

Baruch may have cared about what the rabbis had to say, but Ilana had had no trouble ignoring their various pronouncements. Their words had little to do with her life. But now, like arrows, they landed on various parts of her body. She became nothing but an assemblage of forbidden parts: legs, elbows, arms, thighs. She imagined the rabbis standing before her, surveying her body and shaking their heads in disapproval. Ilana slunk down into her desk as if she could hide from them. She tugged at her skirt, which seemed shorter than it had been just a few minutes before. She felt trapped under the principal's gaze, suddenly, excruciatingly aware of her body. She couldn't remember where she was supposed to put her arms, how she was supposed to sit. Her body felt naked and exposed.

— TWENTY-TWO —

AFTER THEY HAD KISSED, after they whispered "I love you," when they were tired and naked and lay next to each other in their bed, Tzippy whispered in Baruch's ear that she wanted to tell him something.

His eyes were shut, but he said he was listening. They were so close that she could hear him breathing, his heart beating.

"I want to go to college," she whispered.

Baruch opened his eyes, and she waited nervously to see what he would think. She had been afraid to tell him, worried that he would disapprove. But she decided to tell him anyway. Before she was married, she couldn't imagine a boy seeing her in a pair of shorts. But now, lying naked beside Baruch had become the most natural thing in the world. There was nothing she needed to hold back or hide away. He had seen all of her. She hoped he could see this part of her too.

She told him that she had driven by the University of Memphis many times. But she had never thought that the grassy campus, with its libraries, classrooms, and fraternity houses, had anything to do with her. All summer, it had been quiet, with most of the students away. But when she had passed it the previous week, students were starting to return from their summer break. They walked across the campus, arm in arm, in shorts and T-shirts. They sat on the lawn and read. Parents moved their eighteen-year-olds into dorm rooms. The sidewalks were piled with suitcases, stereos, and boxes.

Tzippy had decided to park her car and walk around. On one of the lawns, a table was set up to welcome the incoming freshman class. A woman behind the table mistook her for a student and handed her a registration packet with a course catalogue. Pretending that she was a student, Tzippy sat on the grass and read through it. Each page, each class, seemed to say you could be this, or you could be that. There were so many things to choose from.

In the past, Tzippy had always assumed she would be a nursery school teacher. This was the job she had been born to do—or so everyone had said and so she had believed. But faced with such an abundance of choice, she realized that she didn't want to return to the chaos of young children. She didn't want to rule over a busy classroom where she would put something away and the next minute it would be all over the floor again. Instead, she imagined a world where she could make order. In place of children, she thought about numbers. Lined up in neat, obedient rows, they held their place in line and did what they were supposed to do. She told Baruch that she was interested in taking business classes. She wanted to work. She wanted to have something of her own.

Baruch propped himself up on his elbow and stared at her. He wouldn't tell her what she could or couldn't do. But he looked at her as though he didn't know who she was.

"I had no idea you wanted that," he said.

"I know," she said. "It's not what I thought I wanted either. But now I do."

She knew that this wasn't what people expected of her. Going to college seemed like a radical departure from what her life was supposed to be. It was the litmus test among her friends. It marked you as being modern or not. She knew she should be waiting with bated breath to get pregnant. She should be praying for the month when her period didn't come and the next part of her life would begin. But the voice inside her that urged her to go to college had only become more persistent. She had once thought of this voice as her evil inclination. She had seen it as something to be stamped out, or at least ignored. But now she realized that she had been wrong. It wasn't the voice of her evil inclination after all. It was the voice of her imagination, and it was calling to her.

She wasn't sure where her imagination would lead her, but she wanted to listen to it. In Memphis, she could do what she wanted and no one had to know. She didn't have to tell her mother or her friends about going to college. She could outwardly appear to stand in the same place as always, while inwardly she could come and go as she pleased. Her whole life, she had seen how people quietly made room for what they wanted. They too must have been following these voices, which were inaudible from the outside, loud and insistent only on the inside. She knew people from her neighborhood in Brooklyn who went to movies in Manhattan, where they wouldn't see anyone they knew. Or went mixed swimming with their husbands when they were on vacation, where no one they knew would see them. Or went into dressing rooms to try on clothes they could never wear in real life. Or rented movies and watched them with shades drawn and bedroom doors locked. Or read *Cosmopolitan* in doctors' waiting rooms. Or wore black leather lace-up boots under long skirts. For some people, it was enough to make excursions in the privacy of their own minds. They didn't have to go anywhere at all, but they let themselves imagine the forbidden and the tantalizing. They unleashed their minds to dream even when they were awake.

Her mother, she knew, kept tight controls on what she allowed herself to imagine, living in fear of what others would say. Baruch might think that it was hypocritical to be one thing on the outside while wishing for something else on the inside. But Tzippy didn't have to worry about what they thought. She knew it was okay to chisel out spaces to breathe. She could wish, she could want, she could let her mind, if not other parts of her, roam free.

"What?" she asked when Baruch continued to stare. "Why are you looking at me like that?"

"You should do it if you want to. I'm just surprised," he said finally. "How could I not be? You seem so different."

Under his curious gaze, Tzippy suddenly felt self-conscious. She felt as though she should put on a nightgown. Or at least pull the sheets over her. She did, and Baruch rolled toward her and hugged her. She curled up against him but didn't retract what she had said. She wouldn't pretend that going to college was a whim, a passing idea. She didn't reassure him that the only reason she wanted to go was so she could better support him while he learned. This desire of hers could hide if it had to, but it wouldn't back down. She realized that even being this close to someone, she could tuck away small parts of herself. She could lie here undressed and there were still places to hide.

"Anyway, Baruch," she said softly, as they were falling asleep, "I'm not the only one who seems different."

Baruch fell asleep with this feeling of surprise. He knew that it was technically okay for girls to get an education. They didn't have the same obligation to learn Torah. He knew many couples in which the wives went out into the world while the husbands stayed far away from it. But these wives took classes in the safe confines of Brooklyn or Queens College. They went only so they could get jobs to support their husbands while they learned.

But Tzippy wasn't doing it for that reason. He saw her curiosity and understood that she wanted something more. She knew, as he did, that college stood at the gate to the outside world. And this was what the rabbis had warned them against. In their tales and in their laws, they told of the dangers of going out into the world. They made allowances for it when it was absolutely necessary, when the boundaries of such an excursion were fixed and limited, within a carefully prescribed circumference. But when it was fueled by curiosity, when it was unrestricted and uncontained, they knew there was reason to worry.

His nervous feeling stayed with him all night. It followed him into the next day, when he hurried through the morning prayers so he could get to work on time. Rosh Hashanah was approaching, and The Kosher Connection was busier than usual. Baruch had to forgo the one hour of learning he had promised himself he'd make time for every morning. The pull of the everyday, the needs of the moment, had become pressing. Being busy didn't surprise him. He had accepted the need to work. He had compromised, as so many of the yeshiva boys did when they went out into the world. But no matter how many hours they spent away from learning, they always knew what really mattered. The boys who left yeshiva talked about ways to make time. They debated whether it was better to wake up at five and learn for two hours before davening, or to stay up late and learn into the night. They advised one another on jobs where they could work part-time and still make decent salaries. They listened to Torah tapes on their Walkmans and in the car on the commute. But no one talked about what to do if you liked your job, if you derived satisfaction from this necessary evil.

What surprised Baruch was that he enjoyed what he was doing. He took pleasure in his job. It wasn't what he had thought he would care about, not who he had thought he was. In yeshiva, he had counted accomplishments like grains of sand. Every day, a few more lines were mastered, another commentary on a vast text was studied. There had never been any hope of finishing. But now he wasn't wandering in the infinite. He worked hard and saw results. The job could be finished, the items checked off the list, and he could sit back and see what he had done. It was a feeling he knew well from high school, when he had taken his schoolwork so seriously, when he had cared about something without measuring it against the will of God. In yeshiva, he had forgotten the pleasure of this. He realized that Tzippy was right. He too was different than he had been a few months before. He hadn't been able to go out into the world and remain the same.

Tzippy signed up for four classes: Basics of Accounting, Basics of Economics, Business Planning, and Introduction to Marketing. Though the work was intense, she loved it. In the numbers and equations her professors wrote on the board, she saw a world where everything made sense.

It wasn't just the classes. Tzippy loved college, every part of it. She walked across the campus, and now it wasn't just a fleeting moment when she pretended to belong there. She bought a University of Memphis sweatshirt. She studied in the library. She sat on the steps of the buildings and read. At Brooklyn College, the Orthodox girls sat in groups. In the cafeteria, they ate at tables together. They traveled in these groups for safety, so no one would get lost. But here, Tzippy was the only one. In New York, her name and her long skirt would automatically identify her. People on the outside could look at her and know where she belonged. But in Memphis, no one knew how to make these distinctions. Her name was unusual, her clothes were modest. That was all that could be seen from a first glance.

Tzippy eavesdropped on the conversations that went on around her: dating, parties, sororities, and jobs; families in Alabama, in Mississippi, in Tennessee. The other girls in her classes were a few years younger than she was, but they seemed so much more worldly. She noticed boys who wore jeans and sweatshirts and baseball caps. She was stirred by how they talked to one another, how they touched. In class, she noticed how easily some of the girls raised their hands to ask questions. These girls had a seemingly endless number of possibilities. Marriage was a distant plan for the future. A student in the library saw her rings and asked her if she was married. When Tzippy said yes, the student couldn't believe it; she said Tzippy looked so young to already be married. Tzippy wanted to laugh: She had gone from being too old to being too young. She tried to imagine lives like these. They were so distant from her own, but she sat close enough to peek in. She wondered what it would be like if she walked into the dorm, put on their jeans, and pretended she was one of them. She could remove her rings and her wig, turn back her life, and become someone who wasn't yet attached to anything.

Before, she had existed with walls of glass all around. Her face was pressed up to it, trying to peer through from a safe distance. When she was in high school, she and her friends had gone into Manhattan and passed into another world. They had walked through Times Square and stared in awe and disbelief at the billboards. They were tourists, visiting from a far-off country. The subway that took them home carried them farther away than any 747 could. Now that she was stepping through the glass, she marveled at all there was to see. She was already thinking about what she would take next semester. She wanted to continue her business classes, but there were so many others as well. She wanted to study literature and art history, all these parts of the world that had been deemed dangerous. She thought about the books she had read, and she longed to read more. Every time she went back to the library, she flipped through the book of Degas paintings. They moved her as much as they had the first time she saw them. Something thrummed inside her, and she wanted to open her arms out wide. Nothing she had been taught before could explain how these paintings made her feel.

When she came home to Baruch, she talked about her classes. She read aloud sections from her textbooks and showed him a draft of a paper she had written. But she didn't tell him about the feelings that were stirring inside her. She didn't tell him how she sat in class and imagined being someone else. He might think that she was unhappy with him, that she regretted getting married. But it wasn't that. She wanted to be where she was, and she wanted to be somewhere else at the same time.

Tzippy and Baruch sat together, their books spread out in front of them. It was during the Ten Days of Repentance between Rosh Hashanah and Yom Kippur. Tzippy had missed classes for Rosh Hashanah, and she now had a hundred pages of reading, two papers, and an oral presentation due Monday. Baruch was trying to calculate how much business they had done for the holiday.

They had done better than anyone had anticipated. In the days before Rosh Hashanah, there was always a line ten people deep. The orders poured in. Baruch had hired an extra cook to help in the kitchen. Vats of tzimmes filled the refrigerator, and they sold every bit. Round raisin challahs from Brooklyn arrived in huge crates via FedEx. Within minutes of being unpacked, they were gone.

Two hours before Rosh Hashanah began, Baruch had made a quick switch, from his work clothes into a black suit, from his University of Memphis baseball cap to his black hat. He stood in shul, and the familiar tunes reminded him of who he was supposed to be. He realized how far he had drifted. In his outer observance, nothing had changed. He still prayed three times a day. He wore the same clothes; he said every blessing. But the previous year, he had stood in shul on Rosh Hashanah and trembled from the gravity of these days. The idea of judgment did not loom metaphorical: He had literally felt himself standing before God. He had made a list of his sins, combing through every day of the past year for them, and repented for each one. Now he stood in shul but didn't tremble. When he constantly had to defend his beliefs, he felt them more fervently. Now he had to struggle with himself. He felt God's eye staring at him. Sometimes he looked up to meet His gaze. Other times, he knew it was there, but he was able to turn away.

"What's the matter?" Tzippy asked when she stopped reading and looked up to see that he was upset.

"I don't know what I'm doing. Look at me. I'm barely learning," Baruch said. "I want to, but I never have time. The job takes up any free second I have." He remembered, as if from long ago, the admonition not to waste a second of time, not to be seduced by the pleasures of the world, not to worship false gods, not to veer to the right or to the left. These words, where were they now? From the bookshelves lining the walls of their living room, his books were staring at him. Were he to open one of the volumes from the complete set of Talmud Tzippy had given him as a wedding gift, its spine might crack with rebuke.

"Don't be so hard on yourself," Tzippy said. "It's okay."

"But how can it be okay?" he persisted. "I'm supposed to be learning."

"What are you supposed to do? Make yourself crazy and work all day and learn all night?"

"Maybe I should," he said.

"Do you really believe that?" she asked. "Because I don't."

"What don't you believe?"

"I just think that there's more than one way to be. I don't think you have to learn all day. I don't think that's the only thing that matters. And you know what? I think that you don't even want to be learning all the time. You just feel like that's what you're supposed to do."

Baruch didn't know what to say. It used to feel so clear-cut, the need to choose, the need to separate the holy from the profane. In his silence, Tzippy went back to her books as if nothing had happened. She was so intensely focused on her work. Since she had started college, she had talked about her classes and her professors and about the new people she was meeting. She didn't worry if this was what she should be doing. She didn't feel the struggle as he did. She was enthralled by what she found on the outside. He was struck by every day waking up to someone new. There were no big secrets but a thousand tiny surprises. If he peeked into Tzippy's head, he wasn't sure what he would find.

He glanced at her again. This time she looked up from her books and gave him a conciliatory smile.

"I'm almost done," she said.

He returned the smile. They would finish their work. Then they would talk. It would be like any other night. He thought that maybe he had just imagined this change in her. In her skirt, under the long sleeves and high neckline of her shirt, she looked the same as always.

— TWENTY-THREE —

H ER MOTHER TRIED to get her to talk. Her questions had tiny hooks on them and were designed to elicit everything Ilana felt. Naomi wanted to know if Ilana was enjoying her first few weeks of high school. Was she happy? Was she hungry? Was she interested in a family game of Trivial Pursuit? And did she miss Baruch? Did she want to call him? Did she want to talk about him? To all of these, Ilana gave breezy answers. She pretended to be busy whenever Baruch called. She pretended that school was fine, that everything was fine. Her mother was relieved when she gave these answers. She gazed at Ilana intently. Then, apparently satisfied with what she saw, she moved on to something else. Ilana had perfected the art of doing one thing on the outside, while on the inside she was miles away. She smiled outwardly, while privately she seethed.

Two months into the school year, only three hours into the day, Ilana felt as though she had been there for an eternity. Her teacher, Rabbi Feldman, talked about prayer, but all she prayed for was for the day to end. She looked down at her lap and pretended to be deep in concentration. She didn't care about anything this rabbi had to say. She wanted to hang a sign in front of her desk that said NOT INTERESTED. In her mind, she rebelled in a hundred different ways. She didn't just eat treif, but she ate it in the school cafeteria, in sight of everyone she knew. She kissed boys in the hallway; she wore her bathing suit to shul. She climbed out her bedroom window on Friday night, slid down a nonexistent trellis and into a waiting car. Because there were so many rules, she had an endless combination of possibilities. She imagined dancing at parties in smoky rooms, with people she didn't know, wearing clothes that weren't her own.

She looked at her watch and was dismayed at how little time had passed. She tried to go five minutes without looking at the time again. If she only checked every five minutes, maybe the class would pass faster. Outside the sun was shining. It was one of the last nice days of autumn, and the teachers were trying to find ways to keep the students excited about school. With all the new rules being put into place, they had to do something to lift school spirit. They had planned a school-wide field day for this afternoon. But knowing that there was some respite from afternoon classes only made the morning drag more slowly.

In class, Ilana yawned at her friend Tammy, who returned the gesture. "Help," she mouthed.

Tammy was similarly disinterested and smirked in return. Watch this, she seemed to say, and called out a question, apropos of nothing.

"Why do the boys thank God for not making them a woman and we don't thank Him for not making us a man?"

Getting the teacher off the subject was a small victory. The bigger the question, the more likely the girls were to succeed. Not a week went by without someone calling out, in a particularly boring moment, "But how do we know God really exists?" This question about the morning blessing was the oldest trick in the book. The girls had asked it every year since third grade, when they first knew enough to be insulted by it. In the morning, when they davened, they had stopped hearing the words. In its familiarity, the meaning had ceased to exist.

Their rabbi was happy to take on this question. He waited for moments like these to present themselves, so he could dispel their doubts, melt away their gripes. He stood up and said that women didn't thank God for not creating them a man, because women are obligated in fewer mitzvot, and it would be wrong to thank Him for that. Instead, they were created according to His will, which in itself was a blessing.

"But why are we obligated in fewer mitzvot?" Tammy persisted.

He explained that women were exempt from time-bound commandments, because the rabbis felt it was unfair to require women to do things at a particular time when they had obligations to their husbands and children. And they didn't need the daily cycle of prayers to remind them of God. Women were naturally closer to Him. In their very beings and bodies they carried the will of God, he said, and sounded as if he actually believed it.

They had all heard this a hundred times. Some of them were placated by this answer and some of them weren't. Most of them didn't care. Usually the girls asked more questions just to keep the conversation going and waste more class time. Usually Ilana heard the answers and tuned them out. She didn't let these questions or these answers come too close to her. But now, Ilana wanted to argue against the rabbi. She wanted to prove him wrong.

"But what if you don't feel closer to God?" Ilana called out. "Maybe you're supposed to feel that way, but you don't. Or what if you want to do the mitzvot the boys do. Then what?"

The teacher dashed out a phrase on the blackboard. "Kal kavod bat melech penimah," he read. "Does everyone know what this means?" They nodded. "Good. The glory of the king's daughter is inside. And what does that mean? That girls are different from boys. They're more internal. They don't need to put everything on the outside."

Ilana looked down. These words in white chalk were chasing her. They wanted to cover her, mask her, torment her. She tried to close herself off from the conversation around her. She focused on her lap, until it became the only thing she saw. She stabbed her pencil into the hem of her short jean skirt, which was starting to fringe. She would do this for the rest of the class if she had to. She would do it for the rest of the year. By the time summer finally arrived, the whole skirt might unravel into a pile of faded blue thread.

When the bell finally rang, the girls gathered their books and their bags. They talked and laughed as they pushed their way out the door. Ilana ran out of the room, ignoring the rabbi's request that she come talk to him. She didn't want to talk to him or to anyone.

On the field, the boys were playing baseball, rabbis against students. The girls did three-legged races and potato-sack races. They were tired and sweaty. The makeup they carefully put on each morning in the girls' bathroom had rubbed off. Their smoothed, blown-out hair had come undone, and they had haloes rising from the tops of their heads.

For the last race, they were supposed to put on a big T-shirt with the school logo over their own shirt. Then they were to run down the field, take off the T-shirt on the return trip, and pass it on, like a baton, to the next runner. When it was Ilana's turn, she ran down the field as fast as she could. Her body felt light, as if it were barely there. If she went any faster, her legs might lift off the ground, her hair would sail behind her, and she would be far away from here.

She was almost done with the race. It was time to take off the T-shirt and pass it on. She took hold of it, and in that second, she couldn't be sure—did she intend it, or did it slip through her fingers, two layers of material mistaken for one? Did it just come off, over her head, into her hand on its own? For a second—before the gaping and the laughing and the screams and the rush of wind, before the realization that she had taken off both shirts and was running down the field in her skirt and bra—for that second, something inside her sprang free, and she felt like she was flying.

The rabbi told the principal, the principal called her parents, and that evening Naomi, Joel, and Ilana were assembled in the living room.

"I didn't do anything wrong," Ilana said, hiding her embarrassment under her defiance.

"Why don't you tell us what happened?" Naomi suggested.

"It was an accident. The shirt just came off. I was running and I couldn't tell what I was doing."

"So why do your teachers think you did it on purpose?" Naomi asked.

"Why would I take my shirt off on purpose?"

"I don't know, Ilana. That's what I'm trying to find out."

Naomi wasn't sure whether to believe her. She wanted to. She wanted to feel absolute certainty when her daughter looked her in the eye and said something. But Naomi wasn't sure. On the phone, the principal had also told her that several of Ilana's teachers had commented that she appeared uninterested in class. He said that she had been reminded, on several occasions, about the dress code. It made Naomi search her daughter's face for any sign of the bright, rosy-cheeked girl she thought she knew.

"Actually, I think it's a good thing this happened," Naomi decided. "It gives us an opportunity to discuss what else you're feeling."

"I'm not *feeling* anything," Ilana said.

"You seem different to me, and we should talk about that."

"Maybe I'm different than who you think I am, but so what? You always say that we need room to figure out who we are, and that we don't have to be the same just because we're in the same family. So that's what I'm doing."

"She has a point," Joel said.

Naomi had waited until Joel came home from work to have this discussion. She had assumed he would be equally concerned and thought that they could present a united parenting front. But now she looked at him in dismay.

"This is different," Naomi said. "This isn't about minor variations in observance."

"Minor?" Ilana asked.

Ilana turned to Joel for approval, and Naomi caught the flash of a shared smile pass between them. She suspected he was amused. Maybe he was even proud.

"I want to know why you seem so angry. Are you angry at me? At Baruch? At your teachers?" Naomi asked.

"No. I just don't know if I want to be like any of you. Everyone assumes that I have to be religious just because I was born into this family. But isn't that up to me to decide?"

"Not when you're fourteen years old."

"How can you say that? You never said I had to be religious," Ilana protested.

"Ilana, we've been saying that our whole lives, in everything we do," Naomi said.

She was angrier than she would have liked. She was yelling when she wished she could be speaking calmly. But her anger and frustration flooded past the gates of what she should do, how she should act. Was there no way to live inside the folds of tradition? Did it have to be smoothed out and stapled into perfectly aligned pages? Was there no way to pass it on, full of a contradictory, messy beauty?

"Look around this house," Naomi persisted. "Who do you think we are?"

"That's exactly it," Ilana said. "I *am* looking at our family and everyone is something different. I have no idea what I'm supposed to think. Who are you? Who are we?"

— TWENTY-FOUR —

IT WAS HARD to be far away from Memphis. Herschel drummed his fingers against the dining-room table and tried to imagine what Baruch was doing. It was an hour earlier in Memphis, which meant that he had started closing up for the night. He hoped Baruch remembered to defrost meat for the next day and lock the grating. He wondered how much food Baruch was going through every hour. He wished he had installed a camera so he could watch from afar.

Herschel had finally tasted success. He had gotten something off the ground. The Memphis Jewish community exulted in one-stop shopping. They bragged about it to their out-of-town friends. They claimed that this, more than anything, put them on the Jewish map. There was a ringing cash register and a line of customers. The two tables were almost always full. When Herschel was there, he had walked back and forth behind the counter, around the tables, through the storeroom. He had touched everything, still unable to believe his dream had come to life in the shape of neon signs and cooking appliances, in the gleaming silver of pots and pans, in the shine of a scrubbed white countertop.

In Memphis, Herschel felt like a celebrity. There had been an article in *The Commercial Appeal* about The Kosher Connection, with a picture of him and Baruch smiling from behind the refrigerated-food case. The Kroger employees had taken to calling him rabbi. Over the intercom, they paged, "Rabbi, pick up on line three." In New York, he hardly mattered. But in Memphis, he was someone. The investors invited him into their homes, where large rooms gave way to larger rooms, and he listened to their ideas. They too had dreams. They lamented the shrinking size of the community. They remembered when Memphis was considered the Jewish oasis in the desert of Tennessee. They wanted to restore Memphis to its former grandeur. Herschel said he could help them. They agreed with one another that kosher food was the first step. It seemed impossible that until recently Herschel had never imagined Jews outside of New York. Now, he understood that this was where the true pioneers had come. It was a strange mistake of history that his father hadn't seen the vastness of opportunity and come here.

When Herschel finally left Memphis, he had had to tear himself away. He had been able to disguise his two-week-long stay in Memphis as an extended kosher certification tour. But he had to get back to work, and it had become harder than ever. He was stuck behind his desk, while an idea of his was living, breathing. In his office, piles of papers waited for him. A stack of faxes and phone messages were all marked URGENT. Herschel ignored them. He came in late; he came in when he felt like it. He didn't want to be a slave to anyone else's dream. No one in New York understood what he had created. He had held the world in his hands and now there was no way to hold any less.

On a morning that Herschel spent on the phone with his Memphis investors, Reuben Schachter, the head of the OC's kosher division, came into his office. He asked questions about Herschel's vacation days and the backlog of requests and inspections, and discovered that three companies had not been inspected for six months. Before Herschel could offer excuses, Reuben told him to clear out his desk and leave. He left with pleasure. He collected his files about Memphis and left everything else in a pile on the desk. All these papers, all these requests, had never really belonged to him anyway.

For years, Herschel had been stockpiling frequent-flyer miles. He had been sure that one day he would need them. Now he was able to take at will one of Northwest's three direct flights a day and return to where he belonged. He left without telling anyone what had happened. With visions of Memphis dancing in his head, it was hard to mind that he had been fired. Looking out the airplane window, Herschel waited for the first view of Memphis. As they descended, he saw in the clouds all that he would create, all that he would be.

An hour after Shabbos, which he had spent in Memphis instead of going home, Herschel tried explaining this to Shayna.

"I'm telling you, Shayna. I didn't need it anymore. Now there's nothing holding us back. The Kosher Connection is making more money than I ever dreamed it would. You should see what's going on down here. This is it. This is finally the one," Herschel said.

"No," Shayna said. "Not anymore."

She didn't want him to regale her with numbers and dreams. She didn't want to hear about this rich Memphian or that one. She didn't care which grand home he had eaten at that day. Sitting amid a hundred wedding bills, which she didn't know how to pay, she had no patience left.

Six months after the wedding, it was as if it had never happened. Tzippy had become one of a thousand brides who had walked down the aisle in white. Shayna went to subsequent weddings at the same hall, and each time she expected her wedding still to be assembled. When different brides walked down the aisles, flanked by different mothers, carrying different flowers, she wanted to call out in protest. Shayna was no longer wished mazel tov. She didn't glow with the knowledge that she was the mother of a bride. Worse, her daughter hadn't merely gotten married; she had used marriage as an escape, to run away.

Tzippy didn't call home every day. When they did talk, Shayna hinted about wanting to visit again. Tzippy responded by talking about how busy they were, how little extra space they had. Shayna could visualize every inch of her daughter's apartment. She felt as though she had lived there, as though it were hers. She wanted to hear what Tzippy had made for supper, which wedding presents they used, which ones they wanted to return. She wanted to connect through these details. But Tzippy gave quick, short answers: They were happy, they liked Memphis, everything was fine. There were gaping holes in what Tzippy said. But even when she pressed, Tzippy wouldn't give anything real away.

Her friends who had married daughters bragged about how often they came to visit. They paraded them in shul. A married daughter was the reward for having done everything right. Now, many of them were awaiting the births of their grandchildren. Shayna could never keep up. No matter how much she had, she always had less.

She tried to head off questions about why Tzippy hadn't yet visited. On the phone to her friends, she boasted about the amount of money the Memphis investors had put up. She took pride in saying that her son-in-law was in business with Herschel. She carried on about how the members of the community had begged Herschel to come down there, how they had paid outrageous sums of money to lure Baruch and Tzippy. She said that their efforts had already been rewarded. They were making a fortune.

But now it didn't matter what she told her friends. She couldn't cover the shortcomings that always poked through into her life. It was only a matter of time before the truth escaped and people knew that Herschel had been fired. This was the sort of news that people loved to share. Once they were looking, they would dig deeper and find everything about her family that didn't measure up. This one would hear from that one and tell this other one, and soon she would walk down the street exposed. The nightmares that had always dogged her would come to life: She accidentally left the house without covering her hair. She was sitting in shul and looked down to discover she was wearing only her slip and her stockings. She was at a kosher restaurant with everyone she knew, but on her plate there was a ham and cheese sandwich. It was Shabbos, there was a knock on the door, and Shoshana Schachter came in to find her watching television.

"She doesn't believe me," Herschel called out when Shayna refused to listen to his plans. "Here, Tzippy will tell you how well we're doing. You can trust her."

Tzippy was sitting at the dining-room table, her books spread out in front of her.

"I can't talk," Tzippy said as her father tried to hand her the phone.

"Tzippy's busy," Herschel told Shayna. "But here's Baruch. He'll tell you all about it," he said, and passed the phone to Baruch, who took it willingly.

Tzippy cupped her hands over her eyes and tried to concentrate. The end of the semester was approaching, and she had finals in a few weeks. But she was using all her energy to block out her father.

With no job to pull him back, Herschel was content to sleep on their couch forever. He had unpacked his clothes onto the buffet in their living room. In the bathroom, his toothbrush and shaver cluttered the sink. His papers were scattered throughout the apartment. Tzippy couldn't walk without tripping over something of his. She folded his clothes into neat piles on top of his suitcase. She put away the food he left out. When she picked up the extra cups and plates he used and didn't wash, she intentionally clinked them together.

She was determined not to let her father's presence disrupt her life. Until now, she had managed to keep college a secret from her parents. On the phone, she was careful, screening everything she said for something that might give her away. Even though she was grown up, married, and living away from home, she still felt like everything could be taken away from her if she didn't hold on tightly.

But she wasn't going to let her fear of what they would say stop her. She went to her classes and waited for her father to notice. She also avoided The Kosher Connection as much as she could. With her father presiding over the small space, she couldn't stand to be there. She used to feel that it was partially hers. But now she saw that it belonged to no one but her father. He told Baruch what to do, and he moved things around and messed up the order she had created. He chatted with the customers for hours on end.

But there was no way to contain her father. He talked constantly about his plans. At night, she heard his voice in her dreams. She felt his wakeful presence. In the middle of the night, the light in the living room was on, and Herschel was awake, scribbling notes to himself. The only evidence that he had slept at all was the rumpled sheets in the morning, which he left for her to fold. The apartment had grown smaller. If he stayed one more day, his presence would expand into every last corner, wash across the rooms, spill over the chairs, and seep into the carpet.

"Where have you been, Tzippy?" Herschel asked, and sat down next to her. "The customers are asking about you. They want to know why they haven't seen you around."

"I'm busy," Tzippy said.

"Busy with what?" Herschel asked.

She didn't answer, and he looked at the textbooks that lay before her. "Whose are these? he asked.

"They're mine," she said.

He laughted in surprise. "Tzippy's a college girl," he exclaimed.

IIe picked them up one by one: Accounting. Economics. Marketing. He thought it over. "Good for you," he decided. "I was just thinking that once we start growing, we're going to have to hire more people. We're going to need someone who can help out with the business side. See, Tzippy, I always knew you were like me. Didn't I always say you had a good head on your shoulders? Didn't I used to say that we would make a great team?"

He flipped the pages of one of her books. He nodded as if he already knew everything written there. "But don't let any professor tell you that you can read one of these books and know how to run a business. Believe me, they can't teach you half of what I know."

Tzippy was relieved that her father didn't mind she was going to college. But that feeling was quickly swallowed up. He was already spinning her into his own dreams. Instead, she focused on what was hers alone. Tucked into her notebook, she kept a paper she had written, a sample business plan for an imaginary café. On the front, in red pen, there was a large A. She had worked hard for the grade, but she was still surprised when her professor passed the paper back to her. She liked to take it out and look at it, to remind herself of what she could do.

"We need you, Tzippy. Now this is really a family business, like in the old days," her father was saying. "The father cooks, the mother cleans, the kids wait on tables, the grandmother runs the cash register. And they all live together over the store. How would you like that, Tzippy? All of us in one apartment, one big happy family."

She had hoped to finish her assignment tonight. When she looked at her watch, she couldn't believe how late it was. But Herschel had infected them with late hours. Her parents' house hadn't heeded the clock. Her mother had exerted so much effort to put everything in order and still they had run late. Tzippy had grown up consoling herself with the thought that when she had a house of her own, they would wake up at seven, eat dinner at six, go to bed at ten.

She glanced at Baruch and looked pointedly at her watch. Since Herschel had been here, Baruch had been staying up late, listening to him talk. Then, when Baruch finally came to bed, he repeated to Tzippy the stories her father hold him, all of which she had heard many times before. Instead of spending so much time with him, she wished that Baruch could make Herschel go away. But he didn't mind her parents as much as she did. Distanced from his own family, he enjoyed feeling connnected to hers. He had just hung up from a lengthy conversation with her mother in which he had told her the details of their lives that she was so hungry for. The only thing he omitted was the fact that Tzippy was going to college. Tzippy had told him not to tell. Now, even though her father knew, she still preferred to wait it out. Her father would eventually get around to telling her mother. But she wanted to prolong that inevitability for as long as she could. She didn't want anything to spoil the pleasure she felt.

Herschel finally left her alone and went to join Baruch on the couch. They both had on their Shabbos pants with their white shirts. Black velvet yarmulkes sat atop their heads, both slightly askew, as they bent over copies of *Restaurant Today.*

"Maybe we could try something like this," Baruch said, pointing to an article about a new kind of refrigerated display case.

"I was just thinking the same thing," Herschel said. "It could go across from the cash register."

"Or perpendicular to it," Baruch said.

"Exactly," Herschel said. "Now you're thinking, Baruch. Maybe tomorrow we could order it."

"I thought you were leaving tomorrow," Tzippy said.

"I am, I am," he said.

But she didn't believe him. He would always be leaving tomorrow, and in the meantime, he would live in their apartment and take over their lives. She could be a thousand miles away, but she hadn't really escaped. All she had done was run in a giant circle toward home. Her anger coiled tightly inside her. By focusing on the numbers in front of her, she tried to ignore her father. She tried to forget how easily Baruch went along with everything her father said. As Herschel took out the account books, came over to her, and lay them on the table, she refused to look up.

"Not bad," Herschel said, as he looked them over. He was waiting for her to respond. Nothing could be done quietly, without fanfare, without having to pull everyone in. She kept her head down, pretending not to hear him.

"You're the expert here now," he told Tzippy, and stood over her.

"You look at the numbers and tell me if I'm wrong. Think of it as an extra homework assignment."

"You really want me to tell you what I think?" she asked. "Fine. I will."

She flipped through the pages, looking for a place to begin. She was just starting to feel comfortable with rows of numbers. She looked at the columns, the figures, and began to work them out. But she wasn't looking for the perfect symmetry of a world in order, a business well run. She hoped to find proof of where he had gone wrong. Wrong not just about this, but about everything. She didn't know when it had happened, but she had stopped believing in her father. She wanted to list every idea he had ever had, each of which had magically, mysteriously, unforeseeably failed at the last minute.

In the accounts, Tzippy saw expenses carefully tabulated against income. She saw the amounts the investors had given him, the additional money they were still planning to give. All the other times, her father had been nothing more than ideas. Now he had actually built something solid. To her surprise, the numbers added up. The Kosher Connection was making money.

"It looks good, doesn't it," Herschel said. "I told you we were doing well."

She skimmed the numbers again, hoping to find a mistake and to discover that The Kosher Connection stood on the brink of ruin.

"I could be wrong. I only looked at them quickly. And I'm just learning how to do this," Tzippy said.

"Ha, even Tzippy agrees. We're doing something right."

The good news made Herschel hungry. The refrigerator was crowded with Shabbos leftovers, and Herschel assembled a feast of chicken, potato kugel, and leftover cholent. He was slowly expanding, his belt buckle moving over one notch per week in Memphis.

"Do you want some?" he asked Baruch.

"Why not," Baruch said.

Herschel made Baruch a plate, and the two of them ate, forks and knives clinking against white wedding china.

"Now, this is a meal," Herschel said.

As Herschel ate, he felt better. The failures of the past were replaced with future possibilities. On the phone, he had heard the disbelief in Shayna's voice. He was surprised to hear how upset she was. No matter what the world had to say about his ideas, Shayna had always understood his vision. But he wasn't worried about the change in her. He knew he could make it better.

"Do you want more?" Tzippy asked, seething at her father while holding out the kugel pan. She had given up on getting any more work done. She was going to clean up the kitchen and then go to bed. Baruch could stay out here with her father all night if he wanted to.

"I'm full," Herschel said. He rubbed his bulging stomach and stood up. "We're taking it to the next level," he announced. "We're going to publicize the miracle."

Herschel invited the media. He sent invitations to local celebrities: the weatherman from Channel 3, the wrestler Jerry Lawler, two rival Elvis impersonators. He placed a half-page ad in *The Hebrew Watchman*. He invited the cantors from the local shuls to perform a medley of Chanukah songs. He plastered signs to the walls, ordered hundreds of pounds of potatoes, and strung blue-glittered Styrofoam dreidels and metallic gold cardboard menorahs from the ceiling.

On the first night of Chanukah, The Kosher Connection was wall-to-wall people, assembled for Memphis' first annual city-wide Chanukah party. "I Have a Little Dreidel" played over the store's loudspeakers. Herschel gave Baruch the signal to light the candles. With the investors and their families gathered behind them, they sang together: *Blessed are you, God, for commanding us to light the candles, for doing miracles for our forefathers, and for keeping us alive, sustaining us, and allowing us to reach this time.*

With the candles lit, it was time to eat. Latkes abounded on foil-covered trays. A tray was put out, and almost instantaneously it was picked clean. Two cooks flipped latkes, while Baruch fed raw potatoes into the food processor. There were door prizes and raffles for a year's supply of gefilte fish. While the cantors sang, Herschel and the investors danced a horah around the tables. In a free moment, Herschel popped his head into the kitchen. "Keep 'em coming," he yelled. "Watch your backs. Hot latkes coming through." A table was laden with latkes, deli platters, kugel, and chopped liver. People swarmed around the food as if they hadn't eaten in days.

They left only when there were no more latkes. Alone, Herschel and Baruch sat among the fallen glitter. Herschel put his feet up and shook his head in wonder.

"We could have made a thousand more latkes and they would have eaten them."

"I don't want to see another latke for at least a year. Maybe never," Baruch joked, though it was only the first night of Chanukah and seven more nights of latkes awaited them. But he knew he would wake up early the next morning and be ready to start again. The success of the party would sustain him.

"It was something else," Herschel said.

Baruch and Herschel beamed at each other, too tired to do anything but shake their heads in satisfaction.

"I should go," Baruch said. "Tzippy is probably wondering where I am."

"Where was she tonight?"

"She had class, but said she would try to come after. I guess she changed her mind."

"She couldn't skip class? Isn't that what college kids do?"

"I thought so too, but she said she couldn't miss it."

"You go on without me. I'm going to finish up a few things," Herschel said.

Shayna had insisted that Herschel come home for the rest of Chanukah, and he was supposed to take an early flight back to New York the next morning. There was no point in going to sleep for just a few hours. Instead, he took off his apron and walked around the food case, taking it in from all angles. He backed up, squinted his eyes, and noticed a few feet of empty space on either side. If he moved it over, he could squeeze in a few more tables and chairs. He could add another food case. Once he did that, it would be easy enough to add a full-fledged catering business and free delivery. The new and improved menu could double in size. He saw double-decker sandwiches, a full-size grill, a salad bar, pareve ice cream, and a deep fryer for Southern specialties. Pots of homemade soup began to bubble in his mind. Rotisserie chickens twirled in his head.

— TWENTY-FIVE —

VEN WITH ALL THE PARENTING BOOKS she had read, the years of
accumulated advice, Naomi had no idea what to do. She had given
Ilana space. She had given her time. She had given her empathy. She
had circled her, looking for a way in. But how do you chase a child?
Catch her by grounding her, by punishing her? Surround her with lock
and key, with lectures, with love?

On the phone with her friends, Naomi tried to find the answer. She
wanted to hear that everyone's children passed through this angry
stage on their way to some other stage. Her friends reassured her, but
she didn't feel better. When she talked to Joel, he said that he wasn't
worried. Ilana was a good kid and she was just experimenting. When
she talked to Baruch, she hinted that Ilana was having a hard time and
wondered what he would say. He pressed her for details, and she told
him about what had happened at school. He laughed despite himself.
He said he could just imagine the reaction from the teachers. But after
his laughter, she also heard a silent rebuke.

"What?" she had asked. "What are you thinking?"

"Just that I'm not really surprised, that's all," Baruch had said.

It didn't have to be that way, she wanted to tell him. It didn't have to
be one extreme or the other. For Naomi, being religious had never
been such a struggle. She had always known what she believed. She
may not have investigated it or analyzed it or questioned it. She had
just tried to live it. She had no trouble living in this ever-shifting middle ground, with its mix of sacred and secular. It was always a balancing act, but she had managed to walk tightrope over divergent worlds,

all of which had become her own. She had always felt so much richer for it. The whole world was open to her; the whole world was from God.

What was harder, though, was figuring out how to explain this to her children, how to pass it on. In nursery school, Baruch had learned about the obligation to pray every morning. She had woken up each morning to hear him belting out the Modeh Ani according to the instruction of his teacher. One morning, he had asked her why she didn't always daven. In a rush of words he probably didn't understand, she said that she meant to but didn't always have time. She said she prayed in her heart. She prayed when she had time. It was the truth, but he looked at her and shook his head. "Mommy, I don't think Hashem is proud of you," he had pronounced.

Now, on the phone, she heard this same disapproval. As much as she didn't want to think so, she wondered if there might be some truth to what he believed. Maybe the world made more sense when everything was drawn with strict lines of black and white. For the first time, Naomi thought about curfews and phone limits, all those authoritarian gestures she had once deplored. She had run out of options. Maybe it was time for rules. Maybe it was time to clamp down.

On Friday afternoon, Naomi cooked with a plan in mind. She had decided that over dinner she would catch Joel and Ilana by surprise and convene a family meeting. She had threatened to do this for years, until it had evolved into a joke. There was so much she had said that they hadn't taken seriously, but she had never insisted that they listen. She had preferred to let her ideas rest lightly, hoping that they would eventually seep in. This time, Naomi was ready to make them listen.

For once, she didn't wish for extra hours until the start of Shabbos. She was nervous about what exactly she would say, and she wanted it to be here already. But when the time came to light the candles, Joel wasn't home. She called him at work and on his cell phone, but there was no answer. She waited and watched the minutes tick by. She hoped every clock in the house was a few minutes fast, anything to give him a few more minutes to make it in time.

Shabbos descended on the neighborhood. From her front window, Naomi saw her neighbors lighting their candles. The men were walking to shul. She reluctantly lit her candles without Joel. Her worry alternated with anger. Something had happened. When he got home, she expected to hear a long explanation about traffic, about bridge shut-downs. She was ready to yell at him, ready to scold. Ilana was still in her room, and for once Naomi prayed she would stay there. She didn't want her to see this. She didn't want to have to explain.

The minutes passed. It was five minutes late, it was ten, then it was fifteen. But even one minute late would have been a big deal. They fudged, they bent rules, but Shabbos was a fixed point that couldn't be bent. They cut it close, they slipped in under the wire, but only until the very last minute, when any shades of gray ceased to exist. It either was Shabbos or it wasn't. You were either home in time or you weren't.

The car pulled up in the driveway. The car door shut, Joel's keys turned in the lock, and he walked in twenty minutes late for Shabbos.

"What happened?" Naomi demanded.

"I'm late," Joel said, and shrugged.

He put his briefcase down. He emptied his pockets of his keys, pens, and wallet as if he had all the time in the world.

Naomi, Joel, and Ilana sat through a quiet dinner. Whatever words Naomi had been formulating were now gone. She was grateful for the brevity of their Shabbos meals. For once, she didn't try to break the silence. Ilana and Joel looked at her in surprise. They were so used to her filling in the spaces. But this time she couldn't do it. She looked at her family and had no idea what to say.

After dinner, they read, each in their own corner of the living room. Naomi went upstairs first, then Ilana. Joel stayed downstairs, trying to put off the inevitable conversation. He didn't want to talk about it, pri-marily because he had no excuse to give, no explanation to offer. There had been no traffic jams, no bad weather. He hadn't mistaken the time Shabbos began. It wasn't an emergency. It wasn't beyond his control. His only answer was that he had work to do, and he had let time slip away in order to finish.

On Fridays in the winter, Shabbos started early, around four o'clock. In order to be home on time, Joel was supposed to walk out of his office at three, as if this were perfectly normal. They could go out into the world, but they were expected to carry their Orthodox laws with them. In his parents' generation, they had left their yarmulkes at home. They had tried to fit in. But in this day and age—when they could be anything, when they could go anywhere—they were supposed to have no trouble being different. They were supposed to move seamlessly, proudly, between their different worlds.

But he had work he needed to do, and he didn't want to leave it for later. He didn't want to tell the clients they would have to wait. First he convinced himself that he could stay a little longer and still make it home in time. Then he passed the moment when he could make it home comfortably. Then he passed the moment when he could make it if he had no traffic and if he sped. He ignored the sky that was darkening outside his office window. He stopped calculating how close he could come. He put Shabbos out of his mind and finished what he needed to do. It wasn't intended as a rebellion. It wasn't a theological statement. It wasn't an experiment. It was just his small, private decision.

He drove home, and while he was somewhere on the West Side Highway, it became Shabbos. Candles were being lit in his home, in his community, but they seemed so far off. He kept going. He hadn't called home to say what had happened. He had shut off his cell phone to ignore Naomi's inevitable questions. He pretended that it was like any other night of the week. He was like every other driver in every other car. It was the start of the weekend, the beginning of rush hour. Usually, when he drove home on Friday afternoons, he saw other Orthodox Jews in their cars, all with the same schedules, with the same pressing need to make it home. But at this hour, he was the only one. There were no signs of Shabbos anywhere.

Joel had always heard stories about what people did if they got stuck driving too close to Shabbos. They approached their observance with the gravity of a life-and-death decision. They didn't take chances when it came to Shabbos, because it was unimaginable, it was impossible, that they would ever desecrate it. True belief was stopping a car by the side of the road, locking keys, briefcases, and other prohibited items inside, and walking home along the highway. And this kind of belief was what he didn't have. What amazed him, though, was that he didn't feel bad about it. He couldn't summon the firm conviction that what he was doing was really wrong. In his uncertainty, nothing was fixed. His Orthodox world could exist fully formed. Then he could close his eyes and it would disappear. He had never been late for Shabbos before, and he didn't plan to make a habit out of it. But this one time it had been so easy.

Finally, there was no more putting it off. Joel went upstairs. The stairs were dark, most of the lights upstairs left off for Shabbos. As he neared the top step, he almost tripped over Ilana, who was sitting there waiting for him. She was wearing the Columbia sweatshirt that had once belonged to Bryan. She had taken it out of the discarded-clothes bag and was wearing it as pajamas. It was huge on her; her hands were hidden by the sleeves. As Joel saw the familiar blue lettering, he forgot where the sweatshirt had come from and wondered for a second if it was his. And then he remembered. Of course, it must be the one he had bought for Bryan. He thought wistfully of all the hopes that had been embodied in that garment. It made him remember Bryan and all that he had wanted for his son. But this son didn't exist anymore. Instead, he saw his daughter sitting before him.

"I know we've been ignoring this, but, Dad, what happened to you tonight?" she asked.

Joel sat down next to her on the stairs. With his kids, he never knew how honest to be. As parents, they were presumably supposed to present a coherent vision of the world. They were supposed to have everything all figured out and be ready to pass it on—as if this kind of certainty was one of the prerequisites for being a parent. Yet he didn't have this trait, not for himself, not for anyone. Naomi had always been the one to deal with the large questions children posed unexpectedly, and he had been happy to defer to her. But at the moment, Ilana was looking at him and waiting for an answer.

"I had so much work to do, and I just decided to stay and finish," he said.

"But it's Shabbos. How could you do that? Didn't you think that it was wrong?" she asked.

"Wrong? I don't know. Maybe. But I didn't think about it like that."

"But Mom does. And so does Bryan."

"I know they do. But you know what, Ilana, it's just what happens sometimes. That's real life. We make choices, and they're not always the ones we're taught in school, or even the ones we think we'll make for ourselves."

"But then what *do* you believe?" she asked.

She was looking at him so intently. Even as a little girl she had these piercing brown eyes that could almost look through people. He knew whatever answer he gave would be followed by another question. In her, he saw shades of Bryan. His children, he thought, these seekers of the truth. He wondered where that had come from: They certainly didn't get it from him. Always a skeptic, he was still trying to find a way to live within his world as best he could. The mysteries of the universe didn't nag at him. He could live in the tenuous space of the observant agnostic.

"I don't know," he said. "But it doesn't bother me not to be sure. I can live with sometimes not knowing."

"But then what am *I* supposed to believe?"

"I guess you have to figure it out for yourself."

"That's what I'm trying to do," she said. "But then I ask questions and no one answers me."

She started to cry, softly at first. Then, with no warning, she flung herself into his arms. Her body went limp against him, and she sobbed into his shoulder. He couldn't remember how long it had been since he had rocked one of his children like this. Since they were babies awake in the middle of the night. Since they were kindergarteners with skinned knees.

"So keep asking," he said as he held her close.

After Naomi had taken ten deep breaths, after she had counted to ten, after she had tried to see it from his point of view, she couldn't hold it in any longer.

"Joel, I'm worried about you," she said when he came upstairs.

He got into bed and mumbled a response into the pillow. She couldn't hear what he said, but she wasn't sure she wanted to. She didn't want to hear about work, about being busy, about the kind of pressure he was under. For years now she had worried about his job, and this was the culmination of those fears. When they were first married, he had worked late every night. She was lonely, but she justified it by saying that he was paying his dues now and would reap the rewards later. Then, when she was a young mother alone with two kids, she had called him hourly, wondering when he would leave. She hated tucking the kids into bed without him. She hated having to pretend that it was normal that he was never there. She soothed her children when they missed him. She tried to fill the space left behind by his absence. But the minute he walked in the door, they swarmed him, starved for time with him.

Her worry hadn't subsided once the kids no longer expected him to be home. Now she worried for his sake. She saw the exhausted look on his face when he came home in the middle of the night. Tired had become his most natural state of being. He fell asleep at the Shabbos table. Any outside interest had been swallowed up in the voracious demands of his job. It would eat away at him until there was nothing left. At the annual firm dinner, she saw the partners in their tuxedos, puffed with their sense of accomplishment. Their wives had expensive smiles painted on otherwise blank faces. She bristled at their self-congratulatory words. Money was all they had to show for themselves. This was how they measured their days, their years.

"I lost track of time," he said. "That's all it was."

"No, it's more than that," she said. "I mean it. I'm worried about your soul."

He rolled over in bed and laughed.

"You're not taking this seriously," she said.

"Naomi, what do you want me to say? I'm not going to make excuses. This is who I am. It's who I've always been," he said.

Naomi got out of bed and left Joel to wrestle with his conscience. Which he wouldn't do, she realized. He was content to leave things as they were. But she needed more. Downstairs, she stood at her front window and looked out. Up and down the street, Shabbos candles illuminated nearly every window. At this hour, they were starting to flicker and go out. She sat on the couch and flipped the pages of *The Jewish Week.* The newspaper was filled with notices about events in the area. Usually she read them but gave little thought to going. But this time a notice caught her eye. SOUL SEARCH, it read.

— TWENTY-SIX —

A T NINE O'CLOCK on a Sunday morning, the auditorium at Manhattan's Ninety-second Street Y was packed. There were men in yarmulkes, women in yarmulkes, bareheaded men and women, men with long beards. Rabbinical students and people who knew nothing about Judaism sat together. They were all there for a day-long seminar on Jewish Spirituality. There were sessions on Jewish meditation and prayer, on creating new rituals, on healing services, on finding meaning in the everyday, on elevating the physical to the realm of the spiritual.

Naomi listened to a Jewish Renewal rabbi talk about the divine spark present inside every person. He quoted the sixteenth-century Lurianic Kabbalists, who said that the world was created by the mystical contraction of God. He had diminished Himself in order to make room for the universe. Some of the vessels of the world sheltered the light of God that emanated from this powerful, contracting force. But the vessels couldn't contain the light and they shattered, sending tiny flecks of the divine into the world. The task for humans was to repair these vessels and to restore the light to its wholeness.

In other sessions, a Reform rabbi who had spent ten years as a Zen Buddhist quoted the Lubavitcher Rebbe. Hasidic tales were used as launching points for meditation. The Talmud was cited as a guide for Jewish healing. Some of the rabbis they quoted were the same ones Baruch referred to. But here, in these sessions, they were made over in the language of the new age. Instead of being the strict guardians of tradition, the rabbis sounded so modern. It was hard to believe that these rabbis weren't still alive, living in and partaking of this world.

A year before, Naomi wouldn't have considered coming to this event. Even if she were curious, she would have viewed it as a little too offbeat. It wasn't exactly ouside Orthodoxy, but it was certainly outside the mainstream. No one she knew talked about personal spirituality or soul searches. They regarded these topics with suspicion. Or maybe, as far as she knew, no one else felt the need to delve into them. At first, she heard, interspersed between every word, Joel's cynical, amused laugh. She heard Baruch's disbelief in the authenticity of these ideas. She tried to imagine her friends from shul here. They would roll their eyes; they would view this as "Judaism lite."

But for her it wasn't any of this. She wasn't here to step outside the boundaries of her world. On the contrary. She knew her world was wide enough to contain these ideas and so many more. She could pull them all in with her. She stopped worrying about everyone else and thought only of herself. She focused on the part of her that wanted to be here, that wanted to be moved, that wanted to believe. She listened, rapt, as a woman rabbi told the story of the great Hasidic rabbi Menachem Mendel of Kotzk, who asked his disciples where God lived. Thinking this an easy question, they answered that He lived everywhere. But Menachem Mendel shook his head. "No," he said, "He lives wherever we let Him in."

Naomi bought a stack of books. She signed up to receive flyers and newsletters. She read *Kabbalah for the Layman, God Is a Verb, The Seven Faces of the Soul, The Women's Guide to Jewish Spirituality.* She read hungrily, as if she might uncover something vital on each page. This reading became her solitary pursuit. She didn't tell anyone about her newfound interest. Her longing for God, for spirituality, felt too private.

The ideas worked their way into her life. When she lit Shabbos candles, she thought about how she was bringing more light into the world. When she ate, she focused on the meaning of keeping kosher, of trying to elevate a physical need to a spiritual plane. She did the same rituals she had always been doing, but she peeled back their layers and began to feel them more deeply.

The latest book Naomi had started was *The Art of Jewish Meditation,* which was why she now sat in the lotus position on the living-room floor. She was propped up on a couch pillow so her knees were below her hips. Her shoes were off, her feet planted on the ground. Her spine was straight, reaching up like a ladder toward heaven. Her hands were in a purposeful position, fingers lightly touching one another. She breathed in, then out, trying to find her focus. Despite the ache in her back, she held the position. That was the easy part. The harder part was feeling what she was supposed to feel.

She was supposed to block out everything that filled her mind and reach a heightened sense of spiritual connection. Then she could find her center, direct her mind, and listen to what God and the universe had to say. The first step was to take leave of the noise of the everyday world. Like static on a phone line, this noise made it impossible to hear Him. She was supposed to shut out not only noise but clutter. In their house, books were starting to take over. Their bookshelves were already double-lined. Naomi's night table had three rival towers. The coffee table was buried under the piles. It was a good thing she was supposed to close her eyes.

But then what? She checked the book again. She was supposed to take ten breaths and try to envision a world of white on white. Then she was supposed to imagine the Hebrew letters emerging from this canvas. She tried to imagine herself entering the Hebrew letters. Each letter held a mystical, potent force. She imagined that they were three-dimensional and that she could walk around inside them. She could peer out through the crowns of the letters, which were removable. They were actually keys, and she was receiving them. The white between the words wasn't empty space. It was an all-white room, with white doors that were opening to her.

Naomi breathed in and out, trying to let the world become nothing more than her series of breaths. She focused on the image of a single flame of light and let it push from her mind her usual array of thoughts. If she could do this, her mind would become a gateway to other worlds, and finally to herself. It wasn't easy. There was no straight path to God. The second she cleared away one thought, another took its place. She was still worried about Ilana and Joel. She missed Baruch. The book said to gently push her thoughts away and find her concentration again. But was there a place in her head that was sheltered from the continual rush of thoughts, ideas, and wishes?

The phone rang, and the doors to the infinite slammed shut. If it were up to Joel, they would screen every call. But she usually answered the phone no matter what, too afraid of what she might miss—even if she was in the middle of something, even when Joel shook his head in annoyance at the telemarketers who seemed to know the instant they sat down to dinner. He joked that she should have the phone surgically attached to her ear. Now she decided to let it ring. She tried to breathe through the insistent ringing and view it as one more distraction from which she needed to take leave.

"Aren't you going to answer it?" she heard.

She opened her eyes. Joel was standing before her, smiling, smirking, wondering, and laughing. He was both concerned and amused to find her sitting on the floor in this position.

"So this is what happens when I'm at work," he said.

She jumped up and looked for a book that she could pretend to be reading. She tried to think of an explanation to offer. It hadn't occurred to her that he might come in. It was almost six o'clock, and she couldn't remember the last time he had voluntarily come home this early.

"I'm just relaxing," she said. But he was still looking at her quizzically. "Why are you home?" she asked.

"No reason," he said.

"What," she said, "there was no more work to do?"

"It'll still be there tomorrow, don't worry," he said, and smiled.

She had said this exact line to him so many times, and he had always bristled and said it wasn't true. He had regarded such comments as further evidence of how little she understood the pressures of work. It wasn't true that he could always have come home earlier. It wasn't, as she also liked to say, simply a matter of priorities. He couldn't have survived this job if he gave only half of himself to it. If he always had one foot out the door, he never felt content. He had learned, somewhere along the way, that he enjoyed his work more when he let it become his world.

But she was right that sometimes it was easier to stay at work. There, even after the most demanding of days, he could close the door to his office. He'd look out his window, forty-three floors above the busiest city in the world, and separated by a pane of glass, he'd be alone. From above, the city seemed so spacious. He saw into the windows of the buildings nearby, but the people working in those offices seemed worlds away.

Home, of course, was never like this. Even in their big house, they were crowded together, their needs and expectations bumping into one another. But tonight, a desire for his family had seized him. He surveyed the work he had left. It was the sort of thing he could leave for later, and what surprised him most was how much he wanted to. It had become easier to be home. He had cleared a space for himself, for who he was and what he needed.

Naomi looked at him in surprise. This decision to leave work was a little late, not just by hours but by years. But here he was, and she was glad to see him.

She laughed and decided to tell him the truth. "Well, you're just in time. I'm meditating."

"Are you?" he said.

"Yes. Do you want to join me?"

Now he laughed. "I don't think so. But you go right ahead. Don't let me stop you."

She looked at him carefully. She had known him for so long, through so many events in their lives. But he could still surprise her. She reassumed her position, and realized that she could do what she wanted. He could stand there and watch her. Or he could go upstairs and do what he wanted. They could still be together.

She closed her eyes and once again started to breathe. This time, she started to feel something. From inside each breath, she thought about wholeness. The doors in her mind opened again, and the members of her family began to enter through them. An idea occurred to her. Passover was a few months away, and she wanted everyone to be together for the seders. She wanted Ilana and Joel, Baruch and Tzippy, Herschel and Shayna and their girls, to sit together at the seder table. The image of the entire family, in-law and extended, entered her mind, a series of blinking, flashing lights replacing the single, steady flame.

— TWENTY-SEVEN —

EVERY DAY another box arrived. They came by FedEx and UPS, by messenger and special delivery. One day a jumbo fryer arrived, followed by a second freezer a week later. The next week, it was a snow-cone machine, then an indoor grill and a movie-theater popcorn popper. A month later, a bubble-gum machine. A hot dog broiler. A flashing red neon sign that read ALWAYS OPEN.

"It's growth," Herschel told Baruch over the phone. "It's all about growth."

Herschel had decided that it was time to take it to the next level. He wanted to open a chain of Kosher Connections, and he was traveling, scouting out new sites and meeting with potential investors. He assured Baruch that it takes money to make money. If you're not moving forward, then you're moving backward. You have to be able to see it. Herschel promised him that the investors had approved these new purchases. They knew what a great job they were doing. He had them, Herschel said, in the palm of his hand.

Baruch installed the new equipment, pored over instruction manuals, and added new items to the menu. He assembled the kosher candy display from a thousand small plastic pieces. Baruch tried to trust that Herschel knew what he was doing. He was willing to suffer the hardship of the moment in order to reap the rewards to come. It was like the birth pangs of delivery, the growing pains of a nation.

———

Soon there was no floor space left, and no counter space. It became increasingly difficult to open the refrigerator. Boxes were stacked on either side, leaving only a narrow passageway. The deliveries spilled into the neighboring aisles of the store. The manager of Kroger stopped by several times a day and extracted a promise from Baruch that he would clean it up immediately. His customers shook their heads disapprovingly at the mess. The investors told Baruch that they were worried about the latest expenditures. Bills and invoices were piling up. They requested a meeting with Herschel. They insisted that Baruch give them the books to look over. They said they would give it a little more time, because they knew how hard he was working. They warned him, though, that they didn't trust Herschel.

With all the new menu items, the chef could barely keep up. The customers began to complain about shrinking portion size, about watery soup, about small, rock-hard matzo balls. People claimed that the salads varied from day to day: one day too spicy, the next too bland. Baruch explained that they were just working out some kinks. But even his favorite customers began to turn against him. Their voices took on the rattle and whine of the machines. Now that they had tasted, they wanted more. They had forgotten what it was like to be hungry.

Baruch created theme nights in an effort to appease people. Monday night was Cotton Carnival Night, with a free snow cone and cotton candy to anyone who bought at least twenty-five dollars' worth of prepared food. He advertised with coupons in *The Hebrew Watchman* for people to clip out and bring in. Tuesday was Buy One Kugel, Get One Free. On Wednesday, he offered twenty-percent discounts on fresh meat. It took all Baruch's energy just to keep the place running. Though they officially closed at eight, he had enough work to keep him there for many more hours. Each new piece of machinery seemed to add an extra hour to his day. The equipment became his boss. He remembered, as if from a former life, the verse that claimed, "It is not up to us to finish the work, nor is it up to us to desist from it." Whoever wrote that didn't have a business to run, didn't have to worry about angry suppliers and late deliveries, demanding customers and unruly machinery. To go home would only make the next day worse. Kroger was open twenty-four hours, the fluorescent lights always glaring, and it was easy to forget that there was a separation between night and day, work and home.

———

At the end of a long day, two men showed up bearing a deluxe-model rotisserie, capable of roasting fifty-two chickens at once. It was glass fronted, stainless steel, and six feet tall, with eight removable spits and four separate heating elements. They came, tools in hand, to install it in a tiny sliver of space next to the convection oven.

The phone rang as they were installing and venting it, and Baruch assumed it was Herschel, calling to remind him about this delivery. Instead, it was his mother. He had a hundred things to do, but his mother talked on, this time about *Kabbalah for the Layman*. He tuned her in and out, and it didn't make a difference. Even when he listened, he didn't understand half of what she was talking about. She had stopped filling him in on what was going on at home. She had stopped telling him how nice it would be if he invited Ilana to visit, if he called his father at the office just to talk. Instead, she talked about souls and light, focus and feeling. It was hard to believe that this was the same religion he practiced.

"I was thinking," Naomi said finally, "maybe we could all be together for the seders. You and Tzippy and her whole family could come to us. It's the first Pesach since you got married, and I thought it would be special."

There were rules for how to divide up the holidays, whose parents they were supposed to go to when. The seders were supposed to be at the wife's family's, at least in the first year of marriage. Though Shayna had been reminding them of this for months, they were planning to stay in Memphis. Tzippy wanted this more than he did. She had insisted that she didn't want to go home.

Baruch had agreed because of all the work he had to do for the holiday. He was so tethered to his job that the idea of ever going anywhere felt impossible. Pesach was the highlight of the year for the kosher food business. These days, anything—even cereal, pasta, or bagels—could be made kosher for Passover. People who didn't usually care about kosher made a point of keeping it for this one week. Some bought new dishes and did everything according to the letter of the law. Others made ham and cheese sandwiches but used matzo instead of bread. Herschel and Baruch were planning to stay open until the last minute to capitalize on the pre-Pesach need for takeout as people cleaned their kitchens. Then, in an overnight blitz, they were going to clean and blowtorch the place. The next morning, they would open, ready for Pesach.

"It sounds nice, but we're planning to stay here in Memphis," Baruch said to his mother.

"It would be great for all of us," Naomi persisted. "Promise me that you'll think about it."

He said he would, because that was the only way she would let him get off the phone. Then he got back to work.

Past midnight, he was still there, trying to stay awake. With each task he did, he put off calling Tzippy. He already knew how the conversation would go. At first, she would sound happy to hear from him. Her voice would rise in expectation, as she asked if he was done yet. When he said he wasn't, she would want to know when he would be. He wouldn't be able to give her a definite answer, and she would grow annoyed.

He knew that she was unhappy about their recent expansion. She was critical of the decisions he and Herschel had made. She grew angrier when he told her about his conversations with the investors, who had warned him that they were losing patience with Herschel. In fights that invariably took place late at night, on the phone, when he had a hundred things to do, she blamed him for going along with Herschel's grand plans. She asked him why he was so intent on cleaning up the mess Herschel was creating, when she was sure that The Kosher Connection would ultimately fail. But then she grew tired of talking about it. She turned her attention from him and from the business and focused on her schoolwork. He could see her decide to stop caring about what he was doing. But she didn't tell him what she was thinking. He felt her holding back.

Baruch was so tired that he unwittingly did things twice. He recorded the purchases of the day and fell asleep. When he woke up, he recorded them again. In the haze of sleep deprivation, he paced to keep awake. Each time he meant to call Tzippy, he was distracted by something else he needed to do. This time it was the rotisserie, which was buzzing continuously. Baruch hoped the sound meant that it was working, though it could just as easily be a serious malfunction. It could mean that the machine was overheating and was about to explode in a mess of flames and chicken parts. The noise made the ache in his head vibrate. He searched for a service number. But there were no instructions except for the best way to skewer the chickens. He turned the switch off and then back on. But that only made the noise worse.

"Could you shut up?!" he screamed at the machine.

He was too tired to care that he was yelling at his equipment. The noise continued, whining and rattling. When he couldn't stand it any longer, he kicked the metal bottom of the rotisserie, and the machine grew quiet. All he heard was the hum of the refrigerator and the faint sound of carts rolling by. In this lull, Baruch sat at a table, surrounded by brown boxes and a blizzard of Styrofoam peanuts. He put his head in his hands and fell asleep. He awoke two hours later to the rotisserie rattling, the lights glaring, and his wife standing before him.

"It's almost two in the morning," Tzippy said.

As he blinked and tried to wake up, she couldn't hide her frustration. She was furious that he was making mistakes with the business, furious that he wouldn't stand up to her father. But he no longer saw things as she did. She stared at him and wondered who was this person, her husband. He had become subsumed into Herschel's dreams. He had also adopted Herschel's work habits. Days blurred into nights until there was no difference between the two. She barely saw Baruch anymore. She fell asleep to his promises that he would be home soon. In the night, as she slept, she was aware that he was crawling into bed. She was too tired to say anything to him. Then, when she woke up in the morning, he was already gone.

That night, she hadn't been able to stand it anymore. When she woke up at two in the morning and he still wasn't home, she tried not to care. She tried to let it be his job, his problem. But she had been too upset to fall back to sleep. In a bolt of decision, she had gotten out of bed, thrown on her clothes, and come here.

"It looks like you're having a garage sale," Tzippy said.

She had thought she would feel satisfaction at seeing her father on the brink of failure. As she lay alone in bed, she had imagined The Kosher Connection going up in flames. She had envisioned a batch of chopped liver going bad and poisoning the entire city. She had fanta-sized about the earth opening and swallowing Kroger whole.

But instead Tzippy looked at the mess and felt it calling her back. She was still tied to it, no matter how distant she had wanted to become. She had been determined not to let the mess they made land at her feet. But now here it was, and she couldn't walk away.

There were no signs of the work she had once done. Most of the menus she had made were gone. Those that remained were torn. The once white floors needed a good washing. The five tables were crowded together, and they were sticky. The glass front of the counter had fingerprints across it. Every space was stacked high with food and paper, plastic containers and metal tins, glass and wire and flashing lights. The storeroom was filled with boxes and piles of papers, deliv-eries to be unpacked, utensils to be organized.

At the sight of the flashing red ALWAYS OPEN sign, Tzippy shook her head. "Can you turn that thing off? It's making me crazy."

"I think your father wants it on, in case someone passes by and doesn't notice us."

"First of all, you're not 'always open.' And second of all, I don't think it's possible to walk by and not notice this mess."

She unplugged the sign, enjoying the sparks of blue that crackled at the end of the cord. Then, overwhelmed by the clutter, Tzippy sat down in the only unoccupied space. Baruch joined her, and the two of them leaned back against the refrigerator.

"Are you going to tell me what all this is?" she asked.

"It's equipment."

"I can see that. But why is it here? Do you really think anyone is going to buy cotton candy?"

"A restaurant in Tupelo, Mississippi, was going out of business, and your father bought it for almost nothing."

"How are you going to pay for all this?"

"You have to spend money to make . . . ," Baruch started to say but trailed off. "That's what your father says. Once people see that we have a larger selection, they'll come in more and spend more."

"Do you really think this is going to last?" she asked.

"I don't know, but I can't think about that right now," he said. "I'm just trying to keep the place running. The rest is up to your father."

"Where is he, anyway?"

"Yesterday he called to say he was in Birmingham. He thinks it's ripe for something like this."

"Well, I think my father is crazy," Tzippy said.

Baruch stood up and went back to work. He tried to put away a week's worth of supplies that had been stacked on the countertops and piled on the floor. But he worked slowly. He picked up each pan and stared at it, trying to remember where it went. He read each stray piece of paper before deciding what to do with it.

"Let me do it," she said.

Tzippy grabbed the papers from him. She got rid of the duplicate sheets and filed the packing slips. She hung the inventory list on the wall. She stacked boxes and chased Styrofoam peanuts. When she had created some semblance of order, Tzippy looked at the bills. On the small desk in the corner of the kitchen, there were unfinished financial reports that hadn't been sent to the investors, unanswered letters from their lawyer requesting a meeting. Next to these was a pile of unopened envelopes and pink customer copies for goods delivered, some duplicates and triplicates, having been sent out in thirty-day increments to no avail.

As Tzippy cleared away boxes, she imagined spinning around the kitchen, overturning pots and pans, leaping from the top of one oversized steel appliance to another, her legs extended into a grand jeté. She would stretch out her arms and whirl around, sending cans, forks, and flour flying across the room.

This time, instead of imagining it, she did it. Tzippy took the bills and receipts from their piles and threw them in the air. They floated down, onto the desk, onto the floor, onto her lap.

"What are you doing?" Baruch yelled.

He grabbed her hand and tried to stop her. She jerked away from him, and he dropped to the floor, trying to gather the papers. He was on his hands and knees, scampering after them. But she couldn't stop herself. She laughed at him and tore up more bills and receipts and order forms. She threw the tiny scraps of paper into the air, letting them float down on her hair, her clothes, in Baruch's face, a veil of white fluttering between them.

— TWENTY-EIGHT —

For the remainder of the week, Tzippy and Baruch tiptoed around each other. Sometimes she caught him looking at her, as if trying to decide who she was. He was tentative when he talked to her. On his face was a mixture of horror and awe. She knew she was supposed to apologize for her display of anger. She was supposed to disavow it. But she couldn't. Instead, she held on to how good it had felt to do exactly what she wanted. She didn't talk to Baruch about this, though. He would hear what she said and then wonder how to bring back the sweet girl he thought he had married.

They hid this distance by being busy. Baruch left the house early, before she woke up. She went to class and spent her days at the library. By the time he came home, she was already in bed. She pretended to be asleep as he got into bed next to her. Then, as he fell asleep, she lay awake. She reached over to stroke his back. She could close her eyes and imagine it exactly. There was the birthmark on his left shoulder. The shoulders led to soft arms, which he told her had once been more muscular. She had teased him and said that she remembered. Her hand hovered above his skin. She felt him breathing, but she wasn't quite touching him. If she did, he would turn toward her and instinctively put his arm around her. In his half-sleep, he would mumble that he loved her. She could let herself slide into his words and his embrace. Or she could pull back and remain distant. She could view him across the divide of their bed.

Before she had met Baruch, she used to think "my husband," and these words held unlimited possibilities. She used to imagine lying in

bed next to her husband, never scared or lonely. In the arms of a husband, how could there be room for these feelings? His arms would
keep her safe, would hold her tight. She and her friends had once
debated the pros and cons of each boy they dated. Even on the brink of
engagement, some of them worried whether they were making the right
decision. Sometimes the bride, already dressed in white, asked her
friends for last-minute reassurance. But once they walked down the
aisle, they never looked back. They left behind all possibility of doubt.
In their visions of the marriage house, there was room for everything but
feelings of uncertainty.

But this was what she felt now. Tzippy got out of bed and walked
through the dark apartment. All around her were remnants of the
wedding. In a white porcelain frame, a picture of the two of them
smiled back at her. They had their arms shyly around each other's
waists, and she was looking up at him, her excitement reflected on her
cheeks. The wedding album, their names and the date embossed in
gold, was on the coffee table. The pictures in it had been painstakingly
compiled, selected from the hundreds of proofs her mother had sent
her. This one book would present the definitive version of what her
wedding had been.

She picked up their wedding video. There were three tapes in all,
every single moment recorded. There was also an edited "highlights"
version, and when she put that tape into the VCR, her wedding sprang
to life. In the dark living room, she watched it in fast-forward. At the
end of the video, there was a shot of her and Baruch face-to-face, hardly
noticing the presence of the camera and the entire video crew. Over
their faces, in calligraphy, the words "The End" unfurled. In the next
frame, more words appeared. Now, over their bodies and faces, these
words proclaimed, "This is not The End. It is only the beginning." And
that was it. The wedding that they had been planning her whole life
ended in a static of black and white across the TV screen.

What came next was the marriage, and for this Tzippy and her
friends had not prepared enough. They had thought that being happy
came guaranteed. Dating and engagement were likened to the six days
of creation. Marriage was like Shabbos, the day of rest, when they
could sit back and marvel at what they had wrought. She and her
friends had thought that they could measure someone by a list of qualities. They had thought that three dates or five dates or certainly ten

dates would tell them all they would need to know about someone. They had thought that, at age eighteen, they were fully formed. They had thought that they entered into marriage from fixed, stationary points. Now Tzippy didn't know what to do with her discovery that they were all in constant motion.

She had once longed for the walls of marriage to hold her tightly in place. She had thought she would no longer fantasize about other ways she might be, no longer imagine herself assuming various shapes and forms. Now she wanted to know how much room there was inside a marriage. Were these walls as impermeable as she had thought? Were there any holes in them where she might slip out and explore?

And this was only the beginning. She and Baruch had barely set off, and already their marriage seemed so fragile. It reminded Tzippy of the glass eggs her mother collected and always warned the girls against touching. Of course, her sisters hadn't listened. They liked to rub their fingers across the cold glass. They rolled them over their cheeks, pressed them between their hands, and when they were feeling especially daring, tossed them back and forth in a game of hot potato. Usually the eggs could withstand this; the girls put them back in the breakfront when they heard their mother coming, and there was no way to tell what they had done. Once, though, Dena had picked up an egg, and before she could press it, roll it, or toss it, it shattered in her hands.

It suddenly occurred to Tzippy how much she missed her mother. She needed to know how her mother had managed. She needed to know if any of this uncertainty lay behind the perfectly assembled version of Shayna that she and her sisters had come to expect. Sometimes Tzippy had seen a flicker of anger pass across her mother's face when Herschel wasn't home when he had said he would be, when a business venture didn't go as planned. Sometimes she caught the far-off looks on her mother's face. But these looks always passed. There was no room on Shayna's face, in their house, for them to linger. Even though it was late, Tzippy called her mother. She wondered whether this late at night, when her mother had taken off her clothes and her wig, she might also let out whatever lay behind her smile.

"Hi, Mom, it's me," she said when her mother picked up on the first ring.

"Tzippy!" her mother exclaimed.

Shayna was surprised to hear from her, as if she had long since given up. Usually Tzippy tried to get off the phone as quickly as possible. She stayed on the phone with her sisters to avoid talking to her mother. She asked questions to avoid saying anything about herself. She assumed that her mother knew she was going to college, and she had waited for her to say something about it. But she never did, at least not directly. Shayna laid traps and waited for Tzippy to step in one of them. She asked what she did every day. She asked why she always seemed so busy. But Tzippy navigated carefully, letting this secret that they both knew about remain hidden.

Now, though, she wanted to spill herself out. She wanted to be able to say who she was, without having to hide or pretend. She told her mother that she was going to college. She said that she loved it. She said that she and Baruch were fighting. She couldn't stop worrying she had made a mistake in getting married, in coming to Memphis. And there was no time for them to even talk about it. Baruch was so consumed with work that there was no room for anything else. And even so, The Kosher Connection was on the brink of failure. Instead of wanting to help him, she imagined walking away. By the time she finished telling her mother everything, she was crying, her words caught in her sobs.

"It's not how I thought it would be," Tzippy said.

"You know what, Tzippy? It never is. It's never really like that," Shayna said, and sighed. "It's just what marriage is."

"What's the matter?" Tzippy asked. She was waiting for her mother to become upset about what she had said. She had expected Shayna to be disappointed in her and angry at her. Against this, she now knew how to defend herself. But faced with her mother's relative silence, she didn't know what to do.

"I'm fine," Shayna said.

"Are you sure?"

Her mother laughed, but her voice was still shaky. "Of course I'm sure."

"Are you still angry about our not coming home for Pesach?" Tzippy asked.

"My daughter won't come home for the seders. What's to be angry about?"

"We'll come this summer," she offered.

"Really? I thought maybe you were never going to come."

"Of course we are."

"Well, good. Because the girls can't wait to see you. All they talk about is how excited they are to see their married sister."

"You know it's because of how much work Baruch has. He says he can't leave. As it is, he doesn't know how he's going to get everything done in the next two weeks."

"Is Pesach really that soon," Shayna said.

"How are the preparations coming?" Tzippy asked.

This time of year, cleaning for Pesach was usually her mother's favorite topic of conversation. Tzippy asked about it so she could hear her mother talk. She expected her to light up as she said what she did every year. Shayna spent half the year cleaning, the other half recovering from the effort. Tzippy had grown up watching Shayna tape lists to the walls of the kitchen. Every day she checked off, with a red marker, another item: the girls' closets, the upstairs bathroom, the coat closet, the toy box. The list was in ascending order of difficulty, according to frequency of use and likelihood of finding chametz. When she found actual chametz—pretzels in Malky's tote bag, a peanut butter and jelly sandwich under Dassi's bed—she dangled it triumphantly between her fingers. But this year, Shayna didn't want to talk about it.

"I haven't started yet," she confessed.

—TWENTY-NINE—

Two weeks before Pesach, Shayna's recurring nightmare was that she had cleaned every inch of the house. She had turned every knapsack inside out, checked every pocket of every jacket, and run toothpicks along the grooves of the dining-room chairs in search of crumbs. The seder table was set. The girls were dressed. But she had forgotten to cook. The turkey was frozen, the matzo farfel unmade. The seder was starting, and all she had was a single matzo ball to divide among twenty guests.

This year the dream might come true. So close to Pesach, she shouldn't have time to sit. She shouldn't have time to think. Her broom, mop, and dust rag should have been in constant motion. She should have been done with the bedrooms and been moving on to the living room. A few days from now, she should be ready to take out all the silverware, wipe out the drawers, and line them with fresh shelving paper. But instead of getting ready, she was lying in bed. She saw what needed to be done, but she couldn't stop thinking about how she wished they could go away for Pesach. Every year, her friends went somewhere fabulous. Aruba, they said, because we're tired of Miami. Scottsdale this year, because San Juan didn't live up to our expectations. Shayna always tried to nod sympathetically. "It sounds wonderful," she would say. "But we prefer to be home. I can't imagine not making Pesach." Of course it was a lie. Not to cook, not to clean? If she could, she would run away and leave the kitchen, the whole house, behind.

When her friends asked what was wrong, Shayna insisted that

everything was fine. If they didn't believe her, they chalked it up to the pre-Pesach cleaning that was sapping everyone's energy. But even without the cleaning, Shayna was exhausted. Herschel was home only intermittently. He was working on something new, and when he called, he was always in a different city, surrounded by new people. In one of these conversations, she told him that it would be nice if they could go away for Pesach. She had tried to keep her voice light, as if she were just expressing a preference, a slight wish. He listened and said he would do what he could. He said you never know how things will work out, and then, she was sure, he forgot all about it. She didn't tell him that this wish grew so deeply in her that it had roots that spread into every inch of her body. She didn't tell him that she wished, all night long, for everything she wanted but didn't have. She lay alone in bed but couldn't fall asleep. She looked helplessly at the mess in the house. She ignored the wedding bills, which still hadn't been paid off. She yelled at the girls, who at any given moment were either crying or whining or teasing or screaming. She couldn't daven, she couldn't get dressed. She didn't want to eat, didn't want to move, didn't want to think.

A few days before, Shayna had been at Kosher-Mart, doing her Pesach shopping. She had her list from last year, where she had marked off what she had run out of, what she had left over. With these notes, she hoped to have one year when she bought exactly the right amount. In the macaroon aisle, she was mulling over the different flavors when she saw Shoshana Schachter. Shayna studied her list and pretended not to notice her.

For a trip to Kosher-Mart, Shoshana Schachter wore high heels and a silk blouse. Her makeup looked recently touched up. She looked Shayna up and down and glanced at the contents of her shopping cart. Then Shoshana picked up a box of macaroons and saw the OC symbol. She glanced at Shayna, and Shayna saw a flicker pass across her eyes. Shayna had tried to plug the leaks with a flurry of words. She had claimed that Herschel had quit the OC because he and Baruch were doing so well. With most people, she could pretend. But Shoshana Schachter knew from her husband that Herschel had been fired. She took one look at Shayna and saw right through her.

Shayna swerved her cart and tried to get around Shoshana. But there was no escape. She felt stares and whispers coming from every aisle.

No longer paying attention to what she needed, Shayna piled potato starch, grape juice, and jellied fruit slices into her cart.

When she got to the checkout counter, Shoshana Schachter was talking with a group of her best friends. Though they presumably had been cleaning for days, everything about them was flawlessly in place. Two weeks before the holiday, they were probably finished with their preparations. Those who weren't finished probably had little work to do in the first place; they were no doubt going away. These were the women Shayna had always wanted to become. Their lives and their homes and their clothes all appeared to be smooth and seamless and whole. As if there were no children's sticky hands, no husbands' empty promises. There were no lists compiled in their heads of all they must do. There were no equally long lists of everything that would never get done. Their lives came together in perfect, sharp points.

Just standing near them made her feel bad. No matter how much she tried, she would never be like them. She had chased after them for years, with her clothes and with her home, with everything she had and everything she wanted. And it didn't matter, because she would never catch up with them. Whenever she thought she had finally come close, they effortlessly sailed beyond her reach.

Now Shayna pulled herself out of bed and stood in front of the window. She wondered if her neighbors ever felt what she did. She was so tired of trying. Were there other women besides herself who couldn't do it anymore? Maybe they too wished they could take leave of their hardworking, childbearing selves. They could wind up their bodies and send them off to do housework, while they lay on lounge chairs in a place where dinner was already made, floors swept clean, and they were served frozen tropical drinks topped with paper umbrellas.

Malky, Dena, and Dassi came bounding into Shayna's room as she was getting back into bed. Shayna had stopped watching the wedding video, but the television was still in the living room, and the girls had been spending their waking hours, when they weren't at school, in front of it. They stared at the screen with open-mouthed wonder. It didn't matter what was on. The shows were less thrilling than the commercials, and they went around the house humming jingles from Burger King and Pizza Hut. They knew which toys to request for next

Chanukah. They crafted mock commercials for cleaning products and cars. They acted out game shows and soap operas.

"Can we come in?" they asked as they climbed into her bed.

They had stopped asking what was wrong. They knew that their mother's inability to get out of bed qualified as something you didn't talk about. For the first time in their lives, no one was paying attention to every detail. From hair ribbons to socks, they were on their own. Zahava was doing the bare minimum required of her as the eldest. Her primary chore was bribing her sisters into fending for themselves. Malky, Dena, and Dassi were happy to oblige. They could live out their lifelong fantasy that they were orphans surviving in the wilderness.

"Okay," Malky ordered, continuing the game they had begun in front of the TV. "If you could eat anything you wanted, what would it be? List your first choice for meat and for milk."

They weighed McDonald's versus Taco Bell, Pizza Hut, and Chuck E. Cheese, their evidence gathered from the commercials that brought these images into their imaginations. It didn't matter that they lived in the thick of Brooklyn, on a block lined with kosher pizza, kosher candy, kosher Chinese food. They still wanted more.

"It's not fair," Dassi whined. "We don't even know what we're missing."

"We don't even know anyone who's tried it," Dena agreed.

"I did," Shayna said, "once upon a time."

The chatter stopped, and they stared at her in shock. Dassi instinctively put her hand out and rested it on Shayna's leg, checking to make sure this was still their mother.

"When I was your age, I wasn't religious. I didn't grow up like this."

"Pizza Hut?" Malky gasped.

"And Taco Bell?" Dena asked.

Shayna gathered the girls into a semicircle in her arms. Usually she would have chided them not to say such things. She would have made up a fairy tale about how she became religious. She would have tried to banish the treif food that waltzed through their minds.

"Do you miss it?" Dassi wanted to know.

"Tell us what it's like," Malky begged.

She looked at their expectant faces. The food was so appealing to them in part because it was so forbidden. Treif wasn't everything, she wanted to tell them. Actually it was so little, such a small thing to give up. Not once had she looked back and regretted becoming Orthodox. Without it, her whole life would have been bare, a room with no furnishings, no decorations, no people. But she also understood their curiosity, and it no longer felt as threatening to let it into her home. She knew how hard it was to want something that would always elude her. She felt for their desires, for Tzippy's, and for her own. She thought about it. If she could fling herself out of this world for one minute and taste all the possibilities, fulfill all her desires, what would she compare it to? To a Viennese dessert table where the food replaced itself as it was eaten? To a smorgasbord made according to the wishes and hungers of every guest? To a grocery store where everything was free? To a seven-course meal where you never had to undo the tight waistband of a skirt? To the rabbinic tales of the banquets that would exist in the world to come, where the greatest delicacies would be laid out as a reward for the righteous?

"Imagine being able to go anywhere and eat anything. Whatever you want, you can have."

Teeming with envy, the girls ran off to revise their games. Now Shayna would get a starring role. She would become a main character in the soap operas they were acting out. They would dream up tales of amnesia, kidnapping, and blackmail. They would ask her to tell this story every day. When she grew tired of telling it, they would recount it to their friends and to one another, embellishing every detail. Each word she told them would take up hours of imagining in their minds.

When Shayna finally fell asleep, she dreamed about a world made of glazed sweets and her daughters dancing among them. She lifted her huge skirt and all five of them came scurrying out. They were costumed in jewel-colored glazes and dusted with powdered sugar. They were dancing across the stage, each in her own direction, and it was okay. When Shayna woke again, she saw, standing in her doorway, a Tzippy all grown up, a Tzippy who wasn't supposed to be there.

This Tzippy had her hands on her hips. "What's going on here?" she asked.

Tzippy's eyes adjusted to the dark of her mother's room and zeroed in on what was wrong. It was nine at night. Shayna was in her nightgown, and the girls weren't in theirs. The television was on and a trail of cookies led from room to room. Every bed in the house was unmade. Every cup and every plate had been used and not washed.

"What are you doing here?" Shayna asked.

"Why are you in bed?" Tzippy asked.

"I'm not feeling well, that's all."

The girls had followed Tzippy into the bedroom. After a few moments of stunned silence, they all began to talk at once, telling Tzippy how they had banded together to nurse their ailing mother back to health.

"How long has this been going on?" Tzippy asked.

"Just a few days. I didn't want anyone to know. But I'm feeling better. I was just about to get out of bed when you walked in."

Tzippy had come because she couldn't stop thinking about the sadness in her mother's voice. It didn't matter that Tzippy had wanted to escape. In an instant, her mother could call her home. It also didn't matter that it was almost Pesach and Tzippy had preparations of her own to begin. It didn't matter that Baruch was hoping she would help him out with the work he needed to do. Despite the tension between them, he assumed she would step in and save him. She would cook the food, take the orders, satisfy the customers. She was being pulled in both directions. She belonged here and there. She had left home and she would never leave.

Once she had decided to go back to New York, she waited until Baruch came home from work to tell him. He walked in the door and immediately started talking about how swamped he was. He had barely been able to keep up with the workload before. Now he had to maintain the day-to-day operations while also getting ready for Passover.

"I need to go home," Tzippy said, and she tried to explain how her mother had sounded on the phone.

"When are you coming back?" he wanted to know. He was surprised and upset that she was going. He wanted her help, but more than that, he worried about why she wanted to leave.

"I'm not sure. I haven't thought about it yet," she said.

"You're not going to stay there for Pesach, are you?" he asked in disbelief.

"You could come too," she said.

"I wish I could."

For a second, she thought he would disentangle himself from The Kosher Connection and hand it back to Herschel. They would abandon it: leave the lights on, the food in the oven, and not worry about it. He would come with her, and they would somehow start over.

"I really can't," he decided. "I have too much to do."

"So what? Why can't you just leave? Who cares anymore?"

"I care. You know that. But it's not always going to be like this. I just need to make it past Pesach and then I can figure out what to do."

She shook her head in anger. "No," she said. "It's not okay. Nothing is okay here anymore."

"Come on, Tzippy," he pleaded.

He reached for her and tried to hug her. But she pulled away. All she wanted to do was run. She wouldn't look at him as she threw clothes into a bag. She packed her notebooks and textbooks. She didn't call to say she was coming. She wanted to catch her mother unprepared.

Within an hour of her arrival, Tzippy had a load of laundry going, the dishwasher running, and the girls in their nightgowns. Since she had been married, they had shuffled their bedrooms around. Now Malky and Zahava each had their own room. Dena and Dassi had taken over hers. She knocked on Malky's door, then Zahava's, and wished them good night. Dassi and Dena were excited to have Tzippy sleep with them in her old bedroom. They had decided to let her have her old bed, so they shared the extra bed that had been moved in there. Tzippy tucked them in, but they weren't ready to go to sleep. They asked her every question they could think of, trying to decide whether marriage had taken away their sister and replaced her with a grown-up. Most of all, they wanted to know why she was here.

"Because I missed you too much. I couldn't go one more day without giving each of you a hug," Tzippy said.

Though pleased with this response, they regarded it suspiciously.

"Did Baruch mind that you came without him?" Dena asked.

"He's swamped with work," she said. "Before Pesach is his busiest time."

"Is Daddy there too? Is he helping Baruch? Is that why he's not home?" Dassi asked.

She quieted them with one more kiss apiece and the promise that they would talk more in the morning. Then she turned off the light and got into her old bed. Though the room no longer belonged to her, Dassi and Dena had preserved her presence. Her posters were still on the walls, her china dolls lined up on the dresser. She hadn't brought them with her, not wanting to clutter her new apartment. Looking at what she had left behind, she felt as if she had been away forever. Maybe she had never lived here at all.

When she was engaged, she had imagined what it would be like to come home a married woman. She and Baruch would stay in her room, and this time they would close the door and shut out the rest of the house. It would feel illicit and scandalous, and best of all, it would be allowed. He would hang his clothes in her closet, unpack into the chest of drawers she had had since she was a little girl. They would huddle together in her twin bed. They would pull her pink-and-white bedspread over their heads to muffle the sound of their laughter.

She missed the girl who had imagined this. She missed the nights of her engagement when she and Baruch fell asleep on the phone, in their separate beds and separate rooms, dreaming of being together. She remembered how he looked when she first saw him and followed him, how she felt when she first began to imagine that they might end up together. She remembered when they had first touched, when it had still seemed so strange that they were allowed to live together. She missed all these moments. In the quiet house, this feeling grew until she ached with how badly she missed him. Her small bed felt empty. His absence filled her room; it filled the house. In the dark, nothing else seemed to exist.

Tzippy waited until her sisters fell asleep, and then she called him. His voice was heavy with sleep when he answered the phone and murmured her name.

"Are you awake?" she asked.

"A little," he said.

"So keep your eyes closed," she said. "But talk to me."

Trying not to wake her sisters, she whispered to him. He whispered too, even though he was the only one home. They didn't talk about their fight, about the work he had to do or the worries she had about her mother. For now, at least, they didn't want to think about any of it.

He said he had gone to sleep on her side of the bed. He was pretending that she was right next to him, where she should be. She said that she wished they could spend the whole night on the phone. They would fall asleep together and wake up together.

"Do you miss me?" she asked.

"So much," he said.

"I miss you too. Even when I was home, I missed you."

The house was still. Her room was warm with the steady breathing of her younger sisters. With covers over their heads, phones pressed to their ears, Tzippy and Baruch felt as they had when they were engaged. They remembered the pleasure of these late-night talks when they had yearned for each other across the wires.

In the morning, the house sprang to life, and Tzippy felt as if she had never left home. Her life with Baruch was a brief hiatus, a vacation or a dream. She braided hair, tied shoes, and made sandwiches. "Mommy's fine," she reassured her sisters. "Don't worry. She's tired. Maybe it's a little bit of a cold," she said as she bustled them off to school.

Then the house was quiet. Tzippy thought about trying to wake her mother, shaking her if need be. She was worried about her and wished she knew what to do. She thought about calling, paging, faxing, her father. She wanted to leave a flurry of messages that would force him home. But when she looked around, a more pressing need took over. She saw a house in need of Pesach cleaning. She had watched her mother do this so many times. But it was harder this year. Usually they made order from order. This time, the house was in chaos. Tzippy first had to return it to its usual clean state. All these years, the mess had been waiting for the day when Shayna let down her guard. Drawers were left open and clothing spilled out. Countertops were sticky. Plastic toys crunched underfoot.

Tzippy didn't stop. She didn't think about the fights she had had with Baruch. She didn't think about the mess Herschel had made in Memphis. She didn't think about the classes she was missing, the papers she was supposed to be writing. Instead, she scooped up dirty laundry with one hand while her other hand was already straightening the top of a dresser. She had finally discovered her mother's secret. The busier she was, the easier it became to forget. If she cleaned and cooked and ran the house, there would be no space to think about anything else.

But no matter how much she did, the work seemed endless. Tzippy wished she could pick up the house and shake out the crumbs. She imagined putting her sisters through a car wash. When the girls came home from school, Tzippy put them to work. She made color-coded lists and handed out assignments. Dena was the duster, Malky the mopper, Zahava the vacuumer, Dassi the searcher. By enlisting their help, she took one step forward and one step back. But there was no other way to do it. If she let them loose in the house, they would undo what she had done. She would be farther behind than when she started.

To her surprise, her sisters listened. The fun of disorder had faded, and they were happy to have someone in charge. They gleefully did their jobs, looking for chametz as if they were on a scavenger hunt.

"Good, Dena," Tzippy said when her sister came in to report that she had finished her job. "Now I want you to go through the books on your shelf, open them up, and make sure there are no crumbs between the pages." Her voice was sterner than she meant it to be, but there was so much work to be done. "And no cheating. I mean it. Every single book," she called after her.

Tzippy checked things off her list. She didn't pause before moving on to the next task. There was no time to think about what would happen if they didn't make it in time for the holiday. Kares was the prescribed punishment for those who ate chametz on Pesach. Your soul shall be cut off from your people, the Torah said. As a little girl learning this in school, Tzippy had shivered at the thought. She imagined her whole family cut loose from their world, circling the globe in a never-ending orbit.

Five days before Pesach, Tzippy tackled the kitchen. She started with the freezer, which was usually filled with labeled Tupperwares of lasagna and soup and chicken. Now, though, the Tupperwares were pushed to the side and the shelves were crowded with twelve identical bakery boxes.

Tzippy took them out and lined them up on the counter. She snipped the white string and opened one of the boxes. Inside was a cake in the shape of a lavender hat, with frosted pink flowers and bows. It looked like the spring hats Shayna had in her closet, waiting to be worn on Pesach, when all the women switched from wool to straw. She imagined her mother wearing this cake on her head. She would walk proudly to her seat at shul, waiting to receive compliments on her confection.

It took Tzippy a moment to realize that these cakes were from her wedding. As was true about most of the guests her mother had insisted on inviting, she knew the cakes had been there only from the pictures and the video. She had no actual memory of them. They had been just one more detail that her mother had cared about so deeply and Tzippy hadn't needed or noticed. She still didn't need cakes like this, but now she ached for her mother who had wanted them so badly. At the wedding, these cakes had fit in with the imported satin and organza overlays. Now, they looked like overdressed guests at a party, trying too hard. In their flowers, their bows, their pinks and their purples, they held pieces of her mother, as if she had baked herself into them. If Tzippy cut one open, her mother's desires might come spilling out.

A few hours later, the girls came back into the kitchen and held up stray Cheerios and pretzel rods. Dassi displayed a whole challah roll that she had extracted from under her bed.

"Have you looked in your backpacks? In the closets? In your books?" Tzippy asked.

When they promised her that they had looked everywhere, Tzippy sat them down at the kitchen table. She passed out paper towels as placemats and instructed them to tuck napkins under their chins. Then she laid before them the purple hat cake. The girls couldn't believe their good fortune. At the wedding, the cakes had gone uneaten because no one could eat something so pretty. Shayna had brought them home with her, and for weeks after the wedding the girls had spied on them daily. They'd counted the boxes and tried to fold back the cardboard and peek inside. But Shayna shooed them away from the freezer. She couldn't bear to cut the cakes. She said she was saving them for a special occasion.

Tzippy cut them each a wedge of cake. It was chocolate on the inside, and between each of the three layers was raspberry crème. Dena nodded her head knowingly. She had suspected the presence of crème all along. They stuffed cake into their mouths before Tzippy could change her mind and take it away. They gobbled up their pieces with no thoughts of later.

To their shock, Tzippy asked if they wanted seconds, and they nodded enthusiastically. They ate those pieces with the same fervor. Zahava initially claimed to be on a diet and took only a single bite. Then she took one more, her last, then another, her very last. Soon the girls didn't bother to ask Tzippy to cut them another piece, one with a flower or a bow. They plucked them off with their fingers and ate with their hands.

"Why aren't you eating?" Dassi asked Tzippy.

"I'm not hungry," she said.

They stared at her in disbelief. This was wedding cake, and hunger had nothing to do with it.

"You have to eat," Dassi insisted.

Malky held up a spoonful of cake in front of Tzippy's mouth. "Just taste it," she said.

Powerless against the collective will of her sisters, Tzippy took a bite. The defrosted cake still tasted fresh. After one bite, Tzippy felt like she could eat the whole cake. The appetite that had been hiding since she came home returned with new force. She spooned cake and icing into her mouth, feeling like she hadn't eaten since she had gotten married and left this kitchen.

Soon five stomachs were clutched and bursting. And there was still a quarter of the cake left.

"I think I'm going to vomit."

"Come on, just a tiny piece."

"Pesach is in five days. Someone has to finish it. It's a mitzvah."

"Not me. I've already had four pieces."

"Well, I've had five."

"So throw it away."

"It's *wedding* cake. You can't throw it away."

"Tzippy should eat it. She didn't have her share."

"And it was her wedding."

Tzippy took another piece on her fork, as if she were going to eat it. Instead, she flicked it across the table. A dollop of icing landed on Zahava's cheek. The girls stared at Tzippy in awe. They were certain that even when she was their age she didn't misbehave like this. But unable to come up with a way to explain this as an accident, their eyes danced and their faces lit up.

"I'm telling," Malky said.

"Who are you going to tell? I'm in charge now," Tzippy said.

Zahava placed cake at the edge of her fork and took aim. Tzippy took it gracefully, cake in her face and on her blouse. Then she started to laugh. The girls took this as a good sign and flung cake at one another. Chunks of chocolate cake and purple icing sailed across the table. Dena chased Malky and mashed cake into her hair. They took particular pleasure in messing up Zahava's outfit. Dassi plunged, face-first, into the remaining piece. There was chocolate on their clothes, on their faces, laced between their eyelashes, encrusted in their hair. Raspberry crème was on the walls and all over the floor. They started to laugh, loudly, hysterically, holding nothing back, not worrying about how it sounded or how it would look if anyone walked in.

"Okay," Tzippy said when they grew quiet. "I think we've done enough damage for one day."

She sent them upstairs to wash their hands and faces. The kitchen was messier than when she began. There was now chametz in the crevices of the table, in hard-to-reach spots on the ceiling, tracked upstairs on the soles of their shoes. But Tzippy didn't worry about it yet. Instead, she sat at the table and enjoyed the noise of their stomping up the stairs, jostling for position around the sink. She hoped her mother could hear them as well. She heard the faucet shut off and then the patter of feet into bedrooms, where the girls put on their nightgowns and got ready for bed. There was no need for dinner tonight. The five of them had finished off a cake meant to feed twenty.

Which left eleven cakes that after almost a year in the freezer still looked too good to eat. The first one thumped as it hit the bottom of the garbage can. The thumps grew softer, each cake padding the landing of the next. A pink hat against a yellow one, two butterflies, a treasure box, a lattice basket filled with marzipan strawberries. To the bursting garbage bag, Tzippy added one gorgeous cake after another.

The next morning, Tzippy willed herself to pull off her covers and sit up in bed. But she couldn't move. She closed her eyes and went back to sleep for another hour. She was driven out of bed by a wave of nausea that rolled across her stomach. Everything in Tzippy's body had turned to sloshing water. She hung over the toilet bowl, retching, though nothing came out. When the nausea passed, she didn't want to go back to her room. She cracked open her mother's bedroom door.

"Mommy?" she said softly.

"Come in," Shayna murmured, without opening her eyes.

Tzippy lay down. She pulled the blankets up and curled against her mother, waiting to be taken into her arms, to have her hair smoothed, her stomach rubbed.

Shayna rolled over. "Tzippy," she said, surprised.

"I don't feel well," Tzippy said.

"Here," Shayna said. "I'll draw on your back."

She had played this with the girls for years, scratching their backs, then writing words and drawing pictures for them to guess. Of all the girls, Tzippy deciphered them the fastest. She could tell the difference between a cat and a hot-air balloon. She felt the shape of each letter against her skin.

"This is a hard one," she said, and wrote out the first thing that came to mind: Mrs. Tziporah Miller.

Tzippy knew but didn't say. So Shayna wrote it again and again. Each time the letters became permanent fixtures on her back, penetrating Tzippy's skin, becoming who she was.

"Do you know?" Shayna asked.

"Of course," Tzippy said.

"I still can't believe it," Shayna said.

"Neither can I."

Her stomach calmed, Tzippy lay next to her mother. She was eleven years old again, and there was nowhere she would rather be than with her mother, in a cocoon of blankets, planning a wedding that would never come and never end. She was still the age when she stood in the kitchen as her mother braided challahs and baked cakes. She was young enough to think that from this kitchen her mother ran the world.

— THIRTY —

BARUCH HAD BEEN CALLING Herschel all week, on his home phone, his business phone, his cell phone, his beeper. All these ways to reach him and he was nowhere. Until now, Herschel had been in constant contact. He had called with ideas. He had called to check in. He had called to see if Baruch had unwrapped the latest delivery. But now that Baruch needed him, he was hard to find. He became a series of long messages and hand-scribbled faxes received in the middle of the night.

Finally, when Baruch managed to track him down, Herschel only had a few minutes. He had someone on the other line, he was late for a meeting, he had people waiting to talk to him.

"I don't know what to do," Baruch said, and he began to list the problems. He hoped Herschel would tell him which switch to jiggle on the machine, which bill to pay first, which magic words to use to calm his customers. "And the investors keep calling. They said they've left messages and tried to fax you, but they can't get in touch with you. They're very upset, and they're ready to pull out if we don't get things under control."

"Don't worry so much," Herschel said. "So the investors are nervous. The customers have a few complaints. What are they going to do? Go to the other kosher restaurant in Memphis? Anyway, I have a surprise for you. Guess where I am? Houston, Texas. I've found the next new idea," Herschel said, and he hung up before Baruch could say anything else.

In the beginning, Baruch had been convinced by Herschel's reassurances. He had listened to his grand ideas. He had even become part of them. Despite the problems and the complaints, Baruch had believed.

But now every new piece of equipment chipped away at this belief, and Baruch could no longer keep his doubts at bay. He knew that they had overexpanded. They were spending too much money, and it was becoming more difficult to recoup any of it. They had alienated their customer base and hadn't listened to the investors whose money gave them the right to be in charge. In the spaces between Herschel's dreams, a rational, skeptical voice was creeping in. Baruch was his father's son after all.

Three days before Pesach, the investors came with pained looks on their faces and said that they were pulling out. They had been willing to lose money if it meant that there would be somewhere to eat out. But The Kosher Connection was a money-consuming machine. They had a pile of unpaid bills. They couldn't go to shul without hearing an assortment of complaints. The manager of Kroger was threatening to terminate their lease. After Pesach, they were going to close. But they still wanted somewhere to eat out. They were angry with Herschel, but they had seen how hard Baruch worked. They asked if he was interested in staying in Memphis. He could manage whatever they tried next. Maybe a steakhouse, they thought. Maybe pizza.

Baruch couldn't respond. He had put in so much time, poured in so much of his energy. His job had entered his mind, his body, and expanded until there was no room left for anything else. He had given up his learning because of it. He had let it come between him and Tzippy. He had dreamed of it and prayed for it. Baruch had always imagined belief to be made of solid, impermeable stone. But he saw now that it was made of glass, and it shattered within him.

As soon as they left, Baruch reached for the phone. A few hours before, he had made desperate attempts to get Herschel on the phone. But now he didn't want to talk to him. Baruch didn't want to hear dreams. He didn't want to hear plans. Feeling alone and in over his head, he longed for straightforward advice. He wanted to hear the smart, practical voice of his father, who would know what he should do.

Until now, he hadn't mentioned to his parents that there were prob-

lems with the business. He had answered their questions with a ubiq-
uitous "Everything's fine." He hadn't said anything because he was
afraid his father would gloat at having been right. But Baruch had bigger problems to worry about now.

He called his father at the office and waited for Joel's secretary to
put him through. When Joel picked up the phone, he was surprised to
hear Baruch's voice. He sounded gruff initially, but Baruch persisted,
past the outer layer to where he knew his father would be willing to
listen. Baruch didn't worry about the awkwardness, the distance,
about all that had been said or not said. He told his father what had
happened. He described how hard he had worked and how the business had failed anyway.

"You did all of that by yourself?" Joel asked.

His father sounded impressed. He ignored the ringing of his second
phone line, the voice of his secretary over the intercom. He listened
carefully and sounded more involved than he had in years.

"Did you sign any sort of contract? Are you listed as a partner or an
employee? Do you have any named liability?"

To all of this Baruch said no. He was tied to the counter merely
by the fact that he had believed in it. He had spent years wondering
why his father worked so hard. But now he understood. He knew what
it was to care about a job, to feel responsibility for it resting on his
shoulders.

"Good. So get out of it," Joel advised. "Listen to the investors. It's
their money, so it belongs to them. Sell off what you can. Close it up.
Finish what you need to do. And then come home."

— THIRTY-ONE —

THREE DAYS BEFORE Pesach, Naomi had work to do. Any laxity she accepted during the year was gone when it came to Pesach. She didn't overlook a single detail. "Dirt isn't chametz," Joel liked to tell her. But she didn't want to hear it. She had too much to do.

In this manic burst of cleaning and cooking, she tried to summon her excitement about the approaching holiday. She wanted to connect to generations of women like herself who had turned their houses upside down in the search for the sometimes tangible, sometimes metaphysical crumbs. By cooking and cleaning, she would find her connection to the women of the past. If she scrubbed a countertop until it shone, she might be able to see their kerchief-covered heads, their wrinkled, knowing faces staring back. Her ancestors might have been worn down from the work, from the worry about how to find the extra money to pay for matzo and wine. She, in her well-equipped modern kitchen, might seem worlds apart. But these women were part of her, and she wanted to feel them.

Keeping busy was better than focusing on how empty the dining-room table would look with only three places set. She had wanted to create a seder for her family that would bind them together. She had read up on experimental seders, on the meaning of Passover. She had been sure that Baruch and Tzippy would change their minds and come. She hadn't made other plans. She hadn't invited other guests. As the holiday drew nearer and the change of heart from Baruch and Tzippy hadn't taken place, she found it hard to keep reading and planning. This year, she also found it harder to clean. In previous years, the work had been transformed by the festive feeling of having everyone home and guests expected. But now, with her disappointment hanging over her, it just felt like work.

Naomi finished cleaning. Her counters were covered with sheets of plastic, her burners and stovetop with aluminum foil. The pantry was lined with shelving paper. Her kitchen was ready for Pesach. But there was no chance to rest. It was time to start cooking.

When Joel came home from work, Naomi was knee-deep in matzo meal and eggshells. Ingredients were spread out over the counter.

"Guess who called me today," he said as he came into the kitchen.

She was too tired to play along. She stopped working and sank into a chair.

"I give up. Who?"

"Bryan," he said.

"He did?" she asked, surprised to hear it. "I don't suppose he said that he's coming home for Pesach."

"No, he said that they're closing down The Kosher Connection."

Now she was even more surprised. "Why? What happened?"

He told her what Baruch had said, and she became upset. She was worried for him and for Tzippy. And she dreaded what would come next. The holiday would be swallowed up in Joel's reproach. This would become the conversation around the seder table. They would intersperse the four cups of wine with fighting about what, if anything, they should do to help.

"But what is Baruch going to do?" she asked.

"I don't know. He has a few options, but I don't think he knows yet."

"Aren't you upset about this? This is terrible. How can you be so calm?"

"He's a big boy. He knows what he's doing," Joel said.

She looked at him in amazement. Before, she would have done anything to bring Joel and Baruch together. She would have torn down the barriers between them with her bare hands. But they had done it by themselves. Or started to. Joel was the one who should have been angry. She would have expected him to say that he knew all along that this would happen. Even though it was true, he said none of this. Instead she heard respect in his voice.

Later that night, Naomi was still in the kitchen. She was flipping through her binder of Pesach recipes, trying to decide what to make. Though she rarely followed the recipes exactly, she still liked to collect them. She used them as a starting point for the dishes she made. The recipes had come from her mother and grandmothers, from great-aunts and cousins several times removed. None of her Pesach cakes or kugels were unattributed. Some of the recipes had been typed on note cards and glued onto the pages of the binder. Others were scribbled on scraps of paper, on the backs of grocery receipts. She could have copied them over. But she liked them this way. She liked to see the handwriting of relatives no longer alive. She liked to see the oil spills and the smudged numbers, to feel the sticky, sugary cards.

To her surprise, Ilana came into the kitchen and sat down at the table.

"You have matzo meal in your hair," Ilana said.

Naomi halfheartedly tried to brush it out. "I do? Oh well," she said.

"What are you doing?"

"Cleaning, cooking, everything."

"Do you want help?"

"Sure, if you want to," Naomi answered. She forced herself to stay nonchalant and not let on how badly she did want help. With Ilana, one false move and it would all be over. She would go back to her room. Naomi wouldn't know why she had come down, why she had left.

"So what should I do?" Ilana asked.

"I was hoping to make two desserts tonight. You can start the sponge cake if you want to. The recipe is in there."

Pesach sponge cake was her nemesis, but she felt an obligation to make it every year. The recipe had been passed down from her grandmother to her mother to her. With this recipe, she couldn't improvise or approximate. If she wanted the cake to stay intact, she had to follow it exactly. In addition to the ingredients, the recipe listed helpful tips about the cake: not to shout in its presence, not to check on it, not to stir too hard, not to overbeat the egg whites, not to use too much matzo meal. Even then, it didn't always come out. It worked or it didn't, of its own volition.

Ilana flipped the pages of the binder. She pried them apart looking for the recipe.

"Gross," Ilana said, and pulled out from between two pages a piece of paper, sticky with oil and matzo meal. Dangling it between two fingers, she handed it to her mother.

It was a flyer that had come in the mail the week before. WOMEN'S PRE-PASSOVER HEALING CIRCLE, it read. Naomi had laughed when she saw the date and wondered who would have time to attend. With so much work to be done at home, it was hard to think about uniting the upper and lower realms, hard to worry about centered consciousness or meaningful living. From the mailing lists she was on, she had also received flyers for Passover workshops, feminist seders, and dances of Miriam. She had looked at them wistfully, wishing she had the time to go to all of them. She had almost thrown this flyer away, then had shoved it into a drawer instead. It had made its way out of the drawer, and when she came across it again, on her nightstand, she used it to jot down a phone number. It was then carried downstairs to the kitchen, and from there it became a placeholder in her recipe binder.

Naomi put aside her recipes and turned off the mixer. She had learned to believe in signs, to believe that the world had a way of communicating its wishes. The cake could wait. The egg whites could stand or fall.

"Go get your shoes on," she told Ilana. "We're going out."

"We are?" Ilana asked, but didn't move.

"I mean it," Naomi said.

"Are you kidnapping me?"

"Something like that. Come on. It'll be fun."

"Like this?" Ilana asked, gesturing to the sweatpants and T-shirt she was wearing.

"Exactly like that. It's come as you are," Naomi said

The Women's Pre-Passover Healing Circle was intended to heal the bonds of slavery—physical, emotional, and spiritual. These circles had begun for the physically sick, to heal the soul when the body was also not well. But they were being used more widely to heal whatever ailed someone. When Naomi and Ilana walked into a darkened room in the local community center, the group was sitting in a circle on the floor. Soft music played in the background. Almost imperceptibly, people moved and made space for them.

"You have got to be kidding," Ilana whispered.

"Shh," Naomi whispered back. "You don't have to say a word. Just sit here with me."

A young rabbi sat in the circle. His beard was long, but so was his hair. He welcomed them and invited them to take their shoes off. Plant your feet firmly on the ground so your spirits can soar, he said. Naomi did what he said, and Ilana rolled her eyes but kicked off her sneakers. She sat a few inches back from the circle, afraid that someone might talk to her. Naomi had brought Ilana on a whim. She had wanted to come here so badly. For days, she had done little but get ready for Pesach. But inside, Naomi felt so unprepared. She would go into the holiday exhausted and worn out, having been enslaved by the needs of the kitchen. This year, she wanted to feel the holiday in her heart, not just in her house. She had hoped to share part of that desire with Ilana. She wanted her daughter to see that there was so much more to religion than her anger of the moment. Ilana was only at the beginning of becoming who she was going to be.

"Close your eyes and take deep breaths," the rabbi instructed. "Be aware of each breath."

Naomi closed her eyes. Among other people striving for the same thing, it was easier to concentrate.

The rabbi told the women to imagine themselves embarking on a spiritual exodus. Egypt, he said, was a place of fixed possibilities. With the stone of the pyramids and the mortar of the bricks, it locked people into place. Even its Hebrew name, Mitzrayim, meant "narrow." But the desert was wide and open and empty. It was a space between places, where change could occur. A haphazard band of slaves could be transformed into a nation.

In this desert, where anything could be, they were going to try to connect. "Think of the people you love," the rabbi said. "Let their faces fill your mind and try to connect with them. Peel back the layers that keep you apart, and try to see inside them.

"See the word 'connect' in your head," the rabbi continued. "Let it wash over you. Then try to see yourself. Turn your eyes backward and gaze into who you are. Push away anything that prevents you from seeing yourself. Connect with who you are, with who you want to be. Visualize the whole world in connection. Think of the parts of a tree, a leaf that becomes a twig which becomes a branch which becomes a trunk which becomes roots which become the ground and then the earth and then the whole world."

Naomi did this. She thought of her children and peeled back their masks and veils and outer garments. She trusted who they were on the inside. She was sure she would always be able to find them there. She thought of herself and became the trees. She saw her children and her husband and they all became branches and leaves. Tears sprang to her eyes. As they left her body, she felt herself expanding. Her heart was growing larger.

The group began to sing, and she joined in. It was a Hasidic niggun, a song with no words and no end. A woman she didn't know put her arm around Naomi, and she, in turn, put her arm around her daughter. Ilana's shoulders tensed, but Naomi persisted, and soon her resistance relaxed. In this swaying circle, in this darkened room, something inside Naomi lightened.

During the car ride home, Ilana didn't say a word. She still wasn't sure why her mom had brought her there. She didn't know what her mom expected her to think. She wasn't even sure what the experience had been. Not that knowing would have made a difference. Singing and swaying, deep breathing and communing, didn't do a thing for Ilana.

Instead of singing or listening to the rabbi, she had spent the whole time watching her mother. She had always seen her up close. Now she tried to see her from far away. She imagined that this wasn't her mother. It was just some other woman she happened to be sitting next to. Her mother could have been any stranger. She was singing and swaying, and after a few quick glances in Ilana's direction, she seemed to forget her daughter was there. She didn't smile over at her encouragingly. She didn't try to make her sing. She was just doing what she wanted, and she seemed so happy, so serene.

As weird as the whole experience was, what struck Ilana most was how seriously her mother took it, how into it she was. It was as if her mother had a secret life about which she knew nothing. Ilana had been watching her parents and her brother closely, hoping they would give her what she needed to know. She had heard them say so many things, most of which she didn't believe. But every once in a while, they handed her something she could use. Even if she didn't always know what they meant, she recognized something real when she saw it, and she knew she should hold on to it.

Naomi didn't break the silence in the car. She was content to let it be. Maybe it was an opening for Ilana, the first glimmer of a way in. For Naomi, it was so much more. She had scrubbed and vacuumed and cooked. But only after this evening did she feel truly ready for Pesach, the festival of freedom, the holiday of springtime.

When they got home, Ilana went to her room, closed the door, turned the radio on, and picked up the phone, all the usual varieties of noise with which she surrounded herself. But Naomi had seen a glimpse of her daughter. The outer mask of makeup, the armor of styled hair and trendy clothes, had lifted, even if just for a minute.

"Did you get to meditate?" Joel wanted to know when Naomi joined him in front of the television. "Or levitate?"

It wasn't like that. But Naomi couldn't explain what it *was* like. She was back in her own house, where more cooking and cleaning awaited her. Were she to explain what the rabbi had said, it would sound silly. But she held on to the quiet moment she had felt in the circle. When she had started to sing, it was as if she hadn't used her voice in years. By the time she finished, her voice had come free.

"We sang," she told him instead.

— THIRTY-TWO —

Once they finished cleaning, the transformation would be complete. Tzippy would bring the Pesach dishes down from the attic and unpack them into the newly cleaned cupboards. She had planned menus in her mind, and she would begin to cook. The Pesach grocery order waited in the garage. With thirty-six hours to go until the first seder, Tzippy gathered her team in the kitchen. Holding mops and toothpicks, dust rags and garbage bags, they searched for any last bits of chametz.

When they at last looked up from their work, Herschel was standing in the kitchen doorway. He waited for the girls to jump around him and search his bag and pockets for presents. Instead they stared at him wide-eyed. Their dust rags stopped mid-stroke. Only the vacuum cleaner whirred on.

"No hello? Didn't you miss me?" he asked. "I have a surprise for you," he announced when they remained silent. "We're going to a hotel for Pesach. In Atlantic City."

The girls looked from their father to Tzippy and stood frozen in place.

"I think I have something here for you," Herschel said, and pretended to search his pockets. Then he opened his briefcase and pulled out a white bakery bag.

"One for you. And one for you." Herschel handed each girl a giant sprinkle cookie. When he saw Tzippy, he stopped. "What are you doing here? Where's Baruch?" he asked. He held up the last cookie. "You're lucky I happened to buy an extra," he said, and handed her the cookie, which she refused.

The girls wolfed them down, dropping crumbs onto the floor Tzippy had mopped at two in the morning. She saw her lists coming unchecked, the house spinning backward, toys flying back off shelves, cabinets becoming unlined.

"I'm making Pesach," Tzippy said.

"Why make it if you don't have to?" Herschel asked.

"I want to," she said.

"Going away for Pesach is an incredible experience. Three meals a day and not once do you taste the matzo meal. You have to see it to believe it. These buffets make a wedding look like a fast day. They stretch from one side of a banquet hall to another. You can't stop yourself. You have to try everything."

As the girls drooled, Shayna came into the kitchen. She smiled to see her whole family together unexpectedly. She kissed each of the girls but ignored Herschel.

"Did you hear?" he said. "We're going away for Pesach."

"A hotel." Seemingly against her will, Shayna breathed out the word. Though she tried, she couldn't resist. Herschel had her by the heart.

"I did it for you. It's what you've always wanted," Herschel said. "I convinced my new investors that I needed to be with them for Pesach. It wasn't easy, believe me. These hotels have been booked for months. They have waiting lists as tall as you, Dassi. But even when they say they're booked, they always have a few rooms available. They save them for their VIPs. And that, girls, is what we are this year. You know why? Because I'm one of their partners now. I had an idea and the owner of the Atlantic City Pesach operation wants to do it."

"I was about to start cooking," Tzippy protested.

"So sit down. Relax. Take a break," Herschel said to Tzippy. Then he turned back to Shayna. "The amazing thing is, I didn't even have to go looking for this idea. It came to me. You won't believe it when I tell you."

Shayna put her hands over her ears. "We'll go to the hotel as long as I don't have to hear about it."

"Come on, Shayna," he said. "You know you're curious."

"You can go, but we're not," Tzippy said. "We'll go to Baruch's family."

"You have to come," Shayna insisted. "You always go to the girl's family for seders, at least the first year. And you haven't been here in months. You can't go running off as soon as you get here."

"So we'll stay here. If you want to go to Atlantic City, you go."

Shayna reached for Tzippy's hand, and she held it tightly. "I know," Shayna said. "Believe me, I know. But I need this, I really do."

Once again, Tzippy felt the force of her mother's desire. This time, she didn't know how to say anything but yes.

Herschel worked his way back into his family's good graces. It took only a few minutes and the girls were chattering away to him. Shayna surveyed the work Tzippy had done in the house, exclaiming as if her daughter had performed a miracle. Tzippy held back, though. The previous night, she had felt so close to her mother and sisters. Now, as the girls listened to Herschel and Shayna tried her best not to let on that she too was listening, Tzippy finished the remaining tasks alone. She wondered how she had ever lived here. She wasn't sure where her place was anymore. There was so much noise, but she had nothing to say.

Then Baruch walked into the kitchen, and everyone stopped talking. Herschel clapped him on the back. The girls jumped around him. When they cleared away, he came over to Tzippy. He hugged her, and they ignored everyone around them.

"Is everything okay?" he asked Tzippy softly.

She shrugged. "I don't know."

He had called the previous night to say that he was coming, but in the midst of all the preparations, she had barely remembered. He had also told her that The Kosher Connection was closing, but that the investors had offered him a job if he and Tzippy wanted to stay in Memphis. There hadn't been time to discuss it or even think about it. All she could do was add it to her list of things to worry about.

Now Tzippy looked up at Baruch. They had had such nice conversations on the phone each night. Far apart, she had once again felt like she could say anything to him. Now that he was here, she remembered the fights they had had, the doubts and fears she had felt. Which one was real? she wondered. She was worried about what they were going to do next. She was still angry and disappointed that it hadn't turned out as she had wanted it to. But she was also so glad to see him. She felt her love for him. When she added up these conflicting feelings, they became her husband.

The shiny newness of marriage was being stripped away. What was underneath didn't have the same sheen, but it was more solid, more real. This marriage house was so much bigger than she had imagined. She and her mother and her friends had described each of the rooms to one another. They had thought about the furniture, the wallpaper, and the rugs. They thought they knew exactly what it looked like. But they had seen only a part of it. There were corridors that surprised them, nooks and crannies and closets they hadn't known about. In the marriage house, there were always more rooms to discover.

Herschel's cell phone began to ring. He excused himself and stepped into the living room.

"I'll be right back," Baruch whispered to Tzippy.

He followed Herschel into the living room and waited for him to get off the phone. Herschel had heard that the investors had pulled out. Between phone messages and faxes and registered letters, he had been unable to escape this news.

"I tried," Baruch said. "But it was impossible. It was out of control."

"It doesn't matter," Herschel said. "In the scheme of things, they're small potatoes. We need people who see the big picture. These new investors are the big time. They're going to help us make something bigger than we ever dreamed."

Herschel was tired of grocery stores. He had anticipated the future, and his new investors were willing to make that happen. He had taken several ideas and joined them together: extreme sports meets "Survivor" meets exotic vacations meets kosher cruises and kosher cuisine. For the two days before Pesach, he would run a boot camp in New Jersey, so the participants would get to experience slavery. Each group would be assigned a leader, their own Moshe. There would be pyramid building and simulated plagues. The night before Pesach, they would be taken out of Egypt. They would receive make-your-own-matzo kits and have to bake it and roll it and haul it on their backs. For a small fee, the more adventurous would be able to replicate an actual paschal sacrifice. Then, after a great show of fireworks and festivities, a caravan of buses would take them to the four-star, beachfront kosher-for-Pesach hotel in Atlantic City, where they would spend eight days in freedom and luxury.

"We'll call it Relive the Exodus," Herschel declared.

"Count me out," Baruch said. "I can't do it anymore."

Baruch ignored Herschel's attempts to convince him. He was amazed that Herschel didn't even seem to care that The Kosher Connection was being closed. While he had let their failure eat away at him, Herschel only saw new opportunities that would arise. For Herschel, nothing ever closed. There were now two Kosher Connections. One was being packed up and closed down; the other was always open, always expanding. He had an endless supply of ideas, and he stacked them one on top of another and kept climbing. He didn't look down or back. For a moment, Baruch envied him. He too had wanted to live in the outer reaches of the everyday world. But he couldn't stay there. For him, The Kosher Connection was not an idea, not a plan. It was built from his hard work. It was the minutes of every hour of every day he had poured into it.

Herschel kept talking even after Baruch had left the room. No one needed to hear his ideas in order for them to exist. But Baruch had had enough. He now heard the holes in Herschel's words. He saw how high they reached, how far they fell.

"What happened?" Tzippy asked when Baruch came back into the kitchen.

"You don't want to know," Baruch said.

"You're right. I don't. Anyway, we have something else to talk about." she said.

"I know," he said. "What are we going to do?"

There was so much still to talk about, and on the phone they had only begun to figure it out. Tzippy wanted to go back to Memphis, back to school. Baruch could help the investors with another restaurant in the meantime. He could make time to learn. They would both make space for each other to figure out who they were and what they wanted.

But there was something else now too. She hadn't yet told Baruch about the recurring nausea and the strange flickerings in her pelvis.

"Guess what?" she said, and pointed to her stomach and smiled.

He looked blankly at her. Then his mouth dropped open in surprise. Now things were changing once again. Neither of them knew what to expect. Neither of them was sure how this would continue to change them. They looked at each other, eyes wide with fear and hope at what lay ahead.

The girls crammed a month's worth of toys and clothes into their bags. They spent the day dancing with excitement. Baruch was trying, with little success, to supervise their packing. When they wouldn't listen to him, he gave up and went to help Tzippy with the final preparations in the kitchen. Herschel hadn't packed at all. He was busy on the computer, trying to put together a business proposal. Shayna was still trying to ignore him, but little by little she was softening. She reminded the girls that at the hotel they needed to wear a different outfit at every meal. She took a long, hot shower. She packed her fanciest floral hats.

When they finished packing, there were hanging bags and hatboxes, knapsacks and overflowing shopping bags. On the first attempt, the suitcases didn't fit into the minivan. Herschel and Baruch unloaded them and reorganized. Tzippy checked her watch and tried to hurry them along. Pesach would begin in just over three hours. With no traffic, the drive took two hours. But no one else seemed to notice how late it was getting. Herschel got a phone call. Dassi had to go to the bathroom. Shayna thought she had forgotten her diamond earrings. Then Dassi had to go to the bathroom again.

Tzippy couldn't stand it any longer. Out of deference to her mother, she had agreed to go to the hotel. But she wasn't going to move at their pace. She snatched the keys from her father's hand. "I'm driving," she said.

"Look at that," Shayna said. "Miss Independent."

"Everyone in," Tzippy said. "If you want to go, we're leaving right now."

Though they didn't fully believe that she knew how to drive, they listened to her. Tzippy exiled Herschel to the backseat, where the girls climbed on him and brought forth a steady stream of questions and requests for snacks. She locked the doors so no one could attempt one more trip to the bathroom.

Tzippy pushed away her lingering fear of driving in New York. She remembered how easy it had been to drive in Memphis, and holding her breath, she merged onto the highway. Through Brooklyn she drove, trying to make up for the time they had lost in leaving late. Soon they reached the Verazzano Bridge. It loomed magnificent, the road curving up as if it didn't ever end, didn't do anything so mundane as connect Brooklyn and Staten Island. She could drive across it and it would take her anywhere. The sun glinted off the water underneath. She soared across, feeling like God might give their minivan wings.

The feeling didn't last. When she passed through Staten Island and finally reached New Jersey, traffic awaited them. With less than an hour until the holiday began, they were at a complete standstill.

"We have plenty of time," Herschel assured them.

"It's like yetziat mitzrayim," Shayna said, the exodus from Egypt.

"Where, where?" the girls clamored, expecting to look out the windows and see a nation passing by on camels, matzo strapped to their backs.

Baruch craned his neck, looking for a hopeful sign. The holiday was approaching, all too soon, and every minute they stood in traffic made the possibility of desecrating it more likely. Reviewing in his head the halachic protocol for such a situation, he wondered how many miles they would have to walk, bags on their backs, sisters riding on top of roller suitcases.

"Don't worry," Herschel said again. "We're going to be fine."

Ten minutes later, they had only moved forward a few miles. Undeterred by his placement in the backseat, Herschel called out instructions to Tzippy and came up with alternate routes. No matter how much time passed, Herschel insisted that they were going to be fine.

The girls were yelling at one another, Shayna was yelling at them, and Herschel was still talking, oblivious to it all. The van seemed to rock from the noise. The windows might blow out, Tzippy imagined, if it continued for one more minute. She took her hands off the steering wheel and screamed. Then she leaned on her horn and let forth a deep bellow. Her family stared at her in surprise. It did nothing to move traffic, but it brought an unprecedented quiet.

Baruch touched her hand. "Are you okay?" he whispered.

"I am now," she said.

She didn't want to say more, didn't want to do anything that would disturb the silence. He smiled back, enjoying this moment of being together. As if her entire family were not in the backseat. As if they didn't have miles to go in not enough time.

At last, traffic began to clear and they moved forward. But too much time had passed. Atlantic City was still miles away and Pesach was upon them. Tzippy wasn't going to be swayed to attempt the impossible. She wasn't going to keep driving with the pipe dream that they could make it to the hotel on time. She was in charge, and she knew what she needed to do. She took the first exit she came to, and she turned around. She sped until she finally reached the turnoff for Laurelwood. The minivan screeched as she swerved across two lanes of traffic at once. Other drivers honked and cursed at her, but she made it safely across. Minutes later, they pulled into the Millers' driveway as Naomi was getting ready to light the holiday candles.

— THIRTY-THREE —

FOLDING CHAIRS WERE BROUGHT up from the basement. More places were set. They all crowded around the table and began the seder.

All over the world, seders were beginning and ending. Across the time zones, there was a progression of wine drunk, parsley dipped, stories told. There were vegetarian seders and interfaith peace seders and feminist seders and liberation seders. Communal seders, seders overlooking the beach, seders next door to casinos, and traditional seders led by bearded grandfathers sitting at the heads of long tables. And seders mumbled, seders rushed, seders danced, seders acted out and sung.

On this table, there were three seder plates. There was a Lenox china plate that had belonged to Naomi's grandmother. Next to it was an abstract metal and glass seder plate that Joel had bought in Israel. At the far end of the table was a laminated white plastic plate decorated with Magic Markers that Baruch had made in the first grade. On each plate was the boiled egg, the parsley and salt water, the bitter herbs, the romaine lettuce, the charoset, and the broiled shankbone. They would first sing the order of the night: kadesh, urchatz, karpas. From kiddush to hand washing to the telling of the story of the exodus from Egypt, they would pass through this evening.

Naomi looked around the table, ready to begin. For this Pesach, she had removed the chametz from her house, but she had also removed it from her soul. She had tried to shake out the hard parts, the dry parts, the ungiving, unbending, closed-off places inside her. She had let go of her disappointment that it was going to be only the three of them, and she had planned something special. It didn't matter how many people were there. She would do it this way even if she were having her seder by herself.

And now she had a crowd. There was bibliodrama planned and a modern interpretive dance of the crossing of the Red Sea. She was going to go around the table and ask everyone to describe an exodus in their own lives. She had married new ideas to ancient traditions, and this seder was what she had come up with. It wasn't what anyone here was used to, and they might initially be resistant. She would have to pull them in. But she was prepared for that. She had come to the seder dressed as Miriam. She wore a robe that was royal blue and embroidered at the neck. The sleeves were loose and fringes dangled at the end.

Next to Elijah's cup, Naomi had placed the cup of Miriam, a latter-day addition to the age-old traditions. She was using a cup Ilana had decorated years ago with seashells and beads. She usually brought it out each Pesach as the cup of Elijah. But this, she knew, was the use it was intended for. Instead of wine, the cup of Miriam was filled with water, to remember the sea she had danced across, the well that had followed her through the desert giving water on her behalf.

The cup of Elijah had always been Naomi's favorite part of the night. She remembered being a child at the seder, struggling to stay awake. Near the end of the seder, when the rest of the family went to open the door for Elijah, Naomi stayed behind to watch the wine, to see if he really took a sip. She stared at the cup, willing herself not to blink and miss it. As her family sang in front of the open door, she saw a ripple in the wine's smooth purple surface. In her eleven-year-old eyes, there was no room for doubt. As far as she was concerned, Elijah surely lived eternally and traveled around the world, visiting each seder. He surely had been in her dining room and drunk from the cup. This was what she wanted to bring with her into this seder—her unfettered wonder and belief.

Kadesh, the opening chord of the seder. They filled one another's glasses with wine or grape juice. They all stood as Joel recited the kiddush. He didn't sing it out, relying more on a chant that fell closer to speaking. He had been looking forward to a quiet seder, the first time he could remember when they didn't have a crowd. In his memories of the extended family seders they had gone to when the kids were young, what stood out most was the noise and the domino-like effect of one glass of wine knocked over by another. Now he was recovering from the shock of the unexpected crowd assembled here. It wasn't what he had hoped for, but it was amazing what he could get used to.

Naomi had made sure that Ilana and Baruch were sitting on either side of him, and that made it easier. Ilana insisted on having wine this year, and they had acquiesced. She was thumbing through the pages of the Hagaddah to see how long the seder would take. But at least she was there, ready to ask some questions of her own. Joel and Ilana exchanged glances, reassuring each other that they would make it through this intact.

Ilana had opened the front door for their unexpected guests and had been too shocked to do anything but call out plaintively for her mother. She had felt overrun at the sight of so many people. But then Baruch came over to her and said how good it was to see her. He still didn't hug her, but he came as close as he could, and she wondered if it might be enough.

Baruch sat next to Joel on the other side, a pile of books and commentaries by his plate. Now that he had his books in front of him once again, he realized how much he had missed them. Handwritten notes from previous years stuck out from between the pages. These were ideas he planned to share tonight, questions to ask, answers he intended to give. Joel looked to the right and to the left, and there they were, his children.

The families weren't accustomed to being together, and they joined in quietly, shyly, at the assigned parts. Their voices didn't always fit together. Some went high while others went low, blending together different tunes. Then, in the position befitting kings and free men, everyone leaned to one side, and they drank the first of the four cups of wine.

Urchatz, hands washed in preparation for food, imitating the priests in the Holy Temple long ago. As Naomi passed a bowl of water around the table, Tzippy and Baruch exchanged private smiles. They held hands under the table and separated only to pour two cupfuls of water over each hand. Then they clasped hands again. For them, the seder was infused with the secret they carried. With this news a constant presence in his head, Baruch felt like even more time had passed since he sat as a child around this table. He had changed so much, and instead of pushing him away, this distance now made it easier to come home. He no longer needed to ask whether he was like them or not. He had gone away, but he could still come home, at least to visit. This wasn't home for Tzippy, but there was nowhere she would rather be. She wasn't worrying about the house she had cleaned, the menus she had planned that would go uncooked. Her nausea was still coming and going, in waves and ripples. After taking deep breaths, she felt better and thought about the mystery unfolding inside her. She was sitting directly across from the cup of Miriam, which she had never seen before. She stared at it, and it steadied her.

Karpas, the sprigs of parsley dipped into salt water. The green, a sign of spring. The salt, a memory of tears. Sadness and deliverance in the same bite. Herschel hadn't eaten all day, and he was starving. He took a piece of parsley and dipped it. His fingers tapped his nervousness onto the table. He stole glances at Shayna, but she wouldn't look at him. With the hotel invitation, he had tried to bring her the ultimate gift, and now he was thinking of what they were missing out on. The buffet tables spanned his mind, and he thought of the people they wouldn't get to see, the connections he wouldn't make, the food they wouldn't eat this year. But there was always next year, he consoled himself.

Shayna felt her own stirring of hope. She had passed through something, and it had broken, at least for the moment. It didn't matter that there was no hotel. She no longer felt the same desire for it. At this seder, she was transported back to the first Pesach she had ever celebrated, when her mouth had hung open at the beauty of each ritual. She looked at Dassi. She had grape-juice stains on her dress, but her face was lit with excitement at the prospect of singing the Mah Nishtanah. Dena had a stack of notes in front of her, given out by her teachers, and she intended to read every word before the night was over. Malky was sitting next to Shayna and glancing at her in concern. She was old enough to know, old enough to understand. Zahava didn't notice anyone but herself. Her face was made up, her nails were done, her hair was styled to perfection. She smiled as if she were an actress and this were her opening night. And Tzippy, her eldest daughter, had a strong voice and a sure hand and a wide heart, and she sat happily next to her husband. As she took in each of their faces, Shayna was flooded with love for her daughters.

Yachatz, they broke the middle matzo. One half was returned to the seder plate; the other was put away for the afikomen, which the girls would steal and hold for ransom. Already the younger girls dreamed of what they wanted. For weeks, they had debated the benefits of Barbie dream house versus Barbie luxury car. They had gotten over their initial disappointment that the hotel had turned out to be a house. Naomi had brought out a bag of dress-up clothes she had saved from when Ilana was little, and they had decked themselves out in old bridesmaid dresses, muumuus, and kimonos. With floppy straw hats on their heads, scarves and beads around their necks, they smiled complicitously at Naomi. They were miniature, modern-day Miriams.

Magid, the retelling of the exodus story. The matzos were held high, and they read together: *This is the bread of affliction that our ancestors ate in the land of Egypt. Whoever is hungry, let him come and eat. Whoever is in need, let him come and join us.* The whole world, Naomi imagined. She could open this house and invite them all in.

Dassi stood on her chair and belted out the Mah Nishtanah, asking, *Why is this night different from all other nights?* They began the answer. *Because we were slaves to Pharaoh in Egypt and the Lord our God took us out with an outstretched arm.* This was the short version. From here, they opened it up and expanded. Instead of telling the story of the exodus directly, they added commentary onto commentary. They told the story in words and with food, with their bodies reclining and their fingers dipping into the wine to count out the plagues that befell the Egyptians. They told the story of Yaakov, who went down to Egypt, and Moshe, who led them out. God's might was remembered, the suffering recounted, the miracles recited. They told of the four sons and the sages who stayed up all night, and they told of themselves.

They reached the climax of the story. *In each generation, one is obligated to feel as if he himself has come out of Egypt.* Naomi sang these words to a tune she made up as she went along. She didn't care that everyone was staring at her. This year she substituted "she herself," since she had come out of her own personal Egypt. She felt past, present, and future collapse into one. All this history, and it was still relevant here today, still happening in this moment. The exodus felt so close at hand. They were all, always, going out.

Now that they had told the story, the seder sped up. They crunched through the cardboard-like matzo. They bit into the white slices of maror, until tears came to their eyes and their faces turned red. They mitigated its bitterness with the apple and wine of the charoset. They imitated Hillel the Sage, who made a sandwich of these opposites, mixing the bread of affliction with the bread of freedom, the bitter herbs with the sweet charoset. Then it was time for dinner. It didn't matter that it was eleven o'clock at night, and that after eating the matzos and charoset and drinking two of the four cups of wine, no one was in the mood for a meal. At least for this moment, Naomi had them here, and hungry or not, they were going to sit together and eat the dinner she had prepared.

ACKNOWLEDGMENTS

I am very thankful to Binnie Kirshenbaum and David Liss for reading drafts and offering their insight and advice. To David Wolf, who read multiple drafts, on unreasonable deadlines, red pen in hand. To Mark and Beth Epstein, Jonathan and Jill Lamstein, Malcolm Myers, and Binyomin Gillers for sharing their knowledge with me. To Rachel Mesch, for her ideas and constant encouragement, especially at Starbucks, early on. To the fabulous Laca Tines, without whom I would not have been able to finish. And for their support and encouragement at various stages along the way, I thank the Galper family, Simmy and LE Mirvis, Shana Gillers, Barry Wimpfheimer, Idana Goldberg, Naomi Zelwer Becker, and Sarah Kass Mandelbaum.

I am especially thankful to my parents, David and Lynnie Mirvis, for their love, support, and understanding, and for answering the call and driving a thousand miles to baby-sit at the very end. To Shoni Mirvis, for her ideas, her insight, and her apartment. To Eitan and Daniel, my two beautiful boys. And to Allan Galper, all my love and gratitude, for living this with me every day.

Finally, my deepest gratitude to Jordan Pavlin for her extraordinary wisdom and insight. And to Nicole Aragi, for deadlines, for handholding, for believing, for reading, again and again.

A NOTE ABOUT THE AUTHOR

Tova Mirvis grew up in Memphis, Tennessee, and now lives in New York City with her husband and two young children. She is the author of the novel *The Ladies Auxiliary*, which was a national best-seller. *The Outside World* is her second novel.

A NOTE ON THE TYPE

The text of this book was set in Walbaum, a typeface designed by Justus Erich Walbaum in 1810. Walbaum was active as a typefounder in Goslar and Weimar from 1799 to 1836. Though the letterforms of this face are patterned closely on the "modern" cuts then being made by Giambattista Bodoni and the Didot family, they are of a far less rigid cut. Indeed, it is the slight but pleasing irregularities in the cut that give this typeface its humane quality and account for its wide appeal. In its very appearance Walbaum jumps boundaries, having a look more French than German.

Composed by NK Graphics, Keene, New Hampshire

Printed and bound by Berryville Graphics, Berryville, Virginia

Designed by Robert C. Olsson